HAVANA GIRLS

A gripping tale of family secrets and Cold War intrigue
across Cuba and Florida

THE QUEENPIN CHRONICLES
Book 3

L.L. KIRCHNER

Prologue, Los Angeles, 1950

The ratatat of her typewriter keys slowed as lights across the hillside sparked to life, like a bejeweled cape unfurling. Imogene —usually charmed by this sight—scarcely noticed. Must call Briggs, was all she could think as she absent-mindedly tugged out any curl remaining in her hair. The letter she'd been working on could wait.

She shouldn't be putting off either, really, but Briggs's need to know was immediate. She'd no intention of giving the story of the century to the *St. Petersburg Press*. Not when Aggie had promised her a career-changing byline in the *Los Angeles Times*. She couldn't turn that down for Briggs. Scratch that. *Wouldn't*. She was filing with Aggie the next day.

Tipping her wrist, she checked the time. Three-thirty back home. She could still catch him before the afternoon's editorial meeting. The only task she'd put off longer was the confession in front of her.

Imogene touched the top plate of her Robin's egg-blue Olivetti, tracing its curves. How she loved it. So strange to approach it with anything other than enthusiasm. But this was no ordinary missive for her daughter. Unlike the phone call, she wasn't sure this *was* the right thing to do.

Her source could remain forever confidential. That was how this worked. But she wanted her daughter to know the truth. Sally was only eight, but already she saw the world in black and white. It was up to Imogene to help her understand that, sometimes, the only way to fight a monster was to make a deal with the devil. Otherwise, her reputation as a gung-ho reporter would give the girl the wrong ideas. She would lionize her mother. Until the real story came out. Secrets had a tendency to reveal themselves one way or another.

Besides, her story would change lives.

From a certain angle, the reporting did include her original assignment. If it weren't for the Black Dahlia case, she'd never have done this investigation. She looked down at the newspaper clippings on her desk, her work over the past five years. The 'Beautiful Homes' photo spread of the Juergen mansion was on top because chronological order made sense. Underscored what she was trying to show her daughter. That "story" was essentially a collection of captions. That was all Briggs had ever expected of her. At the start, it was all she'd ever expected of herself, and this was why—she reminded herself—she had to tell Sally the truth.

Shuffling the pile, she found her first big piece. The exposé she had given the *Press*—'Bookie Joint, Crap Game, Houses of Ill-Repute — Tampa's Biggest Crackdown.' Her first investigative report. All because Briggs had sent her out on a puff piece— the Florida Girls beauty contest. That *was* a puff piece. Especially after Briggs got his fingers all over it. Thank heavens for Agnes Underwood.

She had shown her how different work could be. Aggie was her mentor, the first woman Imogene had ever worked for and the only woman she'd ever met who took less care in her appearance than she did. Frazzled hairdos and wrinkled suits aside, Aggie never treated Imogene as anything less than a fully capable reporter. Then again, neither had Sal Giancarlo.

Shame bloomed in Imogene's chest. She'd known all along that while Sal was feeding her stories to take down gangland's most wanted criminals, he was moving in on their territory. She didn't plan to let that happen with Elizabeth Short's murder. Until he told her how vulnerable young women were regularly picked up off the streets for the pleasure of men. Then his motives ceased to be a concern. She had to make Sally understand.

The clock struck the quarter hour. Beads of perspiration formed on Imogene's forehead. She fanned herself with her shirt. She could delay no longer.

Lifting the heavy black receiver off the switch hook, Imogene dialed the operator. She'd just come on the line when a scraping noise sounded at her door.

Who on earth—?

The door knob rattled as she half-rose from her seat. A sudden sharp thud slammed the door on its hinges. Startled, Imogene dropped the phone and turned to face the window, cursing the view. This was no mere interruption and there was no escape down that steep hillside. But she couldn't leave her confession lying about.

Ripping the sheet from her typewriter cartridge as she gathered her clips, Imogene thrust the lot into the Manilla folder she'd prepared. What now?

She made a mad dash for the bathroom and stuffed the envelope into the one place no man would look, where her words could easily disappear—her sanitary napkin box. No matter. After her story about corruption in Vegas was killed, she'd taken steps to ensure that wouldn't happen again. Her story was in her desk at the *Times*. Safe.

The door burst open.

ONE

Sam, Miami-St. Petersburg, 1978

SAM CRADLED THE PHONE BETWEEN HER EAR AND clavicle, grateful she'd splurged on a shoulder rest or she'd be even further behind in her day. Not that she relished the task at hand. Just because she could make a call while she filed meeting minutes didn't mean she wanted to. Hopefully, her father's answering machine would pick up before his wife did. Only Sharon would call on a Monday morning.

"Could you come with me, Sam?" Leonard Filmore and his greasy comb-over stood in her cubicle door. He didn't look happy, but then, he was the department chair. Not once had he seemed happy to see her—*a woman!*—in his halls.

"I have the minutes right here, Dr. Filmore," she said, dropping the receiver and holding up the freshly typed pages.

"You don't need those," he said. "But... maybe your purse."

Later, Sam would replay that moment endlessly.

If only she hadn't drunk so much at the office party. Of course she shouldn't have made out with her married colleague, but weren't universities where people were supposed to experiment? So what if she was a graduate research assistant? It was after hours. She'd been too timid in her undergrad days to try anything even mildly weird. Besides, she was officially a divorcée. Jimmy had finally signed the papers. She should have confronted Filmore.

"Hang on there, pal. If this is about Friday's happy hour, I'd like to know what kind of trouble Ed is in. Do you think I care? You're not putting my name on your precious study no matter what I do. But good luck making your deadline without me."

Watching the squat pastel houses and tidy lawns roll by from her bus window, Sam regretted that she'd not said any of those things. Because what her advisor had wanted, apparently, was to criticize her "erratic" behavior. Suggest she take some time off.

"I bet it'd be different if my name really was Sam and not Sally," she muttered under her breath. Not that she wished she was a boy, but she'd never liked the name Sally. Her father had always blamed her mother, and there was no asking her. Imogene Fuchs was dead.

She almost missed her stop. "Sorry!" she yelled as the bus driver was pulling away. "Would you please stop? Please? Sorry!"

It was garbage day. Metal bins lined the street, tempting her to rid herself of her box of office ephemera, but she didn't want to fill up some unsuspecting neighbor's empty trash can like that. Besides, she'd chucked it all into a milk crate she'd nabbed from storage. She could find another use for that at home. Never again would she load her workspace with so much junk.

Trudging barefoot through Saint Augustine grass—there weren't any sidewalks in Coral Groves—she recalled Jimmy's enthusiasm about the neighborhood's promised shopping mall. As if a mall could make up for moving to the hinterlands of Miami. To a place she hadn't seen until after the deed was signed.

Still, her dread began to lift. Filmore hadn't offered to pay for this "temporary" leave, but her first child support check was due any day. They'd be okay. After taking, distributing, and filing the meeting minutes, she should at least be paid for today. If it came down to it, she vowed, she would seek severance.

She stopped to collect the mail and regarded their one-story concrete block home, identical to its neighbors on Citrus Way. It could stand to be painted. She'd always hated the salmon shade Jimmy had picked.

Inside, she dropped her box, keys, bag, and the day's post in the entry, catching her reflection in the mirror. She'd lost a significant amount of weight in the last year, which she didn't mind, but her blond hair was flecked with gray, which she did. Her cheeks had sunk, and she had dark circles around her eyes. They looked worse than usual.

Leaning closer, she saw the problem. Good lord. She'd rubbed her mascara clean off her lashes and onto her face, quite possibly during the staff meeting.

A noise in the hallway startled her. She stiffened. Someone was in the house, and they were coming down the hall.

"Mom?"

"Abigail!"

"What are you doing home?" they asked in unison.

Abby appeared wearing an oversized T-shirt, her awful shag haircut in hot rollers. "What's with your face?"

"Young lady, you're supposed to be in school."

"So are you."

"I'm taking some time off to do work around the house," Sam lied, cursing herself both for lying and feeling the need to explain.

"I'm going to stay with Dad," Abby announced. "I left school to pack because I knew you'd freak out. Cheerleader tryouts are in two weeks, and he's closer."

"Does your father know about this? Does his girlfriend? Whoever that is this week...."

"Gag, Mom. You don't care about me. All you care about is the alimony."

The phone's shrill ring cut through their standoff. Sam shot out her hand. They didn't have a machine, and it might be work calling, asking her to please come back. Except now she really did want to paint the house.

"Fontana residence," she said, her voice automatically shifting into polite adult.

"Oh, Sam. There you are. Finally." It was her father's wife.

"Listen, Sharon, I'm kind of in the middle of—"

"It's your father," she said. "He's dead."

* * *

Three days into sitting shiva, and Sam could no longer resist the urge to sneak into her dad's office. Sharon would be furious, but the compulsion to ransack was too strong. Sam had to assuage her guilt.

She'd spent so much of her life wanting to know her mother, angry at Sharon's presence, that she'd barely known her father. Other than the foot he'd lost in the war, she'd thought of him as healthy. Immortal. He was only sixty-seven.

Taking a seat at his swivel chair, she noticed the room had the same smells she remembered, a hint of copper pennies mixed with pencil shavings and the scent of pages deep inside a book. She wondered when she'd last been in this room. When *he'd* last sat here. His desk was topped by a 1976 calendar blotter, the lamp she'd bought for his birthday with S&H Green Stamps, even the same three photographs that had always been there—his hand-tinted army portrait, her mother's high school graduation photo, and a smaller picture in a silver case, Sam as a child, maybe five years old.

In the past thirty years, he'd never added an image of the

woman keeping vigil downstairs to the family tableau. Not even after Sam had left the nest. Terrible as it felt to admit, she took satisfaction in this. They'd wed in 1950 when Sam was nine—less than a year after her mother was found dead in Los Angeles. She'd never forgiven him for replacing her.

Her mother, she realized, was the essence of her search. What might she learn about her through her father's effects? She knew the resume—the truth-seeking reporter who died tragically young—but little else. What about their life together? Their love? Something beyond the photographs. They never talked about her, especially after Sharon came along.

It didn't take long to find the key under the pencil tray in the center drawer. Had her father hidden it? The corresponding lock was nowhere to be found. She was crouched over her father's old briefcase trying the clasp when a cough at the door startled her. *Sharon.*

Twisting around, Sam noticed that her father's wife wasn't wearing shoes. No wonder she hadn't heard her. Sharon wasn't orthodox or anything, but for this she was doing the barefoot thing.

Fine. Sam could hardly pretend this was quiet contemplation, and she was ready for a battle. But Sharon merely stood in the doorframe, staring at Sam with her dry, red-rimmed eyes.

Finally Sam spoke up. "I didn't take anything, I—"

"Take whatever you like," Sharon said. "I was looking for you to see if you'd like a sandwich."

* * *

Over perfect Reubens, Sam studied Sharon. She only ever thought of her as her father's wife, never her stepmother. Sharon wasn't evil, but she wasn't someone Sam had ever felt drawn to either. Her interests were gardening and mahjong with her pals. Snooze.

The doorbell rang. "I'll get it," Sam offered.

"Don't be silly," Sharon said, storing their plates. "It's almost sundown. We can eat these when our guest leaves."

Sam really wanted the rest of her sandwich. Surely, they didn't both need to answer. Or was this another custom she was unfamiliar with? The most Jewish thing her father had ever done was go to temple after her mother died. The ladies there had been keen to set him up with the childless, nearly forty-year-old Sharon Marx.

As Sharon headed for the door, Sam remembered Abby leaving with Jimmy, her flowered suitcase and garbage bag of belongings loaded into his Volvo. At least he'd brought Abby to the funeral and not his girlfriend.

"Right behind you," Sam said. She wouldn't abandon anyone like she'd been abandoned.

* * *

That evening, after the last guest departed and they'd finished their sandwiches, Sam washed dishes while gazing out the window. As little as Sharon had changed on the inside of the house, she had transformed the backyard. To the postage-stamp space, she'd added a concrete slab for a grill and some metal chairs. Around the chain-link fence, she'd planted ornamental palms and hibiscus clusters.

Sam hated it. Still, the thought of going back to her own empty house held no appeal.

"Your father wanted you to have this," Sharon said, dropping something metallic on the table. "It's from your mother."

Sam turned, but Sharon had already left. A footlocker sat atop the red Formica. On instinct, she tried the key in her pocket.

The tumblers clicked, and with shaky fingers, Sam lifted the lid. Inside lay a sealed manila envelope that read:

**FOR MY DAUGHTER SALLY FUCHS
TO BE OPENED ONLY AFTER MY DEATH.**

—IMOGENE FUCHS

TWO

Thelma, Havana, 1945

THE CAB CAREENED THROUGH HAVANA'S VIBRANT STREETS, giving Thelma nothing to do but watch the city pass. Women hung laundry from their balconies. Children chased each other down sun-drenched sidewalks. Tourists sipped coffees at outdoor cafés. The mundane rhythms of everyday life made for a surreal contrast to her momentous day.

George is still alive, she repeated. Words that did little to beat back the tide of—*Why aren't I happy?* She knew.

When George had resurfaced after weeks lost at sea, Thelma had rushed onto the first flight to Cuba; of course she had. Her husband had been missing longer than they'd been married. What had happened to him? Would she ever know?

Out of habit she reached for the sapphire necklace George had given her, a placeholder for the wedding ring he had yet to buy, only to remember she'd ripped it from her neck, forcing it on his cousin as she declared she was not part of the Wright family.

The rearview mirror caught Thelma's attention. A black two-door seemed to be shadowing the cab. "Did you see that car behind us?" she asked Peggy.

Her friend cranked around to face the rear window.

"Geez, Pegs. At least try and be a little subtle."

Peggy turned back to Thelma. "Aye aye, Commandant Thelma." She clicked her heels in the footwell. "You're as bad as Kathleen Young, you know that?"

The coupe made a right down a side road, and Thelma allowed a smile. "If Mrs. Young heard that, she'd dock your pay for insubordination."

Peggy laughed. "You'd know."

Thelma risked another glance back to be sure they were still in the clear. "Seriously, though. You weren't with us in Vegas for long. Eyes everywhere."

"Oh, hon, I worked for Mrs. Young for ages. She had opinions about how I should act way before you or the Florida Girls came along."

A memory flashed into Thelma's mind. Elementary school. Trapped in a circle of kids, pointing and shouting, "Bastard. Your mom's a whore." If they'd known who her father was, they would've been afraid to say it to her face.

"All I know is," Thelma said, "I'll feel better when Imogene's story is out. Those wise guys will be so busy fighting each other in Vegas, they won't bother us. Especially since they think"—she caught herself before saying his name because she couldn't be too careful—"my father is dead."

"We're here," said Peggy. "*Muchas gracias,*" she said as she settled up with the cabbie. That was all Thelma could make out anyway. She was grateful her friend spoke Spanish.

From the outside, the hospital looked like any other, but inside, the stench of Cuban cigars and disinfectant competed for attention. Languid fans pushed the air in circles but did little to combat Havana's tropical heat.

A nurse stopped them. She and Peggy exchanged rapid Spanish as Thelma arranged her face into an expression of expectant hopefulness. In their exchange she heard, "Mrs. George Wright," knotting her stomach into a tight coil. Sounds around her muted, reduced to the hammering of her heart against her ribs and the cold plink of water dripping somewhere.

Finally, Peggy squeezed her shoulder. "It's down that hall, but only one of us can go." She motioned to the chairs along the wall. "I'll wait here. And Thelms?"

Thelma slowed, truly looking at Peggy for the first time that day. Her platinum bangs were stuck to her forehead, but her eyes shone with determination.

"We'll see you through. No matter what." She smiled. "But before you go in, here." She pulled a tube of lipstick from her handbag. "Put on some of this."

For the first time in days, Thelma laughed then dutifully freshened her lip rouge.

Walking the corridors, Thelma passed large open rooms where patients lined the walls. Each step felt heavier than the last as she dreaded finding her beloved. She'd gotten no information other than the fact that, after six weeks missing, he'd turned up at a hospital in Cuba. Where had he been all that time?

At the threshold, Thelma drew in a deep breath. She'd watched her mother shrivel and die before her eyes, but the wasting had been long in coming. After years of addiction, the end was something Thelma had hoped for. Planned for.

George was different. He had pursued her against all reason and in return made himself a target. He'd almost been killed. Now he was here in Havana. Alive.

* * *

"Why so glum, chum?" Doris asked as she entered the dining room in their Vedado rental, bearing a plate of fruit for the table.

"We knew Homer was a piece of work, Thelms," Helen said, reaching for a chunk of mango.

She'd described Homer's fit—how he'd ripped a bleeding heart of Jesus picture off the wall as he screamed that Thelma wasn't part of the family—in detail. What she'd yet to confess was failing to tell George that Sal was in Havana and living at their house.

"They didn't make you leave the hospital. And anyway, you *are* married." Doris pulled a signet ring from her pinky. "Here. Flip this around so the initials face in. Voila! A plain gold band."

Thelma jammed the ring on her finger, about to ask her friends' opinion when a moan from Francella Ava DiGruppo, her father's mistress, interrupted their conversation. Mercifully, it was limited to, she hoped, the moment of climax.

An image of George in his hospital bed flashed in Thelma's mind, flat on his back, trapped inside a metal frame, legs suspended by a series of ropes and pulleys and weights. Only time would tell if the guilt she felt now was worse than the shame she'd felt when he was missing. Both situations were her fault.

"Do we have anything to drink?" Thelma asked.

Her friends looked around the dining room as if the taxidermy sporting trophies coating the walls might know. If the stress didn't kill Thelma, the hunting lodge decor in this place might. But then, Helen and Doris had only a single day to find accommodations for them all. "Sal says he's out of the game for good," she'd promised her friends from the airport in Las Vegas. "Just make sure whatever you rent is well off El Centro. He has to stay out of sight."

Thelma rose to commence her booze hunt, but Doris reached for her wrist across the table. "Thelma, hang on." She looked into her eyes. "Mother is coming to visit."

The words stopped Thelma. "Here?" She stared into a long-dead bison's glass eye. Where would they put her? And why was Mrs. Juergen coming at all? Did she know who Sal Giancarlo was?

"We'll stay at a hotel," Doris assured, seeing the worry lines in Thelma's face.

Helen leaned toward Doris and kissed her on the cheek. Thelma envied their ease—Doris, dark and striking, her natural warmth now edged with resolve; Helen, the pale bookworm whose frisky intelligence had encouraged that evolution. Together, they'd shown her how life altering it was to be true to yourself.

"Do you think your mother might"—Thelma tipped her head between Doris and Helen—"accept your romantic friendship?"

"You think the woman who insisted I *pass* would be okay with my Boston marriage," said Doris, looking Thelma dead in the eye. She didn't phrase it as a question. "The more things change, the more they stay the same."

Thelma understood. Less than a year ago, she would've been entertaining a patron in some dim room, praying her mother's cries wouldn't pierce the thin walls and wilt another man's ardor, leaving them unable to afford even the two shabby rooms they called home. Her life now couldn't be further from that, yet she carried that experience. Always would.

"It's not like we don't need to be careful out there," Helen said with a shudder. "Cuban culture is no more enlightened than the US. Why give people a reason not to work with us when we're trying to start a business?"

This was the least of their concerns, Thelma thought, hanging her head.

"None of that, sugar," Doris said. "Whether George stays or goes, we know there's no money. We'll make do."

"We'll just have to scale back," Helen said.

For the hundredth time that day, Thelma's eyes welled. A knock at the door interrupted, sending her pulse racing. "Peggy has a key, right?"

The girls nodded.

"Who—"

"Oh, for Pete's sake," Doris said, rising. "There's only one way to find out."

"Doris, no!" cried Thelma.

"Relax, already. I'm answering the door like a normal neighbor."

"It's probably the bread man, Thelms," Helen said. "Or maybe the rag man? They come around in the morning and before supper."

Thelma watched Doris move down the hall, her stomach knotting with each click of her friend's heels against the tile. A woman's voice carried through the door—American, cultured, familiar. Thelma's relief lasted only a moment before a new worry took hold. If she'd found them, who else could?

THREE

Sam, St. Petersburg, 1978

SAM TORE OPEN THE ENVELOPE. INSIDE WAS A SINGLE sheet of typewriter paper and a pile of newspaper clippings.

DECEMBER 20, 1949

MY DEAREST SALLY,

SAM COULDN'T HELP BUT CRINGE AT SEEING HER GIVEN name on the page. It wasn't a family name, and for the life of her, she'd never understood why her mother had bestowed it. She read on.

THIS LETTER MAY COME AS SOMETHING OF A SHOCK AND NOT simply because I'll have passed away by the time you read this. We will have undoubtedly talked about my work, but there is a great deal I will have omitted. I want to tell you now while I have the courage.

I hope you know how loved you are. You have been my guiding light, the reason I pursued interests beyond my domestic duties. While I cherish being your mother, as a reporter I found I could benefit entire communities. The war showed what women can do for our country. With so much work to be done rebuilding our nation, why should we stop now? Rather than step aside, I want you to have these same opportunities and more.

It's been a challenge. But I concur with our great First Lady Eleanor Roosevelt—"Women are like tea bags. We don't know our true strength until we are in hot water!"

I promised not to reveal these secrets because they could put others in danger. But I am stalling. Briggs, my first editor, would call this entire opener "throat clearing" and cut the whole thing.

I'm writing you from Los Angeles, where I'm cubbing under the magnificent Aggie Underwood, privately still working on Elizabeth Short's murder, more famously known as the Black Dahlia case. What I have learned in the course of investigating the girl's hideous murder has me thinking about the explanations I owe you. I am in part to blame—

THE LETTER CUT OFF THERE.

With a gasp, Sam realized the date. Her mother had begun writing this the day she died. She would've had no way of knowing she was about to die in a car accident.

The urge to call Jimmy struck hard even as she hated herself for the impulse. But she wanted to mull over the letter's contents with *someone*. She considered phoning Ed, her erstwhile office mate, but doubted his wife or the dean would appreciate that. If she was ever going to become an FBI profiler, she was obliged to keep Dr. Filmore sweet.

Now, here she was days later, back in the kitchen talking— albeit in a roundabout way—with the frumpy-looking woman her father had married about the cryptic letter and bizarre assortment of press clippings she'd found. Shiva was over, but no mention of Sam's departure had been made.

She spread the clips on the table like crime scene photos, like she'd learned in the criminology seminars she'd taken the previous semester. Still, the magic eluded her.

"I can't fathom how these stories are related." *Let alone how they connect to anything my mother did that would have made her culpable in a murder.* Sam looked down at the newsprint strewn across the table, searching for possible connections. "Take this one, a home and garden feature on some rich lady's house, and then here"—she pushed aside some clips—"is one about organized crime in Tampa."

"Well, they're both written by your mother," said Sharon. "Which I must say, back then would've been quite an achievement."

Sam held up another story. "Then there's this. Some troupe of traveling swimsuit models? The Florida Girls of Sun City Emporium, lah de dah." She put on a ringmaster's tone. "One million in dough for our doughboys." She shook her head. "My mother did not write that cheesy headline."

"What the heck?" Sharon's hand shot out. "Give me that one." She scanned the clip in silence. "How did Sun City Emporium get *travel* rations?"

Travel rations. The detail triggered something in Sam's memory—her mother at the kitchen table, surrounded by gas coupons. "That's right. You needed coupons to get gas during the war. Mom cursed her editor for that one, sending her all over the city. 'I spend more time waiting on the trolley than writing,' she'd say."

Sharon returned the story to the pile. "A couple of names

keep cropping up. Mrs. Kathleen Young. Miss Thelma Miles? Ring any bells?"

"Nada. But you know, how many people were there to write about in St. Pete? And Mrs. Young drops off the map after Mom left town." Sam picked up a news clipping. "Here is another Thelma at a casino groundbreaking in Las Vegas," Sam said. "But from these pictures, I can't even tell if that's the same person. Last name's Wright. The truly bizarre part?" She fluttered the page.

"What?" Sharon asked.

"I called four one one. There's no such casino." Sam leaned closer to Sharon, eyes bugging. "Never has been." She knew that when a lead turned up false, she should look for who benefited from the lie. But Sharon was already shifting the conversation.

"You remember that Sun City place, though. Don't you?" Sharon patted her wrist. "You used to love their pink candy floss."

Sam did remember begging her mom and dad to take her downtown to see the spinner that churned out cotton candy. She didn't recall ever going with Sharon. "That was a drugstore?"

Sharon shook her head. "More like, well, it was almost like a mall. It was only one store, but the place was enormous. They closed in the early sixties, I think? Once the actual malls opened. But we stopped going at least a decade before then. That store went into serious decline."

The turn the conversation was taking was getting on Sam's nerves. A classic pattern, she thought. Sharon's attempt to change the past by reframing it to include herself.

"Yes, Sun City was quite the place back in the day," Sharon continued. "Though your mother never liked going there. Said the place gave her the creeps."

That caught Sam's attention. Her mother, who'd walked

into mob-controlled casinos without flinching, spooked by a department store? She pulled the press clippings closer, scanning for mentions of Sun City. "What else do you remember about it?"

"Your signal when you wanted to leave. Remember?" Sharon drummed her fingers against the table. "You'd say, 'I want a chocolate malted, Daddy.' Sun City didn't have a soda counter."

Sam smiled, though she recalled no such thing. But she could redirect too. "Look, here's one about some club in Cuba. No date. No byline. Just an announcement—*Bird of Paradise opens in Havana, Lillian Montgomery headlines*. Pretty random."

"Now, this is interesting." Sharon picked up another story. "It's one of those Beautiful Homes features about Ava Juergen's place down in Pinellas Point, where all the old Florida families used to live. Ava still lives down there."

"Ava? You're friends now?" Sam asked, regretting the words as they came out of her mouth. Was Sharon being more annoying than usual, or was impatience how Sam was processing her grief?

To her credit, Sharon ignored her. "This has got to be her daughter." She held up the Florida Girls story. "See that? Doris Juergen. You should pay her a call."

"Where is that?"

"Oh, they call it the Pink Streets now since she sold off her land to developers. But the Juergen mansion is still intact."

"And you think I should just go down there, knock on the door, and ask the old lady about my mother?" Sam fluttered her lips. How could she say what she was really thinking? That all her life she'd blamed her father's wife for what little she knew about her mom. That if this woman had never come into their lives, surely her father would've regaled her with tales of her journalist mother's exploits. But how could he with wife number two around?

When Sharon didn't respond, Sam stalled. "I don't know."

"You don't know?" Sharon was incredulous. "You've wanted to know more about your mother for as long as I've known you. We've *all* been curious. Here, she's left clues, and you don't know if you want to follow them? For someone studying forensics... *Feh.*" Sharon waved her hand dismissively. "*Meshuggener.*"

"I'm specializing in forensic *psychology*." There was no need to mention she might need to find another career now; it would only prove Sharon's point. "I want to understand what makes people do the things they do. Why they make their choices." She looked away. "But to get there, you need a crime scene. Mom's car accident was not a crime." Sam looked toward the window over the sink.

Sharon rapped on the table, bringing Sam's gaze back around. "Listen, *bubeleh*. What is wrong with you? You're not some nebbish, so stop acting like one and show some gumption!"

Easy for her to say, thought Sam. What if all these years she'd been wrong about Imogene Fuchs? What if her mother wasn't the intrepid warrior she'd always believed her to be? What secrets had she meant in her letter?

Her mind veered to Abby.

"I'm moving in with Dad. Permanently." Her daughter's voice warbled over Sharon's recording tape, which was wearing down as fast as Sam's resistance. It made her glad she didn't have an answering machine.

Naturally, Sharon had been standing right beside her. Heard everything. When Sam had said she was taking a little time off work, Sharon hadn't pressed. Still, she couldn't loaf around underfoot all the time. Problem was, Sam had no place else to be.

"For the love of God, Sam, you didn't contest the divorce or go after that man for alimony," Sharon had said after her daughter hung up. "Your daughter is only thirteen. You can't let her tell you what to do."

Of course Abigail could call the shots. She would have her father's blessing and his attorney's backing. Sam couldn't face the disgrace of losing that battle. Her daughter would have to return of her own volition. Contrary to whatever Sharon was thinking, Sam knew that Abigail would tire of Jimmy's girlfriends soon enough. Besides, if Sam turned away from these breadcrumbs her mother had left, wouldn't she be doing exactly what Abby was doing now—refusing to understand her mother's choices?

"I suppose I might as well poke around," said Sam.

"Stay as long as you like. You know you're always welcome here," Sharon said.

For the first time it struck Sam that she and Sharon—the self-possessed, never-at-a-loss Sharon—had both become unmoored.

FOUR

Thelma, Havana, 1945

"LILLIAN WRIGHT! ARE YOU EVER A SIGHT FOR SORE EYES," Doris was saying as Thelma rushed toward the commotion. In the anguish of the past few days, she'd forgotten giving Lillian their address. Of course she had—her cousin George, presumed dead after weeks lost at sea, had suddenly reappeared.

"It's Lillian Montgomery, I'll have you know," said Lillian.

Thelma could practically hear her wink.

"Too right! Thelms said you got married. Congratulations! Is he here?" Doris asked, looking around her into the gated courtyard.

Lillian touched her gloved fingertips to Doris's chin, drawing back her attention. "Sorry to say, but no. My husband, Phil *Skylar*, is on set. Montgomery is my stage name! You like?"

Before Doris could reply, their guest spotted Thelma. "Darling!" She rushed to greet Thelma. Though wearing only a simple white eyelet cotton dress with cap sleeves and a full skirt, Lillian still managed to look like the movie star she was.

"I came straight here. Can we go right to the hospital?"

Thelma stepped forward to give her cousin a hug, noticing

then that she had nothing with her. "Where are your bags? Aren't you staying with us?"

"I couldn't decide what to bring, so I didn't bring anything." She peeled off her gloves and tucked them in her handbag. "I can get everything here, right? El Cantato. That's the big department store everyone says I must visit."

Smiling, Thelma shook her head. She loved her cousin-in-law, but rich people were like a whole other species. She'd never heard of this El Cantato.

"We can't go to the hospital?" asked Lillian.

"No! I mean, I can't. But you probably can."

"What are you talking about?"

"Homer."

"Oh." Lillian leaned in the doorframe. "Lemme guess. Dear uncle has a conniption when he sees you."

"Come in," said Helen, slinking into the now-crowded hallway. "Let's get you something to eat and drink after your journey. That's a long trip from California."

Lighting up at the sight of Helen, Lillian reached to embrace her. "You are such a love. But I can't possibly." She turned and grabbed Thelma's wrist. "My taxi is waiting, and we're going right now."

"Lillian!" The sharp tone in her voice surprised even Thelma and caused her cousin-in-law to drop her wrist. For the life of her, though, she couldn't think of an objection. Why wouldn't she accompany Lillian? Homer Wright could stuff himself. "Hang on, I need to get my pocketbook."

* * *

At the hospital, they found George's room empty, the bed neatly made. Icy fingers clutched at Thelma's heart. She raced to the hallway, stopping the first nurse she saw. "Where is he? Where's George?"

"Perdóneme," she said, before hurrying on her way.

In her shock, Thelma stood stock-still, unsure what to do when—to her horror—the nurse returned with a doctor. "Señor Wright was taken for tests. He will return soon."

Lillian, who'd made her way to the hall by now, thanked them and ushered Thelma into the room. "Don't go all Kathleen Young on these poor people," she said.

For the second time that day, Thelma laughed, even if it was also the second time that day she'd been compared to Kathleen Young. They fell into an easy silence, though she couldn't shake the sense that eyes were on them. "I'm going to go have a smoke," Thelma said. "Do you mind waiting here in case he comes back?"

She barely waited for a response before nipping out into the hall as a man in a shiny suit turned the corner. There was something familiar about him.

Recognition dawned on her. She called to him. "Carlos? Carlos Gonzalez?"

Turning, he twirled the slender tip of his mustache in his fingers. "Thelma Miles," he said. "Or should I say, Señora Wright?"

"Who's this?" asked Lillian, who'd joined them in the hall.

Thelma looked between the two, unsure what to say. She'd practically forgotten about him. "Carlos worked with my father," she said slowly. "And we did a little business too."

Carlos spit out a humorless laugh. "A colleague? Is that how you'd describe my contribution?" He turned to Lillian. "I only kept the entire organization running while this lady was out singing and dancing."

"Delightful," said Lillian. "But right now, her husband is fighting for his life. So if you wouldn't mind...."

Carlos reared back, looking ready for a fight as well.

"Let's talk business another time," Thelma said, feeling the color rise in her face. As far as this man knew, Sal Giancarlo was dead. That should've eliminated any dirt that Carlos held over her, so she'd pushed the man from her mind. She had no intention of jumping into any more unsavory collaborations, nor could she. Not unless she wanted to watch her life fall apart.

"What's wrong with now?" Carlos sneered. "You owe me."

"I don't know what you're talking about," Thelma said, but her voice lacked conviction.

Carlos stepped closer, sounding low and menacing. "Don't play dumb. That's not why I made sure you'd come back."

Made sure? Was he implying he had a hand in George's disappearance?

"Nurse!" Lillian turned away from them in search of help, but Thelma ignored her. Her mind raced. Had Carlos also *made sure* George was *missing* all that time?

"It was you," Thelma accused, her voice low and shaking with anger. "You sabotaged George's plane trying to get to me, and when you discovered I wasn't on that flight, you kept him hidden to lure me back."

A flicker of surprise crossed Carlos's face. "See? You are a smart cookie. But you're in over your head. Your father might be gone, but his sins live on. Yours too. Somebody's gotta pay for 'em."

Before Thelma could respond, a commotion at the end of the hall caught their attention. George was being wheeled back to his room, with Homer Wright striding alongside. "That"—she motioned with her head—"is my father-in-law. He will not take kindly to this news." She didn't mention that he wouldn't take kindly to seeing her either. Luckily, her gambit paid off.

Carlos bent toward Thelma's ear, though he was a bit

shorter so his breath hit hot against her neck as he hissed, "This ain't over. Not by a long shot."

As he walked away, Thelma felt the weight of her past. She'd come to Cuba to start a new life with George, but the web of secrets, and lies, and old vendettas had followed her. Between Carlos's threat and Homer's hostility, it was beginning to look as if finding George had been the easy part. The real challenge still lurked ahead.

* * *

BACK AT THE HOUSE IN MIRAMAR, LILLIAN RAN FOR THE zebra-fur fainting couch, threw herself across it, and covered her face with her elbow. Thelma sat opposite in a red leather club chair, pushing at her cuticles.

"Who was that horrid fellow?" Lillian lifted her arm to look at Thelma. "You know he's in love with you, right?"

The idea that Carlos Gonzalez could love anyone besides himself had never occurred to Thelma, and she didn't want to have that conversation. Not when he'd confessed to causing George's accident. Not when her husband was fighting to recover in that hospital bed and his father wanted to kidnap him. "Hardly. Speaking of love, how's married life treating you?"

Hands now folded across her midsection, eyes closed, Lillian pursed her lips. "Better than it has been treating you, I'd say. But you know, it's Hollywood. Who knows if it'll last." She faced Thelma and put her fist beneath her chin. "For now, I'm head over heels. I'm so glad you got to meet him."

"Me too. He's dreamy," Thelma said, but the words felt hollow. Performative. "I wonder, though, if I failed you in some way. You never mentioned him, and then suddenly there he was in Las Vegas, and you two were engaged."

"What? You mean while your husband was missing at sea and you were having a go at the Giancarlos? Right." Lillian settled in her seat with a mischievous grin. "We'd only just met. On that dreadful little Red Skelton movie I told you about? Not long before I came to Las Vegas. Anyway, I am sorry I wasn't here to help you deal with Homer 'til now."

Was it Thelma's imagination, or was Lillian blushing? That was new. She talked a good game, but she was as lovesick as anyone. Still, she felt compelled to confess. "Lillian, I haven't told him Sal is here."

"Well, of course you haven't," said Lillian, shifting to face her cousin-in-law.

"I—" Thelma stopped herself mid-sentence. "What?"

"We killed Sal in Vegas, remember?" Lillian blinked. "And since Imogene's mafia exposé was also killed, we need to keep all that mum. My cousin is heavily medicated, in and out of consciousness. He could tell anyone. We can't have that."

Thelma watched her lean back and wondered, not for the first time, what it was like to have grown up with the kind of money and love that made you believe you could reshape reality to suit your needs. But then again, wasn't that exactly what they were all doing?

Lillian cupped her elbows into her hands, her mood shifting. "I can't imagine George will waver, but I am worried about Homer."

Thelma's heart sunk. This was what she feared all along, that Homer's money might have more pull than their love. "It *is* a lot of money."

"Oh, Thelms," said Lillian, moving to kneel beside her friend. "That's only part of it."

"What do you mean?"

"Uncle Homer will cut him off from everyone in the family. *Everyone.*"

Fluttering her lips, Thelma couldn't think of anything to say. Much as she wanted to hear Lillian affirm that George would stay no matter what, she didn't want to hold on to false hope. She shrugged. "I'm not going anywhere," she said. "So there's that."

"Good girl." Lillian stood, extending her hand. "Come on, let's get out of this dump and go shopping. I need some clothes."

Thelma looked toward the door. "But I thought we were going to meet Helen and Doris."

"We are! At the Tropicana. You can't expect me to wear this." Lillian indicated her sundress. "And don't tell me you're bone-tired. I've got just the thing for that too." Ever the pharmacist's daughter, she pulled a white packet from her pocket and flicked it between her fingers. "You used to be able to get this in Coca-Cola!"

"Thanks, I'm good with tequila," Thelma said, her mother's own glassy stare flashing through her memory. She would not risk becoming an addict like her mother. Still, as she watched Lillian pour and sniff a line, a new hollowness opened inside her. Here she was, about to go out *shopping* while George fought for his healing in that hospital bed. Lillian was right. There wasn't anything she could do for him. All she really wanted to know was whether he'd still be hers when he finally got out of that bed.

FIVE

Sam, St. Petersburg, 1978

SAM APPROACHED THE GRAND GULF-FACING, Mediterranean-style villa with a determination that soon—like the stone entryways, upper balconies, and decorative columns—crumbled. Its faded salmon-pink stucco and white trim exterior suggested that this mansion's best days were in the past. Feeling more than a twinge of solidarity, Sam swatted down her urge to mow the old lady's yard.

After double-checking the address, she pressed the doorbell. Not a peep. Probably broken.

A gecko skittered past, and she started—the disrepair made her jittery. What if the only people living here were squatters?

To her left, a window faced the wraparound porch. She peered through the pane, only to come face-to-face with the barrel end of a shotgun. Sam covered her face with her purse—a pleather imitation of the Jackie shoulder bag—and let out a bloodcurdling scream.

The door flew open. "What in the devil?" said a tiny woman, still behind the pointed gun. "Who are you, and why are you on my porch screaming like a banshee?"

Why was she on this porch? Hadn't enough of her life been

upended in the last six months? What good would come of digging up the past now?

"C at got your tongue?" the woman asked. She was maybe five five in bare feet, with a braid the color of steel wool piled atop her head like a crown. Round but for her small, delicate feet. She had to be in her eighties. "What is wrong with you?"

Her stepmother had asked the same question, and Sam still had no answer. Was she more afraid of finding out something she didn't want to know about her mom? Or the fact she was not merely the kind of wife you left behind, but also the kind of mother?

"I'm looking for a Mrs. Elsa Juergen?"

"Nobody here by that name," the woman said.

Sam was about to apologize and take her leave when the gun cocked, followed by a blast.

"Nothing like the smell of gunpowder in the morning," said the woman, grinning madly before planting her shotgun by the entry and turning back into the house. "You coming or what? You're in the right place."

The cool gloom hardly beckoned. Knickknacks crowded every surface, all coated by layers of dust. A stench wafted her way, not of rotting food or animal matter but something that might cover either—mothballs. Then again, this lady had already left her weapon at the door. From the way she'd handled the gun—too practiced for someone playing at being threatening —Sam sensed that any danger was over. It wasn't like she was needed elsewhere.

"Shut the door behind you," the woman continued without looking back. Sam followed the braid into what turned out to be a bright-yellow kitchen.

Unlike the rest of the house, this room was tidy and in functioning order, though it hadn't been updated since the 1940s and had its share of clutter. Worn tea towels hung from hooks, chipped mugs and plates sat drying on a dish rack, and an assortment of snow globes lined the windowsill—the Eiffel Tower, the old Hollywoodland sign, and a waterfront building that read Bird of Paradise, Havana. A bongo drum sat in one corner.

"Tea?" the woman turned and asked as she stepped into the tiny kitchen. "Miss...? I still didn't get your name."

"Sam Fontana," she said, taking a seat. "And you are?"

"That's my chair," the woman said without turning. "Anywhere but there."

"Sure." Sam moved to the opposite end of the table, taking the only other seat in the room.

Taking Sam's response to mean she wanted tea, Elsa Juergen poured two cups from a china pot. Premade, as if she'd been waiting for a visitor. Her hands trembled slightly as she poured, causing Sam to wonder if it was age or nerves. The old lady wouldn't try to poison her, would she? She'd poured from the same teapot, the liquid identical in both cups.

"Lemon or milk?" she asked.

Not five minutes ago, this woman had pointed a gun at her, and now they were having tea like it was a social call? The rapid behavioral shift suggested either mental instability or extreme manipulation. After all, a good poisoner could build tolerance, and the strong scent of Earl Grey could mask other odors.

"Neither," said Sam. "Do you have any whiskey?"

"Whiskey? It's eleven o'clock in the morning," said the woman. "How about some honey?"

Sam wanted to scream. *Goddamn right! Far too early to be shot at, lady.*

"Fine," she said. "I take it you know who Mrs. Juergen is?"

Turning back to the counter, the woman extracted a jar of honey from the cabinet over her sink. "You are correct," she said and promptly left the room.

Sam jerked upright. She wouldn't be going back for the gun now, would she? Why had she listened to Sharon? Then a cupboard opened in the next room as Elsa Juergen scrambled through plates and glassware and who knew what else.

But the woman simply returned with a bottle of hard stuff and two shot glasses. "I do know a Mrs. Juergen." She poured two generous shots. "My mother."

Sam looked over the steam rising from her teacup, amazed at her good fortune. "Are you Doris?"

The woman reared back, and her eyes misted over. Sam could feel her pain. Had they been sisters? "I'm sorry, I—"

"Little girl, you have no idea what you're getting into." She knocked back her drink. "Doris was my daughter. Dead going on twenty-seven years now."

The woman let out a deep sigh, and her features went still. Sam gave her silence room to breathe. Losing her mother at eight was awful. She didn't think she'd survive losing Abby. Or had she already?

With a shake of her head, the woman's eyes popped open. "I imagine you're Imogene Fuchs's child. Yes, I can see from your face I got it right. Been wondering when you'd turn up. If I'd still be alive to see it. Seems I can't quit this life before everyone I love."

Her words stunned Sam, though not for the sorrow behind them. No one had ever come out and guessed she was Imogene's daughter.

Taking a seat, the woman placed a box of store-bought short-bread cookies on the table. "Here. This could take a while."

After introducing herself as Miss Elsa Juergen, she pointed at the bongo drum in the corner. "I expect that's why you're here," she began.

Sam leaned closer, but as Elsa spoke of Paris in the 1920s, jazz clubs, and a Cuban musician named Augustín, her hopes fell. As captivating as Miss Juergen's story was, Imogene Fuchs wasn't part of it.

"I loved a colored man back when it was a crime. It's why I never troubled myself over Doris, you see?"

See what? Sam wondered. But Elsa rambled on without pause.

"We couldn't get married of course, and, well, I still wanted my Doris." She turned back, leaning closer to Sam. "We named her after Doris Fleischman. You know her?"

Another person Sam had never heard of, but she held her tongue. "In our work," Dr. Filmore would've chided her, "patience is like film. Rush and you'll blur the picture before it can develop."

"When Doris signed into the Waldorf-Astoria using her maiden name back in 1922, the scandal made the papers all the way to France. This was just after her wedding! Not that Gus and I could marry. I let everyone think my husband died in France." She gestured at the house. "We lived right under everyone's noses in absolute freedom for years. Making music. Making art. Making love."

Her immodesty made Sam blush—Elsa Juergen looked to be in her eighties. Least she's a good storyteller, she thought.

"Your mother figured it out right away, who Gus was. But then, she kept a lot of people's secrets," Elsa said. "I guess that's why I told her the whole story. To the outside world, Mr. Céspedes was my groundskeeper."

Eureka, thought Sam. "That house and garden story?" Sam straightened. "About 'Mrs. Juergen's Immaculate Home,'" she said, using air quotes.

"That was all Gus's doing; he really was a whiz in the garden." Elsa's voice hardened. "But I'm tired of that game. Fact is, I'm just tired. I've told you everything there is to tell."

Except Sam wasn't here for Elsa Juergen's story. She

wanted to know why her mother left that news clipping behind. Don't rush the process, she reminded herself. "It must be exhausting staying on top of all this," Sam motioned around the room. "Was my mother a comfort? Before she passed?"

Elsa looked Sam up and down, as if seeing her for the first time, making her feel self-conscious about her stained peasant blouse and unwashed hair. She really had to get it together.

"You don't remember?" Elsa asked.

Heat rose at Sam's neck. *Remember what?*

"Never mind. I can see you don't. You came here. With her. Back in '48. Your mom's boss, Agnes something or other, had just asked your mother to stay on out in California. Your father was none too happy about that. Said if she left again to never come back."

Sam was stuck on the date. That was two years before her mother died, when her parents were still very much married. Weren't they?

"You should be proud," said Elsa. "But I wouldn't be surprised if her ambition isn't what got her killed."

Killed? Miss Juergen was clearly confused. "My mother died in a car crash."

"Are you sure about that?" Elsa lifted her near-hairless brows. "Did you know what she was working on?"

Sam shook her head. The way she switched between personas—homestead protector, free spirit, bereft mother—indicated significant executive function. But that didn't make her a reliable source.

Fingers snapped inches from Sam's face. "Eh. I guess you're not so much like your mother after all."

Her words sliced into Sam's reserve, that part of herself she kept hidden. Always. Even from Jimmy. Wasn't this what she'd feared from the beginning? How could she measure up to a mother she'd never known? Now her father was gone too. Scooping her purse to her chest, she toppled her teacup.

"I'm sorry, I— I have to go," she said, righting her mug.

Elsa's last words followed her out—"You're not so much like your mother after all"—echoing in Sam's head as she drove mindlessly around her old hometown. Finally, she had to top up her gas tank. The fumes helped ground her. By the time she parked in front of her childhood home, she'd recovered from her daze. Time to get back to Miami and sort out her life.

Sharon met her at the door. "Sam, dear. Someone named Helen Young was here looking for you."

"I don't know anyone by that name." Sam shrugged. "Did she look like a Moonie?"

Sharon laughed. "I wouldn't have opened the door. No! Used to be Fuller. Helen Fuller. One of those Florida Girls."

Why would one of the Florida Girls be looking for Sam?

SIX

Thelma, Havana, 1945

THE TAXI PULLED UP TO THE SPRAWLING SPANISH colonial mansion, its whitewashed walls framed by palm fronds and lush bougainvillea. Thelma's heart raced as she helped George out of the cab, her fingers clutching his arm tight. She was hovering, she knew, but she couldn't shake her dread. In the month since George had told his father in no uncertain terms he planned to stay, she'd found separate accommodations for her father. Yet the nagging sensation lingered.

"Let me do it," George said, his voice strained with the effort of maintaining his dignity. Using the hood for support, he reached for his crutch inside the car.

Peggy clucked her tongue. "Don't be a numbskull, Georgie. You have the use of a left arm and half a right leg. How're you gonna feel when we have to turn this car right back around to San Lazáro?"

A smile pulled at the corners of George's mouth, quickly replaced by a wince. Inside his near-full body cast, he looked diminished, vulnerable in a way that made Thelma's chest tighten.

Lillian threw open the doors, her Hollywood smile plastered on. "Welcome to Dead Carcass Manor!"

"Lills!" George's face lit up. "This is a surprise."

Thelma tried not to be hurt at how much more delighted he seemed on seeing his cousin than he had her. At least the moment passed quickly; as soon as he'd settled in the bedroom, he fell into a deep sleep. The women gathered in the dining room, their voices low and urgent.

"I don't know what you're so worried about, Thelms," Peggy said, spooning rice onto her plate. "I'm not bringing any money to this deal."

"But that's how we set it up to begin with," said Thelma too sharply.

Lillian leaned in, brows knitted. "And I already told you, George will get an allowance from the trust. Enough to live on, especially in Cuba. And once you start making money at the club...."

"That could be a while," Thelma said, immediately regretting her words.

"I can always lend you money," said Lillian.

"No," said Thelma. "We'll be fine."

"Hey, if you're asking," said Peggy, her platinum bob swinging as she leaned forward, "I wouldn't say no to some cash. This hair doesn't bleach itself."

"Do you need money, Peggy?" asked Lillian.

"Oh my God, Lills," said Peggy. "Did you lose your sense of humor in the divorce?"

"Low blow!" said Lillian, but she was laughing.

Her marriage to stuntman Phil Skylar had infuriated her manager—wrong time in her career, his lack of star power, that she'd be the tramp who took up with anyone on set. When Phil dumped her, though, he wasn't about to let that be the story.

Montgomery's Fame Fractures Fragile Phil's Ego!

Marquee Madness: Montgomery Fires Jealous Co-Star from Real-Life Romance!

Stunt Double Can't Double as Supportive Hubby: Montgomery Axes Jealous Phil!

Before knowing an actual movie star, Thelma would've bought those headlines without question. Now she couldn't believe how she'd fallen for those rags. Meanwhile, that movie star was glaring at their dirty dishes.

"At least let me hire someone for you," Lillian said. "With Sal gone, there's no reason not to have some help in here."

As if on cue, the doorbell rang.

"That must be her!" said Lillian, jumping to her feet.

"You already hired someone?" asked Thelma, unsure of strangers even without Sal around. It was hard to shake the vigilance that had followed them from Las Vegas.

"You're a goddess, Lills," said Peggy.

Thelma eyed Peggy as if she were a traitor. "What we need is a nurse," she said.

"I have one of those coming too," Lillian said over her shoulder as she headed for the front door.

"C'mon, Thelms," Peggy said in a low tone. "You gotta admit we need all the help we can get at this point."

In stormed a ball of grandmotherly Italian fury, short and stout in widow's weeds. "You must be Thelma," the woman said, her drooping nose seconding the disapproval in her tone. "We must talk."

Thelma's palms lit up. Her heart pounded. And she knew—this was Sal's wife. Candy? Cara?

Lillian caught up to her. "Excuse me. Ma'am? The agency said you were...." She trailed off before extending a jaunty arm in the woman's direction. "I'm Lillian Wright. You must be?"

Without taking her hand, the woman answered. "I am Mrs. Salvatore Giancarlo, Carlotta Ambrosia Giancarlo."

Peggy gasped.

Red splotches broke out on Thelma's neck.

Mercifully, Lillian stepped in. "Mrs. Giancarlo! My dear! I am so sorry for your loss."

The sudden shift unsettled Carlotta and sparked Thelma's memory—a disgraced mobster's wife had no one. When Sal betrayed Ben Siegel, it put Mrs. Giancarlo in danger. Carlotta wanted cash, not condolences.

"You're that actress. Getting a divorce," Carlotta said, extending her index and pinky fingers toward the floor. "*Facciamo le corna.*"

"I am indeed"—Lillian leaned toward Carlotta—"traveling incognito."

Before the woman could ask for compensation to keep that news to herself, Thelma stood. "Please. Come with me so we can discuss this in—"

The front door burst open. "Carlotta!"

All eyes turned toward the hall into the dining room as in marched Sal, his face blotched with rage.

"Santa Maria!" cried Carlotta, looking as if she'd seen the dead come to life, which in a sense, she had. "I lit candles... Is this some devil's trick?"

Her shock morphed into indignation. "*Ingrato!* Where have you been?" she cried as, with surprising speed, she advanced and slapped him in the face.

Almost as suddenly, her fury crumbled. She reached for his face with her weathered hands, tracing new lines with trembling fingers. "*Figlio mio,*" she whispered, her voice breaking. "You're too skinny, my Salvatore."

"*Mi amor!*" cried Sal as he embraced his wife, planting kisses on both cheeks as Carlotta's tears streamed freely.

Thelma thought she might get whiplash. She kneed the back of Peggy's chair, but her friend merely shrugged. As long as she'd known of Carlotta, she'd believed that the relationship between Sal and his wife was transactional. Yet here they stood, holding one another as if they'd survived a train wreck. Then Sal was holding Carlotta's head, looking into her eyes and murmuring, no less.

That was when she knew—not through one of her premonitions but the simpler certainty of betrayal—that her father had set her up. Remembering his assurances that he was happy to leave when she'd asked, her insides burned. It was only a matter of time before word got out that Sal Giancarlo was very much alive and living in Cuba.

The *clop whoosh* sound of crutches heading toward the dining room roused Thelma from these ruminations. "No," she whispered, but her husband had already made it to the dining room.

"Sal Giancarlo?" George stopped, propped on his crutches, torn pajamas covering what little skin was not beneath plaster. "What the hell are you doing here?" Between his casts and crutches, her husband looked about as threatening as a kitten.

After glancing at George, Sal's eyes locked on Thelma. "It's better this way," he said quietly before addressing the room. "Did your wife not tell you I was in Cuba?"

"Thelma?"

The hurt stamped on her husband's face cut Thelma to the core. She stepped forward, words tumbling out. "George, I can explain—"

"Explain what?" His voice was low, treacherous. "That you've been lying to me? That your father—the man who nearly got us killed—is here?"

Sal clucked his tongue. "Hey, George-o. Watch yourself. I heard my wife was in town, and I came to get her." He turned to leave, pausing at the doorway to address Thelma. "Just remember, *vita mia*, family is all we have in the end."

All we have? Did Sal even know what he was saying? He'd scarred her for life when he discovered she existed, far worse than the mark on her face. She rolled her shoulders back—showgirl posture, signaling a strength she didn't fully feel. "Get out, Sal," she growled, sounding alarmingly like her mother, surprised as Sal merely trundled off with Carlotta.

Her husband's face reddened. Had she made things worse?

"The rest of you too. Go," George said, his voice cracking. "I need to speak with my wife."

Tears blurred Thelma's vision as Peggy and Lillian filed out, their faces etched with concern. George, clearly pained, was still upright.

"Sweetheart, at least have a seat."

"No, you sit down and shut up," he said, the harshest he'd ever spoken to her.

Stunned into acquiescence, Thelma pulled out a chair and sat to face her husband.

"I had to give up my father." George's voice seethed with rage. "My family. And while yes, they come with their own blend of poison, they won't actually kill you. Your family... is another matter."

Thelma dropped her head. "Darling, we haven't really talked about this but"—she looked into her beloved's steely-blue eyes—"I know my father had nothing to do with your plane's ... malfunction."

"I thought you were leaving all that behind," he finally said, taking an audible breath. "But you brought it with you."

Though this was not how she'd envisioned sharing this news, Thelma had failed to make any other plan. Now, there was no promise she could make, no—

"Guys, listen to this!" Peggy shouted and she and Lillian raced into the room with the Zenith portable. Over static, President Truman's voice crackled to life, speaking of scientific marvels. A hush fell, but the words washed over Thelma as she considered the ruins she'd made of her marriage. How coolly she'd assessed Lillian's nuptials mere moments earlier.

"An atomic bomb? What the heck is that?" Peggy asked, bringing Thelma back into the room, where Truman droned on.

"WE ARE NOW PREPARED TO OBLITERATE MORE RAPIDLY AND *completely every productive enterprise the Japanese have above ground in any city.*"

THE SOUND OF GUNSHOTS SENT THEM RACING TO THE courtyard. Even George. People spilled from their homes into the streets. Neighbors embraced. A man blew frantically on a trumpet, the discordant notes somehow fitting the chaotic jubilation.

"They're celebrating," Doris said. "Look—even the soldiers."

Indeed, uniformed men were hugging civilians, passing bottles of rum hand to hand.

"The war is over," Lillian whispered, her eyes bright with unshed tears. "After all these years."

Thelma felt no relief, only a hollowness spreading beneath her ribs. While the world reveled in peace, for her, the siege had just begun.

SEVEN

Sam, St. Petersburg, 1978

Helen Young, it turned out, lived in the next neighborhood over from the Fuchs. She'd left her address but not her phone number. "Tell her to stop by anytime," she'd said, according to Sharon.

Sam had decided to head for Helen Young's straight away. Better than run the risk of talking to her father's wife another moment. She'd take the Juergen lady's story and run with it. "Oh, yes! Your mother and father had been on the rocks for years," she'd say. Or, "Murdered? But why would someone go after your mother?" No, thanks. Talking to a stranger was far preferable.

The address led Sam to a pink cottage where a man in a straw fedora and bow tie stood hosing down the sidewalks. Mr. Young? Indecision seized her, alongside another urge to call Jimmy. She knew nothing about these people she was tracking down.

Jimmy.

She hated that he was still her reflex, but then he was the only person in her life who'd met her mother. Still, why him? They'd stopped communicating ages ago after he'd finally found

47

another job. No. It was even before then. During that long stretch after he'd lost his case. She'd assumed that distance and lack of communication was what had happened with her mother and father, but if Elsa Juergen was to be believed, she was wrong about that too.

"Say there," came a muffled voice. "Are you all right?"

Outside her window stood the man—no longer holding the hose—and a woman, both looking into her car expectantly. Was she all right? She'd lost a few minutes again, her head resting on the steering wheel.

Grabbing her bag, she pushed the door open. "Yes, fine. Sorry," she said. "I was meditating."

Sam's boss—former boss?—had once said this to her when she'd walked in on him napping in his office. She doubted Leonard Filmore had ever meditated a day in his life, but she'd recently adopted the excuse. It was stunningly effective.

"I was looking for Helen Young," Sam continued. "I was told she lived here?"

"You must be Sally! I mean Sam. Sam Fuchs!" The woman clapped her hands together. "It's a pleasure to finally meet you."

She reached for Sam's hand. "I'm Helen Young, and this"— she did a half turn, motioning toward her partner as if presenting an award—"is my husband, Archie Young."

Like her spouse, Helen was a redhead, though hers was more a pale copper shade. They matched overall—both were slender and small boned—but they had the kind of magnetism you'd notice walking down the street.

"Pleased to meet you," said Archie, giving Sam the distinct impression that he was, in fact, pleased to meet her. "Let's get out of this heat," he said. "You two have some catching up to do."

Catching up? Either he was being disingenuous or he was clueless. "I wouldn't want to impose," she said.

"Nonsense. I asked you to come," said Helen. "I've got some photographs of your mother's you probably haven't seen."

Sam deflated. Photos of her mother's would be more pictures she'd taken as a reporter, which so far, had revealed very little. Yet Sam cataloged the disconnect between their casual manner and the urgency that had brought Helen to Sharon's door looking for her. Whatever warning they wanted to deliver, they'd planned this meeting.

"Archie was about to head out," Helen added. "It'll just be us."

They turned toward the house in time for Sam to catch the whoosh of a curtain. She stopped. Who else was there?

Archie gave a slight bow. "I'm off to shuffleboard league. I'll grab my keys and be on my way." On opening the door, a fluff of golden fur bounded into the yard, peed, and pranced back.

"Don't mind Pumpkin." Helen reached down and picked up her dog. "She's all bark and no bite. Isn't that right, my baby?"

After retrieving his keys from a candy dish beside the door, Archie bent to kiss the dog before heading to the carport. "Don't hold supper on my account," he said to his wife before turning to Sam. "We'll have to make plans for another time."

"Oh, love, she's only here a few days," said Helen, reaching for Sam's hand. "Come, let's sit in the Florida room," said Helen. "It's the most comfortable spot in the house this time of day."

Like most of these postwar builds, the house was a single-story concrete box with an open floor plan. Unless someone was hiding in a bedroom, they had to be alone. Maybe the heat was getting to Sam.

Smack in the center of their living room sat an off-white baby grand piano topped by an army of family photos.

"Is that you?" asked Sam as she moved toward the

photographs on the top board. At the center was an eight-by-ten hand-tinted photograph showing six girls posing around a piano in what appeared to be a grocery store's stockroom. A young girl with strawberry hair sat at the bench.

"Oh, that!" Helen marched past her to the piano, picked up the frame, and handed it to Sam, simultaneously turning another, smaller image face down. "Your mother took that, matter of fact. When they didn't end up using it in the paper, she gave it to us."

There was no caption, but Sam was fairly certain that these were the original Florida Girls, and so Helen Fuller must have become Helen Young. In her kelly green shirtdress, the woman before her looked like a retired schoolteacher. Maybe a librarian. Not a former dancing girl. And not the kind of story her mother typically pursued.

"That other picture?" Sam motioned toward it with her chin. "What's that one?"

Helen reddened as she stooped to place Pumpkin on the terrazzo floor.

Sam crossed her arms. "Why did you ask me to come here?"

"Please, why don't we sit—"

This was all too much for Sam. She reached around the woman to grab the picture, unprepared for what appeared when she flipped the frame—an image of Helen at a podium behind a display of books with titles like *Glitter*, *Gams*, and *Girls Who Love Girls*. "You're a writer too?"

Helen slapped the photo face down, right where it had been. "Well, I am. That's why I wanted to talk about what your mother was working on."

"Twenty-eight years ago?"

"Please." She nodded, tucking a loose lock behind her ear. "If you'll come with me, I have a whole photo album I think you'd like to see."

Sam forced herself to pause. It wasn't like this lady had pulled a gun on her. Why was she being so confrontational? "Sure."

Once they were seated in the patio room, Helen produced a photo album. "Let me start by saying, I read about your father's passing. I'm so sorry for your loss. Please accept my condolences."

The unexpected sympathy cracked something in Sam's stony wall. Beyond Sharon's breathy updates—*Joanie's getting married! Stuart landed in jail! Your old gym teacher quit and moved to Alaska!*—Sam hadn't kept up with her schoolmates. Still, she'd noticed that, even during shiva, her classmates had stayed away. Helen addressing her loss directly was disarming. And, she would later reflect, most likely calculated.

The page Helen opened showed a photograph of her with three other women against a salt-scarred seawall, their sundresses whipping in the wind as waves crashed behind them. They looked like the women from the Florida Girls article.

"My mother took this?" Sam reached for the photo album. "When was she in Cuba?"

"She came in '48, I think?"

As Helen dithered about whether the visit was in 1947 or 1948, Sam flipped the page. The black-and-white image there showed the arched entrance to a stone building, topped by a hot white neon sign that read Bird of Paradise, with an abstract flourish suggesting either a bird or a plant. The same as the snow globe she'd seen. She pointed. "What is that? That same building was in a snow globe over at Elsa Juergen's house."

"That"—Helen pointed—"is the nightclub I ran with Doris. Thelma and Peggy too. We called it the Bird."

She continued, waxing on about rum-soaked nights and mambo bands. None of it was tied to her mother, but Sam was loath to interrupt. Whatever it was that bonded these women, it was grounded in shared pain.

"We left in 1953," Helen said, though her tone had changed. "The revolution, well, it wasn't safe anymore. No place for a child anyway."

"1953?" Sam's research focused on family separation after the 1959 revolution. "What happened in 1953?"

Helen slid her readers down her nose and appraised Sam. "You didn't think Castro appeared fully formed in 1959, did you?"

That did it. "Listen, thanks for—"

"Did Mrs. Juergen tell you she thinks your mother's accident wasn't an accident at all?"

Sam dropped back into her seat. "Do you think my mother was murdered? Is that why you asked me here?"

Helen reached into her pocket for a tissue. "Well, dear, your mother did have a way of finding disparate threads and making a tapestry. And she was always investigating things certain people wouldn't have wanted exposed."

"What kinds of things? What was she investigating?"

Helen looked away. "You know she reported on organized crime, but her last story was something else. Have you heard of Elizabeth Short?"

"You mean the Black Dahlia case?"

Helen's head snapped back to Sam.

"It was in some clips she left behind." Sam shrugged, though she'd have loved to take credit for having encyclopedic knowledge. "Still unsolved."

"Folgers?" Helen asked, removing her readers as she moved toward the kitchen, not waiting for an answer.

"I'd love a Coke if you have any," Sam called after her.

When Helen returned with coffee cups, she was all business. "From the moment I read your father's obituary, I wanted to get in touch. Your mother had been in contact with government officials about my Doris, you see. And I was curious if you'd come across anything about her investigations in her effects."

Midway through lifting her mug Sam stopped, struck by the now-obvious clues. The way Archie had kissed the dog but not his wife. Elsa's mention that she'd never "troubled herself" over Doris in the middle of her own love story. The photo of Helen with a stack of lesbian pulp fiction titles. At some point, Helen and Doris had been a couple. The revelation paled in comparison to the betrayal Sam felt. This woman wasn't interested in helping Sam learn about her mother. "Did my mother mention to you that she was leaving me a letter?"

"She left you a letter?" Helen leaned closer. "I didn't know. What's in it?"

Sam was tiring of the coy act. "Mostly press clippings. The name Thelma cropped up a few times. Sun City Emporium. Also the Youngs." She slammed her teacup on the coffee table. How had she not made the connection? "Wait—are you related?"

"My husband's family owned Sun City Emporium. They sponsored the Florida Girls. That's how we met but"—her hand shook as she set down her own cup—"it's not that interesting."

Not interesting? This woman was withholding something. "The Giancarlo name came up a few times. Mean anything to you?" Sam watched Helen's face, sizing her up.

On hearing the name Giancarlo, Helen tilted her head. It was subtle, but Sam caught it. "We all thought we'd live forever back then. Doris...." Her voice caught, and she stood abruptly to face the window. "Well, none of us knew how it would end."

"I'm sorry." Sam knew Doris was dead but didn't quite know how to offer condolences on an unacknowledged relationship. Before she could press further, a ringing telephone sounded but quickly cut off. "But that was nine years after my mother died. You don't think it's related."

"As I said," Helen began again, "your mother—"

"Mom!"

They looked toward the voice. Sam caught Helen's reaction —her mouth had become a straight line—and stifled a gasp.

"Not now, dear," Helen said. "Take a message."

A tall woman in a tangerine bodysuit clicked toward them in wood-soled slides, her bleached blond curls bouncing against her dark eyebrows with each step. The woman looked a little younger than Sam, but she didn't remember any Youngs from high school. Maybe the hair was aging her. Either way, she must have been adopted. There was no way that Amazonian creature had sprung forth from the bird-boned likes of Helen and Archie Young. Sam had thought they were alone.

The woman stopped, her arm extending just short of the room as the phone cord uncoiled to its maximum distance. She waved the earpiece in Sam's direction. "It's for *her*."

EIGHT

Thelma, Havana, 1945

After seeing Lillian to the airport—she was due back on set in Los Angeles—they gathered in the living room. World War II was officially over, but among the animal heads and exotic pelts, the atmosphere inside their Miramar home was anything but peaceful. Thelma dropped onto the sofa as if weighted down by lead.

In an attempt to ease the tension, Doris passed drinks. George declined. "I think I'll hit the sack," he said.

Thelma reached for him, forcing a smile. "All right, darling."

He reversed away from her, maneuvering toward the bedroom foyer in the wheelchair he'd reluctantly agreed to use. "I'll see myself to bed," he said.

His tone reminded Thelma of arriving in Iowa with her mother, her small suitcase still unpacked, the unfamiliar crickets loud outside her window.

A sharp knock at the door sent a jolt through the room. "Who's that?" asked George, stopping before he was halfway to the bedroom hallway.

Before the twinge in her left palm caught fire, Thelma rubbed her hand hard against her thigh and downed her G and

T. Peggy rose to answer, lifting her brows as she passed Thelma. They both knew it couldn't be her father. Sal Giancarlo didn't knock.

"There's someone here to see you, Thelma," Peggy announced, though she sensed her friend knew exactly who it was.

Rising quickly, Thelma knocked over a stuffed mongoose on the coffee table, losing any advantage as Pegs returned, followed by a balding man with round eyeglasses wearing a custom suit.

Artemis Clauer, her father's consigliere.

"Mr. Clauer," she said, righting the taxidermied animal. "I wasn't expecting you."

Artemis scanned the room, scrutinizing the hunting decor and strained faces without a tic. "My apologies for interrupting. But there is some urgent business I must discuss with Mrs. Wright. Alone. Perhaps there is somewhere we could speak privately."

George looked between Thelma and the newcomer, the groove between his eyebrows deepening as anger supplanted confusion. "Anything you have to say to my wife you can say in front of me, *Clauer*."

Thelma winced as her husband emphasized the Germanic-sounding name; she herself had mistaken him as German—and potentially a Nazi spy—when they'd first met. But Mr. Clauer was Jewish.

"I'm under strict instructions," Clauer said.

"Mr. Clauer, this is my husband, Mr. George Wright." Thelma took Clauer's arm and motioned toward George. "Darling, this is Sal Giancarlo's attorney. He—"

"Then that goes double," said George.

"Come on, George," Helen said, standing to grab the handles on George's chair. "You of all people understand attorney-client privilege."

"I'm beat after all this excitement." Doris jumped up, her voice overly cheery. "Nice to meet you, Mr. Clauer."

"I know my cue," said Peggy, moving between their guest and George.

"Helen, don't you dare wheel me off."

"George is right," said Thelma, pulling on their visitor. "We'll go to the dining room. You all just stay right here."

Once she'd dragged Clauer out of earshot, Thelma dropped his arm. "What are you doing here?" she spat, shutting the door behind them. "My father, of all people, knows that my husband is not receptive to such interruptions."

Artemis placed a suitcase on the table. "Your father insisted I deliver this immediately. He is in Miami where recent events have, well, accelerated his plans."

"What plans?" Thelma asked. "And what events? When did Sal go to Miami? Scratch that. I don't want to know. What are you—"

But Artemis wasn't listening. Instead, as she spoke, he placed his briefcase on the dining room table with tender care, sliding his hands along the sides like he was caressing it, then finally unlocking the lid, which popped open to reveal stacks of one hundred dollar bills. All in hard American currency.

Thelma clamped her mouth shut and leaned over the case. "Are you out of your mind? How much money is in there?"

"Five hundred thousand dollars," Artemis stated coolly. "From your father, in light of recent complications."

"Five hundred—" Crossing her arms, Thelma took a step back. "Where did it come from?"

The edge of Artemis's lip turned up, somewhere between a smirk and a grin. "It's your share from the sale of the Casino Royale. Sal felt it was in the best interest of our business concerns if we left that market for now."

"And what does he expect in return?"

"For now? Discretion. And perhaps a more proactive approach to certain business opportunities in Havana." Artemis's gaze flicked back toward the door they'd walked through. "We'll be in touch of course."

An icy dread washed over Thelma as she stared at the trunk. They'd been plenty discrete. This could only mean one thing—Sal was back in the game. But she wasn't interested in playing. "We don't want your blood money. Find somebody else."

"But you're family. And you know that family is everything to Mr. Giancarlo."

It took all Thelma's will to refrain from scoffing. "It didn't seem that way for the first eighteen years of my life, Mr. Clauer."

Whether Artemis heard her, his only reply was to close the suitcase and place it gently on the floor. "Do what you will with the money, but I am leaving it here. Know, though, there are people who won't take kindly to your... career change. Whatever you decide, watch your back."

The sound of George's wheelchair approaching interrupted them, and Artemis pivoted to leave. "Enjoy the rest of your evening," he said, stopping at the door. "If you need anything, you know how to reach me."

Seconds before George entered the room, Thelma kicked the suitcase as far under the table as she could. The front door swished shut as her husband wheeled himself—one-armed—into the dining room with Helen, Doris, and Peggy trailing behind.

"What did he want?" he asked through clenched teeth.

Thelma plastered on a smile, discreetly blocking his view of the table, glad that fuller skirts were once again in fashion. "Nothing, darling. He just wanted to tell me that Sal is in Miami, living discreetly. Nothing for us to worry about."

"Why would he come here to tell you that?"

"You know how strange they are," she said. "They think it's less risky to speak in person than over the phone. I guess? Why don't we head back to the living room for those drinks?"

George joined the group as they settled back onto the animal print couches. Doris fired up the Victrola, and they chattered aimlessly, but Thelma sat mute. The mounted animal heads stared at her accusingly, glassy-eyed witnesses to the brutality of the hunt. Their mistake in plain view, covered over and made decorative. As she smiled and nodded at appropriate intervals, she was painfully aware of the five hundred thousand mistakes waiting for her in the next room. She kicked off her heels and waited for the right moment.

After remaining seated as long as she could stand to, Thelma excused herself. Tiptoeing toward the dining room, she decided that Peggy's room would be the best place to hide the trunk. Why let this money be a tether to her past when it could be a lifeline to her future?

NINE

Sam, St. Petersburg, 1978

"JIMMY?" SAM REPEATED INTO THE PHONE, HIS NAME weirdly unfamiliar on her tongue. Gripping the phone like it might skitter off, she pulled the receiver's cord as far as it would stretch into the Young's living room. She could pull the curtain just far enough to see her rusting Plymouth Valiant in the drive-way, a sad testament to the state of her life. "Is it really you?"

"The one and only. Unless you know some other Jimmy who'd call?"

That familiar touch of condescension in his voice made her press her forehead against the cool windowpane. "Is everything okay? How did you know where to find me?"

"Are you trying to hide?"

She'd forgotten his vexing lawyerly habit of answering a question with a question? Two could play that one. "Where's Abby? Can't this wait 'til tomorrow?"

"Abby's fine. She's got a swim meet, then she's sleeping over at Natalie's. Now's perfect."

Sam closed her eyes, trying to orient herself in time. The days had blurred since Sharon had called her at work. No, they'd spoken at the house. Who was Natalie? She didn't remember any friend of Abby's named *Natalie*. Was that his girlfriend? The thought shouldn't sting, not with everything else she'd lost.

"What do you want, Jimmy?"

"Babe...."

Babe?

"I think, well, I need to see you."

"You what?"

"I need to see you."

"Jimmy, you just saw me at Dad's funeral."

"Right. I know. You got me thinking."

The loud exhale gave Sam's thoughts away, but she tried to refrain from sounding overly sarcastic. "Really. About what?"

"You and me, babe. I need you back in my life."

For a split second, Sam's reserves cracked. For so long she'd ached to hear those words. "You want to come here now, though?" She looked at her watch, the face reflecting the dying light. "That's going to be late. Why don't we talk tomorrow?"

"No, no. I'm calling from the road. I'm already on my way. Unless you have other plans?"

She couldn't picture her ex at a phone booth. Her gaze drifted to Helen's piano, a photograph of Helen and Archie and a little girl with long dark hair—in Cuba, from the looks of it. "I don't think—"

"You're right. You've been right all along. We owe each other more. We owe Abby. She wants us to stay together."

"She said that?"

A heavy sigh came across the line. "I just... I need you."

His words made her heart flutter, a feeling she hadn't felt in... she didn't know how long. Years? She'd been shot at by a crazy lady who claimed her mother's death wasn't an accident. The woman she thought would have some answers only wanted to ask questions about her mother for her own selfish reasons.

She didn't know if she still had a job. And she was still raw from her father's death.

"You're right, Jimmy. We should talk." Sam assessed her car, unsure it could make the trip. "How about I come back tomorrow? We can—"

"I should be there in a couple hours," Jimmy continued before hanging up.

Two hours? He must have gotten on the road while she was at Elsa Juergen's or when she was driving around right after that. Now, he was on his way, confident that the world would bend to his timeline. She'd once hoped that certainty would rub off, but it had only flattened her.

The fact that he'd not waited for her to acquiesce rankled, but it wasn't as if she'd hidden her feelings.

Turning back to return the phone to its cradle, she about bumped into Helen's daughter; she'd scarcely moved. She stood staring, blocking the telephone's base. So Sam held out the phone. The woman scrutinized the receiver like it was some kind of Judas before taking it. "Thank you, ah...." Sam began, but they'd not been introduced.

The woman's response was to stand silently, propped against the wall, arms and legs crossed, clicking her Candie's heel against the terrazzo floor. A pose that forced Sam to squeeze past her to return to the Florida room.

"Why so glum, chum?" Helen asked. "Doris used to say that all the time...."

Oy, enough about this Doris, thought Sam.

Helen knitted her brow. "Everything okay?"

"I think? No. I don't know," Sam began. "It was my husband. Ex-husband. I guess he's coming to town?"

"Jimmy Fontana?" Helen gazed out the window but only briefly this time. "I imagine you need to head out?"

How did Helen Young know her husband's name? This was

all too creepy for Sam. "Look, I don't know what you're up to here—"

"This is no game, love. Your mother thought there was a connection between mafia hot spots and reports of missing girls. Girls like Elizabeth Short." Helen took a sip of her Folgers. It had to be cold and disgusting, but she didn't so much as wrinkle her nose. "I think Doris knew something about it, and that's what got her killed."

Sam felt her jaw set. Helen didn't have anything to say about her mother; she was mining for intel on her lover. Or maybe Elsa Juergen was right and she didn't have her mother's nose for news. "You know, actually? The time has really slipped away. I'm sorry, but I do have to go." Grabbing her purse, she stood to leave. "I'll show myself out."

Helen reached for her arm. "Your mother must've had something, and I'm betting she told Doris and Thelma."

Yanking her elbow from Helen's grasp, Sam sneered, "I'm sorry I can't help you."

As the door slammed behind her, Sam saw the swish of curtain in the front window again. She doubted these freaks could band together to solve a one-piece jigsaw puzzle, but that didn't mean she had to fix their problems. Her therapist would be proud. She wasn't meeting Jimmy for Jimmy's sake but for their family's. That was what she would tell her shrink.

THE STEW OF EMOTIONS RIPPLING THROUGH SAM'S BODY— anger at Helen's fishing expedition, dread about Jimmy's impending arrival, and that familiar ache whenever anyone mentioned her mother—made it difficult to concentrate. She missed the turn to her dad's house and was doing a one-eighty in the road when she realized she was about to collide with one of those hideous concrete dolphin mailboxes. How she loathed them. Not only did these weird approximations of nature fail to resemble anything oceanic, they were an affront to the natural world.

Keeping her eyes trained on the sculptural monstrosity, she swerved to avoid impact, only to be met by the thunderous kiss of metal on metal. The collision was over almost immediately as Sam's car stalled out, but the next moments hung suspended like the air before a thunderstorm as she was thrown into sudden stillness. Echoes from the past shot through her mind.

"It was a car accident."

"Fatal."

"Burned almost beyond recognition."

"Your mother is gone."

Her hands gripped the sun-warmed steering wheel. The dashboard radio crackled but went right on playing its tinny rendition of "Stayin' Alive." Sam thought she might be sick.

"Acute neuroses," Dr. Filmore had diagnosed, referring to Sam's tendency to filter events through the lens of her mother's death. She'd worked hard to rid herself of this trait, looking at photographs and reports of car accidents as part of her therapy. Even congratulated herself for choosing a field that required analysis alongside her coursework because she'd never have been able to afford it otherwise.

The smell of Froot Loops pulled Sam back to the moment. Looking past the steering wheel, Sam saw that the right-front corner of her Valiant was creased. The car lurched at an awkward angle, and her eyes traveled to the source of the smell —the radiator was spewing antifreeze. Her car was not driveable.

Was it neurotic if she'd been in an actual car accident?

"Hey," someone yelled.

Sam lifted her gaze to see the other driver. Coming at her.

Long lean muscles under overalls. No shirt. Shaggy hair teasing his brow.

She wanted to brush the hair from his eyes, run her fingers along his washboard abs, take him in her back seat.

Contain yourself, Sam, she scolded.

But the admonishment didn't work. As she rolled down her window, she wondered if this guy might have a thing for middle-aged ladies in distress, forgetting—for the moment—all about Jimmy.

TEN

Thelma, Havana, 1946

THE WAR'S END CHANGED EVERYTHING. RESTRICTIONS lifted, ships returned to the harbor, and soldiers returned home —their scars both visible and hidden. Sal's cash made a difference too. They could be choosy. After months of looking at properties, Thelma had secured an appointment at an abandoned warehouse in Havana's coveted Vedado neighborhood.

She'd told the girls right away about the money. To her shock, they didn't force her hand.

"You don't need to buy your way in, Thelms," Doris had said. "Especially if you think Sal is going to want something in return."

"Yes, dear," Helen had agreed, squeezing Doris's thigh. "But we could certainly use the additional funds."

Helen was right—Thelma had reviewed the books. They needed the money. What could her father really do as a dead man?

With that decision made, they'd all agreed it was best to keep George in the dark. The truce that she and George had settled into after he'd walked away from his family was, as yet, uneasy. Until the Bird opened, he was content to fill his hours with tennis at Club Vedado, remarkably incurious about the nightclub's finances. "Too many cooks in the kitchen," he'd said, with that trust-fund casualness that still caught her off guard.

"I told you," Lillian had teased across the miles in a rare phone call. "He was never terribly interested in business. But trust me, he'll be terrific with the guests."

Now, as the weathered stone building came into view, Thelma knew they'd found their home. Sunlight filtered through cracks in the boarded-up windows, revealing high ceilings and a vast open floor strewn with crates and other debris. Apart from the dust, cobwebs, and musty smell of neglect, the place absolutely reeked of jazz and late-night dancing. Thelma could picture the nightclub to come—top-shelf liquor, the very best acts, and thanks to their cash infusion, no mafia.

While the agent described the building's highlights in rapid Spanish to Peggy, they marveled over their find.

"I love it," said Doris, clapping her gloved hands lightly.

Helen looked pointedly at a crack in the concrete floor. "Don't tell him she said that, Pegs," she said over her shoulder. "There are some details we need to discuss."

"Ask him about concessions for friends of Mr. Grau," Thelma added. They'd greased far too many palms to pay retail, as far as she was concerned.

The broker raked his jeweled fingers through his slicked-back hair. "Do you need to speak with your husbands?" he asked, his English perfectly passable.

The excitement and determination that had led to this moment erupted in laughter. They agreed to a price on the spot, leaving plenty of room to make the place their own.

* * *

Spring melted into summer, the days marked by the clang of hammers and grind of saws. Ongoing shortages followed the war, making building materials dear, but they learned who to sweet-talk, which warehouses might have an extra crate of nails, and how to spot talent.

By day, they overhauled the building. Peggy worked with the contractors, translating their ideas for dining and dancing into a reality—no improvised green rooms at their club.

Nights belonged to Havana. They'd drift from club to club, taking turns on the dance floor. George would spin Thelma while Doris and Helen danced with visiting sailors, always within sight of each other. Peggy's Spanish improved the fastest as she traded more than glances with bartenders and musicians in search of steady gigs. Every night taught them something new about what their club could be, but mostly they just danced until dawn.

By late September, they were almost ready. The last rays of sunset filtered through the skylights, washing the four of them in golden hues as they gathered around the newly installed bar. Opening night plans covered the gleaming marble top.

"How's everything coming along?" Thelma couldn't keep the grin off her face.

"We should have enough for beef Wellington, lobster Newburg, and oysters Rockefeller to last a month," Peggy said, ticking items off her list. "Same with the baked Alaska."

"Our house band has already started rehearsing," Doris said. "They're going to blow the lid off this town."

"*We're* going to have to start rehearsing." Helen grinned. "Any word on Lillian?"

"Still a no. She's stuck on set," Thelma said, though the news couldn't dim the mood. "We're agreed then? November first?"

The sound of footsteps echoing from the foyer cut through

their moment of celebration. A man's voice called out, "Hello? Anyone here?"

Like a cockroach emerging from the dark, Carlos Gonzalez darted toward them. "Ladies," he said, his slender mustache becoming a straight line in his joyless smile. "I'm glad I found you."

Thelma stepped forward, her fingers curling against her palms. "You remember Carlos Gonzalez," she said, watching Helen and Doris. They didn't know him like she and Peggy did. "What brings you here?"

Carlos scrutinized their work, deliberate as a buyer at auction. "I heard about your little venture. I must say, I'm impressed. But I thought we should have a chat before you open your doors to the public."

"What kind of chat?" Peggy's voice carried an edge Thelma hadn't heard before. But then, her friend knew who exactly Carlos was and what he'd done to keep her father's business from imploding.

"Carlos," Thelma said. "I think we should talk. *Alone.*"

"No," said Doris. "If there's something to discuss, we should all be there."

Thelma bit back a curse. So long as Sal stayed buried, Carlos had nothing on her—but Doris's newfound sass could change that fast.

"Oh yes. Let's all sit together," said Carlos, his casual tone belied by those eyes that missed nothing. "We have some things to discuss."

They moved to a dining table still wrapped in kraft paper, its crackling surface echoing the tension. Carlos settled back, lacing his hands behind his head, the stink of too many days without bathing wafting off him.

"You've done well for yourselves, ladies. But now you need my services. Havana can be a challenging place for newcomers. Especially those with, let's say, *interesting* backgrounds."

Thelma's eyes narrowed. She was hardly the first former call girl to run a nightclub. "What's that supposed to mean?"

"It's not what I mean, Thelma." Carlos pulled a cigar and guillotine from his pocket, the metal catching light as he nipped the head. "It's what I know. What you know."

The cords in Thelma's neck pulled tight. He couldn't possibly know about Sal, could he? There was no starting over somewhere else. They'd sunk everything they had in this place. Keeping her face impassive, she spoke in a low purr. "You don't know what you're talking about."

"You want to make me say it? Fine." He paused to suckle his stogie. "You cannot do business in Havana." He pointed his Cuban at Helen and Doris. "Not if certain indiscretions come to light. Not with two confirmed bachelors. No."

Thelma narrowed her eyes. "You wouldn't."

"Wouldn't I?" Carlos chuckled, clicking open his lighter and toasting the end of his cigar. "You know what I can do."

The girls exchanged glances while Carlos rotated his smoke with practiced ease, drawing three quick puffs.

"What's he talking about, Thelms?" asked Peggy.

Thelma looked into her lap, clacking her fingernails. She hadn't mentioned Carlos's visit to the hospital, and her gut twisted at the memory. "George's plane... Sal didn't... Carlos...."

Peggy cut her off. "*No tienes ninguna prueba.*"

"Your Spanish is much better, Peggy," said Carlos. "But you should know that I don't need proof."

"Creep," Peggy said.

Carlos's gaze swept over the women, lingering on Doris and Helen, both of whom had gone silent. "They really have no idea how this works." He turned to Thelma. "Are you sure you want to be in business with them?"

The dream they'd given everything for hung in the balance. In a voice taut with rage, Thelma asked, "What exactly are you proposing?"

"In exchange for my protection"—Carlos waved his cigar around the club—"you add a few gaming tables. And I get forty percent of your take."

Peggy slammed the table with an open fist. "Forty percent!"

Before she could continue, Doris lifted her hand and pumped it slowly, as if to lower the temperature of the room. "How do we know we can trust you?"

A near-genuine grin slithered across Carlos's lips, smoothing the pockmarks on his skin. "I love secrets." He scanned Thelma. "Isn't that right?"

The time had come to call this meeting to an end. Though her reign at the helm of Sal Giancarlo's empire had been brief, she knew how to deal with such a man. She stood.

"Okay, Carlos, here's my offer. We don't tell Homer Wright about what you can do...." She paused, unsure if he was aware of the violence Homer had unleashed against his own striking workers and wanting to be sure it sank in. "Because my father-in-law doesn't care about one dinky club. So it's best for you that, as far as the Wrights know—and that goes for George—you don't exist. You don't eat here. You don't play here. You don't show your face. We just decided it made business sense to add a casino."

Carlos looked around the room. "I don't see a George," he said, standing and jabbing his arm forward.

Thelma looked from Helen to Peggy to Doris, each of whom gave a slight nod. For the first time in months, she felt her palms light up, and she was grateful for the barrier it would put between her and Carlos's clammy grip. "Twenty percent," she said.

The mustache quivered.

"Plus five for your, ah, discretion." Thelma took his hand. "You know we're going to make a fortune."

"Twenty-five, then. I look forward to our partnership," he said with a bone-crunching squeeze. "I'll be in touch."

As he sauntered out of the club, the women exchanged grim looks. Their dreams for the Bird of Paradise may have been tarnished, but what choice did they have? Thelma should've known by now that too good to be true was the same as waiting for the other shoe to drop.

ELEVEN

Sam, St. Petersburg, 1978

"LADY, CAN YOU DRIVE?"

The kid coming at her, the other driver, couldn't be over twenty-five. *The little shit.*

Sam looked between the cars. His pickup didn't have a dent, but his bumper had sliced into her Valiant like a can opener. "Me? What about you? Your truck is in my lane."

"You were doing some kinda sixteen-point turn, not paying any attention. I was trying to get out of your way when you ran right into me."

Could that be true? Sam wondered. God, he was even more magnetic close up. "I need to see your driver's license," she said. That would tell her his age.

"My license?" He sounded incredulous. "How about twenty bucks and I won't call the cops?"

He must have smelled her weakness. "I'm sorry, but I'm going to need it for my insurance company," Sam said. Reasonable, she thought.

"Insurance? Are you nuts? You wanna pay for this little fender bender in higher premiums for the rest of your life?

A headache was forming behind Sam's eyes. Her neck, she realized, had seized from the impact.

"You can probably get this fixed, straighten out that axle, repair the leak... Maybe two hundred bucks, tops. Your car won't look pretty, but well, it's kind of a piece of crap, isn't it?"

Sam rubbed at her temples. *Piece of crap*. The same thing Jimmy always said. But the kid wasn't wrong. After introducing leaded gas, the geniuses at Plymouth had slapped an Unleaded Fuel Only sticker on their cars and put them into the market. The engines began corroding immediately, but Sam knew none of this when she bought hers at what she thought was a tremendous price. Her second clue something was amiss had been when she stalled out at the stop sign down the street from the previous owner's house, necessitating that she jump out, pop the hood, and flip the intake valve to start the car back up. She'd been so embarrassed she hadn't said anything to Jimmy, thinking she could push for a new car when she finished grad school.

Now, she couldn't afford a new car. Or a used one. Or higher premiums.

"I'll give you that twenty," Sam said. "If you have a tow bar."

He didn't have a tow bar, but in the end, he agreed to drop her down the street at Lee's Automotive.

"I'm Sam Fontana," she said, sticking out her hand. "What's your name?"

When he took her hand, she felt a jolt. "Nico Antonini," he said.

Antonini, thought Sam. She'd have sworn she'd just met someone by that name. Or...

No. She recalled, a furrow forming between her eyebrows. The surname had been in one of her mother's mob exposés. Maybe this kid was related.

"Hey, did you know—" she began. But stopped herself. That

wasn't the kind of thing you could say to someone. *Say, are you part of the mafia?* That was letting her schoolwork rub off in an unhealthy way on her day-to-day life. So she pivoted. "I went to school with someone by that name. What year did you graduate?"

He grinned. Her heart leapt even as she mentally kicked herself for still trying to determine his age. *God, she was pathetic.*

"I'm not from around here" was all he said before heading on his way without another word.

After her car finally made it to the shop, Sam walked home, mind racing. Jimmy would want to know the kid's license plate number. Type of truck. Address. *Something* more tangible than a name that could be fake. She'd gotten no such information.

Yet, upset as she was about the accident—the estimate came in closer to four hundred dollars, fifty bucks more than she'd paid for the car—the idea of seeing Jimmy thrilled her. The attraction to Nico—if that was even his real name—was of no substance. Much as Dr. Filmore had critiqued her ability to recognize trauma in her own life, even she could see that the pull to that kid was avoidance. An escape from the vulnerability she felt.

But was she feeling powerless? Susceptible? Open to attack?

Or was it something else? Something more like a feeling of invincibility. Scarcely a week had passed since she'd seen Jimmy at the funeral. They'd barely spoken, and Abby could hardly look at her. That was awful, she shuddered to remember.

But hadn't Jimmy mentioned a girlfriend? He was always dating someone. Since he'd moved out of their house a year ago she'd had no indication he missed her. Until now.

What was going on with Abby that prompted him to change so dramatically? Had she missed a parent-teacher conference? Or had he simply tired of his girlfriends? Or was it the loss of control? At least when they were married, he always knew where she was. And Abby too.

Then she remembered his words on the phone—"I need you." The many foot rubs after her long shifts at the restaurant. How he'd planned their first trip—a getaway to the Everglades. Hope fluttered in her heart. She deserved this break. Everything else would work itself out.

By the time she crossed into her childhood home, Sam was in what could reasonably be called a good mood despite the totaled car. Then she saw Sharon.

Her father's wife leaned inside the archway to the kitchen, arms folded across her chest as she shook her head in a slow, withering motion. She didn't need to say it; that move asked the question for her. *What were you thinking, talking to Jimmy?*

Unless she'd found out about the car.

"Did Lee's call you about the accident? Is the car fixed already?" She could follow Jimmy to Miami.

Sharon stood upright. "Accident? What? No, I just got off the phone with Jimmy. What happened to your car?"

Crap. "Nothing."

"Fine," she said, though her glare did not relent. "Why *are* you talking to Jimmy?"

"Why wouldn't I?" Sam said. "He deserves a chance."

"A chance? You gave him fourteen years of your life already. Supported him while he earned his law degree. Stood by the man after he lost that big case, kept earning for the both of you. And how did he repay you?"

Sweat began escaping Sam's armpits. She hoped there was time enough to shower and pack. "He wasn't always like that," she said, fanning herself with her blouse.

"Well, he is now."

Sam groaned. "He's the father of my child," she said. "You wouldn't understand."

It was a cruel blow, but she didn't want to talk about her marriage with Sharon, a woman who'd never bothered with having children of her own. Besides, her words had the desired effect. Sharon marched past and slammed out of the house. Relief flooded over Sam as she heard the car start, leaving her alone with the sound of the clock ticking above the sink. *Dammit!*

Despite having spent much of the past year lost in fantasy that the old Jimmy would come to his senses and return to her and their life would go back to the way it was, she'd never envisioned their reunion under these circumstances. Now, Jimmy would be here any minute, and she was nowhere near ready.

TWELVE

Thelma, Havana, 1946

INSIDE BIRD OF PARADISE, THE AIR WAS THICK WITH CIGAR smoke, perfume, and possibility. Thelma retraced the path she'd walked many times, heart hammering against her ribs as she passed the green room—where the plush seating came with a fully-stocked bar to calm pre-performance jitters—and the well-appointed dressing rooms, each with vanity mirrors lit by bare bulbs. Helen, Doris, and Peggy were doing final costume checks before taking the stage with the house dancers. Tonight, their opening number would echo the Florida Girls days, but they had a full roster of talent to come, imported and local. Like the old days, Thelma's main role would be emcee.

Backstage, Thelma forced herself to take a moment to admire the polished hardwood floor, warm under the glow of footlights. Through a gap in the crimson velvet curtain, she watched Havana's elite pour in, their jewels glinting like stars. Above them, the high-stakes tables waited behind discreet doors —Carlos's price for this night but, also quite likely, their key to real money.

"Is everyone ready?" The words barely carried over her pounding heart.

A chorus of yeses answered, and Thelma signaled the band. She strode out to thunderous applause, only to spot none other than Carlos Gonzalez watching from a corner booth, surrounded by his men. Unsure how to respond to his flagrant disregard for their pact, she ignored him. He was a problem for later.

Near the entrance, a ripple in the crowd drew her eye. As the guests parted, Thelma's mood turned. Veteran showwoman that she was, Thelma seized the moment as if it were planned, announcing into the mic, "Ladies and gentlemen, tonight we have a very special guest, star of the big screen and our humble stage, my cousin, Lillian Montgomery!"

Having reached the stage, Lillian swept in for a hug, her signature scent of Dior as familiar as family. "Surprise, darling! I wasn't about to miss this. We're opening with 'Choo Choo Ch'Boogie.'" She winked. "We figured even you could sing that!"

"Me? What about you?"

"Honey, please. I'm famous. I don't have to sing well."

Thelma lifted her brows and smirked. "Everyone else knew you were coming?"

"We only found out a couple days ago, sweetie. Figured you could use a surprise." Lillian backed away, waving as the audience erupted in cheers.

When their performance reached its crescendo, Thelma caught Carlos leaning forward, his eyes fixed on Lillian. Every cell of her being screamed no.

The song ended with a flourish as the club exploded in applause. Lillian blew kisses to the room as the band struck up a sizzling rumba and the real Havana Girls dancers took over.

George met them at the bar. "A round for the house," he called to the bartender.

"There you go, cousin." Lillian smirked. "Trying to upstage me."

Amid the hugs and congratulations, Thelma scanned the crowd. Carlos hadn't moved from his perch, monitoring everything with his calculating gaze.

"Are you all right, darling?" George bent close, his eyes bunching with concern.

Thelma kissed his cheek to hide the worry on her face and arrange her features into a smile. "I'm caught up in the excitement, love." The lies came so easily now. "Lillian, you never cease to amaze me."

After a toast, George headed back to the front of the house to greet guests as the girls returned to the stage, leaving Thelma at the bar to watch their sultry rendition of "Rum and Coca-Cola," a crowd favorite from their war bond tour days. The music swelled and the dancers' movements became a blur of motion. No sooner had Thelma allowed herself to savor their success when the bar manager whispered into her ear that Carlos's tab had hit a thousand dollars.

Resolute, she turned toward his booth. But a movement by the door stopped her cold. Salvatore Giancarlo stood inside Bird of Paradise—the club she'd built with his money. Had he lost his mind, showing himself in public? Or had he come to collect?

Their eyes locked for one electric moment before her father slipped out the door. How had she missed her larger-than-life father? She turned to follow, only to feel a tap on her shoulder. Her pulse jumped as she spun around.

"Quite a night, Thelma," Carlos Gonzalez said, his voice low and smooth. "If I do say so myself."

Thelma didn't know what that was supposed to mean. Nor did she care. "You're not even supposed to show your face here, Carlos."

He leaned in, his lips nearly grazing her ear. "We both have arrangements to remember, then. I'd hate for anything to complicate your success. Or your cousin's."

Before Thelma could respond, George appeared at her side, sliding his arm around her waist. "I don't believe we've been introduced?" His tone would sound friendly to someone who didn't know him. "I'm George Wright."

"This is Mr.... Gonzalez, is it?" Thelma said, the pretense of ignorance bitter. "He wanted to congratulate us before he left."

The air crackled between them, but George maintained his smile. "Thank you so much," he said, extending his hand.

"I was just telling your wife how I look forward to the casino opening. I love a good high-stakes game."

Strain creased George's cheeks. The gambling had been a point of contention, though they'd shown him the numbers. With or without Gonzalez, that income was vital. "I thought we were going to do things differently," he'd said. His last attempt at input in the club.

"Perhaps we can arrange a proper tour of the tables another time?" asked George, putting on his house manager affability.

Thelma stepped in. Her heart pounded in her throat, but she spoke clearly, keeping her eyes locked on Carlos. "Darling, I tried, but"—she smiled brightly—"unfortunately, Mr. Gonzalez only enjoys the tables from afar or he gets in too much trouble."

Puzzlement flashed in George's eyes, but only for a moment. "Well, we sure do appreciate your well wishes, Mr. Gonzalez."

Carlos faced George and gave a slight bow, which infuriated Thelma. But she didn't dare let on. "I am expected at the Hotel Nacional."

"We won't keep you," said Thelma.

She kept the smile plastered on until Carlos finally took his leave and George returned to the front of the house. Only then did she scan the street for Sal. If he'd ever been there at all.

The sun was climbing over the Bay of Havana by the time

the last patrons stumbled out. George helped with cleanup while Thelma closed receipts at the bar, the girls long since home. Carlos hadn't only stiffed his bill—the dining captain reported he hadn't tipped either. She got their waiter's name, making a note to pay him herself.

She would make Carlos pay. Maybe I can get Sal's help, she thought, waiting for Vivian Miles's sardonic voice in her head. But for once, her mother stayed buried.

"Course, I'll have to find him first," she muttered.

"Find who?" Peggy pulled up a barstool. "Let me guess. That deadbeat Carlos."

"Everyone knows he stiffed the table?"

"Yup, we gotta find that bastard," Peggy said.

"Before we can kill him," they said in unison.

They were joking, but the words sent ice through Thelma's veins.

THIRTEEN

Kathleen, Havana, 1947

LITTLE CORA NESTLED AGAINST KATHLEEN'S CHEST, breaking her heart in two. Since arriving in Havana, a single thought had driven her every action—*leave the baby*.

The idea was preposterous. Absurd. It would be like leaving her heart outside her body. And yet...

She'd never felt so betrayed by her heart. Since Lloyd's passing, she wanted nothing more than to succumb to that same darkness. To join him. The only time it didn't inform her every thought was when she practiced yoga.

The sheer physicality of the postures was all-consuming. Not since riding horses as a young girl had she done anything of the sort. Nothing physical, really, beyond running around Sun City Emporium all day. More so than sex, the asanas allowed Kathleen to fully inhabit her body without the nuisance of thought.

How dare he leave her? He was doing so well after his lung surgery. Up and about. *Whistling*. Then suddenly, trouble with his words. His motor skills. "A tumor in his brain," the doctors said. The lung cancer had metastasized. He died right before

Cora was born. "See that she's loved," he'd said. "As much as I've loved you." His last coherent words to Kathleen.

But she couldn't.

It was impossible to look at the child and not see Matteo—dark hair, dark eyes, dark complexion. The girl had nothing of either Kathleen or Lloyd. Strangers on the street even commented. "Must look like his father." One woman had casually said, "Oh, I can't wait to have grandchildren." *Grandchildren.*

The need was constant. She'd forgotten how helpless babies were. All the washing. The feeding. The diapers. Endless diapers. Thank heavens for advances in formula. And money. She couldn't have afforded to keep her boys in disposables and store-bought milk, but Cora could have the best of what the modern world had to offer. Good thing too. Her breasts were as dry as dust.

She had nothing for this baby.

These young women, on the other hand? How they'd fawned over her appearance. The old Kathleen would never have admitted it, but young Cora had never experienced such an onslaught of admiration. Archie had yet to meet his baby sister; he was still serving the Navy in the Pacific. And Bertie —Lord, the disappointment—had gone and married that hideous Hattie May Harper and had a child of his own. No, Kathleen and the baby had been on their own. Alone in California. Even after Lloyd had died, her parents would not relent. They never responded to her letters, but she'd checked —they were both still alive, and still living on Grand-père's farm.

The house in Cuba, too, was exquisite. A grand manor in Havana's posh section. They'd need to make some accommodations. A smaller bed. Some chests for toys. With the money she'd leave, Thelma could afford to hire a live-in. This guest room was perfectly adequate space for two. If the nanny was good, perhaps Kathleen would hire her when she returned.

That was the thing too. Of course she'd return. The invitation from Guruji had been for a six-month course. Cora would hardly know the difference. Didn't men do this sort of thing all the time?

The course was mandatory to becoming a teacher, and she did plan to teach. On the *Helldorado Days* set where she'd learned to practice, the whole cast and crew fell in love with yoga. Yet there were no teachers outside of movie sets. Nowhere to continue her studies. If she could become a teacher, she'd make a fortune. And an educator's schedule was perfect for raising a child on her own.

Raising a child. At her age? She'd be in her fifties by the time Cora was going to her prom. Preposterous. It was only ever meant to be her and Lloyd in California. Not her and Lloyd and a newborn. Certainly not her and a newborn.

But no, she'd long since reconciled with the idea of being a single mother. It was the practice of it that was killing her. The time away would help clear her head.

Thelma Miles was family, after all. And why not offer some exposure to Doris and Helen? She didn't think that her *Helldorado Days* dalliance with Maxine Lewis had changed her natural inclinations, but she felt so mixed up in every way, she'd lost sight of who she was anymore. The only thing she knew for certain was that she could not leave Cora with Bertie and Hattie May. Their marriage was unlikely to outlast her stay in India.

Inside the top desk's top drawer, she found writing paper and a pen. She took a seat at the bureau desk and began writing.

Dear Thelma,

I must write quickly before I lose heart. By now, you'll have been awoken by Cora and wondering where I am.

The truth is, I can't love her. Not as I am. I have nothing to give. The only thing that kept me going these last years, through Lloyd's illness, the store's financial troubles, and well, raising Bertie, has been the idea that we'd have some time alone. Just Lloyd and I.

Now, I'm so tired all the time... unless I'm practicing. My teacher has invited me to study with him in India. But only me. His ashram is no place for a baby.

KATHLEEN SAT BACK AND REREAD WHAT SHE'D WRITTEN SO far. That last line wasn't a lie, exactly. More of an extrapolation. Why else would Guruji specify she come alone?

Should she mention the affair she'd had with Maxine Lewis? The attraction had taken her by surprise on the set of *Helldorado Days*. Ultimately, she'd given in. But no. There was no reason to be explicit. Besides, the out-of-wedlock baby she'd conceived with a gangster was enough information for Thelma to have on her. It was unnatural enough for a mother to leave her child. If she mentioned her own proclivities—no matter how open-minded the girl was with Doris and Helen—she might never see her child again. That wouldn't do at all. She hadn't gone off men. Far from it.

She would, instead, make a nod to the unusual arrangement.

BETWEEN YOU AND GEORGE AND DORIS AND HELEN, THIS child will be well cared for while I'm away. It shouldn't be for long. A few months.

In the meantime, my contracts in Vegas proved quite lucrative. I've left you some cash here but will also send regular funds to see to it she's raised in a manner fitting a young lady of means.

This is by no means an inducement. I can see you and the girls love her—George will come around; men can lag a bit—and she is your family, after all. Try to keep her away from Sal if you can. Otherwise, I trust you. I no longer trust myself.

I understand this may seem strange, but I beg you will forgive me. And as I say, I'll be back soon enough.

Namaste, Kathleen

ONCE SHE'D SIGNED HER MISSIVE, SHE HAD TO LEAVE immediately for fear of changing her mind. Her bag was packed and ready. Cora was nestled in the crib she'd improvised from a dresser drawer. The only thing left to do was get to the street and meet the car and driver she'd arranged. Taking in her baby girl one last time, it took all her will to turn away.

She would be back in no time.

And didn't men do this sort of thing all the time?

FOURTEEN

Sam, St. Petersburg, 1978

SHARON HAD MADE SOME VALID POINTS ABOUT JIMMY. SAM
had her own qualms, of course. Until he arrived and scooped
her up in his arms. "I've missed you," he said. "I've missed this."

Her heart melted—she'd missed *this* too. Not just any kiss,
this was something long and deep. Like they hadn't shared in
over a decade, not since they first started dating. But that was
long before their troubles began. When was it that Jimmy had
first drifted?

She'd known him since grade school, when he was the
smartest boy in their class, even if he wasn't the best looking.
Too tall, too skinny, and bespectacled to boot. Then his family
moved to Miami, and they lost touch. When they reconnected
in college, Jimmy felt like home. He was the only man she'd ever
been with who had met her mother. In his arms, all her anxieties
faded. Or used to.

All that changed when he lost his job. They bickered but
not terminally. Not yet. The real problems began after he
found work again. Started wearing pomade, custom suits, and
contact lenses, though their issues went beyond the superficial.
The swagger notwithstanding—Sam was not a fan of his new

look—after teaming up with his mystery client, he basically checked out. Lost interest in family nights in, camping weekends, and spontaneous trips to Dairy Queen. Forgot about foot rubs.

But this Jimmy felt different yet again. There was an urgency Sam didn't understand, but she could feel it in his touch.

At last they broke apart. Sam asked Jimmy if he wanted anything to drink. "No, baby, I came to get you. We should get on the road."

She blinked. "What? You mean, you want to leave tonight? I thought—"

"Of course I wanna leave tonight. Why else would I come rushing out here?"

He kissed her again, and Sam went weak in her legs. She wanted to take him directly to her bedroom, but Jimmy deferred. "I want to wait. Do it the right way. Not sneaking at your parent's house."

"What about my car?" Sam asked, angling for a little more time.

He wasn't interested in her hesitation. "That POS? What about it? Leave it. Come with me. We'll get you a new car."

A new car? She'd never had one. Despite his new job, Jimmy had been unmoved by her appeals for another car. Not even something new. Just *something*. "You just got that thing," he'd said. "And I'm paying for your school, aren't I?"

Grad school was definitely when their troubles began, when she'd started noticing his lack of presence. How could she not? She was studying psychology and in therapy as part of her criminology coursework. But then, her heart never had answered to common sense. She wanted her old life back. And a new car. She hadn't even told him about the accident.

"What about Abby? Babe, you know I still love you, but we

can't do this frivolously. If you don't mean it, we can't do this. It will destroy her."

It will destroy me, she thought. *And I'm not willing to drop out of school either.*

"I told you, she's staying at her friend Natalie's."

So Natalie was a friend of Abby's. "I don't know...."

"Babe, tonight is the first night of the rest of our lives. Why don't you go pack?" His hand curled around the back of her neck as he kissed her again, steering her toward the stairs. "Grab all your stuff."

Sam, who'd been through several emotional upheavals already that day, felt the last of her reserves break away. Other than "grab all your stuff," those were the same words he'd uttered the night they eloped. She'd never felt more ready to comply with her husband's wishes. Technically, her ex-husband. But it looked like all that was about to change.

THE RIDE WAS MORE AWKWARD THAN SAM WOULD'VE liked. She wanted to ask Jimmy about his life, but a larger part of her didn't want to know. Whoever he'd been dating. Why they'd broken up. She could live without that knowledge. There was at least as much about herself that she didn't want to reveal. The car accident was bad enough without adding the potential for losing her job. And why? *Trifling with Ed at work. What had come over her?*

She didn't know what to say about her mother's letter either. Her encounter with Elsa Juergen would make for a funny story but lead to more questions. Questions Sam couldn't answer, so what was the point? All Sam had learned was that a crazy lady suspected her mother's car accident had been premeditated. Also, that she was cool with lesbians, but they could be as scheming as anybody else. And apparently, that she was no Imogene Fuchs.

They didn't talk until they'd been in the car for close to two hours, almost to Alligator Alley. "Any chance you're hungry?" Sam asked.

"Babe, we just got in the car."

Jimmy hated making pit stops. Even when Abby said she had to go to the bathroom, he put up a fuss. Before she could protest that there was nowhere to stop on the long stretch to the Glades, Jimmy said something she'd never heard him say before.

"You know what? Whatever you want, baby. We can stop at the next exit."

Swoon would not be too strong a word for how his words made her feel. But there was no holding back her questions any longer. "What happened, Jimmy? What made you change your mind now, after almost a year?"

"I guess when I saw you at your dad's funeral," Jimmy said, looking not at her but straight ahead at the road. "You looked so brave and strong. But I knew you needed someone to lean on. I couldn't stop thinking about it because I knew that person wasn't Sharon. Especially after I talked to her today—"

Her husband had rarely strung this many sentences about their relationship together unless they were fighting, but Sam had to interrupt. "I thought you said Abby made you reconsider?"

Jimmy shook his head like he was clearing cobwebs. "So are you asking questions or interrogating? You should've gone to law school. Why do you get so hung up on things?"

Another question that didn't answer what she'd asked, she noted briefly before chastising herself. Nitpicking had driven Jimmy away. *Best to make a joke of it.* "Well, I never met a detail I didn't like."

He appraised her then, and Sam felt very aware of her wrinkled peasant blouse and hair in need of a dye job. But those had never been the details that interested her, not like the messy bits of human nature.

Jimmy was right. She was turning this into analysis when not everything required cataloguing and cross-referencing.

What mattered now was that they would make their marriage work. Rekindle the love that had been. For Abby.

Forcing herself to relax, Sam curled up her knees and hoisted her feet onto her seat, her back against the door to sit facing Jimmy. Study him. They were both thirty-eight, but he looked five years younger. In that vexing way men could, he was getting better looking as he aged, though his dark head of hair—thinner than when they first met—showed no signs of turning gray. Then there was that stunning Italian skin of his. She liked to say his portrait must be in an attic somewhere. Not that he got the Dorian Gray reference. He was book smart, but his pop culture catalogue ended with the Hardy Boys.

"You know, if you can wait, I know of a good place. Best conch fritters in Florida." Jimmy took his eyes off the road, flashing his dimples. "If you can wait 'til after we get there."

Nestling back into her seat, Sam decided she wasn't that hungry after all. "Sure, babe. Why not?"

They drove on in silence a while longer, Sam's eyelids growing heavy, when out of nowhere Jimmy spoke. "Sharon said you might be upset. Something some old lady said about your mom's car accident?"

So he already knew about Elsa. Sam tried to piece together the events of that morning. First, the woman had pulled a gun. Then she implied the mob had Sam's mother killed. Meanwhile, the house was straight out of Grey Gardens.

"You know the more I think about meeting that woman, the more I think she was a sad old lady with nothing better to do than spin tall tales and accumulate garbage."

No need to mention the gun.

"What'd she tell you? I mean, why were you there in the first place?"

Sam had to think. An involuntary yawn escaped. "Honestly, Jimmy, it's all a blur. I'm exhausted."

Jimmy waited a beat before responding. "You've had a rough day, babe. Why don't you take a little nap? You know you can push that seat back, right?"

Sam inhaled deeply. She would not let Jimmy's habit of explaining the obvious detract from her contentment.

* * *

THE SKY WAS PITCH-BLACK WHEN SAM OPENED HER EYES. They were pulling up to a small shack, not the parking lot at a diner. "Where are we?"

"My buddy's house," said Jimmy. "He's letting us borrow his place. I need to stop here before we grab a bite. Come on in. Meet him."

Sam took in the dark structure. A wooden shack in the middle of nowhere. What *buddy* did Jimmy have out here? "I'm not in a headspace to meet someone new right now. I'll wait here."

"Aw, c'mon." Jimmy leaned toward her. "Come say hi."

"Are you sure he's even here? Who is this guy?"

"You won't find out by sitting here," he said, grinning weirdly.

"That's okay. I'll wait."

"Don't be such a stick-in-the-mud."

Sam's stomach clenched. He knew that was her weak spot; she'd always been a serious girl. "That honeymoon didn't last long."

He backed away in his seat. "Don't make this harder than you already have."

"What?" The fog in Sam's brain was starting to lift.

"Get out of the car."

"No, really. I'm fine–"

Before she could finish her thought, Jimmy was getting out of the car. He slammed his door shut and came around to her side, wrenching her handle open. Grabbing her elbow, he spoke in the voice he used when Abby was in trouble. "I said, get out of the fucking car."

Fear gripped Sam. She was wide awake now. He had taken her deep into the swamp. Miles past civilization. What was happening?

FIFTEEN

Thelma, Havana, 1947

THE GENTLE CLINKING OF ICE AGAINST GLASS PUNCTUATED the quiet evening in the Vedado mansion. A stark contrast to the vicious thoughts racing through Thelma's mind. She'd almost had to beg the girls for a night home with Cora.

True, she'd almost called for backup at bedtime. The child had been rubbing her eyes, drooping. Until Thelma shut off the lamp. After three jack-in-the-box rounds of "One no, TT"—translation: *one more story, Auntie TT*—which Thelma had obliged, Cora hopped out of bed and raced to her toy box. After toppling the crate, she picked up and examined each item before throwing it across the room screaming, "Mine!"

Now, Thelma sat with her legs hoisted up on their plush sofa, nursing the goose egg on her shin left behind by a wooden block. The tiny dictator had only relented when Auntie TT, too exhausted to try to get the girl back to bed, let her fall in a heap on the living room sofa. Looking over at Cora's sleeping form, she winced as she iced her leg.

The *Vogue* in her lap was no help. The essay she'd been trying to read—provocatively titled Meditations on a Single

Theme—turned out not to be about divorce but womanhood. She hadn't made it past a quote on the first page. Some O. Henry fellow saying women were "the most helpless of the young of any animal, with the fawn's grace but without its fierceness." He'd clearly never met actual women. Especially not any of the Young women.

Her thoughts drifted to George, half expecting he'd breeze in, suitcase in hand, ready to return to the life they had planned. He hadn't sent divorce papers. Maybe he missed her too.

She took the last sip of her gin and tonic—her third already? —relishing the burn. A pounding at the door jolted Thelma from her melancholy. She froze, heart thumping. For a split second, hope flared in her chest. George?

"Thelma? Sweetheart? Open up. It's me."

The voice sent a chill down her spine—her father. Salvatore Giancarlo. The man who was allegedly dead. Should she confront him? Murder him? Or pretend she wasn't home?

Before she could decide whether to answer, a sonorous wail erupted from the living room. So much for pretending. Worse, he'd know his grandchild was still in Cuba.

"One minute," she called as she pivoted back to the living room. He'd heard the child, sure, but if she could get her out of sight... Letting Cora meet her grandfather—the man the papers had dubbed Florida's Emperor of Crime—would raise far too many questions, questions that would threaten the careful fiction they'd constructed around the girl's parentage.

Before she could snatch up the girl, the door swung open and Thelma was face-to-face with her father. His height and girth made him an imposing figure still, but when it came to scare tactics, she'd learned his every trick. Cora, suddenly silent, stared, wide-eyed, over the back of the couch.

Sal's eyes landed on the girl, his face lighting up with genuine joy. "Is that...."

Positioning herself between Sal and Cora, Thelma hissed at her father. "You shouldn't be here."

His smile faltered a moment before returning, albeit more forced. "Come on, Thelma. Is that any way to greet your old man?"

A bitter laugh escaped Thelma's lips. "Given that it's you, yes."

His jovial act fell away, replaced by grim determination. "Well now, speaking of giving... I gave you half a million dollars. And I know you've put it to good use. I came because—"

"Sit," Thelma said. "I need to put Cora down."

She moved to the sofa and drew Cora into her arms. In a rare obliging move, the toddler curled into Thelma's neck. With her arms around the child protectively, she strode toward the staircase, wondering what to say about the strange man who'd barged into their home. Yet for once, with nary a bedtime song, Cora dozed right off. Thelma hadn't made it all the way into the living room before Sal started in.

"Look, I know I've made mistakes. I shouldn't have... What I mean is, I wish I knew you when you was little." Sal's voice wavered. "Francella had a boy last year and...."

Tears welled in Sal's eyes, but Thelma was unmoved. Nothing new about Sal getting sentimental over his male children.

"Anyways, I'm proud of ya."

At last, her reserve broke, and Thelma's vision blurred even as she hated herself for her sentimentality. She crossed her arms over her chest but could not deny the solace she felt.

"And from here on," Sal continued, "I'm going to be spending more time in Havana."

Any warmth Thelma felt evaporated. "No. You can't. Sal...."

"Whoa, whoa," said Sal. "Before you get twisted up, you should know—Bugsy's gone. It's safe for me to come back."

His words seared like a red-hot poker. She knew Benjamin Siegel had been murdered. Everyone knew. He'd been executed in his own living room, strafed by bullets shot from a moving car. "That's exactly why I want you to stay away from me. From us."

Sal didn't flinch. Instead, he sank into the armchair. "Sweetheart, I hate to tell ya, but that club of yours? It's mine too."

She remembered the day she realized her mother could no longer service her clients. That she would have to do it. George's love had diffused the memory, but she now knew that shame could never truly be erased. Nor should it. She'd allowed herself to believe she was free. "Carlos is *your* rat fink, isn't he?"

Sal sighed heavily. "What's that supposed to mean?"

"Really, though. Forty percent? What were you thinking?"

"Forty percent?" The vein in Sal's forehead popped as he jumped to his feet.

"Keep your voice down," said Thelma through clenched teeth. "You know damn well I didn't go over twenty-five."

"Twenty-five percent! Of *what*?" His voice was low, almost a growl.

"Don't pretend you don't know what I'm talking about, Sal. You taught me better than that."

"I don't have any idea what you're talking about," he shouted.

Thelma grabbed her father's arm and yanked him toward the door. "If you can't be quiet, we're going outside."

He pulled away and shook out his cuffs. "Anybody else did that...." He looked up. Thelma's implacable stare shut him down.

"I'll deal with Carlos," he said.

"No." Thelma lifted her hand. "You've done quite enough already."

"No," said Sal, listing toward her and lifting his hand.

Was he going to hit her? Reflexively, Thelma shrunk into herself and felt for the scar on her cheek, the scar he'd left behind the first time they met. She was the only one of his children he'd seemed to hate on sight.

But Sal merely placed his palm on her shoulder and squeezed. "You don't get it. I'm already paying him. Carlos. To protect you."

The feeling she'd forgotten something important clawed at Thelma, like those mornings she woke up in a stranger's bed. She looked around for her drink and found her glass empty. Sliding out from under his grip, she reached for the tumbler, took it to the bar, and spoke as she poured herself a hefty gin. "Carlos demanded payment. Threatened to expose Doris and Helen. But... you were paying him? What were you thinking? Why didn't you tell me?"

"What was *I* thinking? I seem to recall you were the one sitting at my desk making Carlos feel like a big man."

"After your stroke? Now, we know you saw everything, but at the time? You were like a vegetable. It was eat or be eaten."

"All's I'm saying, you built him up. That was your choice. Now, I'm making mine." Sal reached for her glass and drained it. "Carlos needs to pay."

Thelma's palms flared with that old tingling sensation. Her father was right. Carlos did need to pay. And she did have a choice.

"Sal, before you sold the Vegas place for parts, you wanted me to run that casino legit. The Bird of Paradise can be the same. And I can do that for you." She paused. "But I make the final call about Carlos."

Sal moved away. "No, you ain't the boss."

She spun him around and looked her father dead in the eye. "I am if you ever want to see Cora again."

"You threatening my family? Really?" Sal shook his head,

but a smile played at his lips. "That's going for the jugular. I did teach you right."

Cupping her elbows, she looked into her father's eyes. "Sal, I gotta know." She turned away and leaned against the sofa. "Your brother...." She didn't have to say more.

As the night deepened, Sal talked about his daughter Stephanie. "She was, you know, special. I needed money for her. I was always going to need money for her." He could never afford to leave the life, but his brother had been a different story. "My brother tried," he said. "And they killed him. Capone started a rumor it was me. That was that."

Thelma rubbed her stinging palms against her thighs, nodding. Relieved.

THE SOUND OF SAL GIANCARLO'S SHOES CLICKING AGAINST the Bird's marble floor filled Thelma's ears as she watched her father circle Carlos Gonzalez like a shark. Sal might have been dead to the world for some time, but in this moment he was very much alive and dangerous.

"You took my money," Sal said softly, his voice carrying that calm that Thelma knew signaled violence. "Money that I paid you to protect my daughter."

A bead of sweat trailed down Carlos's collar. "And the club is thriving."

"No, you also skimmed from her profits, which means you stole from me." Sal smiled, but it didn't reach his eyes. "That wasn't our arrangement."

Two of Sal's men stood by the doors, their presence a clear message. Thelma's stomach churned as she ran her fingertips over the scar on her cheek.

"Your mother still lives in that pretty house in Santiago, yeah?" Sal asked casually. "With your father and grandmother? Such a lovely family."

Carlos went very still. "Leave them out of this."

"Oh. Now, you're worried about family. What about my family? You didn't leave my family out of it."

Carlos's jaw tightened as he assessed Thelma. "There's stories I could tell about the Florida Girls."

Narrowing her eyes, Thelma tried to get a bead on him. Hiding the fact that Kathleen Young had killed Sal's firstborn, Matteo, had been Carlos's attempt to muscle into the organization. "You want to tell that story now? After all this time."

"Choose," Sal continued. "Walk away from this club right now and never come back, or...." He frowned, shrugging. "Well, family is everything, isn't it?"

That was the moment Carlos recognized that this exchange was not a negotiation.

"My men will escort you out," Sal said.

Thelma's cue to leave.

"You sure you don't want me to fix this clown for good?"

"Sal, we've been over this. He's not worth going to jail for." Thelma dropped the cigarette smoldering in her hand and ground it out with her heel. "I need some air." This time, no one tried to stop her as she hurried out of the club.

Fifteen minutes later, Carlos stumbled out the back door, supported by Sal's men. His face was bloody, one eye swollen shut. As they frog dragged him past, he watched Thelma, his good eye filled with hatred. Thelma felt nothing but revulsion, for his appearance and her part in it.

Inside, Sal approached. "It's over, sweetheart. He won't bother you again."

"Never again, Sal."

"He had to know we were serious."

Thelma grimaced. "I mean it."

"No," he said finally. "You think he'll be the last wise guy to try something?"

There it was again, that sensation that she'd forgotten something.

"Don't worry, beautiful. Moose and Chickie"—he thumbed toward the door— "they're your new muscle. They'll make sure the Carloses of the world stay away."

"Is this the world you want for Cora. For your boy? Francis, did you say?"

"Speaking of...." Sal was the master of a quick change. "I'm going back to Miami. You can run this place without me."

"What? After all this, you're leaving?"

He nodded. "How can you be surprised? I've got a new baby at home. Gotta keep bringing home the bacon. Speaking of, you can send that twenty percent to me now."

Thelma cupped her elbows. "What for?"

"Moose and Chickie," Sal said, pointing an elbow in the direction of his bodyguards.

"But I'm getting rid of the casino. We won't need Moose and Chickie."

Sal pursed his lips. "Sweetheart, with or without a casino, you *need* Moose and Chickie. Besides... you taken a good look at the books lately? You can't afford to run this place without chips."

Clouds gathered behind Thelma's eyes, the weight of memory. She'd allowed herself to forget there was no getting away.

"Another thing," Sal said, already halfway out the door. "I know Cora don't know who I am. But she will. You'll see." He tapped his pointer finger to his eye, gave a mock salute, and was gone.

Thelma didn't know how long she stood in the encroaching darkness before Doris drove up. "What's cooking, good-looking?" she called from the driver's side.

"Heya," Thelma replied, attempting to mirror her friend's cheer.

"Jesus Christ," Helen breathed, taking in the splintered pile of tables and chairs. "What happened?"

"Sal happened," Thelma said flatly.

"Your father's back?" Doris's eyes widened.

"He was. Briefly." Thelma began picking up scattered papers. "Now, Carlos is gone, but we're keeping the gaming tables."

"Were we not keeping them at some point?" Doris asked, reaching for a busted table leg.

"I was hoping to get rid of them when we got rid of Carlos."

Helen, who'd joined the cleanup, stopped mid reach. "By get rid of, you're not suggesting a capital crime took place here this afternoon?"

It was the wrong thing to do, but Thelma burst out laughing. "No," she finally said. "But we will have some new help around here." She motioned toward the door, where her father's men stood just outside. "Moose and Chickie."

Doris sat up. "We're not going anywhere, Thelms. We've all got our secrets."

"Seriously, though?" Helen said. "The next time your mobster father decides to drop by, a little warning would be nice. We have to talk about everything that affects the Bird."

"I agree." Thelma smiled, nodding even as that nagging feeling came back. *Was she forgetting something?*

As they cleaned up together, however, something tight in Thelma's chest began to loosen. This was what she wanted for her family. Not a collection of secrets kept through threats and violence but quiet support and gentle teasing. Helping each other pick up the pieces.

Her gaze drifted to the bottles behind the bar. If only her dark thoughts would stay buried. Some ghosts, Thelma knew, were harder to outrun than others.

SIXTEEN

Sam, The Everglades, 1978

SAM HAD BARELY PROCESSED JIMMY'S HARSH WORDS AS HE forced her by the arm across the cabin's threshold. The emotional shock hit as hard as the physical pain. Then she saw the love seat. The one from their first apartment.

"Since when do you own a swamp cabin?" she asked, her cheeks burning. Sam had spent hours poring over their assets, and nothing in the Everglades had ever surfaced. Not that the place struck her as love nest material. As her eyes adjusted to the gloom, all she could make out in the single room besides the love seat were a twin cot, a plain table and chairs, and on the wall opposite, a propane stove. Plus, the place reeked. Some ghastly combination of Florida wetlands and something chemical that made her throat itch.

"I told you, it's not my place; it's my friend's." Jimmy lit a kerosene lantern, sending shadows across the plank floor. No sign of a power supply meant no generator. Not even running water. There had to be a hand pump somewhere close.

"If this is your idea of rekindling our—"

"Sit down," Jimmy demanded, scraping a chair into the center of the space. "And shut up."

"I'd rather we leave." Her voice came out steadier than she felt.

He laughed, a hollow, performative sound. Classic intimidation technique, she thought. *Exerting control with your mood swings.* Once she'd observed the pattern in their relationship, she'd written a paper about it, naming the phenomenon *anxious anticipation.* Somehow she'd fallen for it again.

But she could rake through this with her analyst later.

"First we need to talk," he said, patting the chair. "Have a seat."

He was back to sounding accommodating. Two could play at this game. She didn't want this jerk back even if Abby thought they should be a family. She sent up a wish—*May this experience flush this fool from my heart.*

"Why on earth would you bring me here, Jimmy? Did you forget who won the Gulf & Western case? The Everglades won, Jimmy. Not you. You said 'the bog rats can have the swamp.'"

"Why do you think I brought *you* here?" he sneered, pushing the chair against her knees so she dropped into the seat.

"Ouch! Jesus!" Sam rubbed the back of her knees but kept her eyes trained on her ex. "What's this about, Jimmy?"

He paced, running fingers through his hair—a nervous tic she remembered from when they first met and then all those years he struggled. "It's about you needing to mind your own business. Stop digging through old stories. Stop asking questions about Cuba, about the girls."

About *Cuba?* "What are you talking about?"

He stopped. Turned to her. Crossed his arms to look her up and down. "C'mon, Sam. Don't be coy with me. Sharon told me you got that letter. What was in it?"

The half-written page from her mother? What did that matter to Jimmy? *I want to tell you now while I have the courage,* she'd written. But courage in the face of what? She'd never finished the thing. Never said anything about Cuba, though it had been in that article. Then there was Elsa's weird connection to the place. Helen too. Some nightclub. The Bird of Passion or something. But girls? Helen hadn't said anything about girls in Cuba, just Florida.

"Did you hear me?" Jimmy asked. "I asked you what was in that letter."

Sam crossed her arms, scheming. Was the smarter move to pretend she knew what Jimmy was talking about or confess her ignorance? Neither. The smarter move was buying more time.

"I need water."

"Jesus, Sam. Always so goddamn needy."

The heat rose in her cheeks again. The man knew how to push her buttons. But she'd rehearsed this one in therapy. The key was to not react. Continue on getting her needs met. She rose and marched toward the sink, only to remember there was no faucet. Resting one hand on the counter, she spun to face Jimmy. "Where's the pump?"

He moved to the door. "I'll leave you here to figure that out."

"Gimme a break, Jimmy. You can't leave me here."

He smiled, precise and cold. His witness interrogation face. "You seem to be confused about what's happening here. You need to remember who you are, Mrs. Fontana. You're not getting out of here 'til you do."

A sharp, humorless laugh escaped Sam's lips. She was definitely changing her name. "I'm not Mrs. Fontana anymore."

"Doesn't matter what your goddamn name is, Sam. You're part of the family. And in this family, we don't talk to outsiders."

"Are you kidding me right now, Jimmy? You sound like you're reciting lines from *The Godfather*."

Jimmy's eyes bulged, his lips compressing into a thin line as he clutched the door handle. "You're either going to tell me what was in that letter now, or you'll be here until you remember. Either way, you're gonna stop digging in the past. Go back home, and take care of our daughter. Because if you don't, you won't see Abby again."

Sam's breath went shallow and rapid. As he opened the door, she forced herself to count—one one thousand, two one thousand—before speaking. "If you're leaving, I insist you take me with you."

He pivoted on the heels of his cowboy boots, still holding the doorknob. This time his smile was genuine. Much more terrifying. "Believe whatever you want. You'll see."

The panic returned to Sam full force. "Jimmy, there is nothing in that letter. Take me back to Sharon's right now, and I'll show you."

"Nice try," he said, again with the surgeon's smile.

She had one last ace. "If you were any good as a lawyer, you'd know that threatening to withhold visitation is grounds for losing custody altogether."

"You think I care about some custody threat?" Jimmy jabbed a finger in her direction. "Sharon told me you destroyed that letter."

Destroyed the letter? Did Sharon—

"No, babe. You won't see Abby because *you* won't be around."

The door slammed as Jimmy's threat lodged. Had her ex-husband just threatened to kill her?

Get a hold of yourself, Sam. He hadn't threatened her with murder; he'd threatened her with custody. She was catastrophizing, which—as Filmore loved to point out—was how she undermined her analytical potential. She hated when he was right.

Outside, Jimmy's car growled to life. Gravel crunched under tires. Then silence, broken only by the whine of mosquitoes. Sam's purse was in the car. Even if he didn't mean to kill her,

Sam had no money, no ID, and no clue where she was. She wouldn't last long out here.

Think, Sam. Think.

An alligator bellowed in the distance. It was mating season. What were they again? Crepuscular? Did that mean they were active all night? No, that was nocturnal. Was it twilight? Dawn? Both? Not that alligators were the only predators in the Everglades. A cold sweat broke out across Sam's torso. She was trapped.

I promised not to reveal these secrets, her mother had written, *because they could put others in danger.*

She'd followed these clues in hopes of learning more about her mom. Maybe even herself. Instead, now she was in danger. And she had no idea what secrets her mother had meant. Worse, she was beginning to suspect that her stupid note was *all* about her work. That her mother would forever be an enigma.

She did need water.

Most likely, the pump was out front. With a groan, she headed for the door, only to find her push met resistance. She pushed again. Pulled. Twisted the knob back and forth. It turned freely, but the door refused to budge. There was no visible locking mechanism on her side, and the metal plate surrounding the handle was smooth. *Am I* locked *in?*

She peered into the gloom, making out a set of horizontal glass slats glinting in the lamp's faint glow—jalousie windows! She raced to test their ancient cranks, but they didn't give an inch.

Desperate, she grabbed the cast-iron kettle from the stove. Water sloshed inside. After draining it dry, she smashed the heavy pot against the window. Several slats shattered with a crack, but the metal frame remained intact, now lined with a row of jagged teeth.

She pushed her arm through the window, hoping she might

be able to manipulate the panes from the outside. A sudden burst of pain made her gasp—the glass had sliced her arm. She jerked back, cursing, blood seeping into her white sleeve. Even if she broke out all the glass, the metal frames would keep her prisoner.

As the shock subsided, her stomach growled. She resumed her search. Baked beans and Spam turned up but no can punch. Nor a lighter or matches for the stove. Her only remaining out was sleep, but both the bed and the couch made her queasy.

She slid down the wall facing the windows, panting as her mind cycled through the past four years, stopping on Jimmy's mystery client. The one who had resurrected his career, allowing her to quit both jobs and return to school. That was when they'd stopped talking.

She didn't know how long she'd sat there when the crunch of gravel sounded outside. She stood, arms akimbo, ready to give Jimmy a piece of her mind. He was going to be mad about the broken glass. She shook her head. Why was she worried about making him mad?

The door swung open, and to her astonishment, there stood Cora Young, her bleach-blond perm forming a halo around her backlit face. Still in her body-hugging tangerine bodysuit, her Candie's shoes hammered the floor as she stepped inside.

Friend or foe?

SEVENTEEN

Thelma, Havana, 1950

THE JANUARY SUN BATHED THE ROOM IN A WINTRY GLOW
as Thelma watched the baby sleep, her little chest moving up
and down with a determination that about broke her heart.
Baby, she chided herself. The kid was three. They hadn't heard
from Kathleen in almost two years, but her checks still came.
They socked it all into a trust fund. *Trust fund.* This hardly felt
like Thelma's life.

"She is precious," whispered a familiar voice. "Hard to
believe she came out of Kathleen Young."

Thelma startled. Turning, she put a finger to her lips as she
urged her friend back out of the room. For a moment, she questioned the compulsion to invite Imogene Fuchs, but she knew
well why she had. Staying busy kept her from sinking into
despair, and Imogene had troubles of her own.

"Come on. Let's have a sit on the balcony. *Terraza,* we call
it. I'll scrounge us up some cocktails."

Tray in hand, by the time she joined the reporter on the
veranda, Thelma felt rejuvenated. Then the courtyard's enormous banyan tree came into view. When they'd first bought this
compound, the tree reminded her of George—solid at the center

even as its branches reached for more. Her heart felt tender as she wondered how he might be expanding his life without her.

Straightening, Thelma put on a smile, heartened that Imogene had taken advantage of the silk robe she'd left in the guest room. The woman still refused to style her hair or polish her nails—forget about makeup—but her edges had softened a bit. The old Imogene would not have accepted a free robe, let alone a free trip.

"Thelma, I cannot thank you enough for inviting me to your beautiful home. I needed a break."

"Of course." Thelma dropped into the wicker chair beside her. "I still owe you that lesson on how to drive a stick."

"That sounds like too much work," said Imogene. "Maybe next visit?"

"Oh, thank God. I still hate driving a standard." Thelma laughed then rattled the ice in her glass. "Ever had a Cuba Libre?" She poured from the cut-glass pitcher José had made earlier.

Imogene took a sip. "I have now. And I must say, they're quite good."

For a few moments they sat in silence as the sounds of Havana's evening traffic drifted up from the street below. But Imogene could never sit for long without asking questions. They'd barely left the airport parking lot before she'd started in on Kathleen's visit and George's departure. Thelma hoped those topics had been exhausted. "So, when did you decide to add the casino?" she asked. "Did Sal push for that?"

Thelma reddened, wishing they could go back to talking about Kathleen or George. She hadn't mentioned anything about Sal's cash infusion or Carlos's involvement with Bird of Paradise and didn't intend to. "Oh, you know, without George's trust fund, we needed another source of revenue. And now that he's gone...."

Imogene scoffed. "I'm not here on assignment."

It was work to refrain from groaning. If she'd learned anything from Imogene, it was that a good journalist was always on duty. And Imogene was a good journalist. "Times change," Thelma said, light as a feather. "And our tables do a brisk business."

Imogene shook her head. "Back in Vegas, you were so dead set against having a casino."

Though it relieved Thelma to have another friend who knew the truth about her father, Imogene could be terribly one-track. She put down her drink and leaned forward, clasping her friend's hands. "I know you don't like talking about yourself, so the fact you mentioned trouble with Bill in your letter has me worried. Tell me. What is going on with you and your husband?"

It was Imogene's turn to deflate. "One thing I'll say about Kathleen Young, she did manage to find herself a man who supported her ambitions."

Thelma sat back in her chair. She doubted old Doc Young would've appreciated his wife jaunting off to the subcontinent and leaving the baby behind. But she didn't want to get into one of those husband-bashing conversations. She knew damn well why George had left, and it wasn't because he felt threatened by her success. It was her family.

"For a long time, I thought Bill was all in," Imogene continued before taking a long sip of her drink. "But he's not. Not really. He was happy enough when I was in St. Pete covering charity luncheons and society weddings. And at first he celebrated my assignment in Las Vegas. Not anymore. He wants me to come home."

Not long ago, Thelma would've offered her opinion immediately. Now, she knew better. "What do you want to do?" she asked, draining her drink.

"I don't want to drop this story. I can't. You saw the clips." Imogene rested her chin on her fist. "The Black Dahlia case."

"You're still working that story?" Thelma shuddered. "I can't believe it. Do you have some new leads?"

Imogene folded her hands across her lap. "Yes and no. I told you the *Times* moved Aggie to city editor, right? That job has been the kiss of death for the last couple of people they pushed over there."

"Death?"

"Career ender."

"Oh," said Thelma, still confused.

"They did it because of what we discovered." Imogene glanced around as if the tropical plants might be listening. "And it's bigger than Elizabeth Short."

"Bigger than Elizabeth Short's murder? But that story is still making headlines."

"Her disappearance is part of a pattern," Imogene said, her eyes weirdly aglow. "When we started looking at other unsolved murders, cold cases, across the country, we found these similarities—"

"More brutalized corpses?" Thelma recoiled in horror.

Imogene put her drink down. "Nothing so horrific as what happened to Short. But an alarming number of these missing girls are young aspiring actresses with long, dark hair."

Thelma felt a chill despite the warm evening. "Like Elizabeth," she said, her voice suddenly hoarse. *Like me.*

"They promise big contracts if they're willing to move far away from home—where no one will recognize them—then they get these girls addicted to drugs. It's no wonder—"

The color drained from Thelma's face as a small sound escaped from her throat. Addicts. *Like my mother.*

"Thelma?" Imogene looked alarmed. "Are you all right?"

"I'm fine," she said, wondering if Imogene knew about her

time in houses of ill repute. But that was impossible. Thelma reached for a newspaper to fan herself, collecting her thoughts. "My mother was addicted to drugs. Toward the end of her life, so it feels personal."

"That's not even the half of it, sister. I found ties to Mickey Cohen, who I know for a fact works with Ben Siegel. Did you meet him in Vegas?"

Midway through a gulp of her cocktail, Thelma choked. "Mmm, no," she wheezed, thumping her chest as she coughed.

"Bill thinks I'm seeing things that aren't there because they killed my Vegas story." Imogene sat back, her voice still low. "But that has nothing to do with this. Every girl I spoke to mentioned mafia nightclubs."

Mafia. Like my father, Thelma thought, barely remaining upright.

"Okay, sure. Maybe I'm more keen to go after these guys." Imogene lowered her voice even further. "But they've got to be stopped. One fella Cohen works with, Mark Hansen? He runs these small-time juice joints, dime-a-time dance halls, and underground clinics. Back in the day, he discovered Lili St. Cyr. You remember her? She was playing the Frontier that night Sal... We...." She waved her hand. "Well, you remember."

Thelma's head swam as she tried to conjure up St. Cyr's performance, anything but what Imogene had just implied about her father's involvement with such horrors.

"Hansen's a real sicko." Imogene leaned in closer, her voice dropping to a whisper. "Rumor is that Hansen sits in at his clinics so he can assist with the girls' procedures. We can't even print most of this stuff."

Imogene, however, felt no such stricture. Thelma tried focusing on the tree as her friend rattled on, but her old trick was no match for the graphic descriptions. Thelma's vision tunneled. The last thing she heard before darkness enveloped her was, "They're running them through Havana."

Like my nightclub.

When her eyes fluttered open, she was lying in her bed still fully dressed as Peggy hovered overhead, worry stamped on her face.

"How'd I get here?" Thelma tried to get out of bed, but her friend gently pressed on her shoulder.

"You fainted, Thelms. Now, rest."

Thelma shook her head, wincing at the movement. She noticed Peggy had on her formfitting red velvet tunic dress. "Shouldn't you be at the Bird?"

"José called. Somebody has to be here for Cora." She fished in her pocket and placed two pills and a glass on the bedside table. "Aspirin."

"Any gin in there?" Thelma smiled.

Peggy frowned.

Thelma reached for the water but left the pills. How she longed for George. The best life she'd known had been those first exuberant weeks they'd shared in Cuba. Knowing that era was years ago did nothing to ease the ache of missing him. He was the only person with whom she'd been fully herself. "Until you started lying to him too," she heard. *Vivian Miles.* The more she drank, the less Thelma heard from her mother. So almost never these days. But her Ma was right; Thelma could no longer say George really knew her.

"What the hell happened?" Peggy continued, worry clouding her deep brown eyes.

The fog was clearing, and Imogene's words floated back. She'd always known the mafia traded in women, but her father didn't even deal heroin. He was all about gambling, graft, and racketeering. For a moment, she considered brushing her off. But the events of the evening had left her raw and vulnerable.

"That Black Dahlia case. Imogene was telling me things that haven't been in the papers. Horrific details...." Peggy squeezed her arm reassuringly, but Thelma doubted she understood. "That could've been me," she said, her vision blurring. "Still could."

"Aw, sweetheart, no." Peggy leaned closer. "You wouldn't want to be that person. When I first met you at Sun City, you were wound so tight, you wouldn't give the time of day in case it revealed too much. You wanted to be a secretary in Miami." She chuckled. "Same here. I thought St. Pete was the cat's pajamas. Never thought I'd leave. And now? We run the hottest night-club in Havana. We live in a mansion. Hell, Frank Sinatra is doing a drop-in tomorrow night."

"I just miss him, Peggy," she admitted softly. "I miss George."

"Of course you do, *chica*. But Thelma, you're stronger than you know. And you're not alone. You've got me, and Helen, and Doris. We're all here for you."

After Peggy left the room, Thelma closed her eyes as her mind reeled. Even if she couldn't find her way back to George, she wanted to be the woman he'd fallen in love with. The woman she used to be.

"And how do you think you'll manage that?" asked Thelma's mother, already roaring back into her head.

Thelma jerked awake, her hands burning as she snapped on her bedside lamp. There was no starting over, like when she'd left Keokuk. She couldn't betray her friends any more than she could her niece. But she could speak to Imogene.

Tomorrow. Right now, I need to find the gin, she thought, padding out of her room in the direction of the liquor cabinet.

EIGHTEEN

Sam, The Everglades, 1978

The wooden soles of Cora's Candie's slapped the floor as she circled Sam's chair, like water torture. The woman was imposing—*tall but not big-boned*, as Sharon would've said, a snarky compliment—but that wasn't why Sam stayed glued to her seat. Every word out of her mouth was crazier than the last, and crazy people were unpredictable.

"They're going to kill you." Cora's voice was matter-of-fact. "Not quick either. They do it the Sicilian way. Dissolve you in acid until there's nothing left."

Sam's stomach lurched. Was that the chemical scent she'd smelled? But that made no sense. Jimmy was squeamish—he couldn't even handle Abby's scraped knees. But the Jimmy she thought she knew seemingly never existed.

"I'm sorry, but what makes you think you know what Jimmy's going to do?"

Cora stopped in front of Sam. "Because I'm family. I've seen it happen."

Family?

Disparate evidence clicked into place with each clack of Cora's kitten heel—her mother's clips, Jimmy's mystery client/benefactor, and just now, his weird reaction to her mention of *The Godfather*. Before now, she'd missed every single clue—Jimmy worked for the mob.

If Cora was family, too, did that mean Helen and Archie were gangsters? "So you're in on this? That's why you refuse to help me escape? What makes you think I won't run away?"

"Good idea. Solves the problem for them."

With a sigh, Cora pulled a wooden chair across from Sam, fishing a pack of Virginia Slims from her bodysuit. Sam wondered where she'd hidden them as Cora extended the pack in her direction. "Want one?"

Sam shook her head as Cora lit up. Jimmy will freak out when he smells the smoke, she thought. Then she noticed an ashtray on the end table, right next to the lantern. She really didn't know him at all.

"Your husband, he wasn't always like this, right? Frankie Giancarlo changed him."

"Frankie Giancarlo?" Sam had no clue who she was talking about.

"You know. He's Sal Giancarlo's son. *The* Giancarlos."

That name Sam did recognize. Salvatore Giancarlo. Head of an old Tampa crime family. She'd studied the forensic accounting that was supposed to put him in jail not long after the second World War. It didn't begin to touch his crimes, but—as Dr. Filmore loved to point out—"Our work is not about retaliation, it's about justice." She'd assumed justice won—his name had faded into obscurity after his death.

Enough. Sam had to get this woman on her back heel. "You mean the guy who checked out rather than face his crimes? I've heard of him."

Cora stabbed the ashtray with her cigarette. "He's my grandfather."

The victory was small, seeing she'd annoyed Cora Young,

but she'd take it. "Yeah? Well, I'm sorry but Jimmy's not, as you say, family. He's an employee."

Cora jerked up, shoes clacking across the floor, back and forth. "An employee who can't get work anyplace else."

Sam's mind whirled back to the old days, before Jimmy's environmental case went south. He'd been so adamant about defending Gulf & Western. "This is how legal precedents around environmental responsibility get set," he'd said. He was so sure that case would make his career. After he lost, no one would touch him. Instead of going back to school, Sam took a second job cleaning houses. That company was forced to remediate the damage to the Everglades, but nothing could bring back their dreams. Then along came Jimmy's mystery client.

She twisted toward Cora, hoisting an arm over the chair-back. "In case you haven't heard, we're divorced."

The shoes stopped a moment before Cora started laughing. "You think that matters?" The shoes resumed. "Guys like Frankie, they're good at spotting people who are desperate."

Sam's head bobbed up sharply. She'd been struggling for some leverage; maybe this was it. "Desperate? You? You don't seem desperate to me. Even if you do still live at home."

The clacking stopped as Cora halted. "I don't live at home, dumbass. I was talking about you." She pivoted to face Sam. "My parents owned Sun City Emporium. You remember it? The old department store?"

"Sun City was owned by the mob?" That had never come up in the tax fraud files she'd researched.

"No. Keep up, *Jesus*." Cora returned to pacing. "The people who raised me aren't my parents, but we are related. Helen and Archie Young are my aunt and uncle. It was just easier to call them Mom and Dad."

Sam was genuinely confused. Was Cora deluding herself into thinking that she didn't live at home because the people she called Mom and Dad weren't really her parents? Sam didn't care. All she had to do was distract her because it was obvious Cora left her keys in her car. There was no place to hide them in her formfitting outfit. The key to the cabin was probably right outside the door under a goddamn doormat.

"The Giancarlos bought Sun City's debt in my name on the condition I run it," Cora continued, oblivious. "It's not exactly running drugs across state lines, but it keeps me comfortable. And alive."

And beholden. Not that Sam cared about Cora's résumé, but she did need to ingratiate herself if she was going to get this woman's help. "Run what? Isn't the store, well... Sorry, but isn't it out of business?"

"Do you even read the papers? It's a recording operation now. Sun City Records and Tapes. Bootlegging, mostly. You know, those penny clubs that advertise in the back of magazines? We press the vinyl, package it up nice. Only instead of paying royalties, we kick up to the family."

This was something Sam could grab onto, flatter the skill and ignore the crime. "Wow, how did you figure out how to do all that?"

"I do love music." She smiled, momentarily lost in either rhythm or fantasy. She came back abruptly. "I fucking *love* music. But I didn't come up with the business plan. I inherited that when I came of age too."

So her parents had died when she was a child. Maybe the buddy route was the way to break through to her. "I'm so sorry. Both my parents are dead too."

"You sure are sorry about a lot." Cora frowned.

Sam had to bite her lip to refrain from apologizing for that. She knew she was guilty of this, but it didn't seem like the worst maladaptive trait possible.

"And didn't your dad *just* die? I never even met my real

dad." Cora shook her head. "And my mom's still alive. I think. I have no idea where she is. The only family I have left is Frankie Giancarlo."

And Archie and Helen, Sam thought a beat before realizing —"You're Salvatore Giancarlo's granddaughter?" She wished she could take back her incredulous tone.

"Weird, right? I only found out when I turned twenty-one and the family bought the store. But yeah, turned out the man I thought was my father was a cuck, and dear old mom was sleeping with the enemy. My guess is it was because of Uncle Bertie and his gambling debts back then too. Same thing that killed the store."

No one had ever accused Sam of being overly sentimental— ideal for her chosen field, she'd always thought—but even she found Cora's revelation shockingly flippant. Looking at her now, it all made sense. Her studied nonchalance, the way she wielded her cigarette like a shield, and the deliberate looseness in her shoulders were textbook traits of an abandoned child, the flip side of Sam's hyper-accommodator response. They'd both learned to hide their wounds early.

Also, who was Bertie? Who the hell was this woman's father? But she knew better than to press her on the finer points.

"It's hard, when you realize you don't know your family at all, isn't it?" Sam ventured, keeping her voice neutral despite her racing pulse, hoping common ground could be an in. But even as the thought formed, Cora's expression hardened.

"You and me are nothing alike," she said.

Sam's chest tightened. She'd misjudged badly. This was no therapy session where shared trauma created trust. This was survival. Where she'd seen connection, Cora saw weakness, the kind that got people killed in her world. Cora wasn't there to commiserate. She'd come to deliver a warning.

Sam needed a new strategy.

"You're right," Sam said, trying to keep her voice steady. "I didn't grow up in your world. I know for a fact that my father's wife will be calling the police if you don't at least send her a message so she knows I'm still alive. Tell her...."

Sam's mind flipped through the possibilities. What kind of coded message could she send to Sharon? "Tell her I'm good. Tell her... Jimmy promised to take me for banana splits at some place he found like Sun City." She smiled at Cora as if to suggest she had not been part of her family store's decline. "We used to go there all the time." She swallowed hard. "That way, she'll know I'm fine."

Cora raked her fingers through her hair. "You don't get it, do you? I'm not your errand girl."

"Please. She's probably already called the police—"

"Let her." Cora stood, smoothing her bodysuit. "When Jimmy explains Frankie's got it all under control, they'll drop it. Happens all the time." Cora lit another cigarette. "Sometimes you gotta take what's offered. At least you have choices."

"Choices? I didn't choose this. I was minding my own business."

"Yeah, 'til your business became a conflict of interest."

Conflict of interest?

Cora moved toward the door. "Make the smart choice, Sam. For Abby's sake if not your own."

Sam thought of her daughter, probably sitting at Jimmy's kitchen table right now, doing homework and wondering when her mother would call. How many other daughters had waited for calls that never came because their mothers proved *inconvenient* to the wrong person?

"Wait," Sam said, lunging for the door. "My mother... Did they—"

But Cora was already in her car, leaving Sam alone with the mosquitoes and the growing certainty that her mother's car accident had been anything but accidental. She watched the tail-lights disappear into the darkness, praying Cora would relay the message despite her refusal. Sharon would understand that Sam was in danger, and she would not stop until she found her.

The sounds of the Everglades roused her—frogs croaking, crickets chirping, and alligators splashing. Ordinarily, she loved the natural beauty of the Everglades, but without even a flash-light, the swamp did nothing but ramp up her anxiety. She turned back to the love seat inside, shaking her head in frustra-tion. Out of the corner of her eye, a streak of black and pink flashed beside the ashtray. A matchbook.

Picking up the pack, Sam read the cover: Bird of Paradise.

That nightclub, she thought, a moment before it struck her —the cabin door was wide open.

NINETEEN

Thelma, Havana, 1950

The morning dawned hot and restless. Thelma lay sprawled across the couch, an empty bottle of rum on the floor beside her. The sounds of shouting in the streets filtered through her office window, mixing with the pounding in her head. Her eyes were still gummed shut, but she was aware of the dried saliva on her cheek.

What time was it?

Had she missed the day's planning meeting? In the year since Carlos Gonzalez had threatened to return, Chickie and Moose had come through, but the situation required constant monitoring. Thelma was constantly looking over her shoulder, more trapped than ever. The only time she slept was if she passed out, but that had been causing other problems.

"Thelma?" Helen's voice cut through her hangover haze. "Georgie's here."

Her heart stopped. She didn't remember a Georgie from the night before. She thought the guy's name was Ted. Or Ed. Ned? This was bad. "Who?"

"Your husband? George Wright."

George? As Thelma struggled to sit up, she ran shaking

fingers through her tangled hair. She caught a glimpse of herself in the office mirror—hollow-eyed, makeup smeared, dress wrinkled from sleeping on the couch. In the three years and million scenarios she'd imagined since he'd left, such a faceoff was not one she'd envisioned.

Then he was in her office, tan and glowing with health in a light summer suit. The smell of his aftershave pierced her consciousness, and she folded in on herself. Though she couldn't smell herself, she didn't doubt the office reeked of stale cigarettes and the stench of unmetabolized alcohol seeping from her pores.

"Hello, Thelma," George said softly.

Helen retreated, closing the door behind her.

"George." Thelma scrambled upright. "It's good to... What brings you here?"

"I need...." George paused then pulled a thick envelope from his jacket. "I need you to sign these."

"What are they?" Thelma asked, searching in corners for the bottle she'd dropped earlier.

"Annulment papers." He set them on her desk. "My advisor says it's cleaner than a divorce. Better for my political career."

Thelma laughed, but the sound stuck, erupting as a nicotine-infused cough instead. The flicker of hope she'd carried, the flame that burned for George, sputtered out with each hacking cough. "Can't have a divorced senator, can we?" she finally managed as she located the bottle. *Empty.*

"I'm not getting that far ahead of myself. It's just a run at city council," he said.

The sickening little grin that appeared on his face told her he thought she was being serious. But there was no coming back from this failed marriage. She'd destroyed him as surely as he'd destroyed her. She began scrabbling for her cigarettes. "And you couldn't mail these papers because...."

"Because I wanted to see for myself if the rumors were true."

"What rumors?"

"That you're drinking yourself to death. That you're sleeping with dangerous men. That you've completely abandoned any pretense of caring for Cora."

Thelma stopped moving abruptly. "Don't you dare," she said, her voice a hiss. "You left. You don't get to judge how I raise her."

"Raise her?" George's voice rose. "From what I hear, Helen and Doris are the ones raising her while you drink yourself into oblivion every night."

His words hit like a physical blow. Thelma struggled to her feet, swaying slightly. "Get out."

"I suppose you're not waiting for cocktail hour anymore." George moved closer, perching on the edge of her desk. "What happened to you?"

"What happened? That's rich. You were there," she snapped. "Let's see, after doing everything I could to save my husband's life, my old boss showed up and left me with her baby, who happens to be my niece. Then my husband, who supposedly wanted children, decides he can't handle an actual kid and races back to Daddy Warbucks. Sound about right?"

"Let's not relitigate this."

"Ooh, that law degree is really paying off, isn't it? I heard you went back. Harvard, was it? Nothing but the best now."

"Yale, actually," said George, studying his hands. The beautiful hands that had taught her how good being touched could feel. "I thought you might be upset about Imogene's car accident."

The mention of Imogene made her feel queasier. Moving to the seat behind her desk, Thelma clamped shut her eyes and wished the room would stop spinning.

"She wanted me to tell you about some story she was working," George continued. "Something important. She implied you might... But I don't think you're in any condition to—"

"Stop. Just... stop." Thelma turned away, unable to meet his eyes. The tingling in her palms flared up, that cursed premonition she tried so hard to drink away. "You want something juicy to prosecute and ramp up your campaign?" Her voice cracked.

George was quiet for a moment. Then he pulled out another envelope. "This is for a dry-out clinic in Miami."

Thelma stared at the envelope, her vision blurring. "You want to pay me off so I'll cooperate?"

"I want to save your life." George's voice strained with emotion. "For what we once meant to each other. For Cora. For Imogene's memory."

Outside her office window, a crowd began chanting. Something about Batista—his return had not been universally welcomed but those protestors were risking their lives—and Thelma wondered how she might explain any of this to Cora in terms a six-year-old might understand.

Thelma returned her gaze to the second envelope that George had handed her. "Thanks, but I don't need your help. I'm doing fine on my own," she said as she tore his offering in two.

"Things are changing, Thelma. Not only in Cuba but back home too. People are sick of the corruption," George said, gesturing toward the window. "When the dust settles, you'll need to be clear-headed enough to protect what matters." He stood, straightening his tie. "Help yourself or don't. That was just an admission brochure. There's a bed for you, starting tomorrow. I've arranged everything."

"Why?" Thelma's voice was barely a whisper. "Why do you still care?"

George gazed at her for a long moment, and she saw in his

eyes the echo of the love they'd once shared. "Because after everything, I still believe in the woman I married. The question is, do you?"

He moved toward the exit, pausing before he crossed the threshold. "Sign the papers, Thelma. Let's both move on. And for God's sake, take the help I'm offering. If not for yourself then for Cora."

After he'd gone, Thelma sat in silence, staring at the envelopes on her desk. She reached for her lighter and a cigarette, but her hands were shaking so badly she could barely spark a flame.

Helen appeared in the doorway, head tilted, her strawberry blond hair framing her head like a crown. "Well?"

"He wants an annulment," Thelma said, motioning toward the envelopes. "And he thinks I need rehab."

"And?" Helen moved into the room, picking up an empty rum bottle. "What do you think?"

Thelma peered up at her friend, really took her in for the first time in months. She saw the worry lines around her eyes, the tension in her shoulders.

"How bad is it?" Thelma asked quietly. "Really?"

Helen's eyes filled with tears. In all the years she'd known her, Thelma could not recall ever seeing her cry. "We love you," she said. "But you're scaring us, Thelms. All of us. Even the staff at the Bird. And Cora—"

"I'm sorry, I was wrong," Thelma held up her hand. "I'm not up for hearing more of this. Not right now. Please. Look, I hear you. I'll do better. But I don't need to go off to some clinic. I'm not a drug addict."

She stood, legs feeling somehow shakier as she moved to the window. "Things will be different. You'll see."

* * *

As Thelma lay in bed that night, wide-eyed and alert, she wondered how long it had been since she'd fallen asleep without alcohol. She hadn't had anything to drink since George had left her office. Now, her mind would not stop. She found herself remembering the life she used to dream of, before she left Iowa, when all she wanted then was a beach bungalow in Miami. Alone. She'd never envisioned a husband or a child. Just the freedom to look after herself and not having to hide. Now, she knew that life would've been lonely. She loved the family they'd built in Cuba.

She would slow down her drinking. Only at night. Only clear alcohol, vodka and gin. And tequila on special occasions. She'd show Helen.

Unlike Thelma, that woman had blossomed under Cora's influence. Her cheeks were fuller. She seemed perfectly content to sing and play with the girl for hours, repeating the same songs and stories over and over. It drove Thelma to the brink. Was it possible she'd never really wanted children? The only time she'd really considered it was when she was with George.

George.

She missed his height, burrowing into his neck. The way his touch opened her. Made her want to hold on to things. Now she could barely remember who she'd slept with, she hadn't seen her father in years, and she'd utterly failed Cora.

There would be no sleep. Thelma moved to her bureau, where she dredged up the annulment papers from the bottom of her purse. Her vision blurred as she read: *Petitioner seeks declaration of invalidity.*

Invalidity? The word left Thelma breathless. Another lifetime, maybe—before Vegas, before the Bird, before Cora—but their marriage had not disappeared and left no trace.

"Sign the papers like you should've done years ago."

This was not the voice of Vivian Miles but Thelma herself.

She *had* intended to sign the papers, back in Las Vegas when George was presumed dead. Wasn't he as good as dead now anyway? She no more wanted to spend her life looking over her shoulder for him than for Carlos Gonzalez.

She uncapped her pen. "George is right. We both need to move on."

But as she signed each page, her hand and heart grew heavier. By the time she was done, she knew the truth—she couldn't sign away her feelings. She was no longer George's wife nor was she any freer. Only empty.

After folding the papers back into the envelope, she took them to the entry table downstairs. She would ask Luísa to take them to George's hotel. From there, she padded toward the bar to pour herself a drink—tequila. This certainly qualified as a special occasion.

TWENTY

Sam, The Everglades, 1978

The lantern's glow caught Sam's attention once more. Though it barely penetrated the room, that lamp was all she could think about. Her only hope. Her only weapon.

Her eyes swept the cabin, cataloging the possibilities. There were no knives in the kitchen, nothing electrical. No additional kerosene. This place seemed to have only one nefarious purpose —disposing of unwanted bodies. Not on her watch.

The cot in the corner stopped her. Despite the military corners, nothing about the sickly metal frame suggested order. She ran her hands across the sheets, an institutional-grade cloth that felt rough against her fingers. She thought of the other women who might have touched sheets like these, wondered if the cloth doubled as a burial shroud. *Focus.*

The material was sturdy. Too sturdy to tear with bare hands. Feeling her way along the frame, she found what she needed—a sharp burr where the paint had bubbled and peeled, exposing raw metal beneath. The sheet caught easily on the jagged edge. She bore down as the first satisfying rip of fabric tore through the room. Once she had a good hole started, the rest pulled apart easily. With each pull of the fabric, her hands grew steadier, echoing the separation from everything she'd believed about her life, her marriage, her past. Sam was shredding more than sheets.

Her next task was risky. Stuffing fabric into the lamp's glass chimney posed multiple problems. The hot glass could shatter, sending out a spray of burning kerosene, or the flame could be extinguished. Her best bet was to put out the light then douse the sheet in the fuel chamber. Maybe for the first time in her life, Sam found herself thanking God for sending a smoker.

Beside the ashtray, right where Cora had left it, sat the matchbook—black and pink against the worn wooden table, its edges softened by the decades. The words emblazoned across the pack however—Bird of Paradise, Havana—seemed to pulse in the lantern light, as if they were alive. Yet the matches felt impossibly delicate, like a pressed flower that might crack or crumble at the slightest touch.

Stop digging through old stories, Jimmy'd said. *Stop asking questions about Cuba, about the girls.*

Cora hadn't used these matches to light her cigarette. Had she left them, or had they been there before? Did Cora have something to do with Cuba?

Once the lamp's glass chimney had cooled sufficiently, Sam twisted it open, dousing the strips of fabric. The pungent, oily smell rose to meet her, combining with the chemical tang in the air. Nausea rose, but she forced it down. *Focus on the details.*

Her hands shook as she opened the pack. The first match crumbled between her fingers, leaving only a trace of phosphorus on her skin. Like the person she had become with Jimmy.

The head of the second match was fused to the match cover and broke away from its stick when she tried tearing it loose.

The third rasped against the striker and died, taking a piece of her hope with it.

Sam counted the remaining matches. Four. The same number of years since Jimmy had landed the wonder job that saved their house. She'd been so grateful, she hadn't questioned where the money came from. Now that she knew, there was no going back. She had to escape this cabin and figure out what was missing from that letter despite whatever misdeeds her mother might have committed.

The fourth match caught with a flare so sudden she flinched. As quickly as she dared move, Sam touched the struggling flame to the corner of the torn bedsheet. The flame crawled along the fabric, tentative at first then gaining confidence.

At first Sam was mesmerized by a plume of smoke curling toward the ceiling in a lazy spiral, reminding her how Jimmy used to trace patterns on her skin when they first met. She hated that she couldn't stop thinking about him. Mid recrimination she noticed it—a hiss from the corner, followed by a bubbling sound that made her blood run cold.

Her plan was simple: set a blaze big enough to bring help, even if it took hours for anyone to spot it this far out. As she slipped into the velvet darkness, Sam left the door open. Let the oxygen feed those flames.

Run.

Sam's Keds caught in the wet muck outside, so she kicked out of them, feeling the ground beneath her bare feet. Something slithered past in the dark. She couldn't tell if the pounding in her ears was her heart or the sound of chemicals beginning to react behind her.

She was barely twenty feet away when the first explosion knocked her forward onto her hands and knees. Heat rolled over her like a solid wave as a second, larger blast tossed her into a stand of sawgrass that sliced into her arms, her face, her peasant blouse. She rolled onto her back as the fireball bloomed against the star-strewn sky, beautiful and terrible at once.

She'd wanted to attract attention—counted on it, in fact. But she hadn't expected this magnitude of devastation. Even when the flames started spreading faster than she'd expected, feeding on something more volatile than old wood and cotton sheets.

Acid, Cora had said. *The Sicilian way.*

Another wave of sickness came on. To push away the rising gorge, she retrained her focus on the likely chemical composition. The rotten egg stench could've been sulfuric acid, which like the swamp itself could dissolve bone. But underneath that was a sickly sweet almond scent. Hydrochloric acid, or pool cleaner, would've been easy to obtain without raising suspicion. Ideal for dissolving flesh. This strategy wasn't helping.

She looked back toward the cabin. The smoke column created by the blaze would be visible for miles, but the nearest town was still hours away. Whoever spotted it would have to alert authorities in Naples or Fort Lauderdale. The mafia hadn't been a major area of her studies, but she knew an explosion like that would bring out the Giancarlos' cleanup crew long before anyone official. That left her no choice.

To venture deeper into the tangle of cypress and mangroves was akin to disappearing into the dark heart of the wilderness. She was going to have to find the access road—a dirt track barely visible in the moonlight—and get herself back to the highway. There was only one problem. She had no clue which direction to take.

Looking skyward, she found the North Star, steady and true above the wet dark of the swamp. That was it. If she kept the star over her right shoulder, she'd be heading northward, toward salvation. As if confirming her choice, the distant call of a night bird sounded across the water, music as ancient as the Everglades itself.

As she set off in the dark, every rustle reminded Sam that humans weren't the only predators in these wetlands. Her blouse clung to her skin as the muck pulled at her bleeding feet. Her throat, too, was stripped raw. But she kept moving forward, trudging along for what felt like hours.

Dawn was just pearling in the eastern sky when she heard the rotors of a helicopter whirring. Official rescuers would come by ground. That had to be the Giancarlos. She dropped down into the sawgrass, hoping the thick stems would hide her from view.

She'd dropped beside the road when headlamps appeared, cutting across the path. It was too soon for emergency vehicles. Highway 41 was a thin strip of asphalt cutting through the swamp. Barely traveled at night. There was only one explanation for who could have reached her so quickly.

Then she saw it through the grass, a familiar Cadillac coming toward her.

TWENTY-ONE

Thelma, Havana, 1950

Afternoon sun sliced through the nightclub's skylights, catching the sequins and feathers still littering the floors. The distant strains of street vendors' calls filtered in, a drowsy counterpoint to the muffled clinking of ice as the barman prepared for another night of spectacle. The time for Cora's afternoon nap had finally come, and since George's visit, the time of day Thelma had deemed suitable to commence the day's drinking. She reached for the English paper that had just arrived and asked Miguel for a bourbon.

'POLICY' GAME TIES FOUND IN MIAMI INQUIRY; Kefauver Says Tax Files May Be Used

Thelma's stomach dropped. Imogene Fuchs was either rolling in her grave or sharpening her pencil. *Those yahoos better have got hold of her notes.* The story her friend had been working on had never come out. Thelma didn't know what had become of the piece, but unfinished tasks weren't the kind of thing you asked about at a funeral. And that was the last time she'd seen any of the Fuchses. She'd actively avoided them, her little girl looking so brave, her husband looking so lost. Rationally, she knew Imogene's death wasn't her doing—she could've had a car accident anywhere—but if she hadn't encouraged her friend to pursue work so far from home...

Miguel placed a glass on the bar before her. "¡Salud!" he said.

"¡Gracias, Miguel!" said Thelma. Her Spanish was nowhere near as good as Peggy's or Doris's, but she was trying. With Carlos gone, she spent nearly all her time at the Bird of Paradise.

Looking down at the paper, Virginia Hill's name caught her eye. The reporter described her as "smooth-browed, blue-eyed, with a classic profile," noting she was "easily the most photogenic witness" while barely mentioning her actual testimony. Morons, she thought, downing her glass. Small wonder they couldn't focus on the women trapped in this web.

After Imogene had revealed her suspicions about the mafia-backed prostitution network, Thelma had done some digging. Turned out trading women like cattle had become Carlos Gonzalez's primary business after Sal kicked him out. She sent up a silent prayer—*please let someone uncover the evidence*—before remembering God was unlikely to listen to her.

Miguel must've slipped to the stockroom. The girls would be along soon enough, so she went behind the bar to get herself a more generous second pour. Once they arrived, she'd have to start hiding her drinks, though she was looking forward to their upcoming session. Benny Moré was starting a run, and they were going to choreograph a few new dance numbers with their now-famous in-house troupe, the *Birds* of Paradise. Part of her still felt that old familiar excitement burbling up at the thought of planning the coming shows.

"Breaking news from Miami," she heard an announcer's voice crackling across the radio waves. "Following his arrest in Miami on charges of tax evasion, Salvatore Giancarlo, the criminal mastermind once presumed dead, has finally met his maker after falling on the courthouse steps, reportedly from a stroke. His attorney, Artemis Clauer, said no further comment was forthcoming at this time. I repeat—"

She found the dial and shut off the switch like it was radioactive. Sal... *Dead*? Her father was no more? The news hit her with physical force, a hollow opening beneath her ribs. There'd been no call, no telegram. She'd heard the news along with everyone else, which was, perhaps, fitting. Their relationship had always been defined by absences and what they implied.

An unexpected surge of grief hit Thelma, mingled with something more complex—regret. She'd spent years distancing herself from Sal, building walls to protect herself from both his criminal legacy and his ego. And yet somehow, his death felt like losing a future she hadn't realized she still imagined.

Worse still, pushing him away repeated the model she'd grown up with. Cora was only five, but growing more withdrawn by the day as Thelma drowned her responsibilities in gin and tonics. The irony wasn't lost on her. She'd become what she most despised in her mother and her father—someone who couldn't be counted on. Someone who'd failed the child in her care.

In burst Helen, Doris, and Peggy, chattering away. They stopped on seeing Thelma behind the bar.

"Did you hear, doll?" Peggy asked. "On the radio, they said—"

"Yeah," Thelma cut her off. "I heard."

Chair legs scraped against the floor as Helen and Doris took seats, waiting. Peggy moved toward Thelma. "What are we going to do about it?" she asked.

"Do?" Thelma asked, still processing. Her father was gone. Really gone. Not "dead" like in Vegas, but really and truly dead.

"I told you," Helen said to Doris out of the side of her mouth. "This doesn't change anything."

"Thank you, Helen, but that's not quite what she said." Peggy eyed Thelma. "Is it?"

Time slowed. Or at least Thelma's brain had. Without Sal, who could they trust? Like Carlos, anyone they knew that well knew about Helen and Doris. Stumbling slightly as she came out from behind the bar to join her friends, she noticed a look pass between them. She was, as yet, quite sober; nonetheless, her glass flew from her hand to the floor, sending out a shower of razor-sharp fragments.

"Auntie TT?" Cora called from Thelma's office.

"Stay put, sweetheart," Helen answered smoothly as she crouched to the floor, picking up the shards. "We're just cleaning up a little mess."

"Mama Helen," the child cried.

When Doris stood to join Helen, the pit-a-pat of bare feet rushed toward them.

"Mama Doris!"

Helen and Doris froze. "Cora, love, please stop. Stay still," cried Doris.

Thelma hadn't moved, had barely registered the exchange. She was still processing the news. Her father. The man who had indirectly taught her everything she knew about survival, cold in some morgue in Miami. Reduced to another statistic in the government's display of a crusade.

The irony was not lost on Thelma. Had she been successful in her bid to take down the Giancarlo empire in Las Vegas, the charge would have been the same—tax evasion. What if this was another ruse?

A glinting shard caught her attention. It would be a while before she could pour another drink, she thought, as she simultaneously realized that Cora was about to reach them. Glass crunched beneath her heels as she raced to the girl and swept her up. "Oh, clumsy Auntie TT did it again," Thelma said as Cora wriggled in her arms. She turned to the girls. "I'll take her home. Whatever you decide about the show is fine with me."

Helen, who had resumed collecting glass slivers, looked up from her work.

Peggy blanched. "Really? What about our protection?" she asked. "Without Sal...I hate to say it, but we still need someone watching our backs. We—"

"I need to think," Thelma said, shielding Cora's ears. "I need to figure out where we stand now."

As if on cue, the front door burst open. In walked Carlos Gonzalez, dressed for a night out despite the early hour. His limping gait evidenced the beating her father had meted out three years ago, but his smile was triumphant, confirming what she knew to be true. The world tilted; this confirmation hit Thelma harder than the radio announcement.

"Ladies," he purred. "I trust you've heard the news?"

"You son of a bitch," Peggy started forward, but Doris caught her arm.

"How dare you come here?" Helen's voice was a razor.

"How dare I?" Carlos laughed. "I dare because I won. Your father is dead, Thelma. Gone. Now it is time to renegotiate our arrangement."

Bile rose in Thelma's throat. "There's nothing to negotiate," she said quietly, hugging Cora tighter.

"No? You still think you can run a casino in Havana without

my help?" He looked down at Helen and Doris. "What about those two?"

Cora's voice pierced the silence. "Mamas?"

"Helen," Thelma said softly, "would you take Cora to my office, please?"

She heard Helen's quick steps, felt the weight lift and murmured reassurances as the door closed, but she did not take her eyes off Carlos. "You think you've won?" Thelma turned slowly, drawing herself up to her full height. She was taller than Gonzalez by six inches in her heels. "You think my father's death means you can threaten us?"

"I think it means you need new protection," Carlos stepped closer. "I think it means—"

"It means nothing," Thelma cut him off. "Because you've forgotten something important, Carlos."

"And what's that, *querida?*"

"I'm still Sal Giancarlo's daughter."

Carlos's smile faltered slightly. "Meaning?"

"Meaning he taught me things. Like how to make problems disappear." Thelma moved forward, her height forcing Carlos to look up at her. "Like what to do with men who threaten my family."

"You wouldn't—"

"Wouldn't I?" Thelma's voice was deadly soft. "You knew my father, Carlos. Did you really think he'd leave us unprotected? That he wouldn't make certain arrangements?"

Peggy and Doris exchanged glances, catching on.

"Those arrangements still stand," Peggy added, her voice hard. "One phone call is all it takes."

"You're bluffing," Carlos said, but beads of sweat formed at his hairline.

"Try me." Thelma smiled, her mother's smile, the one Vivian Miles had used to deal with troublesome clients in Iowa.

"And find out exactly what Sal taught me about dealing with threats."

For a long moment, they stood locked in silent battle. Then Carlos's eyes dropped.

"Perhaps it is still too soon," he said smoothly, adjusting his tie. "We can discuss this another time."

"No," Thelma said. "We won't. Because if you ever come near this club, my house, or my family again, they won't find enough of you, or your family, to bury."

"You're not like him," Carlos tried one last time. "You're not a killer."

"I'm whatever I need to be to protect what's mine." Thelma's voice was steely. "Would you like to test that theory?"

Carlos backed away, his facade cracking. At the door, he paused. "Silly girls. This isn't over."

"*Comemierda,*" Peggy hissed as he walked past the three women glaring at him.

As soon as he'd gone, Doris whooped. "Brilliant." She grinned. "Absolutely brilliant."

Helen peeked out from behind the office door. "What do we do now?"

Thelma smoothed her skirt. "Now, we throw the biggest damn party this city has ever seen. Show everyone that we run this club."

"And Cora?" Helen asked softly. "That man has local connections. Power...."

"He's like a bad penny." Peggy groaned. "Impossible to get rid of."

"Now hang on, gang," said Doris. "Take a look around. We've built something solid here. Not just the Bird but relationships. People trust us, respect us. And I'm a local too. A Cuban citizen anyway. And I know for a fact, Carlos has made some enemies. Thelms, let's ring up Moose and Chickie. We are gonna get through this."

Doris's certitude had an immediate effect. Helen went back to cleaning up the broken glass while Peggy retrieved fresh party-planning papers. Doris joined Helen, humming as she did. Inside the office, they could hear Cora singing to herself, safe and oblivious. Soon they were all singing, morphing the tune into the old blues number that had rocketed them to radio fame back in their Florida Girl days.

Wiggle, wiggle
Ooh, wee!
What's that I see?
Got to be jelly
What you say?
Must be jelly
No way!
Don't you see?
Got to be jelly 'cause jam don't shake like that

DEEP INTO THE NIGHT, AFTER THE CLUB CLOSED AND they'd all gone home, Thelma sat alone in her bedroom. "I'll Be Seeing You" played softly on the phonograph, another song from the Florida Girls' repertoire, though this was Billie Holiday's rendition. As she sang along, grief and anger tangled inside her. She couldn't say what hurt most—the loss of a father she barely knew or the marriage she'd torpedoed.

She pulled out a photo from her desk drawer, Sal and Thelma on a makeshift stage in St. Petersburg, christening a new fleet of sanitation trucks. Her first inkling that the Youngs were in deep with the mafia and that they weren't quite aware of this fact themselves.

"You bastard," she whispered. "You saddled me with another mess."

Her gaze fell on a drawing left on her desk. A crude rendering of four figures holding hands—Doris, Peggy, herself, and a smaller figure—standing in front of what must be the Bird.

What was family anyway? She'd never really been Sal Giancarlo's daughter. She didn't want to spend the rest of her days trapped between her father's legacy and the woman she longed to become. After all, she had built something worth protecting, worth fighting for, even if gin and regret clouded that path.

"To you, old man," she said, raising her glass to the empty office. "May you rot in hell."

The first sip tasted like surrender

TWENTY-TWO

Sam, The Everglades-Miami, 1978

SAM FELT SHARON'S ARMS SURROUND HER AS SHE surrendered for the first time in thirty years to the embrace she'd been resisting.

Briefly.

"Don't say a word. Get in the car." Sharon opened the passenger door, patting a mountain of beach towels. "Wrap yourself in these."

"How did you find me?" Sam asked, earning a scowl from Sharon as she marched to the driver's side of the car. "If you could find me, I can't imagine Jimmy won't."

Despite the million *other* questions forming in her mind, fear pushed Sam into the car. As she wrapped the lattice of angry red lines strafing her feet, she couldn't help but notice the stark contrast between Sharon's fluffy clean towels and the swamp and smoke smells emanating from her own body.

The car jerked forward. "You need something cold to drink," Sharon said. "There's a Mobil station up ahead. We'll stop there."

Sam regarded Sharon. She was as frumpy as ever, hair escaping out from under the checked scarf she'd wound around her foam rollers, yet she radiated a steely determination that Sam hadn't seen before. Or, she was beginning to suspect, hadn't noticed.

"What?" Sharon asked, not taking her eyes from the scarcely visible path the Cadillac's headlights made in the pre-dawn light. "I have connections."

"No," Sam said. "You don't get to play mysterious. I don't know where my child is, and I've been threatened with never seeing her again. All while I was being kidnapped by my ex, who is working for the mob, and apparently, so is my dad's wife? Oh, and I was shot at. All because I went on a hunt *you* sent me on."

"Well, when you put it that way...." Sharon gave a lopsided grin but dropped it when she stole a glance at Sam's face. "Sweetie, it didn't take a genius to know Jimmy's sudden interest in you was off-brand. So when you said you were heading to Miami, I drove straight there. That way, when he dropped the act, I'd already be there to collect you. And Jimmy wouldn't be able to keep that up for long."

"We never made it to Miami."

"Exactly. When you didn't show, I started making phone calls. That's how I found out about that cabin. I was already on my way when I saw the fireball."

Sam sat a moment with her stepmother's explanation. Did Sharon know what had gone on in that shack? "Speaking of my mother's letter, I can't believe you destroyed it."

"Destroyed it? Because Jimmy said so? Look in the glove box."

Popping open the door, the familiar manila folder almost fell into Sam's lap. Relief washed over her. She'd best have all the evidence she could lay her hands on.

"Where are we going?" Sam asked, her navigational stars now obscured by the car's roof.

"We need to get to Miami," Sharon said.

"What? No, we don't. That's suicide. Jimmy's mystery client? It's none other than Frankie Giancarlo. He practically owns Dade County."

"Exactly why they won't look there first." Her fingers, Sam noticed, were white-knuckled on the steering wheel. "Besides, Meyer's offered us a place to stay."

"Meyer who?" Sam asked, though the name sounded familiar.

"Lansky," Sharon said. "Meyer Lansky."

"Who's that exactly?"

Sharon took her eyes off the road to look Sam up and down. "Aren't you getting a PhD in criminal psychology?"

Maybe it was Sam's fault no one knew what she was studying. "That doesn't mean I study criminals. The paper I'm working on looks at the traumatic fallout of Operation Pedro Pan."

"Operation what?"

"Pedro Pan. Back in the early sixties, when the US government got the bright idea to let minors into the country so they could escape the Castro regime? Didn't work out well for a lot of them."

"Oh, yes. I remember that." Sharon shuddered. "They set up camps for the kids. *Camps.* Will we never learn?"

A set of headlights appeared in the road ahead, approaching quickly.

"Get down," Sharon commanded.

Sam slid down in her seat.

"It's a cop," she said. "Stay down."

The car slowed, and Sam panicked. Pulling over, even for a policeman, would be a disaster. Even if he wasn't dirty, an arrest would lead Jimmy straight to her. When the car stopped and Sharon got out, Sam wanted to scream. She molded into the footwell as she covered herself as best she could with the towels, and the door opened on her side.

"You pump; I'll pay."

Sam burst up from the towels. "Geez, Sharon. You could've told me."

"I did tell you I was stopping at the gas station." Sharon pointed at a towel. "Clean yourself up a bit. I'll get us some Cokes."

"That's not what I meant," Sam said. But Sharon was already heading for the station.

Holding the nozzle, Sam looked out across the parking lot. At least the place was empty, she thought, exhaling tension she barely allowed herself to feel.

Now it came to her—Meyer Lansky was the mob's accountant.

Limping toward the toilet, Sam recalled reading about the longtime mafia figure who'd mostly beaten charges of tax evasion. Part of his power came from his low profile, as she remembered from the story. Sharon never did respond to her mention of the mob.

A pay phone stood beside the bathroom. Sam felt the urge to call Ed. But how would she start that conversation?

"Hey, it's been a while."

No.

"Sorry about the collect call."

Ugh. And what if his wife answered?

By the time she got back to the car, Sharon was inside with two bottles of Coca-Cola, condensation beading on their surfaces. As she put the key in the ignition, Sam stopped her.

"Tell me, Sharon. How does a nice Jewish lady from Florida end up with an apartment courtesy of Meyer Lansky?"

Sharon's laugh had a bitter edge that Sam had never heard before. "Nice Jewish lady from Florida? Sweetheart, you know I was born in Germany. I was twenty-four when I was sent to Britain in 1937. One of the twenty thousand *lucky* ones." Her voice hardened. "They called us domestic servants. We were servants, all right. Least we were alive. My mother and father and brother were sent to Auschwitz."

Guilt twisted in Sam's gut—all those years resenting this woman, never asking about her past. She knew Sharon's family had died in the camps, but she'd walled herself off from the reality of it. Here she was studying the trauma of family separation, and all this time she'd been living with someone directly impacted by it. In the harsh morning light, she could see the painful memories etched in Sharon's face. Maybe her stepmother hadn't been solely responsible for the distance between them. Sam had blamed Sharon for erasing her mother's memory when maybe Sam had erased just as much.

Sharon started the car and peeled out of the Mobil lot. "I don't know Lansky from bupkes. But I know evil when I spot it."

Glancing at Sharon's profile, Sam saw not an interloper but a survivor. She'd rebuilt herself from the ashes of war, like her mother had tried to do. Like Sam herself was doing now, driving toward answers she doubted she was ready to hear.

TWENTY-THREE

Thelma, Havana, 1953

Angry shouts filled the streets outside Thelma's office, voices raised in unified anger. Despite the media lockdown, reports of protesters' mutilated corpses had seeped out. The noise intensified the already intense throbbing in her head. She knew how to blunt the pain.

Special occasion, she thought, moving to her desk. She drummed her fingers on the drawer before sliding it open to reveal a silver flask. She'd scarcely touched the cool metal when the door opened abruptly.

"Someone here to see you, Thelms," Peggy said. "Very pushy."

Behind her stood a man Thelma had never seen before—tall, bad haircut, and possessed of the kind of anonymous look that screamed government agent. She re-capped her flask and shoved it deep in her drawer. She thought she'd finished with this lot back in Vegas.

"I'm busy," she grumbled.

Paying no mind, the man stepped forward and offered his hand. "Charles Miller. I was hoping we could speak privately."

A Southerner, she reckoned from his accent and deep tan.

Between his rumpled suit and slender neck, she figured he was a desk jockey to boot. Peggy was already mid retreat but Thelma called her back. "Pegs, why don't you stay? Whatever you need to say, Mr. Miller, you can say it in front of my partner."

Miller smiled—practiced, professional. "I'm afraid this is rather sensitive."

"It's fine," Peggy said quickly. "My pile of invoices won't review themselves, and like I said, this guy's a clown."

As she filed out, Thelma noticed how Miller's eyes followed her, calculating. She waited until the door closed before speaking.

"CIA or FBI?"

His smile widened slightly. "What makes you think I'm either?"

Thelma pushed away from her desk. "Cut the act, Mr. Miller. What do you want?"

He settled into a chair, unbuttoning his jacket with practiced ease. "We're concerned about certain meetings being held here at your club."

"Meetings?"

"Led by your partner Miss Juergen. Discussions about Cuba's future, independence, revolution. That sort of thing."

"Doris is a Cuban citizen, proud of her heritage." Thelma shrugged. "Nothing illegal about that."

"Perhaps not. But some of her associates have concerning connections to Fidel Castro's movement."

"What's it to you?"

"Come now, Miss Miles, you know darn well that we can't allow communism to flourish less than fifty miles off a US coast."

"Communism? Castro's against Batista, but he isn't communist," Thelma's voice raised. "He's said so himself."

"And you believe him?"

"I couldn't give a fig about Fidel Castro, but I believe in my friend. Doris wants what's best for Cuba. That's all." She looked agent Miller up and down. "She *is* Cuban."

Miller leaned forward. "Miss Miles, we're not here to shut down your club or arrest anyone. We just want information. Your cooperation would be appreciated."

Thelma felt a familiar anger rising in her chest. "That and a dime'll get a cup of coffee." She stood. "I'm through working with you lot. If you have questions for Doris, you need to ask her. Now get out."

Miller stood as well, straightening his tie. "This is probably for the best, Miss Miles." Miller looked around her office at the velvet furnishings, high ceilings, and gilt embellishments before zeroing in on her face. "I've heard the reports—"

"Reports?"

"Sure. We keep tabs on everyone who's been in the field for us."

An involuntary groan escaped Thelma's lips. "You're joking, right? You people left me high and dry—"

"You mean Mr. Nelson?"

The hammering in Thelma's head intensified.

"That was OSS. A different time. Everything went to hell when we were trying to get out of that war. You shouldn't have been left in the field like that. But as I was saying, judging from your broken blood vessels, the bloating, and generally poor hygiene, I'd say you're not fit for service. But if you could get yourself cleaned up...."

Thelma's chest tightened. "How dare you come in here, ask a favor, then insult me?"

He flicked a card on her desk. "Think about what I've said. If you change your mind—"

"I won't."

Tapping the card, he added, "Just in case. And Miss Miles? Be careful who you trust. Even old friends can surprise you."

She looked down at the card: C. Miller, Special Agent, Central Intelligence Agency. *As I suspected*. "That's rich, coming from you."

After he left, she sank into her chair, hands shaking as she retrieved her flask, reflexively taking a swig to smooth the ragged edges. It had been years since George suggested that dry-out clinic. But she wasn't that bad. Wasn't near as bad as her mother was. She didn't do dope.

She had no idea how long she'd been lost in thought, swilling liquor, when the door popped open and in walked Helen and Doris, the last people she wanted to see her day drinking. She jumped up, flask still in hand.

"Mind if I join you for a snort?" Helen extended a hand.

Doris followed suit. "There's something we need to talk to you about," Doris said, uncharacteristically somber.

"Okay." Thelma tried to pretend this was normal. "Do I need to sit?"

"I think we all do," said Helen.

Thelma's heart sank as she dutifully took a seat on the sofa across from Helen and Doris. She hadn't yet decided what to say about the visit from the spook. Or if she should say anything at all. She would regret her choice.

"It's about Cora," Helen continued.

Thelma blinked in surprise. "What about her?"

"The riots are getting worse," Helen said. "You know the political situation here is deteriorating. We don't think it's safe for a child."

Shifting in her seat, Thelma protested. "Oh come on," she said. "The bearded rebel? Castro was grandstanding. You don't storm the military with a hundred and fifty students carrying machetes."

Doris lifted her chin. "My friend Haydée was one of those students," she said. "Her boyfriend... They sent...." But she could not continue.

"You might not think much of him, but Batista is taking this fellow very seriously." Helen took over. "Batista's henchmen sent her boyfriend's eyeball to her in her jail cell. His *eyeball.*"

Thelma's mind reeled. Batista had seized power a few months earlier, but the takeover had met with little in the way of protest. "But why would he worry about such a small group? The people support Batista. There was some shouting in the streets, but that was about it."

"Are you sure about that?" Helen asked.

Thelma wanted another draft from her flask already. Denial was the logic she'd been using on the regime change for some time, but if a CIA agent was visiting her, that meant the US government was taking this threat more seriously too.

"Batista has taken control of the media," Doris said. "We only hear what he wants us to hear."

Helen rested her hand on Doris's thigh. "Getting back to Cora... Now that the Korean War is finally over and Archie is leaving the Navy, the timing seems right."

Understanding dawned. None of them had heard from Kathleen Young in years and—as her son—Archie Young was Cora's older brother. He had as much family right to be part of the girl's life as Thelma, if not more. "You want to take Cora to Florida."

Helen and Doris both nodded.

"Archie and I would get married, give her a stable home," Helen said. "Sun City Emporium needs the help too. Bertie has run that place into the ground."

"And you?" Thelma eyed Doris with skepticism. "Are you planning to live with them the same way your father lived with your mother?"

Doris's face fell, and Thelma wished she could take back her words. Would she ever learn that lesson?

"For now, my plan is to stay here." Doris took Helen's hand. "It's easy enough to travel back and forth. But someone needs to mind our interests here, and well, you can't."

Heat rose at Thelma's neck, and her pounding heart drowned out her drubbing head. She studied her friends—Helen's face, creased with practical concern; Doris's, lit up with conviction. They'd been the ones raising Cora while she drank herself into oblivion. Much as it grieved her to acknowledge the truth, they'd earned the right to make this choice.

But the humiliation was almost more than she could bear.

"What about Kathleen?"

Helen and Doris exchanged a look, deciding without words who would take the lead. "No one has heard from her since '49," said Doris. "We don't even know if—"

"She still sends money every month."

"Thelma," Helen said, very obviously trying to avoid sounding condescending, "we stopped getting checks from her in 1950."

"You'll still be part of her life, of course," said Doris. "We both will."

They went on, but Thelma knew that everything had already been decided. While they talked about their plans, her eyes welled as she looked for cigarettes in her purse. A picture Cora had drawn for her that morning was inside. A picture of Doris and Helen.

"You're right." Thelma closed her purse without retrieving her smokes. "Cora deserves stability. Safety."

"You'll always be her Auntie TT," Helen assured her.

Thelma laughed softly. "She won't even remember me. She shouldn't. I want her to be happy, to be protected. And safe. You two have given her that all along."

"All three of us," Doris corrected. "Soon to be four, with Archie."

* * *

A FEW WEEKS LATER—OR MONTHS, MAYBE?—THELMA awoke with another pounding headache. She reached for the bottle on her nightstand, only to realize she was not in her bed and there was no bottle. The girls had told her she couldn't come back to the Bird unless she quit drinking. Even then, it had taken a while for her to ship off to the sanitarium in Miami. In one of her more lamentable protests, she said aloud that she feared running into George.

Could she run a nightclub without drinking? Hell, could she get through a day without drinking? She'd let everyone she loved down. How would she ever make it up to them? What if her problems weren't caused by her drinking? What if she was rotten to the core?

"What if I can't do it?" she asked aloud of her empty room, her voice small. "What if I can't get better?"

"Then you try again. But you have to try, Thelma."

Vivian Miles.

Thelma hadn't heard from her mother in years. Was she hallucinating? It hardly mattered. Dreams were something that could not be taken from her. Her single remaining liberty. To have even one sparked a flicker of hope.

Her life might not be over yet.

TWENTY-FOUR

Sam, Miami, 1978

UNLIKE EVERYTHING ELSE IN SAM'S LIFE, COLLINS Avenue had remained unchanged since she'd left Miami, reflections of one art deco hotel after another sliding across the Cadillac's hood as they drove past. *Was that only two weeks ago?* They turned into one of the enormous condos where Sharon eased into a numbered spot over oil stains blooming on the floor.

"I need to call Abby," Sam said as soon as they stepped into the garage, fighting the hum of ventilation fans and the thick Miami air.

Sharon's mouth dropped open. "Wh-What?" She huffed out. "You're going to call Jimmy's house?" Sharon regarded her in disbelief.

"I'll hang up if he answers." Though in truth, Sam hadn't thought about that.

"You sure he's not using Abby as bait?"

Another possibility Sam hadn't thought through. Not that she cared. She had to know that Abby was all right.

"I see you thinking, Sam," her stepmother said. "I should be the one to call. Just a quick check. No alarm bells."

The doors opened into a penthouse apartment with

commanding views of the Atlantic. Until that moment, Sam hadn't considered how out of place they both looked. A luxury building, even one in decline, was no place for swamp grime. At least Sharon had her shoes.

One wrong move would put them both in harm's way. Sam nodded. "I pretty much told Jimmy you'd be calling."

"By now that numbskull should expect I'd be calling. And if he doesn't let me speak to my granddaughter, I'll call in the cavalry." She pointed at the entry telephone. "Don't touch that dial. I'll be right back."

"Hurry, we should ring before she's off to school," Sam said.

Seconds after Sharon had trundled off toward the bathroom, Sam reached for the ivory phone. The contrast to her skin made her pull back her arm. Mud and ash clung to her hair and skin. She should at least wash her hands.

Moving into the kitchen, Sam clocked the Italian marble floors, the Danish modern furniture, the Brazilian rosewood bar —a snapshot of 1950s sophistication, complete with discoloration seeping through the silk wallpaper. Abby would love this place, she thought with a pang.

Without thinking, Sam flipped on the transistor radio sitting on the counter.

"...STILL MONITORING THE SITUATION AFTER AN EXPLOSION along the Tamiami Trail that officials today are calling a 'suspicious incident.' While no casualties have been confirmed, witnesses reported hearing automatic weapons fire before the explosion. Portions of the highway have closed as federal agents...."

. . .

"Oy," Sharon said, coming up from behind and clicking off the radio. "Automatic weapons?"

Sam turned to face her, aware of how filthy she was. "Do you think they planted false information on purpose?"

"Pfft, what do I know?" Sharon placed a bath towel on the counter. "Use this after you wash your hands. It's going to take a lot more than a quick rinse to clean that off. I'll hit the Kress downtown after we call Abigail."

They sat on opposite sides of a small kitchen table, wall phone between them. Panic washed over Sam. "Oh my God. Jimmy said she was staying at Natalie's. I don't know who that is."

"It's fine, I should be the one to call anyway." She smiled at Sam. "How would I know she's at Natalie's?"

Was Sharon implying she shouldn't speak to her own daughter? Her muscles braced as she watched Sharon's fingers work the rotary dial, each number taking an eternity. Her mind cataloged the facts: Jimmy was a lawyer, not a murderer. Just because Abby had never mentioned a Natalie before didn't mean the girl didn't exist. If it was Jimmy's girlfriend, then Abby must not like her much. Or maybe she liked her more than she wanted to admit...

"Jimmy!" Sharon's bright tone made her flinch and would have put her ex on edge, except he suffered from the belief in his undying likability. "How are you?"

Yet her performance was perfect—concerned grandmother checking in after a family funeral. But the signs were all there: Sharon's iron grip on the receiver, the slight catch in her voice asking about Abby. A long pause. Sam's heart thundered as she pictured Jimmy weighing his response.

Then Sharon's shoulders relaxed. "Oh good, would you get her?"

Get her?

Sharon drummed her fingers on the Formica. Sam leaned closer. "What about Natalie?" she mouthed. More silence.

"Sweetheart," Sharon exclaimed.

Now the blank spots in the conversation were excruciating. Sam pointed to her ear then mimed a receiver, pointing and mouthing, "I can't hear." Then suddenly she did hear Abby's voice—distant, small, and uncertain.

Dr. Filmore's words sounded in her ear. "As a woman, you're susceptible to blind spots in your investigations." She didn't believe that had anything to do with her sex even as she knew that Abby was hers.

Sam yanked the receiver from Sharon's hand. "Baby, it's Mom."

"Mom? Are you okay? Dad said—"

For Sam, this was one of those rare moments in life where she saw herself making the same mistakes her mother made. Perhaps with more time, it wouldn't have been so rare. But she knew then, at least for a little while longer, she planned to shield Abby from information. Keep her safe. Even if secrets corroded.

"Listen carefully." Sam kept her voice low, steady. "I need you to do exactly as I say."

TWENTY-FIVE

Thelma, Havana, 1953

THE GROUP THERAPY ROOM WAS STUFFY DESPITE THE winter chill outside. Thelma pulled her mohair cardigan around her shoulders. "Look who's the wilting lily now," she heard her mother say, reminding her of how she'd viewed her friends when they'd first met in Florida.

"But they were wearing open-toe pumps," Thelma muttered, shifting in her uncomfortable metal chair.

"What's that, Thelma?" Dr. Buddlemeyer asked, pulling Thelma into the session.

Since she'd detoxed, Thelma had been hearing from her mother more than ever. And she seemed to have a lot of opinions. "Nothing," Thelma said.

"Since you have the floor, let's reopen our discussion from the last session," he said. "How does it make you feel knowing that your niece was removed from your care because of your drinking?"

Thelma swallowed hard. "I think they did the right thing. Cora deserves a real family, not...." She gestured vaguely at herself. "I'm just the drunk the poor kid got stuck with."

"Let's not fall into martyrdom and self-pity," Dr. Buddlemeyer interjected. "I asked how the situation made you feel, and you went right to what you thought. That's how the rationalization starts. In our brains. We have a disease that tells us we aren't sick. Tells us we're weak. And it gets stronger when you fall into the poor mes."

"I know," Thelma said meekly. "Poor me, poor me, for the love of God, pour me a drink."

The room tittered.

"So, let's talk about strategies."

Dr. Buddlemeyer was annoyed by her "avoidance," Thelma could tell. He'd been telling her that the key to her recovery was opening up and getting honest. But her family was her secret. She was taking lots of notes.

"Strategies for all of you, for when you return to your lives," the doctor rolled on, now addressing the room at large. "How will you maintain sobriety in the face of such emotional challenges?"

A chorus of rehearsed answers filled the room.

"I'll pray to my higher power."

"Call my sponsor immediately."

"Go to a meeting."

"Read the Big Book."

Beside Thelma, Ruby snorted derisively. "Oh sure, because a prayer will definitely stop me from drinking when my pimp tracks me down and slips me a mickey."

The room fell silent. Ruby, a sharp-featured woman in her twenties, had been assigned as Thelma's roommate when she was admitted two days earlier. They were the youngest people in the facility by far. Her previous bunkmate, Gladys, would've been Vivian Miles's age, if her mother were still alive. Gladys had the irksome habit of saying she'd spilled more booze than Thelma could've drank. Then, two days before she left, Gladys had offered a profound insight when

Thelma was fretting about a boozeless future. "Oh, honey, keep it simple—one drink is too many and a thousand never enough." From then on, anything separating them had fallen away.

"Ruby," Dr. Buddlemeyer said carefully, "would you like to share what you're feeling?"

"Feeling?" A laugh like rusted metal ground out. "I'm feeling like this is all bullshit. Pray? Read a book? Some of us have real problems waiting for us out there."

She stood abruptly, her chair flipping to the floor behind her. "This isn't Sunday school. This is life and death."

As she stormed out, Thelma caught Dr. Buddlemeyer's eye and nodded toward the door. He blinked. Permission to follow.

Thelma found Ruby in their shared room, angrily packing her rucksack. Not that she had much to take.

"Going somewhere?" Thelma asked, closing the door behind her.

"What's the point of staying? They don't understand. None of them do."

"I might," Thelma said quietly. "Try me."

Ruby paused, studying Thelma's face. "Yeah? You ever been forced to service men in fancy hotels? Multiple men at the same time while your john mixes up your next bump? Oh, but you get a beating if you didn't smile pretty enough?"

A cloud landed on Thelma's heart. Elizabeth Short's murder notwithstanding, never before had she felt so fortunate to have had her experience and not someone else's. As she'd often reminded herself, no one had forced her to take clients—or drugs, for that matter. "You're a goddamn miracle."

Ruby stopped squeezing her small canvas bag to regard Thelma with disdain. "Not you too?"

"No, I—"

"Listen, I know I'm a drunk. I'm not in denial like those

bozos out there. My problem is I got nowhere to go, and I only know one way to make money."

Thelma sat back and folded her arms. "You think it's going to get better if you leave? Go out and tie one on?" She sounded like Gladys.

Ruby sank onto her bed. "Easy for you to say. You're loaded."

"I'm a lot more like you than you might think, Ruby," Thelma said. "You really should give people a chance." Her breath caught on her last words. How many times had George suggested she do the same?

After a few silent moments, Thelma spoke again. "Who brought you here? That's a start."

"You still don't get it. I ran away. That's how I wound up here in the first place." Ruby patted at her hips. "Can I bum a smoke?"

"Sure," Thelma said, fishing into her pockets for a cigarette. She lit one for each of them before continuing. "Where did you run away from, though? You didn't arrive from nowhere."

"You sure ask a lot of questions."

If she was going to get through to Ruby, she was going to have to offer her something more than platitudes. Something of herself. And something about the girl made her want to get through.

So she told her everything. How, when her mob father had discovered her existence, she and her mother fled to Iowa. Her mother's failing health and subsequent addiction. How Thelma took on her clients but fled after her mother's death. How she met her husband while touring as a Florida Girl then lost him not only once but twice after she'd moved to Havana to open a nightclub.

Ruby lurched up. "Havana? That's where I was! Is it the Bird of Paradise?"

Thelma gasped. "It is. How do you know that place?"

"The girls used to talk about it. Said it was run by women. Some thought about asking for help, but"—she shrugged—"we were too scared."

"Girls?"

Now, it was Ruby's turn to talk. "I was lucky. God, I was so naive." She laughed again, a sound as dry and cold as old bones.

"What happened?"

"This woman came to town, scouting for talent. All I ever wanted was to be an actress, you know? Anyway, she promised auditions in LA. Said all these Hollywood producers would be there. But when I got there, they said the real work was in Havana. By the time I realized they were lying, they had my passport, my money, my everything." Ruby twisted her hands in her lap. "They kept me in a room at the Hotel Nacional. I couldn't leave."

Thelma felt sick. Had this woman been caught up in the prostitution ring Imogene had told her about? "How did you escape?"

"Luck. This one businessman, very important guy so he had an exclusive. A whole weekend of whatever he wanted. But he passed out almost right away. After I, well, you know. Anyways, his wallet was right there. So I took everything he had and ran. It was enough money to get me on a night boat to Miami." Ruby shuddered. "Carlos Gonzalez probably still has a price on my head."

"Carlos Gonzalez?" Thelma couldn't believe she'd heard correctly.

Ruby's head snapped up. "You know him?"

The weight of every drink she'd ever taken to dull her suspicions fell on Thelma's shoulders. She'd spent years trying to quiet the voices in her head, quell her unpredictable internal warning system. What if she could enhance her perceptions by simply being open to them? "I thought...." she began, unable to fully articulate how she'd known something was wrong. "But I couldn't face it." Suddenly she was thirsty, itching for what would soothe the raw ache she felt inside.

"Hey." Ruby touched her arm. "You couldn't have known. They're careful."

"But the girls," Thelma said. "How many...."

"Too many to count. They keep us scattered around the city. Move us between hotels. The Nacional, the Riviera, private houses in Vedado...."

Vedado? That was her neighborhood.

"And now I'm out of money," Ruby went on. "And I only know one way to make money."

Her words broke through Thelma's—good Lord, she hated to admit what she'd been feeling even to herself—*self-pity*. But she knew the exact feeling Ruby described, counting pennies to put off selling yourself another day. "I can help," she said. "You and them. I can hire you."

Ruby stared at her. "Come again?"

Thelma's mind whirred. Between the Bird, Peggy's sharp eyes, and Doris's Havana connections, they could use Imogene's network to set these girls free.

There was a knock at the door. "We'll talk more later," Thelma said in a low voice, waiting for Ruby's nod before answering. "Come in."

Dr. Buddlemeyer poked his head in the door. "Everything all right in here?"

Thelma regarded his graying temples, horn-rimmed glasses, and doughy frame, and wondered how this man had gotten here. They weren't in a competition, so why was she so testy with him? If anything, he wanted to help the women in his charge lead full and independent lives. Was she acting out of guilt?

* * *

LATER THAT NIGHT IN HER ROOM, SHE DREDGED AGENT Miller's card up from the bottom of her bag.

The truth weighed heavy on her, raw and undeniable. Whatever her parents' failings had been—and they were legion —Thelma had chosen her own. Each time she'd reached for a bottle instead of reaching for Cora, she'd made that choice. Each time she'd stayed out until dawn instead of being there for breakfast, she'd made that choice.

What if helping Ruby could become something more? Something bigger. A pathway for many.

She felt the familiar tingling in her palms. Instead of trying to dull the sensation, she stilled her mind. This was why Imogene had told her about the network, not only its existence but how it operated. She would use the very routes the network traversed, but instead of one-way trips to locked rooms, Thelma would establish safe houses and escape routes.

It would be dangerous—for the women, for her partners, for herself. A single misstep could bring the whole operation crashing down. Miller might use her intelligence for his own ends, or abandon her when the stakes grew too high. But she knew, with a clarity that had eluded her through years of drinking, this was a risk she had to take.

A secret railroad running right under Carlos Gonzalez's nose, through the very city he thought he controlled. This time, she wouldn't look away.

"That's my girl," she heard. To her shock, it was Sal.

TWENTY-SIX

Sam, Miami, 1978

SAM WOKE UP IN A BLAZE OF WHITE LIGHT, SWEATING through the silk Nehru jacket and lounge pants she'd found in the drawers. She let the disorientation settle. *I'm back in Miami. In a condo with Sharon. Meyer Lansky's condo.* Had Sharon's blowsy appearance been a facade all along?

This line of thought was going nowhere fast. She wanted to talk to Ed. Figure out what in the hell was happening out in that cabin. The cabin she'd torched. Clean and somewhat rested, she had a dawning notion—whatever nefarious purpose that place had served, she'd rendered it harmless. She grinned like a madwoman.

You need to stop them, or they'll be back at it.

Scrambling out of bed, she was about to call for Sharon when she almost tripped over a shopping bag. Clothes. Her stepmother must have gone out and gotten them while she slept. The phone caught her eye as she struggled to her feet.

She and Ed hadn't spoken since that happy hour, when grief and loneliness led to their desperate kiss behind the copier room. The dean's response had been swift, but at least he'd paid her last two weeks in full.

He'd be at his office.

"Ed?" She steadied her voice. "It's Sam."

The pause that followed was long enough to make Sam wonder if calling him was a huge mistake. "Jesus," Ed finally said. "I heard about your dad. I'm so sorry. But... I... We thought you'd be back by now. Are you still in St. Pete? The department's in an uproar."

"I need your help." The words came out raw.

"Sam, about what happened...."

She pictured him running a hand through his thinning hair, his wire-rimmed glasses sliding down his nose. "This isn't about that, Ed. Please. You're the only person I know who has access to the kind of records I need."

Through the floor-to-ceiling windows, the gaudy neon of Miami's beach hotels blazed ineffectively against the bright sky. Nothing could outshine the truth.

"I think my mother discovered something about the mafia," Sam continued. "And I need to find out what it was. Ed, I think she may have been killed for it."

A moment passed that felt like an eternity.

"What do we know so far?" Ed said finally.

"Not much. Press clippings my mother left behind mention organized crime in Florida before she started working on the Black Dahlia case out in California."

"California?"

"It's where her car...." Sam hesitated, no longer sure how to refer to her mother's death. "Where she was found dead. She worked on a few big stories out there, in particular the Black Dahlia case. Remember? We studied that one."

"I can't believe they never caught that sicko," Ed said, oblivious. "You don't just go from something like that to being a model citizen. For all we know—"

"Ed," Sam interrupted, "this is important. My mother was

writing about the mafia. In particular, the Giancarlos. And I... I just found out my ex works for Frankie Giancarlo."

"*The* Giancarlos?"

Was she the only person who *didn't* know about them?

"They're all over the news, Sam. 'Mysterious Explosion in Everglades.' They're saying it was Frankie Giancarlo's drug lab."

Sam sat up straighter. "A drug lab?"

"Cocaine. Or that's the rumor. FBI's been watching Frankie Giancarlo for months, supposedly. Something about Cuban supply routes."

The pieces started clicking together. The chemicals she smelled, the remote location. Of course it was a drug den. *Dissolving bodies.* Jesus, Elizabeth Short's murder was getting to her.

Even so, that still didn't explain why Frankie Giancarlo would care about her mother's thirty-year-old letter. What could she have been killed for thirty years ago that was still a secret?

"Ed, I need you to look for anything connecting the Giancarlos to Cuba. Especially around 1948. Or '47. That's when my mother visited. Also...." Maybe this was Sam's imagination working overtime again, but she had to have answers. "Look for any connections to the Black Dahlia case."

"I can check the archives, maybe some old case files. But Sam...." He hesitated. "If you think the Giancarlos had something to do with Elizabeth Short's murder, you need to stay up north. These are dangerous people. Salvatore Giancarlo killed his own brother."

She swallowed hard. Keeping Ed somewhat in the dark was probably the best call—he didn't need to know she'd been the Everglades arsonist—but she had to tell him where she was. She would want him to send over any documents he found. "Ed, I'm

back in Miami. But don't worry, I'm keeping a low profile, and...
I have Abby to think of too."

"Christ. Of course. Give me a few hours. Where can I reach
you?"

Sam glanced around the luxury condo. She hadn't a clue
what the address was. "I'll have to call you back. And Ed?
Thank you."

After hanging up, she caught her reflection in the mirror
atop the dresser. The woman looking back wore determination like armor, reminding her of her mother. Imogene Fuchs
had never bothered with makeup, which Sam had always
assumed was a byproduct of her ambition to be taken seriously. Now, she questioned that assumption. Perhaps her
mother's appearance had been its own kind of armor—a way
to be overlooked, underestimated. That seemed to be so with
Sharon.

She dug into the bag her stepmother had left—matching
joggers and a T-shirt with a line illustration of two nude figures
with enormous heads and childlike bodies that read, "Love is... a
warm hug." Mercifully, the hoodie zipped shut. Then her hand
found mascara and a tube of lip gloss. What a relief. Her mother's generation had their thing. Sam had another.

* * *

"Who were you talking to?" Sharon asked over a
couple of Swanson's frozen dinners.

"My colleague, Ed."

"They're okay with you taking some time off?"

"Well, I'm not teaching this summer and...." Sam held her
breath. "No. The truth is they put me on leave. I, uh—" Honesty
didn't mean sharing every last detail. "I was having trouble separating my personal life from work."

"*Mazel tov*," Sharon said, not even looking up from her foil tray. "You need the break. You've been going nonstop."

Sam was astonished. "I need to call him now, as a matter of fact." She pushed back her chair to leave the room, but Sharon reached for her arm.

"Call from here. We should combine all our resources."

"I don't think...." Sam rubbed her forehead. "Your friend Meyer Lansky can't know what we're doing."

"First of all, he's not my friend. Second, who said anything about him? He's been out of the game a long time now. But like I said, I have connections."

"That's what scares me. I do this by the book. I can't lose Abby."

"Honey, my connections aren't what you're thinking. Though we do call ourselves the Mahjong Mafia."

Sam blinked at the phrase. Repeated it in her mind until she was giggling. Then Sharon caught the bug, and they laughed, like they'd survived an apocalypse, which in a very real sense, they had.

Ed picked up on the first ring. "Found something," he said without preamble.

"Ed! How did you know I'd pick up? Remember what we said about being careful?"

Sharon whacked her on the shoulder.

"Do you wanna hear this or what?" Ed asked.

"Of course I do," she said, stopping short of apologizing.

"I came across an unsealed diplomatic pouch. Letters between your mother and George Wright before he was a senator."

"George Wright?" Sam asked.

Sharon leaned forward so Ed could hear her. "He's loaded. His family, they're Wright Industries. War hero. Almost died in a plane crash near the end of the war."

"That's the one," Ed said. "Uh... speaking of careful, who's that?"

Sam put the phone on its back in the center of the table. "That's Sharon Fuchs. My stepmother."

A small sound escaped Sharon's throat. Never before had Sam introduced her father's wife as her stepmother, and the occasion had not gone unnoticed. "She's helping," Sam said. "Speak up so we can both hear you."

"Hi, Sharon. Anyway, several of the letters mentioned someone named Thelma."

"Thelma?" asked Sam. The name sounded familiar.

"They were trying to get her to a dry-out clinic."

Sharon pointed at the manila folder. "Didn't you say there was a Thelma who showed up in different articles under different names?"

"That's right." Sam opened the envelope and spread the newspaper clippings across the table. "Ed? See if you can find a Thelma Miles. Or... hang on. Here she's called Thelma Wright. Good Lord, do you think they were *married?* See what you can find out. And have a courier send over any important documents you find."

Sharon gave him the address and phone number before they hung up. "Wish me luck," she said, strapping her purse over her shoulder.

"Good luck," Sam said. Half-hearted. She fervently hoped Sharon wouldn't need it to pick up Abby at school.

TWENTY-SEVEN

Thelma, Havana, 1954

THE CALL FROM RUBY CAME JUST BEFORE MIDNIGHT.

"Her name is Ellen," Ruby said without preamble. "Long dark hair. From Ohio. Looks like they've got her in one of those mansions off Línea Street."

Línea Street. Thelma pictured it—the thick canopy of royal palms lining the avenue, the wide, cool sidewalks and low limestone walls that separated the gardens from the road. Only a few short blocks from where she lived.

But she felt none of that familiar tingle in her hands.

"You sure she's there?" Thelma asked. Six months sober, and the sensations had become more frequent, though not necessarily more reliable. All she felt in her palms now, besides the phone, was sweat.

"One of my contacts from the Hotel Nacional said she asked for help when she was there, then she disappeared. Resurfaced today on Línea. Housekeeper told him about a girl there who fit that description."

"Are we sure it's the same girl?" Thelma tried to unclench her jaw. "I mean, she might not even be at the house anymore."

"Roger that," Ruby said. "But I don't know how much more solid the intel is going to get."

She sounded so different than when they'd met at High-brook. Beyond the staccato spy-thriller lingo she'd suddenly adopted, though that was new too, it was her determination. It filled Thelma with pride. "You're right. It's the best lead we've had so far. Great work."

There was a rhythm to life in Vedado, where the houses bustled with deliveries and house staff from predawn until the wee hours. The Bird would be closing soon—it was now or never.

* * *

Two hours later, Thelma and Peggy crouched behind the massive trunk of a ceiba tree, its thick roots providing the perfect cover. The summer night was heavy with jasmine.

Peggy peeled her blouse away from her chest, tenting the fabric back and forth as she wiped the sweat from her brow. "Three guards," she whispered to Thelma, counting the cigarette glows in the darkness. "Two by the gate, one walking the perimeter."

"Count on Carlos to be cheap," Thelma murmured, checking her watch in the dim streetlight. Every fifteen minutes, one of the men disappeared from view for exactly three minutes, presumably checking the service entrance around the side. Their planned entrance.

Peggy fidgeted with a hairpin. "You sure about this, sugar? Not too late to call it off."

Guilt wracked Thelma. "Are *you* sure about this? I—"

"Oh, can it. Me and Doris wouldn't have volunteered if we didn't want to do it. All's I mean is, maybe we should just watch tonight. Stake the place out and come back tomorrow."

"Tomorrow the kid might be somewhere else." A sudden noise startled them. In one of the houses nearby, someone had started up a phonograph. Something by Benny Goodman. "You hear that? I think it's next door to the house. It'll help cover sound."

"Let's hope the floorboards aren't loud like ours," Peggy said but quickly caught herself. "Least we know how to handle that."

Thelma looked back to the house. The border wall was lower near the southeast corner, obscured by the cascading roots of a jagüey tree. "We'll use those roots to drop into the garden," she said, noting that the guard had begun his hourly circumnavigation of the place. "We take off as soon as he gets back."

Ten minutes later, they darted across Línea, their rubber-soled ballet flats silent on the cobblestones. In the neighbor's yard, Peggy boosted Thelma up with cupped hands. From the wall, Thelma reached back to help Peggy up before they dropped together into the garden.

Pressed so close to the wall, it took a moment to get their bearings. Ellen's room appeared to be on the third floor where a light still burned behind gauzy curtains. Despite the summer heat, the window was shut. All they had to do—once they made it inside—was find the stairs.

A guard's footsteps crunched on gravel. Thelma and Peggy froze. The beam of a flashlight swept past, illuminating a maze of ornamental shrubs and orchids. They held their breath, counting seconds. Had he heard them? This was a break in his routine. Or had the pattern been in Thelma's imagination? Her hand went to the switchblade in her pocket, hoping they wouldn't need it.

After an eternity, the footsteps receded. Thelma released her grip, and they slowly began making their way to the back. The service stairs were steel, practical and plain compared to the mansion's grand front entrance, though every step risked a betraying creak. Thelma led the way, testing each tread before committing her weight, her heart pounding so loud she was sure it would give them away. Peggy followed in her exact footsteps.

She reached for the door handle as they heard the sound of a toilet flushing. Then silence. Thelma checked her watch. Less than a minute to get inside unless the guard had changed his schedule. If he had a schedule. She tilted her head toward the door. Onward.

With only moonlight guiding the way, they slipped through the kitchen into the hallway. But they were in luck. The landing revealed carpeted stairs, sure to muffle their steps. Upstairs, Thelma recalibrated. Five doors to Ellen's room.

As she eased open the door, which was unlocked, they both winced at the slight creak of hinges. They found Ellen curled on a window seat, shaking slightly. She couldn't be older than seventeen. Her eyes met Thelma's with a look of jaded recognition—she thought they were more clients.

Three stories below, a guard laughed at something his companion said. A car passed on the street. The girl turned to speak, and Thelma saw the bruise on her cheek, poorly concealed with powder. Any last doubts about their mission vanished. Shaking her head, she pressed a finger to her lips.

"Shh," Thelma whispered, tiptoeing forward. "We're here to help."

Ellen's head snapped up, eyes wide and glassy. "Who the hell are you?"

"I'm Thelma. This is Peggy. Ruby sent us."

"Ruby?" A flash of recognition.

"She made it out of this life. So did I. You can too."

Ellen rolled her eyes up and down Thelma. "You? I don't think so."

"I haven't had to sell myself for money in almost ten years."

Ellen hugged herself tighter, her thin arms covered in track marks. "Why should I trust you? Some lady promising me fame got me into this mess in the first place. I have no money, nowhere to go...."

"We ain't promising fame, kid," Peggy said. "Just the chance to get out of this hellhole."

Footsteps sound in the hallway. Ellen's face contorted with panic.

"The closet," she hissed. "Quick!"

Peggy and Thelma barely made it behind the hanging dresses before the door opened. Through a crack, they watched Carlos enter, a small case in his hand.

"How's my favorite girl?"

His baby-talk pitch sickened Thelma.

"I need it," Ellen whimpered. "Please."

"Daddy's here." He set the case down, opening it with practiced movements. "But first, tell me about your visitor."

Thelma's heart stopped.

"What visitor?" Ellen's voice was steady despite her shaking frame.

Carlos's hand shot out, gripping Ellen's jaw. "You can't be that far gone already. You know what happens when you can't play nice?"

Thelma couldn't hear what she said.

"That's right." Carlos moved her head up and down like a puppet. "Then nobody wants you anymore. I have no use for you. Then you have to leave. You'll have no one." He released her with a slight push. "Now, tell me. Señor Lobo. You made him happy?"

Again, Thelma couldn't hear the girl's reply, but she could see Carlos studying Ellen's face for a long moment before he turned back to his case. She watched, feeling ill, as he prepared the injection. Ellen's face slackened with anticipation.

"There we are," he crooned as the needle found its mark. "Better?"

Ellen nodded, already drooping with relief.

"Rest now." Carlos stroked her hair. "Big party tomorrow night. Important clients."

Once he'd gone, Thelma and Peggy emerged.

"We need to move fast," Peggy whispered. "Is she gonna be able to walk out of here?"

"Get out," Ellen said.

Thelma and Peggy exchanged a look. "What?" Thelma asked.

Ellen's eyes were cool and chemical. "I said get out. I don't want your help."

"You don't mean that," Thelma said.

"Oh, but I do." Ellen laughed harshly. "You think you're going to save me? Smack is the only thing that saves. And Carlos takes care of me."

"That's the drugs talking." Thelma gestured toward her bruised face and arms. "This is not what being saved looks like. He's destroying you."

"I was destroyed before he found me." Ellen turned away. "Now go."

"But—"

"Before I call for help."

"Thelma." Peggy's voice was urgent. "We can't make her."

"Get. Out."

Thelma backed toward the door, her chest tight. "If you change your mind—"

"I won't."

Other than the wait by the back door for the guard to complete his round, Thelma scarcely noticed the reverse journey, letting Peggy lead the way. Her mind replayed Ellen's words. *Smack is the only thing that saves.* It was a different substance, but Thelma knew exactly what she meant. When she needed comfort, booze was always there. By the time they were back at the house, she'd made up her mind.

"Peggy I'm going to walk around a bit, try to shake that off."

"You sure?" she asked. But she was yawning.

On the way out, Thelma reached into the glove box, right where she'd left her flask. All these months later, and she hadn't forgotten. She'd kept it there *in case*. For moments like this.

She walked aimlessly through the streets, the cool metal bottle tucked into her bra, against her heart. At the waterfront, she stopped, listening to the waves crash against the Malecón like a pounding heart.

Every choice had brought her here—choosing to join the Florida Girls, choosing her father over George, choosing liquor over everything. Each decision had narrowed her path until she'd found herself alone in a foreign country, fighting battles that were as much about her own redemption as anyone else's freedom.

And now Ellen had chosen too. Chosen drugs and Carlos over whatever freedom Thelma offered. The same way Thelma had once chosen gin over responsibility. The reality of what she'd done to others was devastating.

Even her sobriety—that hard-won accomplishment she clung to—seemed hollow in this moment. What good was being sober if she couldn't actually help anyone? If she couldn't undo the damage she'd caused?

A drink wouldn't erase Ellen's dead eyes or track-marked arms, but it would dull the edges. Help her forget her own failure.

"Or make the darkness a thousand times worse," she heard Vivian Miles say.

The words startled her. She didn't believe them, but the thought of her mother, lying in a stupor, unable to care for either of them snapped her out of her misery. Ellen's tragedy was merely an excuse to drink. *Poor me*, she thought. *Pour me another.*

Thelma's hand tightened around her flask. So easy. So tempting.

Then, with a sudden movement, she hurled it into the ocean. The splash lost in the crash of waves. She raced home to her phone.

"Hello?" Ruby sounded half-asleep.

How could she fall asleep at a time like this? "She wouldn't come," Thelma's voice cracked. "I tried, but she wouldn't."

"Oh, honey." Ruby sighed. "You can't save someone who doesn't want saving."

"Yes, but...." The breath caught in Thelma's chest. She wanted to cry. Or scream. Or both. "What if I can't help these girls?"

"You don't have to, Thelma."

Don't have to? Thelma slumped in her chair as her heart fell to the floor. She was using the telephone downstairs, nearest the door. She wanted to rip out the cord and hurl the whole thing outside.

"But 'faith without works is dead.' They said that a million times at Highbrook—I stay sober by helping other people get sober."

"Not quite. Helping others is the work. The faith part is knowing that they have their own path. You're just doing what's in front of you to stay sober for yourself. It's like Buddlemeyer said. Sobriety isn't for people who need it, it's for people who want it. We want it because we know where that life heads."

As she spoke, a weight lifted off Thelma's chest. She couldn't believe how much lighter she felt. But there was one last thing she had to admit. "I almost drank."

"But you called me instead. Now, go to bed."

A calm settled over Thelma as she hung up, touching the poker chip tucked safely in her pocket. A symbol of her resolve that they'd given her in rehab.

"I won't lie to you, it's going to be rough running a nightclub in Cuba without a sober network," Dr. Buddlemeyer had said. "But our boys made out well on the front with only the literature. And you have a fire in you. I don't know where it came from, but I can see you want this."

She wanted it because she knew that liquor had stopped working for her. Far from comforted, she had emotions that ran from guilt ridden to paranoid.

Back at the Vedado home she now shared with only Doris and Peggy, she climbed the stairs to her empty bed, exhausted but resolute. She'd stayed sober another day. Faced the darkness without drowning in it. There was no changing her past mistakes, but she could choose differently now. Choose to stay sober. Choose to keep fighting. That was the difference between the woman she'd been and the woman she was becoming—she could look at her failures, learn, and move forward.

TWENTY-EIGHT

Sam, Miami, 1978

THE CORAL-AND-BEIGE SPANISH COLONIAL SAT BACK FROM the street behind a curtain of bougainvillea and a set of black, wrought iron gates. Sam squinted at the brass numbers bolted beside the entry, hoping this was the place. She turned to wave the cabbie away, relieved she'd slipped away before Sharon returned with Abby. At least her daughter was being looked after.

Before Sam could touch the bell, the door swung open. A tall platinum blonde in white linen palazzo pants stood inside, exuding an intimidating authority. Sam instinctively straightened her spine.

"Can I help you?" the woman asked, making clear there was nothing she'd rather do less.

Forcing herself to maintain eye contact, Sam stepped forward. "I'm looking for Thelma Miles."

The woman tilted her head. "And you are?" she asked, blocking the entry.

This person might not be Thelma, but from her defensive behavior Sam knew she'd have one chance. "I'm the woman who just blew up Frankie Giancarlo's cabin in the Everglades. Imogene Fuchs's daughter? I believe you knew my mother."

The woman showed no reaction. Did she not watch the news?

From inside came another voice, an even more commanding tone. "Let her in, Peggy."

Peggy hesitated, forehead creased, before stepping aside. "If you say so, Thelms."

The foyer opened into a sunken living room with a view of Biscayne Bay. Chrome and glass caught the morning light, but what struck Sam was the absence of personal touches—no family photos or framed newspaper stories or tourist tchotchkes. She could've been at the library room of an upscale men's club, brimming as the space did with books, records, and ashtrays. The owner obviously had no children.

Thelma Miles rose from a white leather sofa, elegant in a patterned wrap dress that probably cost more than Sam's monthly salary. Her cropped black hair was striped with silver, but her eyes—an arresting amber color that hadn't translated across newsprint—fixed on Sam with unnerving intensity. "I didn't think you were dead."

Some greeting. "You must be Thelma." Sam dithered a moment. This wasn't going to be the tearful reunion she'd half-expected. This was an interrogation—and she wasn't the one conducting it. "Miles? Or are you going by Wright today? You were married to the senator, George Wright?"

A flicker of something—surprise, irritation, sorrow?—crossed Thelma's face before disappearing. "Impressive research. That marriage was annulled. Decades ago." She gestured to a chair opposite her. "Please, sit. Peggy, should we have something to drink?"

Peggy moved silently to a bar cart in the corner. Sam

noticed it held only mineral water and juices—no alcohol. Good for her. But no thanks.

"How about we skip the pleasantries?" Sam remained standing. "I know you've been working with the Giancarlos, who apparently had something to do with my mother's death. So maybe we start there."

Peggy set a glass of lemonade on the coffee table with unnecessary force. "How about we still act pleasant?"

"It's all right, Pegs," Thelma said, taking a glass. "She's Imogene's daughter. She has questions."

"My mother ended up dead in a car crash that we both know was no accident," Sam shot back. "Maybe her instincts weren't that great."

Thelma blinked. "Okay, well." She took a seat then sipped her drink. "You're the one who married Frankie Giancarlo's right-hand man."

Sam bit her lip, unnerved at what these women already knew about her. One of the things she loved about her chosen field was the anonymity of being the one who came onto a scene and asked all the questions. Now more than ever, she was desperate for answers.

"That was the man I divorced, not the one I married," Sam said. "And now I need to know what my ex is mixed up in."

"So, let me get this right," Peggy said. "You think we're also involved, but you came right to us."

Sam took a steadying breath. "I think you're involved, but I don't know how. Only that my mother trusted you. At least enough to keep those clippings."

Thelma's eyes fixed on Sam but with a different kind of scrutiny. "Your voice—it sounds exactly like your mother's."

The unexpected observation caught Sam off-guard. She found herself sinking into the offered chair, thrown by the sudden shift in tone.

"What the hell happened at the cabin?" Peggy asked, her posture still tense.

"First things first," Thelma interrupted. "Sam, I need to know exactly what you found in your mother's papers."

Sam recognized this tactic—show warmth then extract information. But she needed help more than she needed the upper hand. "When dad died—" Her voice wobbled.

Thelma reached forward and squeezed Sam's knee, somehow conveying sympathy even as she urged her to continue.

"That's when I got my mother's letter. But the only clues she left behind were stories she'd written. But the stuff was all over the place—coverage of the Florida Girls, Sun City Emporium, some casino opening. And a letter she didn't finish. Though she did mention secrets that could put people in danger?"

"And that led you to blow up a drug processing facility?" Thelma asked, her tone carefully neutral.

Sam tried to match the evenness. "My husband kidnapped me, took me to that cabin. I didn't know what it was. I didn't even know who *he* was until then, at which point he informed me that if I wanted to keep my daughter safe, I also had certain responsibilities. But I can't just forget...."

Thelma's hands worked at her cuticles. "Forget what?" she prodded, leaning forward, amber eyes intent.

Sam sat upright, as if to move away. Based on what she and Ed had actually found, she had no reason to think that cabin was for anything other than processing coke, that her fears were heightened by circumstance. Yet those fears nagged. If Frankie Giancarlo was so worried about what was in her mother's letter, there had to be a connection to the here and now.

"I believe that when my mother was working the Black Dahlia case, she discovered it was part of a larger operation, and that's why she was killed. The mafia was involved. Specifically, the Giancarlos."

Something registered in Thelma's eyes, but it came and went so quickly it could have been surprise or concern. Her fingers paused their nervous movement. "That's quite a theory," she said.

Sam pressed. "It's more than a theory. Looking into the names in my mom's articles is like a *Who's Who* of American mobsters. Some of them crop up repeatedly. Like the Giancarlos. You. *And* your nightclub in Havana which, coincidentally, is still running under the same name, and for some reason, Cora Young carries around a pack of matches from."

The two women exchanged a look Sam couldn't decipher.

"You've been digging," Thelma finally said. "But you're connecting dots without understanding the pattern."

"Then help me understand," Sam said. "Because right now, what I see is my mother investigating a murder, linking it to something bigger, and then dying in a crash that may or may not have been accidental. I see my ex-husband working for the same family she was investigating. And I see you somehow in the middle of all of it."

Thelma studied her for a long moment. "Your mother was careful about what she put in writing. For good reason."

"What reason?" Sam asked.

"The same reason you shouldn't have blown up that cabin," Peggy interjected. "Some operations need to stay underground to work."

Sam looked between them, fragments starting to align in her mind. "You're suggesting my mother was doing something more than investigating these networks? That she was... what? Using them somehow?"

Thelma took in a deep breath. Sam feared the worst.

TWENTY-NINE

Thelma, Miami, 1978

THELMA WAS STILL RECOVERING FROM HEARING GEORGE'S name tossed out so casually when Sam shocked her by suggesting her father was working with Carlos Gonzalez. Had she incorrectly assessed the woman's threat level because she'd shown up on Thelma's doorstep in a tracksuit? The woman looked ready to hit the K-Mart, not the mafia. But here she was, dangerously close to piecing together the network it had taken years to build and protect.

"There's always more than one game being played," Thelma finally replied.

From the look on her face, Sam didn't like ambiguity any more than her mother. Thelma had to remind herself that if Imogene Fuchs hadn't shared how women were being shipped into Cuba like cattle, Thelma wouldn't have known how to help them escape Gonzalez's clutches.

"You haven't figured out who I am yet, have you?" she asked, daring Sam to piece together the puzzle. When she didn't speak, it was with no small amount of pride that Thelma realized she'd finally done it. She'd erased her past. But the victory was pyrrhic. "My father was Salvatore Giancarlo."

"And you think my family is the threat?" Sam spat. "Talk about glass houses."

Taking a breath, Thelma reminded herself that she and Sam were on the same team. "Like I said, it's not Jimmy we're worried about. I could tell you that Frankie corrupted what was once a lifeline, but that would be a lie. It was always corrupt. But trust me, Frankie is bad news."

Sam slammed her lemonade onto the glass coffee table, causing a clattering that seemed to startle even herself. "Compared to the man who killed his own brother?"

"You said it yourself." Peggy paused and lit a cigarette, the flame momentarily illuminating her face. "You don't know much about Frankie."

Thelma rolled her eyes and faced Sam. "That story is a myth."

Sam frowned. "Look, I get that he was your dad and all—"

"Now you listen." Peggy jabbed her smoke at Sam. "She didn't grow up with the man. Trust me, she's got no rosy view of Sal Giancarlo."

Thelma's eyes swam. Thirty years of friendship had its advantages. Peggy, whose own father had been destroyed by war and addiction, understood the painful complexity of loving and hating your father. "The important thing is that we get to the bottom of what's happening now. Agreed?" Thelma looked between Sam and Peggy until she was satisfied they were all of one mind. "Good. First things first, we need to make sure your daughter is safe—"

"Jimmy wouldn't hurt her," Sam said.

"Have you been listening?" Peggy asked. "It's not Jimmy we're worried about. And how would you know anyways? You didn't even know your ex was connected."

"I spoke to Abby this morning," Sam said, defiant.

Thelma had to give her credit for not being fazed by Peggy. The platinum blonde had intimidated men twice Sam's size with nothing more than a well-timed glare.

"Her grandmother is picking her up," Sam added. "She doesn't know anything."

"Ignorance does not equal safety." Peggy stubbed out her cigarette and returned to the window, resuming her surveillance.

This conversation was taking a dangerous turn. Thelma could see Sam reassessing everything she thought she knew about her ex-husband, about the Giancarlos, about the danger her daughter might be in. Panic would make her unpredictable.

"The thing is, Sam," Thelma said, her tone taking an edge, "Sal wasn't afraid to hand out beatdowns, cheat, steal, you name it. But he didn't deal in drugs or women. Even your mother worked with Sal. A lot of the guys back then—"

"Worked with?" Sam's breath caught. "What are you saying?"

Thelma met her eyes. "Your mother wasn't just reporting on the mafia. She had an... arrangement with Sal Giancarlo."

"An arrangement?" The word felt dirty in Sam's mouth. Her mother—her crusading, dogged investigator mother—had an *arrangement* with the mob? Her hands curled into fists. "She took payoffs? Is that what you're telling me?"

"No. God, no. Nothing like that." Thelma leaned forward. "Imogene knew how to work the system. She'd gather information on Sal's rivals while building her stories about corruption. She'd tip him off about raids sometimes in exchange for intel on politicians or businessmen in his pocket. In exchange, she kept him out of the papers."

"I don't believe you." But even as Sam said it, puzzle pieces were shifting in her mind—the Black Dahlia case, the fragments about girls going missing, the cryptic line in her mother's letter about secrets that could put people in danger.

"It's why she knew about the trafficking network," Thelma continued. "Sal despised it, thought it was beneath him. He might've been a killer and a cheat, but he had his limits. Imogene discovered what Carlos was doing and brought it to Sal."

"My mother knew about women being trafficked, and she didn't report it?" Sam's voice was a squeak.

"She *was* reporting it. If not the way you think." Thelma hated bursting Sam's bubble like this. "She was gathering evidence, building a case that would expose the traffickers and everyone connected to them—judges, cops, businessmen. She couldn't go public until she had it all, until she could make it stick."

"But she never did," Sam whispered.

"No, she never did." Thelma's eyes grew distant. "When Sal died, things got complicated."

"Yeah," Peggy said. "And like we said, Frankie is another story. Now that you've blown up his cabin, you're on his radar."

Sam chewed her lips as she considered their words. "I didn't know it would go up in flames like that," she said finally. "I think... I think they were storing chemicals besides nitric acid. Like hydrochloric and sulfuric acids. You know? Dissolves bodies."

Thelma's stomach lurched. Back in Havana she'd heard a rumor that Carlos used similar methods to make his problems disappear before Castro put him in jail. Had Frankie used the cabin as more than a drug processing center?

Before she could respond, a car screeched to a halt out front. Peggy leaned toward the window, parting its gauzy curtains.

"Burgundy Cadillac," she said, a note of warning in her voice.

Sam jumped to her feet. "Sharon?"

"Who's Sharon?" Thelma and Peggy asked at the same time, both jumping to their feet. This was exactly why Thelma didn't want to bring Sam in—too many unknown variables.

"My stepmother," Sam said, already heading for the door.

Peggy gave Thelma a quick nod. "Lady looks like somebody's grandma."

Thelma winced. "So does Kathleen Young, and she's only gotten more dangerous with age. Stay here," she said, following Sam to the front.

On seeing Mrs. Fuchs at her door, Thelma did a double take. Sam's stepmother looked disturbingly like Imogene Fuchs; Sam's father had a type.

"You must be Mrs. Fuchs," she said, squeezing in next to Sam and extending her hand. "Nice to meet you."

Sharon Fuchs peered at Thelma's hand and scowled. "Wish I could say the same. What kind of trouble have you gotten us into?"

Thelma couldn't hold back a half smile, appreciating the Mama Bear instinct. This woman had more in common with Imogene than looks. Maybe there was something more calculated in Bill Fuchs's choices.

"Where's Abby?" Sam asked.

"She's fine," Sharon answered without answering. "What are you doing here?"

"How about we all move this into—"

"Another incoming," Peggy called from her window seat. "Black Camaro pulling up."

Time to end this chat. "Take them out the back, Pegs," she said, ushering them back down the hall. "I'll handle this."

"Like hell," Peggy said. "I'm not leaving you alone with—"

A fist pounded at the door.

"Get them into that bedroom," Thelma said, turning to face

the entry, hoping like hell they listened. Whoever was at the door, they weren't going to find Imogene's daughter. Not on her watch.

THIRTY

Sam, Miami, 1978

"CORA!" THELMA'S VOICE CARRIED TO THE BACK OF THE
house as Peggy hustled Sam and her stepmother the last of the
way into the bedroom.

"What brings you here?" Thelma continued.

Sam leaned closer to the door, straining to hear the reply as
Peggy backed out of the bedroom. "You two stay put," she
growled. "You don't want Cora Young knowing where you are."

In truth, Sam had no desire to see Cora. She'd seen exactly
who she was at that cabin, suggesting women were being
dissolved but leaving her there with zero actual help. She would
learn more by eavesdropping.

No sooner had she formed that thought than a needle
dropped audibly onto a record player. Horns, piano, and conga
drums pulsed, muffled but insistent through the door. Cuban
mambo. No way was she going to make out what anyone was
saying over that.

Sam widened her eyes at her stepmother, mouthing *fudge*
before slumping against the wall, wondering who these two
women were to each other. She watched Sharon idly walking

around the room when suddenly she slid open one of Thelma's bedside drawers like it was her own.

"What are you doing?" Sam whispered, alarmed.

"What does it look like?" Sharon opened another drawer. "I'm seeing what I can find out."

Sam rushed over. "Cut that out!" She reached for the handle to push it shut, but what she saw inside stopped her cold. A snubnose special nestled in velvet. What was Thelma Miles doing with a gun in her bedroom?

With the confidence of a burglar, Sharon picked up the weapon.

"Stop it. You'll get us both killed!" Sam snapped, no longer bothering to whisper.

"I grew up in Germany during the rise of the Nazis." Sharon checked the chamber and began sliding the bullets out one by one. "You think I don't know how to handle a gun?"

The woman Sam had dismissed all these years as a replacement wife kept surprising her. "Put those back!" she snarled.

Bumping the drawer shut with her hip, Sharon held up her hands, still holding the gun and ammo. "Do we want her using these on us?"

"If she wanted to hurt us, we'd know by now." Sam jerked the drawer back open and pointed inside. "The last thing we need is for her to find out her gun isn't where it should be."

Sharon's eyes flashed with something—respect, maybe—while she made a show of reluctant compliance. As she closed the drawer, the music from the living room swelled. Perhaps Thelma was trying to drown *them* out.

To minimize the chance of arguing further, Sam moved across the room toward the closet. As she absent-mindedly flicked through the hangers, it struck her that *here* were Thelma's mementos—a floor-length pencil dress in deep burgundy with a ruched bodice, a rayon crepe gown in the same color, and another in fuchsia. All custom, all pointing to the life she'd lived in this dangerous game. No wonder the woman kept a gun handy.

If Sam was going to keep Abby safe, she had to keep Thelma on her side. She turned back to Sharon. Her stepmother was still looking through drawers. Sam opened her mouth to criticize as she recognized she herself was doing the same thing in the closet. "Psst," she hissed.

Sharon's head whipped around.

"Did you bring my mom's letter?" The letter would prove that Sam's intention was to keep Abby from harm. It was the only thing she had to convince Thelma to tell her what thirty-year-old secret was so dangerous that Frankie Giancarlo would kill to keep it buried.

But Sharon shook her head no. "The letter's safe. Hidden," her stepmother whispered, going back to her ransacking.

Before Sam could start another fight, laughter erupted from the living room—an unguarded sound, not the tense politeness of adversaries. Her stomach knotted. What history did those women share?

Without warning, Sharon stormed by, charging the door with the fury of a loose bull.

"What are you—" Sam began, but Sharon was already across the threshold.

"What is going on around here?" Sharon's shrill tone was one Sam had only heard once before, when on a visit to Miami, she'd tagged along to a PTA meeting. It so happened that *To Kill A Mockingbird* was on the agenda for removal from the school's library. "What is going on around here," she'd begun, "when we ban a book about moral courage? What will happen when they're faced with real moral dilemmas? How will they learn, as Scout Finch did, that isolation breeds fear, while moral courage is the taproot of strong communities?" Mortified as Sam was that her father's wife had butted in, she'd agreed. Theirs was the only school district in the area that did not ban the book.

Now, Sharon's fist was raised, clutching something Sam couldn't quite see. "I've had enough of this family's secrets for two lifetimes!"

Sam sprang forward, her heart racing as she entered the living room. The scene froze her in place. Peggy had returned to her lookout while Cora and Thelma huddled on the sofa, hands clasped. Thelma's amber eyes were still glistening—from the laughter?—while Cora's expression suggested Sharon had brought in a foul odor.

"My stepdaughter nearly died in that godforsaken drug den, and you did nothing," Sharon continued, waving her arm. "From what she's told me, I'd say it has something to do with this."

She unfurled her fingers to reveal a black-and-pink match-book identical to the one Cora had left in the cabin. The one Sam had used to start the fire. Sharon must have found it while she was pawing through Thelma's things.

Cora leveled her gaze at Sam. "I guess *she's* not dead."

"Don't you ignore me, missy," Sharon snapped.

"Mrs. Fuchs, ma'am," Peggy intervened, stepping between them, "I can assure you, our Thelma is not hiding anything. She's done nothing but as much good as she possibly could."

"Oh, can it, Peggy," Cora said, dropping Thelma's hand as if it had turned toxic. "We all know Thelma's no saint."

"Sweet as always, Cor-adorable," Peggy replied with a brittle smile that didn't reach her eyes.

"Hang on." Thelma held up a hand. "Before this goes any further, there are things you need to understand. You're going to want to sit down for this," Thelma said, her voice taking on a gravity that made even Cora straighten in her seat. "What I'm about to tell you will change everything you think you know about the past thirty years."

Sam felt a chill run up her spine as she took a seat. For the first time since this nightmare began, she sensed she was about to learn the truth.

Settling deeper into her chair, Thelma Miles began her story. "Before she died, Imogene told me she'd discovered a human trafficking ring between the States and Cuba."

"What's that?" Cora asked, her eyes widening.

Sam knew what Thelma meant but was too stunned to speak. Was the cabin part of a prostitution ring her ex ran?

"Prostitution," Thelma said. "Only the women—girls, really —didn't know that's what they were signing up for. They were promised contracts. Then they got them addicted. Used them."

The room went dead quiet.

"It's why we stayed in Cuba and Peggy eventually went to Vegas. To get women to safety. Then the revolution finally came."

"I thought you stayed to run the Bird," Cora said, pointing at the matches still clutched in Sharon's hand.

"Let me tell the story," said Thelma.

THIRTY-ONE

Thelma, Havana, 1958-59

THE LIGHTS OUTSIDE THE BIRD OF PARADISE BLINDED against Havana's night sky, but Thelma Miles kept her eyes on the shadows. Five years of sobriety had sharpened her instincts. She could spot a tail or a trap in pitch-black.

"Is everyone ready?" she whispered to Peggy, glancing at her reflection in a darkened window. The emerald silk dress was perfect—expensive enough to command respect, practical enough to run in. She'd need both qualities tonight.

"Ready," Peggy confirmed, nodding toward the club. "We should move the girls out before midnight while everyone's watching the clock. Not us."

As New Year's Eve 1958 roared toward midnight, they were readying their most daring transport yet—five women in one night. But the risk felt necessary. Castro's rebels had intensified their attacks, and Batista's reprisals grew more brutal by the day. Still, something felt off.

Since sobering up, Thelma had learned to reach for her premonitions, and they'd become a gentler rippling through her body, like a glimmer. But of late, the constant turmoil made it difficult to discern the false alarms from the fires. Between Doris's *compañeros* and the Bird's many donations, they'd prepared for any outcome.

Maybe New Year's was simply too much for Doris to handle alone.

"I won't be alone," Doris had insisted, reminding Thelma they had a fleet of trusted staff that managed their day-to-day operations. "Nothing bad's going to happen on the same night as the biggest party of the year, and I'll feel better if I'm here. Those girls need you. I don't."

The sound of the band tuning up wafted through the doors, mingled with laughter and clinking glasses. Thelma thought about the women inside checking coats, selling cigarettes, taking food and drink orders. They had a well-oiled machine in place to help women escape Gonzalez even if they'd never traveled in a pair on an evacuation. Only extractions.

She thought back to their first few devastating attempts. How that had led Thelma to the women Gonzalez discarded, women who'd become too old or too ill for clients. Women at their proverbial bottom. They proved more inclined to take help when it was offered.

They hid them in plain sight, first getting them cleaned up, then taking them on as employees at the Bird, and then finally— once their papers were in order—moving them out using the same routes that had gotten them here. Routes that Imogene Fuchs had told her about all those years ago.

Closing her eyes, Thelma sent a prayer of thanks to Vivian Miles. Not that her mother was her higher power. Thelma trusted the collective good in the universe for that. But without her mother's voice in her head, she'd never have gotten sober in the first place. If she hadn't gotten sober, she'd never have been capable of helping others escape Gonzalez's clutches.

Thelma gave Peggy the signal. "Let's move."

Inside the Bird they put in motion their practiced choreography, moving through the swelling crowd, a quiet word here, a meaningful glance there. These ladies knew the drill—lose the uniform, walk don't run, meet in the alley behind the Bird. No one in the crowd would notice their departures. Their replacements—the women who were next in line to escape—would take their places.

Doris caught Thelma's eye and made a slight shooing motion with her ostrich feather fan. *Git*, she was saying. *I've got this covered.* But one of the girls, Isabel, was trapped in conversation. Thelma's heart hammered. Doris was setting out bowls of grapes for the revelers to eat once the countdown began. They couldn't delay their departure. She rushed to Isabel's side, risking the attention. "There you are! Excuse us please," Thelma told the red-faced patron. "We need help with the champagne." She practically pushed the girl to her office. She'd have to jump through the window, but it was a contingency they'd discussed.

Once Thelma was finally outside, she noticed the metallic tang of gunpowder. Fireworks, she thought.

"Police presence seems lighter than usual tonight," Peggy murmured as they neared the bay.

They were almost at the docks, so close Thelma could taste the salt air, as welcome as her first sense of it all those years ago in Florida. The women kept moving, silent as they turned the last corner. There, at the end of the alley, instead of the familiar waterfront sights, she saw the five women they were to meet, bathed in the headlights of a police car. For the first time in the six years she'd been running this operation, the women they'd promised safe harbor to were face-to-face with a police car.

On instinct Thelma raced forward, excuses forming on her

lips. The false papers were stiff against her breast, too dangerous to distribute until they were safely aboard. A single girl caught with forged documents would expose them all. Though it was fairly typical to conduct staff transfers at night, to send a whole raft of women off at midnight on New Year's Eve was bound to raise questions. But the car crawled past without slowing. The officer behind the wheel looked distracted, radio crackling with urgent voices. Thelma captured Peggy's gaze, their eyes a wordless collusion pleading, *Let's get to that boat.*

The speedboat was waiting as arranged, engine idling. "*Llevarlas* a Miami," Peggy whispered to the captain as she helped the women aboard. *"¡Vamos!"*

Thelma pressed a roll of American dollars into trembling hands as the women boarded. "You're hat-check girls being transferred to the Miami Beach Hotel, remember? Nothing more. Your papers are in order. Make sure your stories are memorized. You'll arrive by midmorning, and Ruby will meet you once you've cleared the port. Don't look back."

The boats disappeared into the darkness, leaving only ripples in their wake. Thelma let out a breath. Another five souls freed from Carlos Gonzalez's web of exploitation.

In that brief moment of relief, the faces of women they'd helped over the past five years surfaced in Thelma's mind. María, the former dancer who'd been beaten so badly she'd lost sight in one eye. Thelma had gotten her papers that identified her as a distant cousin of their cook, with a clean record and a recommendation for work in Miami.

Then there was Barbara, who'd left her small Pennsylvania town at seventeen for the promise of a modeling contract. But her one-way ticket took her to a locked room at the Hotel Capri, servicing businessmen day and night. She was turned out by Carlos before her twenty-second birthday. Now a secretary in Tampa, she sent coded postcards every few months.

Isabelle, the university student who'd been on spring break, drugged at a party hosted by government officials then blackmailed with photographs. She'd refused to give up the locket with her mother's picture. Against her better judgment, Thelma had relented. It was no small relief to hear she'd made it home successfully.

There was never any fanfare. It was against the rules. And anyway, most girls didn't go home.

No, the successful extractions were but a quiet victory against systems of power that treated these women as disposable. Their network had grown slowly, cautiously—a bartender here, a cleaning woman there, a cab driver who could be trusted, a customs official who looked the other way for the right price.

"Do you remember Rose?" Thelma whispered to Peggy. "The young woman who left with her baby strapped to her chest?"

Peggy nodded, a small smile playing at her lips despite the tension. "She sent word through Manuel last month. The baby's walking now. She's got a job at a beauty salon but didn't say where."

Thelma felt a warmth spread through her chest. These were the moments that sustained her through the fear and doubt. Beyond merely escaping, these women were rebuilding. Creating lives that would have been impossible here.

Tonight, five more would join that number. Five more chances at freedom. If they survived the next hour.

A plane roared overhead. "We should get back," Peggy said, her words casual but her voice urgent. Planes didn't fly out of Havana after midnight.

Then another sound. The fireworks had ended; that was gunfire. Shouts echoed off colonial facades. Had the revolution arrived? Or was this simply another rebel incursion spilling into Havana's streets? They'd had trouble like this in Santiago.

As they neared the Bird, Thelma and Peggy could see its lights were still blazing but the music had stopped. Bodies streamed out the front doors. They broke into a run, high heels clattering on cobblestones.

"Doris!" Thelma shoved her way inside against the tide of fleeing patrons. The club was in chaos—overturned tables, broken glass crunching underfoot.

She found her, crumpled beside the stage, still clutching her ostrich fan. Dark stains spread across the front of her white silk New Look gown. Her eyes were open, but it was clear to Thelma she saw nothing.

"No, no, no." Thelma gathered her friend's broken body, heedless of the gore soaking into her own dress. "Why didn't you come with us?"

"Thelma." A familiar voice cut through her grief.

She lifted her gaze from her friend in disbelief. Was she dreaming? Hovering at the threshold was none other than George Wright, looking grim in his flight jacket. Where had he come from? The plane that had flown overhead earlier couldn't have been him; it was enormous. Besides, that bird was heading south. "We have to go. Now."

"You would leave Doris here?" Thelma's voice cracked. She remembered the time in St. Petersburg when George had helped save Doris by taking them to the so-called colored hospital. What had become of that man, the man she'd fallen in love with? "No, I won't leave her."

"This isn't a debate, Thelma. Castro's forces are moving block by block. The city's falling."

"This will blow over," she insisted. "These things always do."

"Batista has relinquished the presidency."

Peggy, her face streaked with tears, dropped to her knees

beside Thelma. "George is right, Thelms. Doris must've had some inkling. She practically forced us to get those girls out tonight. Why she wanted to stay behind... Don't waste her sacrifice."

Thelma looked down at Doris's still face. Together they'd built something remarkable here—not a successful club but an underground railroad. A place for women to escape the fate that had nearly claimed Thelma.

"Go," she said finally. "Both of you. Go. I'll be along, I promise. We have friends in high places—"

"Thelma, I don't know if you will after tonight." George extended a hand toward her, speaking gently now. "Please, my love. The plane's waiting. Please."

Once more, wild-eyed and unseeing, Thelma looked up at George. Some small part of her had heard him call her *love* and almost broke. But she would not leave Doris. Who knew what these brutes might do to her corpse. They'd all seen how captured revolutionaries were tortured. She could scarcely imagine how Castro's people might retaliate now that they were in power.

"I have to make sure she's buried properly. In Cuba. She'd want to stay here. No matter what."

George started to argue but Peggy caught his arm. "Let her do this. You know how stubborn she is."

They embraced quickly, desperately. Thelma watched them from the stoop, saw as a revolutionary flag was raised against the star-filled sky. The New Year was coming whether anyone was ready or not.

Then they were gone, and Thelma was alone with Doris's body. She smoothed her friend's hair back from her face. "I'll make sure Helen knows how brave you were, Doris," she whispered.

* * *

"But you didn't let me in your room when I came? Remember?" Thelma asked Cora, urging her to say something. She'd been remarkably still for the duration of this tale. Did she sense there was more to the story?

THIRTY-TWO

Sam, Miami, 1978

"You're saying Doris was killed by her *compañeros*?" Sam asked. "Because I didn't think—" She stopped herself. She'd only read about the revolution, Thelma had lived it. Still.

"Didn't think what?" Peggy asked from her seat by the window.

Sam hesitated, measuring her words. "Everything I've read suggests that the internal purges came later."

"Your reading?" Thelma snorted. "I told you my story would change what you thought you knew about the last thirty years. Those books were written by people who weren't there."

But Sam had read firsthand accounts for Filmore's study. She wanted to challenge Thelma but knew that lived experience trumped theoretical knowledge. Her studies were categorized into distinct phases, but revolutions were messy, human things where ideology collided with opportunism, heroism with betrayal. And anyway, the timeline hadn't been her focus. Why was she even hung up on this? She was reading into things, the same as when she'd mistaken the drug operation for a murderous den. Though she was prepared to blame Cora for that.

"People disappeared from the beginning," Thelma continued, her voice softening. "Some publicly, some quietly. But Doris believed in the cause completely."

"That made it easy for them," Cora spat. "The ones you trust are the same ones who can destroy you the most thoroughly."

"Sweetie, your auntie Doris spent the first half of her life knowing the *gardener* was her father," Thelma said. "She was happy in Cuba. She was finally able to embrace her heritage."

"What are you saying? Since her people shot her, that was okay?"

"*Oy vey*," Sharon said. "What choice did your aunt have?"

Cora turned to Sharon, murderous.

Recalling her stepmother's defense of Harper Lee's novel, Sam interjected. "I think what Sharon is trying to say is that trust makes us vulnerable, but without it, there's no love. Only separation."

Cora shook her blond curls. "Whatever," she said. "I'm just finding out that one of my aunties was murdered by her own people. So maybe keep your quaint little philosophies to yourself?" She turned, glaring at Thelma and Peggy. "Why didn't you ever tell me how Auntie Doris really died? You know how much I hate secrets. Especially family secrets."

Thelma and Peggy traded a look. They weren't even being subtle at this point. What were they leaving out of this story? She had to get to Ed. She had so much more information for him.

"For the same reason you're reacting this way now," Thelma said. "Doris insisted we keep our work from you, and Helen, and Archie. Protect all three of you from any danger. What comfort would stories about how we were helping other women offer a teenage girl anyway? And telling you after Doris was gone? Our work would've felt like a slap in the face of your very personal losses. And yes, of course I know how you feel about family secrets. But this is different."

Sam noticed that Thelma used the present tense, as if the need to keep this secret was ongoing. But that made no sense either. The mafia had been the first out of Cuba. They may have been running women before then but not recently. Maybe it was an imprecise way of speaking, but she doubted that too. What if her mother had discovered something she'd never shared with Thelma? Maybe that was why she'd asked about the letter too. If only the pieces would connect.

"How so? Doris was as much my mother as you ever pretended to be." Cora stubbed out her smoke and returned to her prone position, but Sam noticed how her words made Thelma's face pucker. A cruel blow.

"I need a chart here," Sharon said. "A family tree? Something. I can't tell who's related to who."

Peggy stepped out from behind Sam. "They're making it sound more complicated than it is." She shot a look at Thelma, who gave the smallest of nods. "Kathleen Young, she owned Sun City Emporium with her husband. Anyway, she left Cora in Havana with us—me, Helen, Doris, and Thelma—when she went off to India. But then she kinda fell off the map. Then the dominoes started falling in Cuba. That's when Helen and Archie got married so they could take Cora back to Florida. Cora's father is Thelma's brother, Matteo Giancarlo, but he died even before Kathleen's husband. Cora is Thelma's niece, but we're all her aunties."

Sharon shook her head. "That sounds pretty complicated."

A quick laugh escaped Thelma's throat, but this one was genuine, not bitter, causing Sam to steal a look around the room. Surviving the Great Depression and a world war must do something to a person. Maybe that explained her mother—none of them seemed terribly concerned about a woman leaving her child behind. For that matter, they didn't seem worried about this Kathleen Young either. Her stepmother hadn't batted an eye at the woman's affair with a mobster.

"That's what we bonded over, finally," Cora said cheerily, now looking at Thelma. "We both found out as adults that our fathers weren't who we'd been led to believe."

Cora's emotional ricochets were bumpier than the inside of a pinball machine.

"Whose side are you on, Cora Young?" Sam asked. "You came to the cabin to warn me about Jimmy then took off and left me to rot. But you left the door open. Then you show up here? Why should I trust you? Any of you?"

Before she'd finished her tirade, it was clear from Cora's slackened jaw that she hadn't intended to leave that cabin door open. Had she left the matches on purpose?

Like a cop telling traffic to stop, Thelma's hands tapped the air. "Honestly, Sam, we were all hoping you might go home with your tail between your legs and pretend this never happened but... you're definitely Imogene's daughter."

Several reactions coalesced for Sam. First, her knees buckled. She almost crumpled on the spot. Words she'd longed to hear her whole life came at her like a freight train.

Second, she recognized that she'd been sleepwalking through these last years, her studies the only thing keeping her going. In every aspect of her life, she'd tried to make herself smaller, thinking that when she had her degree, things would be different. But feeling seen had nothing to do with her degree. If that was going to change, it was up to her. Starting now.

Third, Sam sensed the pieces of this puzzle clicking into place. Dr. Filmore would've discouraged her—he always frowned on Sam's intuition—but he wasn't here.

"There's no reason to keep your twenty-year-old operation hidden unless... unless it's still active."

There it was again, that look between Peggy and Thelma.

"Like I said, there's a lot you don't know."

"You're not going to tell them—" Peggy began but, seeing Thelma's face, stopped herself.

"I am," she said. "Cora, I know where your mother is."

Sam's jaw dropped. Did Thelma mean she was working with Kathleen Young? Did that mean Kathleen was in—

"You *what!*" Cora bolted from the couch. "Where is she? That bitch!"

"Sit down. Calm yourself. That's another story."

Itchy as Sam was to talk to Ed, no way was she leaving now.

THIRTY-THREE

Thelma, Havana, 1961

THE COMMUNIQUES ARRIVED IN THE DEAD OF THE NIGHT, but Thelma rarely slept anymore, so she always heard the drop. Made sure to get the package before it could be intercepted. Tonight was different, though. It was not yet ten p.m. when Agent Miller strode into her study like he owned the place.

"Time's up, Miles," he said, tracking mud across what remained of her threadbare Persian rugs. "Castro's nationalizing everything that's left. You need to get out now."

Despite the change in routine, Thelma didn't bother looking up from the letter she was writing. Though he was the first person she'd contacted after telling the Youngs about Doris, she'd kept up the pretense that this Castro situation would blow over. She had to, for her own sanity. His CIA had only reluctantly agreed to help her move women out of danger off the island once she'd proved valuable, feeding them intelligence about Soviet shipping routes and Castro's growing military presence. The arrangement was morally flawed, but she'd learned long ago that pure motives were a luxury she couldn't afford.

"As I've told you," she said, carefully folding the letter, "I'm not going anywhere. I'm still doing good work here, and as long as I have this house, I'm staying."

"It's not a request anymore." Miller pulled up a chair, its gilt finish now dull and chipped. "We're moving ahead with the operation. April 17. You don't want to be here when it happens."

Now, she did look up, taking in his rumpled seersucker suit and the sweat beading at his temples despite the hour. "The invasion? That's suicide, and you know it."

"We have intelligence—"

"You have shit." Thelma stubbed out her cigarette. "Your intelligence comes from the same exiles who told Eisenhower that Cubans would rise up against Castro. How'd that work out?"

Miller's face reddened. "Things are different now. Kennedy—"

"Spare me. You boys and your plans." She stood, moving to the French doors that opened onto her once-beloved, now-crumbling terrace. The night air carried the salt tang of the ocean mixed with exhaust from Soviet trucks. "I've seen better schemes hatched by drunks at the Bird of Paradise."

"Speaking of which." Miller's tone shifted. "I have intelligence suggesting they're reopening your old club. Under new management."

Thelma's hands tightened on the doorframe. The Bird had been her pride, her redemption after George left. Until Castro's men had seized it three months ago. The closure was brutal. Now, to hear the Bird was reopening? Worse. *But how?* She turned back to Miller.

"What's it going to be, a soup kitchen? They can't even make proper rum in Bacardi's facilities, and they think they're going to run a whole nightclub?"

"They're bringing in some Russian woman to do the job,"

Miller said. "Going to turn it into a tourist spot for visiting comrades."

"Are you going to bomb that too?" There was no disguising the contempt in Thelma's voice. Not that she tried. This was all too much. "If you'll excuse me—"

She pressed past Agent Miller, but he got hold of her elbow. "Thelma," he said, stopping her short.

She couldn't remember the last time he'd used her first name.

"This isn't something to make light of." He let go of her arm and wiped his brow. "Diplomacy is not working."

"Diplomacy? Is that what you call cutting off medical supplies and closing the embassy?" She stomped her foot. "What you seem to forget are the very human lives affected by your games."

She left him calling after her about extraction plans and safe houses, letting the house's heavy mahogany door cut off his words, though she scarcely understood her petulance. She'd no affinity for the new regime. They'd not only failed to bring about promised changes, there was less of everything to go around. Havana's streets at night were different than before— fewer pedestrians, more soldiers, and virtually no tourists. Still, she knew every obscure entrance and hidden courtyard. Her presence still served a purpose.

Absent-mindedly walking into the night, her feet carried her toward the harbor and, inevitably, to the Bird. The art deco facade was dark, but when she crossed into the alley, light spilled from the rear entrance. A woman's silhouette moved behind the frosted glass.

Intelligence, thought Thelma with derision. More like observation. The Russian lady was, apparently, already ensconced.

Knowing for a fact that the boarded-up window beside the

front door was not attached to anything, Thelma moved swiftly back to the front and lifted the plywood out of the way before she could think the better of it. Inside, the club was an unswept, dilapidated time capsule. Tables stood sentinel, draped in dust covers. The stage, where she'd showcased acts from Miami to Madrid, was now silent. Artwork had been removed from the walls. Her office was, however, ablaze.

Moving stealthily, Thelma headed for the back room. She had no plan, which she realized as she heard the unmistakable click of a gun's safety being pulled back.

"One more step, and I'll blow your head off."

That was no Russian woman. That was—

"Kathleen Young! What are you doing here?"

Her former boss stepped out from the office. Fine lines etched her face, and her hair had gone a bright silver. She was as petite as ever, but the plain navy dress she wore concealed her curves. And no makeup or nail varnish. Thelma almost didn't recognize her.

"Quick, get in here," she said, motioning with the revolver toward the office. *Thelma's* office. "Did anyone see you?"

"Where did you—?"

"I mean it." Kathleen forced her in by the elbow and closed the door. "I only arrived yesterday. They told me the capitalists who ran this place were long gone, but I was hoping I'd find you before...."

"Who is *they*? Did you sneak in here?"

"In a sense, yes." She closed the door behind them and pulled out two glasses. "Drink?"

"Sober eight years now. You'd know that if you'd bothered to read my letters."

"Letters? More like an alphabet. I'm lucky if I can put together a single sentence from what I get."

They regarded one another across Thelma's old desk, a momentary standoff where each sized the other up. Kathleen Young was not dead, nor was she the broken woman Thelma had long assumed she'd become. No, whatever fire she'd been through served as alchemy. Yet for all that, Thelma could read her pain.

"Your letters are the same," she said. "Barely make any sense."

"Right, then. We'll skip the hugs." Kathleen sat in Thelma's old chair and poured herself two fingers of rum.

The smell turned Thelma's stomach.

"Where is Cora?"

"In Florida. Safe. Helen and Archie took her back to St. Pete," Thelma said, settling into the chair across from her desk. Her old desk. "Back in 1953. They have a... convenient marriage."

Kathleen's face fell. Whether it was because of Cora, or Archie, or both, Thelma was unsure. "She's been gone eight years—" She stopped with a rapid intake of breath, as if she'd been about to say more.

The air stilled with unspoken anguish. Thelma finally broke the silence. "I guess we both failed her."

"Is she happy?" Kathleen reached for her glass. "My little girl?"

But Thelma didn't want to give her that. *My* little girl. "Cora's a fifteen-year-old," she said simply. "What fifteen-year-old girl is happy?"

Kathleen merely nodded. "What about Doris?"

"Doris was killed here. By the revolutionaries." Thelma's lips twisted. "I suppose you'd call them comrades."

"They're not *my* comrades." Kathleen's shoulders sagged. "Listen, Thelma, I've been trying to get back here since 1950.

When I heard they needed people in Cuba to run businesses for the good of communism, I broke my arm to get here. I had no idea Cora was no longer in the country. Not a clue where any of you had gone."

Thelma sensed the truth in her words, but she wasn't ready to forgive her transgressions. "Whose fault is that, eh? How in the hell did you end up in Russia?"

"If you insist on doing this now...." Kathleen exhaled in frustration, opening and closing her eyes with deliberate slowness. "As you may recall, when I left Cora with you, it was to study with my guru. I thought it would be six months. Nine at most. The practice had helped me heal after Lloyd was gone, and I wanted to teach." She shook her head.

"But the training took thirteen years? Is that what you're saying?" Thelma didn't care if she was interrupting.

"No," Kathleen said, boring into Thelma's eyes. "What I'm saying is that my teacher didn't think I'd come. He didn't think women could teach."

Her frustration boiled over again. "So why didn't you come home?"

"You think he came right out and said I couldn't teach?" Kathleen scoffed, daring another snappy retort.

A parade of half truths floated in Thelma's mind—Sal's promise that his casino would be legitimate, Carlos's offer of protection, her own reticence with George. Crossing her arms over her chest, she leaned back. "So, what *did* happen?"

"My teacher sent me to Tibet. Said I needed to quiet the agitation in my mind. I was trapped in a silent monastery in a country where I didn't speak the language. The fact we weren't speaking scarcely mattered. And I had no money. I'd begun cobbling together an escape plan when the People's Army arrived and ransacked our temple. They murdered most of the nuns before my eyes, so I guess I was lucky. They put me in a reeducation camp where I had no communication with the outside world."

"You were in *China*?" The idea of Kathleen Young at a temple was difficult enough to conjure, but the reeducation camp begged disbelief.

"No, the camps were in Tibet." Kathleen sipped at her rum. "God, this is awful."

"That's communism right there," Thelma pointed at the shot glass. "These past two years, I've learned more than I ever wanted to about communists. And I'll tell you this, I'd never have pegged you for one. You could be the poster child for capitalism."

To Thelma's surprise, Kathleen regarded her with something like compassion. "This should explain everything. Or a lot anyway. I have stacks of them I've written over the years." Kathleen bent to open a satchel at her feet and produced a slim volume.

Thelma clocked the diary in Kathleen's hand but made no move to take it.

Kathleen dropped it into her bag. "You can read it later. There isn't time to explain now."

"Try me."

Kathleen knocked back the rest of her drink. "Honey, I'd have done anything to get out of that camp. If anyone would've understood, I'd have thought it would be you. I was a prisoner. Still am. But I can help you. You should leave tonight."

"Leave? Are you out of your mind?"

"Castro has a list of names, and he's crossing them off." Kathleen pursed her lips. "Your name is at the top."

Thelma froze. She'd seen the bodies of "traitors" left in the streets as warnings.

* * *

"So what you're saying is," Sam asked, breaking the silence that had once more descended on the living room, "Kathleen Young helped you escape Cuba, but she stayed behind?"

Thelma took in Imogene's daughter—her face burning with her mother's same intensity as she spouted more facts she'd learned about the revolution—though she was only half listening. Her thoughts were mired in that night when she'd finally taken the journey she'd sent so many others on. Though she'd crouched among the crates in Havana's harbor often, that night everything looked and felt different.

* * *

Despite the chill in the night air, her shirt clung to her skin. All around, searchlights swept the docks in lazy arcs as Thelma pressed herself against a warehouse wall, counting seconds between passes.

"Señora Miles?" The whisper came from behind a stack of crates.

Manuel Herrera emerged from the darkness. His cousin Rosa had been one of the first women she'd helped escape Castro's crackdown on prostitution, a purge that—while cloaked in revolutionary righteousness about "reform"—had simply traded Gonzalez's form of exploitation for another as the women were sent to agricultural work camps. Manuel had been the first person Thelma thought of when she decided to trust Kathleen.

They moved together along the abandoned pier, the only sound the gentle slap of water against wood as they made their way in the dark. Beside a derelict warehouse, Manuel had moored a rundown rowboat. They climbed in without a word, Manuel taking the oars while Thelma kept watch.

Unlike the women she'd sent before her, Thelma had her identity papers. She'd gone straight to the Harbor from the Bird. Kathleen had produced a few American dollars for her, but otherwise she had only her purse and inside—most precious of all—the coded logs of every woman they'd helped escape, women she still felt the need to protect. But she had no plan beyond that.

As they puttered out of the harbor, Thelma watched the city lights recede. The Bird of Paradise's neon sign was dark now, but she could still pick out its silhouette against the sky. Farther down the Malecón, somewhere inside the Hotel Nacional, Kathleen was reporting to her handlers. In principle, they'd agreed to continue the work, this web of helping hands stretching across the water, but they hadn't worked out any details. Leaving now felt like another broken promise.

Three miles out, they cut the engine and drifted. Minutes stretched like hours until another small boat materialized from the darkness.

"Marco," Manuel called softly. "¿*Todo bien*?"

"*Todo bien*," came the reply.

The boats drew alongside each other. Marco helped Thelma aboard then passed a package to Manuel. "Letters from Miami," he said. "Take them to the usual drop points."

As Thelma looked between the two men, a plan formed.

Manuel offered a lopsided grin. "Senora Miles, I hope you are not upset—"

"Upset? Manuel." She squeezed his hand. "Far from it. I think you're a genius. Both of you. And I plan to stay in touch." She looked pointedly at the bundle in Manuel's hand. "That is, if it's all right with you."

"You will continue to help?" Marco asked.

"Any way I can," she vowed, knowing now she could.

As the boat turned north, Thelma watched Manuel's running lights disappear toward Havana. The city glowed on the horizon like a beacon, dimming but not extinguished.

THIRTY-FOUR

Sam, Miami, 1978

"When was that? 1961, was it? When Kathleen Young helped you escape Cuba?" Sam didn't wait for Thelma to respond. "What I can't figure out is how this got my mother —" Sam's mouth worked, but no words could pass the lump that lodged in her throat.

"Killed?" Sharon offered. "Your father always thought there was something fishy about that accident. Said your mother was the most careful driver he knew."

Her father had never said as much to Sam. Jealousy stabbed at her as she considered the idea of them discussing her dead mother. Coming to conclusions. All without her knowledge or consent. Then again, after graduating high school early, she had never returned home to live. Only as a visitor.

Three slow claps came from the corner of the room where Cora lay prone on the couch. "Nice story, Auntie TT." She sat up. "You two did all that because of *her* mother." Cora tilted her head in Sam's direction. "What about me?"

Sam wanted to take the crystal ashtray from the table in front of her, now filled to the brim with butts and ash, and throw it at Cora. She'd give anything to hear a story like that about her mother. Following the clues she'd left behind was supposed to make her feel closer; instead, the quest was making her more opaque. If her mom was taking down a human trafficking ring run by the mafia, why did she need "courage" to tell Sam about it after she died?

"You egotistical wastrel."

Sam's head shot up abruptly. *Sharon?*

Her stepmother snorted. "Your mother, missing since 1948, resurfaces, and your reaction is to feel sorry for yourself?" she asked Cora, though her frustration could well have been directed at Sam. She'd been thinking almost the same thing— *What about me?*

"I knew she wasn't dead," Cora said flatly, examining her nails with deliberate nonchalance that didn't quite mask the hurt underneath. "Obviously."

Sam reached for her stepmother, gently placing her hand on her arm, feeling the surprising warmth beneath her cardigan. "I think—"

"No, she's right." Thelma stood, making brief eye contact with Sharon. "You both are. Let me show you." She disappeared down the hallway, returning moments later with a carved wooden box clutched to her chest.

"Letters?" Sam asked as Thelma settled back into her chair.

Tapping the box, Thelma sat in the overstuffed leather club chair. "No. The few letters we did exchange were so redacted, it was ridiculous. This is one of Kathleen's personal diaries. She gave it to me when I left Cuba."

Cora lunged, but Thelma lifted the container out of reach. "Settle down, Cora. Your mother never meant for you to read these."

Reminding Sam of her daughter, Abby, Cora crossed her arms and asked with an exaggerated sweetness, "May I please see my mother's diary that you've been keeping from me?" She returned to churlish. "Is that what you want?"

Sam bit her lower lip, trying to maintain her composure as she wondered how she'd feel if a trove of private thoughts from Imogene Fuchs were to suddenly appear, especially one that had been kept from her.

Thelma pushed the ashtray aside and put down the box, tantalizingly emblazoned with a gold-embossed stamp that read S.G. Cigars.

SG—Salvatore Giancarlo, thought Sam.

Lifting the lid unleashed a spicy tobacco and cedar scent mixed with the musty vanilla fragrance of aging paper. Cora plunged her hand into the box and pulled out a small leather-bound notebook, thumbing through it before tossing it aside.

"What does it say?" asked Sam.

"Here," Thelma said, handing over another notebook with care. "This one's from the first few months after she left. She gave it to me before I got on that boat. Must've been carrying it with her in the hopes of running into one of us."

Sam opened the journal, noting the perfect Palmer script. The handwriting of a well-bred young lady.

MARCH 22, 1947 - MYSORE

I WAS ON MY MAT LONG BEFORE THE PREDAWN BELL, *practicing so I didn't have to think. The asana effect lasts a while but only a while. I've found this journaling helps, too, though quite by accident. What began as a record to share with Cora, when Guruji told me outside contact was forbidden, has become a respite.*

. . .

CORA SNORTED AND FLIPPED FORWARD A FEW PAGES. "HOW touching. The woman abandons her child to find herself then writes about it like she's some kind of martyr."

APRIL 3, 1947 - MYSORE

CORA WOULD BE FIFTEEN MONTHS OLD TODAY. I WONDER IF *she's walking yet. Talking? Does Thelma read her bedtime stories? I hope she leaves the singing to the other girls.*

I tried writing a letter to my baby girl yesterday, but I couldn't finish it. Guruji has forbidden contact anyway. "For the duration of your training," he said. As if distance would quiet my heart. I am here, supposedly becoming the parent Cora deserves so the darkness I feel inside doesn't poison her. I didn't have this problem with Bertie. Certainly not Archie. But then, they had their father. Cora will never meet hers, neither one.

I fear I've made a terrible mistake.

"OH, PLEASE," CORA SAID AS SHE PAWED PAST MORE PAGES.

Sam wondered how she could be so angry she'd pass up this chance to discover her mother. Finally, she stopped. Sam read over her shoulder. Was it her imagination, or had the hand-writing changed? What began as a flowing, confident script became condensed. Anxious, almost. Even the words appeared to be pressed harder into the page.

DECEMBER 1947 - RISHIKESH
I was on my cushion long before the bell. "Too much agita-tion of the mind," Guruji told me. "You must study vipassana."

Now, I can barely sleep, my thoughts roaring like the Ganges below.

But the meditation isn't helping, and now, I'm forbidden from even the physical practice—

CORA FLIPPED VIOLENTLY TO ANOTHER SECTION WHERE the writing had grown tiny, desperate, like someone trying to make the pages last longer. Sam could no longer read it, but Cora read this one aloud with bitter emphasis.

MAY 28, 1948 - RISHIKESH

THIS HAS GONE ON FAR LONGER THAN I EVER THOUGHT IT *would. On the one hand, I am wracked with shame. On the other, desperate loneliness for my Button—*

"BUTTON?" CORA RAISED HER EYES FROM THE PAGE. "WHO the hell is Button?"

"Your father," Thelma said. "That was her nickname for him."

"She called your brother *Button?*"

"No, Mr. Young. Lloyd Young. Her husband."

"Oh, you mean the poor guy who died while mommie dearest was filming that Vegas promotional movie instead of taking care of him at home. That's the one you mean?"

"That's one way of looking at it," Thelma said.

"It sounds like Kathleen Young was having a nervous break-down," Sam said.

Cora stood, towering over Sam. "Are you saying my mom's

crazy?"

Sam tipped her head up at Cora, noting her sharp edges and practiced nonchalance. The way she held herself apart from everyone. Fierce though Cora was, Sam recognized the survival strategies. Cora's presence here said volumes more about who she was down deep. Considering her life story, it was hardly surprising that she looked out for herself above all else. Frankie had sent her to that cabin in the first place; only a fool would have helped Sam escape. "Honestly, I can't imagine how all this must feel to you."

Cora's shoulders slumped as she fell back into the sofa cushions before looking back at Sam. Were they bonding?

"You have no idea what it's like growing up without a mother," Cora scowled.

"Oh come on, chickie," Peggy interjected, "you didn't exactly lack for maternal attention. You had four aunties at home, and everyone at the Bird loved you."

A mist crept across Cora's eyes. "I barely remember Cuba. I came here in second grade, and it's like I had scabies. I was blackballed before I even knew what that meant."

Sam thought back to her own experiences in second grade. Her mother had died the summer before. By the time the school year was out, her father had remarried. It marked a person, being ostracized in elementary school. "Second grade was hell." She nodded. "I was shunned. Especially after...." She caught sight of her stepmother, who'd done nothing but prove Sam was wrong about her, before adding her usual phrase: *after he married Sharon.* It was not, she admitted to herself at long last, the truth about her classmates' banishment. "Well, after my mother's car went over a cliff off Highway 1."

Ice clinked in someone's abandoned glass. The afternoon light had shifted, catching on the layers of stale smoke that wound through the room.

With a jolt, Cora straightened. "Oh my God, your mother was Imogene Fuchs? The reporter? I remember that story," she said, more animated than before. "Happened before my time, but in high school we did a civics project about groundbreaking local reporters. That story really stuck with me, how she died out there. Alone. So far from her family. Such a terrible accident."

The precise opening Sam needed. "That's the thing. I'm not so sure it was an accident."

She had everyone's attention now.

"What do you mean?" asked Sharon.

"Elsa Juergen said it was no accident."

"Pfft," Cora said, lifting a blond tendril off her forehead. "Consider the source on that one."

"Hang on." Thelma put her load on the table,

"What else did she say?" Thelma continued.

Sam struggled to recall their conversation. It had been a mere three days earlier, but it felt like a lifetime had passed since she'd met Elsa Juergen. "Something like, 'That's what they want you to think. Check the records.' But, you know, I've already gone down that path. My mother's body was burned beyond recognition, but they did have dental records."

"Those can be faked," Peggy said, sending a searing pain through Sam's heart.

"You're not suggesting Imogene isn't...." Sharon whispered the next word. "Dead?"

"Then who was in that '48 Super Deluxe?" asked Cora.

"Wait, what? No!" Thelma said. "But did you say a Super Deluxe? A Plymouth Super Deluxe?"

"Uh, yeah. They didn't make another one." Cora blew a smoke ring. "Sweet ride."

"Wait, wasn't that the same car we rented in Vegas?" Peggy asked.

"It was. But ours was a '41. 'Course they didn't make any cars during the war." Thelma turned to Cora. "Was the '48 also a manual?"

"Yup, a three on the tree."

Sam had lost the thread. "What's that?"

"A stick shift," Cora answered. "Where the shifter is on the steering column."

"Oh," said Sam. "Okay."

"Cora, are you sure?" asked Thelma.

"TT, if there's one thing I know, it's cars. They only made them that way."

"Sam," Thelma said with a gentle urgency she found alarming, "you're right about one thing. Your mother couldn't drive a stick. Imogene couldn't have been driving that car. Unless—"

A sharp knock at the front door cut her off. Through the door's stained glass, Sam could make out the silhouette of a man in a hat.

"You expecting anyone?" Peggy asked, already moving toward her window perch.

"No, no one at all." Thelma's hand disappeared beneath a sofa cushion.

A casual movement but one that failed to disguise its purpose. She was reaching for a weapon.

The knock came again, more insistent this time.

THIRTY-FIVE

Thelma, Miami, 1978

"CHRIST. IT'S LIKE GRAND CENTRAL IN HERE WITH ALL these arrivals." Peggy looked out the window. "Black sedan." She leveled her eyes at Thelma. "Our tax dollars at work."

Thelma smoothed her dress, making sure her gun was not visible. Thirty-odd years dealing with men like him had taught her to never be caught unprepared. "Ladies, this is a, uh, business associate I forgot was coming. It's, well, it's nothing important...."

"What she's trying to say is scram. Come on." Peggy rose to shepherd the women to the bedroom. "You're not missing anything."

As she closed the door on them, Thelma dropped a new record on the turntable—Artie Shaw, better for muffling the conversation—and assembled herself in an air of mild boredom. This had long been their game, that they didn't need each other.

Had he noticed the cars out front? Cora was always driving something different, and surely Sharon's Caddy wouldn't be on his radar. No reason to assume the vehicles had anything to do with her. Thelma opened the door wide

"Agent Miller, always a surprise." The words came out

smoothly, but Thelma felt her shoulders tense—a reflex she'd developed over decades of dealing with men like him, men who appeared only when they needed something. She'd learned the hard way that the CIA's definition of "mutual interest" tended to favor one side—and it wasn't hers. How many times had she provided intelligence only to be left hanging when she asked for something in return?

His rumpled summer suit and military haircut remained unchanged since their first meeting in '53, the very picture of a Southern gentleman. His first lie.

Today, there was no bothering with any pretense. Miller barged in like it was a raid. "Where is she?" he yelled around Thelma's shoulder. "Cora Young?"

So much for not making Cora's vehicle. "Agent Miller," Thelma began, but he was already pushing by.

As he passed the record player, he sliced the needle across its surface, silencing Artie Shaw. The scratch made Thelma wince—that record was out of print. Her hands pulsed as if to remind herself this was the least of her worries.

She followed Miller into her main room, mentally taking inventory of her exit routes and the amount of time it would take to extract the .38 at her hip. Before she'd finished, Cora came flying out of the hallway to the bedrooms. Mercifully, Sharon and Sam had the good sense to stay put.

"Yeah? What?" Cora said, undaunted. Despite that she was clad only in a halter top and short shorts—or maybe because of them?—her niece looked ready for battle.

She stopped Miller cold, but he didn't exactly relent. "Word is you torched that cabin."

"Who the fuck are you?" The girl was playing with fire, but Thelma felt a surge of pride. Her niece put her hands on her hips and turned. "Auntie TT?"

Miller cocked a fist on one hip, pulling back his suit jacket to flash his service arm. "I'm your worst nightmare."

Time to intervene. "He's CIA, Cora. We've... I've known him since Cuba."

For once, Cora dropped her veneer of nonchalance. Her jaw dropped, and her eyes went wide. No words came. Thelma had never seen her so thrown.

Miller did not slow. "I don't know what you think you were doing, but we needed that operation."

That was all it took to bring Cora back. She crossed her arms and tilted her head with a frown. "We who? And listen, pal. What do I care what you're doing? I didn't set that fire."

That information was all Miller needed. Smiling, he took a seat on the armchair—Thelma's seat—and produced a toothpick from his jacket pocket. He pointed it at Cora. "I didn't have you pegged for stupid. You know as well as I do whatever you did or didn't do don't matter. This isn't a hunt for the truth."

In the ensuing silence, Miller popped the toothpick in his mouth, rolling it around before settling on a spot. Thelma saw the rage building in her niece, half expected her hair to lift up.

"Cora," Thelma cautioned. Useless.

"I didn't do it!" Cora blurted, somewhere between an avowal and a tantrum.

Peggy moved toward Cora and threw an arm around her. "Listen, tootsie, everything's going to be fine. That's why he's here." She was looking at Miller, who'd never been her favorite, as if to insist. *There was nothing like the solidarity of a lifelong friendship.* "What do we need to do now?"

But Cora was already wiggling out from under Peggy's arm, scrambling for her handbag. "I don't know what you all are doing"—she fished her keys out of the purse, flashing them at Thelma as she walked past—"but I need to go find Frankie."

Find Frankie?

"You don't want to do that—" Thelma began, but it was too late. Her niece continued on as if she'd said nothing, her heels clicking a furious rhythm over the threshold down Thelma's driveway as the door swung shut behind her.

"Aren't you going to stop her?" Peggy asked Agent Miller.

A look crossed over his face, one that told Thelma he was about to make some smart aleck remark. He was enjoying this. "I was going to ask what brought you all the way from Las Vegas, Mrs.... *Lowry*, is it now?"

To her credit, Peggy didn't blanch at the dig. So what if she'd had several husbands? Though for the life of her, Thelma couldn't understand why she kept marrying them.

"I haven't laid eyes on you," Miller continued, "since your warm greeting in Havana."

"You don't say," Peggy said. "I don't remember even meeting you."

Thelma wanted to pump her fist in the air, but the last thing she had any interest in was getting sidetracked by their age-old battle. "Frankie won't hurt Cora. He needs Sun City Records to wash his money clean."

"It's not Frankie I'm worried about," Miller said, all serious again. "Did you hear what I just said? We were funding that coke operation in Frankie's cabin. The money was for the anti-Castro rebels."

His words took a moment to land. So much to parse. She feared her hair might stand on end. She'd been avoiding her nephew Frankie almost since she'd landed in Miami back in '61. As handsome as his father had been, he'd inherited the worst of Sal and Matteo's temperament. Kid was a powder keg, liable to go off at any moment. And the CIA was using *him* to funnel money?

Thelma's operation may have dwindled, but she did more than service Miller's need for Soviet intelligence. There were plenty of women in Cuba who had no one to help them besides her and Kathleen. In that regard, Miller had always been skint. Expected far more than he gave, but he was her only access to legitimate paper. Never gave them a damn dime, though thanks to Lillian, that hadn't been a problem. "International Business Machines, darling. I have no idea what they do, but it's absolutely legal and sure to make a killing," she'd told her back in '46 when Thelma still thought business was something separate from crime. Hoping to go legit, she'd invested heavily.

She had to get this conversation back on track. "I doubt very much Cora cares about your problem. She's more concerned with what Frankie thinks."

A raised brow suggested Miller's contempt for Frankie's thinking abilities. "The brass will not take kindly to it," he said. "She's going to jail for a very long time."

"I know she didn't do it."

"Miles, you disappoint me. You *should* know as well as I do, her guilt or innocence has got nothing to do with what happens to her. They'll do anything to keep the stink off."

"How did you know Cora was here?"

Miller sat back, crossing an ankle over his knee in that inconsiderate sprawl Thelma found vexing. "Her T-bird's out front," he said. "But that's not why I came. I came to tell you Carlos Gonzalez is out of jail."

The news hit her like a physical blow, Carlos Gonzalez was responsible for more misery than any human should be, but she kept her face carefully neutral. Why now? Miller never shared intelligence unless he wanted something in return. The timing was too convenient, with Frankie's cabin explosion all over the news.

She studied his face, but the leathery mask hadn't changed. What game was this?

THIRTY-SIX

Sam, Miami, 1978

"Yeah, I heard all that," Sam said as she and Sharon emerged from the bedroom, moments after Agent Miller's departure left the house in charged silence. But she didn't care about Carlos Gonzalez, whoever that was. "I have to go get Abby."

"She's fine," her stepmother said. "I left her not an hour ago."

Of course Sharon would think her thirteen-year-old was fine. Sam had still been in grade school when Sharon and her father started leaving her at home with the TV and Swanson's most weekends. She was such a goody two-shoes she hadn't taken advantage of the freedom, but Abby was different. Sam had to leave this zoo and get Ed digging for records.

"Sharon," Sam said, her voice firmer than before, "we need to get back." She tilted her chin at Thelma and Peggy. "You understand, right? I need to make sure that Abby stays put."

Thelma's face hardened, as if she was weighing her options. "Of course," she finally said. "But Sam." She put a hand on her shoulder. "Be careful who you talk to. After that explosion...."

Sam didn't need the reminder but thanked her anyway before hurrying away.

* * *

SHARON HEADED NORTH ON HIGHWAY ONE, TOWARD THE condo on Collins. The twilight made it look as if Miami's skyline shimmered. Sam rested against the leather seats, letting them cool her skin as her mind burned with possibilities.

"I think my mother discovered something about the Giancarlos before she died," Sam finally blurted, breaking the silence. "Something Thelma doesn't know."

The skin smoothed across Sharon's freckled knuckles. "What makes you say that?"

"I think she came to town for Sal Giancarlo's funeral."

"He was buried in St. Petersburg?" Sharon asked.

Sam was always forgetting that her stepmother hadn't lived in Florida much before marrying her father.

"When was that?"

"1950," Sam said, mildly shocked this detail could be fuzzy to Sharon. Had she been unaware Sam's mother's corpse was barely cold when she'd married her father? *Focus!* "That's why I had to get out of there. I need to feed Ed all the new information we got, and I need to catch him before he leaves school."

Sharon, focused on navigating a difficult intersection, said nothing. When she did speak again, her voice was soft. "Your father never liked to talk about those days. He said the grief nearly killed him."

The revelation hung in the air between them, another piece of her father that Sam had never known. The bitterness she half-expected was muted, blunted by exhaustion and her growing admiration for Sharon.

They drove in silence the rest of the way as Sam thought of her mother's involvement. Not only had she been documenting this story as a reporter, she'd actively fought it. Despite what it must have cost her emotionally to collaborate with Salvatore Giancarlo. The revelation shifted something fundamental in Sam's understanding of her mother. Imogene Fuchs was more than a crusading journalist; she'd risked everything to help women escape situations most people preferred to ignore.

Despite what Elsa or Helen said or thought, Sam was like her mother. Her work with Cuban families that had been ripped apart through careless government programs was not merely documentary; it was to prevent such tragedies from recurring. Her ultimate goal was to tell a story people could not look away from. To show how all trauma rippled out into society as a whole.

* * *

THE CONDO WAS SUSPICIOUSLY IMMACULATE, CAUSING SAM to panic over Abby's whereabouts. But the spare key was right where Sharon said it would be, and moments after entering the unit, asynchronous noises erupted from the bedroom. Her daughter was there.

"Abby!" Sam called, racing back toward the bedrooms.

Seeing her daughter's textbooks spread across the bed filled her with relief, but Abby hadn't noticed her mother's appearance as she pogoed around the room, homework forgotten. Sam faced in the direction of the noise emanating from the television. The words Iggy Pop appeared onscreen just before she shut it off.

"Mom!" Abby stopped. "I was watching that."

"Is that what you call what you were doing?"

"Mom!"

"You didn't even hear me come in. It could have been anyone. And for what? What was that?"

"Some show called *TV Party*. It's... Oh, never mind. You wouldn't get it." She put her fists on her hips. "Where have you even been? Did you see Nana? She went looking for you."

"Yes, she's making us something to eat." Sam sat on the edge of the bed, patting the seat beside her. "C'mere, Abby. We need to talk about some things."

Abby's eyes narrowed with that familiar teenage skepticism. "Like what? You said you were taking me out."

Sam paused a breath, centering herself. "Here's the thing. Sharon is going to take you to St. Pete tomorrow. It's not safe for us here. I need you to—"

"St. Petersburg? Gag! No!" Abby's face contorted in horror. "Cheerleader tryouts are Friday!"

Of all the things to worry about at a time like this. But then she remembered her own all-consuming teenage passions, the scaffolding that held her together after her mother's death. "Honey, I hate to tell you this, but you aren't going to be here for that."

"I'm calling Dad right now." Abby reached for the bedside phone, her jaw set in that stubborn line Sam recognized from her own mirror.

Sam wrenched the phone from her daughter. "No, you won't." In their struggle, she saw Sharon lingering by the door. *Great.* "I need to tell you something about your father."

She paused, wondering where to start. "Do you remember when your father lost the big Gulf & Western case?" she began, and the rest poured out—the hard times, the distance between them, the job she'd only just found out he had.

"Daddy's working for the mob?" Abby asked, sounding awestruck.

"I only told you that so you understand this is very serious," Sam said. "Your father is not the man I married."

Abby's face crumpled slightly. "But Dad wouldn't let them hurt me."

The childlike faith in her voice sent a pang through Sam's heart. "I don't think he would. But he's not the one calling all the shots." She went on—the cabin, the explosion, and finally, her suspicions about what had really happened there. "It's an ideal location for their dirty work."

"Why didn't you say something before?" Sharon finally asked.

"You set that Everglades fire?" Abby's eyes widened, something like respect washing over her features. "Radical."

"I didn't mention my suspicions because they're still a hunch. Cocaine is a perfectly plausible explanation for the explosion," Sam said. "And young lady, there is nothing *rad* about dissolving human beings in vats of acid. I told you that so you understand the consequences. Your father is working with dangerous people. People who would think nothing of hurting us if we were in their way."

After Abby agreed to lay low, Sam heard the microwave fire up—a strange domestic counterpoint to their crisis. "I have to go make a call," she told her daughter. "You wash up for dinner."

Sam found another phone in the master bathroom. *What's with this guy and telephones?*

"I found out a few things," she greeted Ed. "We already knew my mom was friends with this Thelma Miles. Apparently, she told her about a prostitution ring the mob was running, and Thelma used that info to help women escape some network in Cuba run by a guy called Carlos Gonzalez. Ever heard of him?"

Ed whistled. "Never."

"That's not all. Thelma ran a business with a Doris

Juergen—write this down, it's not spelled how it sounds: *J-u-e-r-g-e-n*. She was part of the initial movement to overthrow Batista."

"A lot of middle-class Cubans wanted to see the back end of Batista," he said.

"But Thelma is Salvatore Giancarlo's daughter! I mean, the mafia were among the first people Castro kicked out."

"That's one of the things I wanted to tell you," Ed said. "Though, near as I can tell, Thelma hasn't had anything to do with the family in decades. She was tied to the family back in the late forties but not after Sal died."

"When was that?" Sam asked. "Sal's death."

"Hang on. I just had that." She heard the sound of papers shuffling. "May 28."

"So he couldn't have done it."

"Done what, Sam?"

"Killed my mother. Her death...." Her voice caught. "That was no accident. I thought maybe he did it."

"You all right?" Ed asked.

Sam took a breath. "I'm fine," she said. And she was. The despair, she knew, would come later. Now, was the hunt. "So... you don't think the nightclub was connected?"

"Doesn't appear that way." Ed shuffled through some more papers. "Have you come across anyone named"—more shuffling—"Francella DiGruppo? Francella Ava DiGruppo?"

They went on like this for some time, sharing what they'd learned, making guesses.

"Sam!" Sharon appeared in the door, still yelling despite her proximity. "It's time to eat."

She turned away, crouching over the receiver. "Listen, Ed, I should go."

Sharon was still standing in the door.

"I'll call you later."

"Sam?" Ed said, sounding more hopeful than she liked. "You know I'd do anything for you."

Her stomach lurched. She didn't want to encourage him, but she didn't need any more enemies either. "Thanks, Ed. We may take you up on that."

As Sam hung up, she stared at the telephone, her mind raced. The academic perspective was detached—dates, names, business dealings. But what Thelma had shown her was the human cost. The women who'd been trafficked weren't footnotes in a case study but people with names, faces, dreams. The cold facts of trafficking meant nothing without understanding the terror of a locked room, the desperation of addiction used as control, the courage required to run toward an uncertain freedom. Those stories made her work matter.

The mood was quiet over their suspiciously orange macaroni and cheese. The kitchen phone jangled on its hook, cracking the silence.

"You get it," Sam told Sharon. "If it's Jimmy...." She trailed off. If it was Jimmy, they were screwed.

"Thelma!" Sharon cried as she turned the mouthpiece toward her chest and whispered, *I gave her this number*.

After a lot of uh-huhs and sure, okays, they hung up.

"What'd she say?" Sam asked.

"She wants us to come back."

"Tonight?"

Sharon nodded.

"I'm coming," Abby said.

"No," Sam said firmly. "Absolutely not." She gave her daughter the look that had ended countless arguments over the years. It worked this time, too, but she couldn't ignore the hurt flickering behind Abby's eyes. "I'll explain everything when we get back," she added more gently. "This is just something I need to do."

Abby nodded reluctantly. "Fine. But I want the whole story when you get back. No more hiding things."

The parallels weren't lost on Sam. Wasn't this exactly what she'd resented her father for all these years? The secrets, the omissions, the way he'd "protected" her from the truth about her mother?

"Deal," she said.

THIRTY-SEVEN

Thelma, Miami, 1978

THELMA SPED TOWARD DOWNTOWN MIAMI, LOST IN thought. For as long as she'd lived here, she'd avoided the press. But if Kathleen Young had taught her anything, it was that the media could be a powerful weapon when deployed strategically. Now was that time. But these women were showing all the sparkle of a turnip.

She almost missed her exit. As she hit the blinker, she found Sam and Sharon in the rearview, each looking out their own window. Sharon had inserted herself into the evening, which Thelma didn't really mind. She wasn't going on TV, but she could keep Peggy company in the green room. Sam was another story. Her, she needed. "Almost there," she said. Nothing.

She had to turn this mood around. "Gosh, I hardly recognize the pair of you. You look like movie stars. Excellent work, Pegs."

"I always say you can get away with anything when you're wearing the right shade of lipstick," Peggy said, her broad, gap-toothed smile betraying her modesty. "Those designer outfits of yours don't hurt either."

Thelma wanted to hug her old friend. She'd caught on and was trying to get this pair in the right headspace too. Despite that she had found the perfect looks—an Adrienne Vittadini wrap dress for Sam and a Pucci caftan for Sharon—these women were not ready for prime time. She pulled onto the shoulder, draped an arm over the seat bench and looked into the back seat. "What's wrong?"

"We don't know what your plan is here," Sharon said.

"Thank you, Mrs. Fuchs, but I was talking to Sam."

Sam squeezed her stepmother's knee. "Reporters make me nervous."

She said it so quietly, Thelma wasn't sure she'd heard correctly. Reporters made Imogene Fuchs's daughter nervous?

But Sam went on. "And I don't know how my advisor will like me talking about his research."

"Didn't you say you did all the work?" Peggy asked.

"So?" Sam asked.

"Sam. Honey." Thelma leaned farther into the back seat. "You're not just window dressing here. You're the credibility this story needs. You blew up Frankie Giancarlo's cabin, alerting all authorities that he's processing coke out there. And no one has done a thing about it. Not the cops. Not the Feds."

"Not helping," Sam said.

"I'm trying to point out what we're up against. The thing is" —Thelma lowered her voice, making sure Sam was really listening—"without your credentials, your research background, I'm just another woman with a grudge against the Giancarlos. They'll write me off as Sal's bitter daughter with an axe to grind. But you?" She tapped Sam's knee. "You're the daughter of the most respected investigative reporter in Florida history, with academic credentials and legitimate research showing how drugs are one of the ways immigrant communities are vulnerable to exploitation. You give this story weight."

Sam glanced up, something shifting in her expression.

"The women I've been helping?" Thelma continued. "Official channels pose as much risk to them as men like Frankie and Carlos. You're our way around that."

"You're still running your operation," Sam said, sounding less like she was asking and more like she was confirming a hunch. "That's why you and Kathleen Young have stayed in touch."

Dammit. Now Thelma had no choice but to confess, and well, at this point the secret hardly mattered. "I was. Not after tonight. My contacts will be blown. But Carlos Gonzalez has to be stopped, and you're the only one who can make people take this story seriously."

"But I thought we were only going to talk about the historic aspects of the prostitution ring," Sam said.

"Exactly right. That's why you're here. The expert, connecting the dots between all these nefarious activities and the exploitation of immigrant communities. Nobody else can do this."

"So my job is to bore them out of being interested in the juicy story while simultaneously making them care enough to report it?"

Thelma laughed, as much from relief as Sam's words. Humor was a good sign. "Let's just say that between your mother and Cora's, I've learned a thing or two about how to play the press. I know exactly how Frankie is moving his product because it's the same networks that were used by Gonzalez. Miller and the boys at the CIA might be obsessed with communists right now, but they have to listen to public outcry. That's where the media comes in."

Sam said nothing, but Thelma could see her thinking it through.

"If you can't do it for me, do it for Abby. Do it for all the daughters who deserve better than men like Frankie deciding their futures."

Tension flickered across Sam's face. "Of course," she said, straightening her shoulders. "I'm ready."

"Good." Thelma returned to the wheel, relief washing through her. "We need all hands on deck, but your focus matters most tonight."

Not that Thelma took her own advice. No, her mind went right to the last time she'd laid eyes on Kathleen Young. Her story about the reeducation camp had been so outlandish, it had to be true. If anyone could sweet-talk a passel of commies, it was Kathleen Young. But she'd understood Cora's anger; a few words couldn't undo the damage inflicted by her years of absence.

Not like it had for Thelma.

* * *

"Help me what?" she'd asked Kathleen as she fished a cigarette out of her pack while tipping back on her chair's legs.

"Let's not be coy now." Kathleen's expression went stern. "Do you want to end up like Doris? We both know you've been helping girls disappear from the island."

"What? I—" How had she failed to destroy the evidence?

"Come now, Thelma. I may be many things, but I've an excellent head for business. I pieced it together from records I found in your files."

Thelma's neck turned to flames as her chair slammed forward. "Are you planning to turn me in to your superiors?"

"Turn you in? I see your listening skills haven't improved. No, dear. When you're gone, I can run this side. Help women escape."

An involuntary grin teased at the corner of Thelma's mouth. "Then you don't know what I'm doing. Not really." She stubbed out her smoke. "You want to help women escape prostitution, but the women here, still in that line of work? They don't want to work on farms or in factories. They want to do the work they know they're good at and that they'll be well compensated for. I help those women —women who don't have families or friends in high places—get to the States. If they want, they can go right on plying their trade."

Kathleen's eyebrows shot up. "You're a madame?"

"You would think that. No, Kathleen. I'm not their new middleman. I help them escape. That's it. They can do whatever they want, but for the most part...."

"But—" Kathleen began, but then a faraway look crept into her eyes. "I can help you do that too."

It was Thelma's turn to be shocked. "You would do that? But... Why?"

"Don't you see? It's the same old story, different flags." Kathleen's eyes met hers. "Men think they can do anything they want to women and get away with it. I'm through with that game. And, well, in my own way... It's for Cora. But you mustn't tell her I'm here. I won't put her in danger."

Outside, a military truck rumbled past. Both women instinctively stilled 'til it passed.

Thelma studied her former boss, the woman who'd once saved her life by killing her half-brother but then betrayed her trust by abandoning Cora. But that was all another life. None of that mattered now. Looking into Kathleen's eyes now, she saw they shared the same determination.

"But... do you really think we can work together?"

"Of course we can. We've done it before."

That was what worried Thelma. She rose.

"Where are you going?" Kathleen asked.

"To get a club soda," Thelma said. "We've got plans to make."

"There isn't time." Kathleen had waved her off. "You need to leave as soon as you can."

* * *

OF COURSE IT WASN'T KATHLEEN'S FAULT SHE'D BECOME alcoholic, no more than it had been her mother's. They'd both been born with the disease. But if it wasn't for Kathleen, maybe she and George...

Stinking thinking, she told herself. *I need to get myself in the right headspace for this interview too.*

Her last moment of clarity before the lights—

THIRTY-EIGHT

Sam, Miami, 1978

EVERYTHING HAPPENED SO QUICKLY AT THE TV STATION, Sam only remembered the events in bursts. First, the green room. Sam had never been in a green room. Couches lined the walls, and in the center sat a coffee table, loaded down with mixed nuts, cheese and crackers, and—oddly, thought Sam, for people going on television—deviled eggs. Three large televisions played the network stations, but the volume was muted. There was no telling what anyone was saying.

A young woman with a clipboard and a headset swanned in with questions about her research. Her stomach knotted. "Dr. Filmore's research," she'd clarified, earning a glare from Sharon. The reality of what they were about to do landed. This wasn't a classroom presentation. It was live television. People across Miami would be watching, people like Jimmy and his boss.

But as she asked how separation policies had impacted Miami's Cuban community, her confidence stirred. This was why she was here—to use her expertise to give their story credibility.

"Great," the woman said admiringly before checking her watch. "Five minutes to air."

Her next memory was being on set. She and Thelma were seated on weirdly shaped, uncomfortable chairs facing a row of cameras. That didn't seem so awful until they turned on the lights. Sam began to perspire straightaway.

"Try not to squint," a technician advised as he clipped a microphone to her blouse. "And don't look directly into the lens."

A makeup artist rushed forward, dabbing powder on Sam's forehead. "The lights make everyone sweat," she said in a low tone.

Sam nodded her thanks, mentally rehearsing her talking points as the activity around them intensified. Technicians adjusted equipment, producers conferred in hushed tones, and the tension in the room seemed to build by the second.

The reporter appeared, looking not at them but at her clipboard. Sam recognized her—"This is Kathy Campo for WTVJ"—but couldn't remember her beat. If there was an introduction, Sam didn't recall it.

Beyond the lights she heard, "Three, two, one...."

The red light blinked on, and Campo transformed. Back straight, face to the camera, smile wide. "Good evening, Miami. Tonight, a special report on organized crime in South Florida with two women who claim to have insider knowledge."

This wasn't the angle they'd discussed.

"Ms. Miles, you're the daughter of Salvatore Giancarlo, one of the most notorious crime bosses in Florida history. What can you tell us about your family's operations?"

"I'm here to discuss existing vulnerabilities that have been exploited since Carlos Gonzalez—" Thelma began, steady.

"Is it true that you've maintained your connections with organized crime figures since your father's death?" Campo interrupted, her smile neither faltering nor reaching her eyes.

Thelma's jaw went tight. "We're here to talk about how

vulnerable communities are more susceptible to criminal networks—"

"Is that how you would characterize your family's current activities? As criminal networks?" Campo pressed.

The interview was spiraling out of control. Sam leaned forward, desperate to redirect. "Ms. Campo, research shows a direct correlation between—"

"And you"—Campo shifted to face Sam—"daughter of the long-deceased investigative reporter, Imogene Fuchs. Did you know your mother was looking into Thelma Miles right before her fatal accident? Had even visited Havana?"

The half accusation hung in the air, shocking in its bluntness. Sam felt the blood drain from her face. This wasn't an interview. It was an ambush.

The next three minutes felt like an eternity as this woman took fragments of information and turned them into salacious quotes. Sam went mute as Thelma struggled to regain control of the narrative. But Campo was quick to interrupt with shocking accusations that, Sam would realize later, all came without proof.

The producer finally called, "Clear!" Campo removed her microphone and was whisked off by her assistant without a word to Sam or Thelma, leaving them stunned in their seats. Before Sam could catch her breath, the producer was thanking them for their time as she ushered them out the back entrance to "avoid other reporters who might be waiting."

The phone was ringing when they arrived, and the group stood staring at the phone, a colorful assembly in Thelma's white Bayside paradise.

"We should go to our place," Sharon said. "Hide out there."

"Go to Meyer Lansky's? Are you nuts? That's just asking for trouble." Peggy snorted.

Before Sam could ask why, there was a pounding at the

door. They'd drawn the curtains but hadn't heard anyone pull up, which ruled out Cora and, most likely, Agent Miller.

"I know you're in there," came a woman's voice.

Thelma shrugged, and Peggy herded them into the living room a moment before the door opened.

"As I live and breathe," Sam heard the voice say. "Not since your father's funeral."

Sam was seized by the urge to race to Thelma's bedroom and retrieve the pistol she'd seen there, but there was no time. Stilettos were already stabbing out a purposeful march toward them. At least it wasn't Frankie.

The woman stopped when she saw them all assembled. "Aww, look. The gang's all here. Ain't that the sweetest?"

The intruder was old-school glamorous, her dyed black mane wrapped in a leopard print scarf that matched her car coat. Though she was shorter than Peggy and Thelma, she moved with the same elegant step. Now, she and Peggy were hugging? Could this be another long-lost Florida Girl?

Sam slid a sidelong look Sharon's way, but her stepmother was watching the proceedings with rapt attention. If they made it out alive, this experience would make for a landmark case study. Dr. Filmore would... *Nothing*. That jerk would probably reject her idea out of hand. Then steal it.

Pay attention, she scolded herself. The chummy behavior was tricking her into inattention.

The woman in the scarf broke away to face Sam and Sharon. "Francella Ava DiGruppo." This was the woman Ed had told her about, Sal's mistress and Frankie Giancarlo's mother. The woman who, according to Ed, had kept the family business alive after Sal passed.

Francella extended her hand, first to Sharon then Sam. "I hear you blew up my son's cabin." As she spoke those words, she tightened her grip on Sam's hand. Terrifying.

Francella let go of Sam's hand and gave her face a light slap. "Cute."

Sam was flummoxed. There was no rule for this. No guide. Nothing in her coursework covered wild cards like this. Francella was Sam's primary suspect in her mother's murder. Where was Agent Miller?

"Do you talk at all?" Francella clucked her tongue. "I thought that was an act for the TV but...." She turned back to Peggy and Thelma. "Some friend you got here."

"Francella, I think we know this isn't a social call," Thelma said. "Where's Frankie?"

"Thirty years you don't call, you don't write, and this is how you greet me?"

"I helped you get work on Broadway, didn't I?"

"As I recall, that was your friend Lillian."

"When did you last speak to my mother?" Sam asked. "Imogene Fuchs."

All eyes turned to Sam, except for Francella's. She fluttered hers as if flipping through a mental Rolodex. "Imogene, Imogene... Fuchs, you say? I don't think." Her eyelids burst open. "Nope, never talked to her."

A scoff pushed through Sam's nose. Involuntary. She marveled to think how many times this woman might have used that act to get away with murder. "No. Tell me, Francella. What do you know about my mother?"

Sharon kicked her shin. "Ouch!" Sam said, creating the perfect distraction for Francella, who brushed past them toward Thelma's kitchen counter.

"You got anything to drink in that bar?"

They had no choice but to follow her lead.

THIRTY-NINE

Thelma, Miami, 1978

"I do have champagne," Thelma said, drawing a stare from Peggy. The bottle had been gathering grease and dust in the back of her kitchen cabinet, but it had been a gift from one of the families she'd helped. It would be a good label. "I'll go get it. Peggy? Maybe you can help me?"

"I have a better idea," Francella said. "I'll help you while Pegs takes a load off."

In the thirty years since they'd last seen one another, Francella hadn't changed at all. In Thelma's book, that was not a plus.

She was deep in the tall cabinet beside her refrigerator when Francella pinched her hip. She shot upright and banged her head as she located the champagne in its hiding place. "Jesus, Francella, what?"

"Listen, you know as well as I do, nobody cares about the amount of product Frankie is moving."

Thelma's kitchen was narrow, not much of a kitchen as she barely cooked. They stood so close together, she could smell Francella's breath. She must've had garlic at supper. "Our story brought you out of the woodwork, didn't it?"

She cocked a fist on her hip. "Who do you think showed Frankie what to do?"

In a sudden glimmer, Thelma understood that Francella had been involved in getting rid of Imogene Fuchs. There was no one else to raise Frankie after Sal died. But Francella, embittered over losing her career, left much of the job to Sal's Sicilian wife—Carlotta brought Frankie up. It didn't matter to Carlotta that Imogene had kept their Las Vegas secret; she wasn't family. With her father and his ilk, it was always about family, as if family spawned trust.

But Thelma knew better.

She hadn't fully loved her own mother until she understood her untrustworthiness. Saw that she hadn't caused Vivian's shortcomings as a parent. Real love meant accepting someone's limitations. Intimacy meant trusting someone enough to know they'd hurt you but not destroy you. Perhaps this was what had been missing with George, not the absence of love but the absence of this trust.

"Why did you do it?"

"He's my son. He had to know his father." Francella said.

"No, I mean kill Imogene Fuchs."

Shaking her head in disbelief, Francella clucked her tongue. "You want to do this now?"

"That girl in there? That's why she's here." Thelma lowered her voice. "That's Imogene's daughter."

Francella looked toward the sunken living room. "Jimmy's wife is Imogene Fuchs's daughter? Ha! Then you better hope this story doesn't come out."

"What do you mean?"

"Imogene's story? She was going to expose Kathleen Young."

Expose Kathleen? "For what?" she asked, realizing the answer even before her words were out. For the murder of

Matteo Giancarlo, Cora's father. The murder Thelma had helped cover up. Her expression must've given away her thoughts.

"Yup, that's why."

"Does that mean Imogene's death was my...." But the thought was too terrible for Thelma to continue.

That didn't stop Francella. "It's not your fault she was murdered."

The fact she'd said it belied the truth. But... "Who would've wanted to kill Imogene for that besides Sal?" Again, the answer came before she finished her sentence. No one. Sal had put the hit out before he passed.

Francella scowled. "The guys who did it didn't know that he was dead. And...."

She hung her head, alarming Thelma; this was not an expression Francella wore.

"I had to pay them," she said. "Carlotta made sure of it."

Sal's wife. Another glimmer. Carlotta had come straight from Sicily. Thelma remembered reading her obituary not long after she'd returned to the States from Cuba. Frankie would've been a teenager by then. Exactly when the stories about his recklessness started swirling. Why she'd avoided the remaining Giancarlos other than Cora.

"So, what? You're here to blackmail me? Be my guest. After tonight—"

An exasperated grunt stopped her.

"I came to warn you. This is bigger than Frankie. They start digging? A lot of people are going to get hurt."

Thelma regarded Francella. The fine lines around her eyes. The incongruently jet-black hair swept up in a scarf. Her father's one-time mistress almost pulled off the well-to-do older upper-class lady, but—Thelma brushed the scar on her own cheek—she, too, bore the mark of Salvatore Giancarlo. Francella's long straight nose was no more, forever pushed to one side. "*Going* to get hurt? A lot of people have been hurt already."

"Look, your little side hustle? The men involved are prominent men. Famous men. If that all comes to light...."

Side hustle? Thelma was so outraged to hear, for the second time in one day, her life's work reduced to something inconsequential, she barely knew where to start. "Why is it okay that so many women have gotten hurt?"

"Sweetie, I don't make the rules. But I think you know if the names of certain politicians and businessmen come out, well, they won't. That will get buried. Right next to you." She paused, but Thelma remained unconvinced. "I'm not trying to make you out to be the bad guy. I know you've been moving paper for decades now, helping women stuck in Cuba who are, well, women who are like us. That won't matter to these—"

"Women like *us*? You think some women ask for it?"

Sadness bloomed in Francella's features. "Oh, honey, no. I mean women who want more out of life. Women who don't want to be treated like they don't matter."

Their eyes locked, and something broke free in Thelma. Another chip in her armor.

"A long time ago, you told me that men would kiss my ass but women would save it. You remember?"

Thelma nodded.

"Well I rode on men kissing my ass a long time, even after Lillian got me work on Broadway. I always felt like life had never been fair to me. You know what I mean?"

"I do. Like you had to play by their rules to get anywhere." She thought of her days behind Sal's desk, the businesses she'd had burned to the ground, her half brother Matteo, letting her father's money fund the club—all her choices. "It took a long time to break that habit. And I caused plenty of damage along the way."

"That's why I'm here. When I saw you on TV... I thought you should know that Frankie is working with the CIA. They aren't going to stop him."

"I know they're working together, Francella. The point of going on television was to make it impossible for them to hold Abby hostage."

"Abby?" Francella sighed, eyes moving heavenward before focusing squarely on Thelma. "I don't know who that is, but after that little show you put on TV, you should leave town."

Sam appeared at the counter. "We're all ready for drinks out here."

"Here," Thelma held out the bottle. "Take—"

Tires screeched up to the curb. Thelma looked from Sam to Francella.

"Shit," said Francella.

* * *

EVEN CONTORTED WITH RAGE, FRANKIE'S FACE IN THE doorframe made Thelma catch her breath. He could've doubled for her half-brother Matteo. "What are you doing here?" she asked.

What came next ended in a matter of seconds but proved what they said about crises. So much happened in those crucial moments, the retelling would take far longer than the unfolding.

First, Francella had already beaten Thelma to the hall, hence the question. "Baby, listen to me—" she began.

"You looking for me?" Thelma asked, packing into her cramped entryway behind Francella.

Sam was deep into the foyer before anyone saw her, carrying that dusty bottle of champagne. "Let's have a drink," she said, almost mid hallway now. "It's a very nice bottle."

Frankie cursed on seeing her, but Francella whispered

something in his ear and pulled him into the bungalow toward Thelma's living room.

Directly behind Frankie came Jimmy Fontana, though Thelma didn't know who it was until Sam called out.

"Jimmy?" Sam asked. "What the hell?"

But Sam didn't wait for an answer. Instead, as mother and son tried to squeeze past, Sam turned. Frankie was behind his mother with his hand on the small of her back, like he was guiding her.

Sam raised her hand. Thelma froze as she caught the glint of something sharp slicing through the air. The blade descended in a perfect arc—not into Frankie's back but onto the neck of the bottle. The action caused the cork to burst, pop forward, and glance off the side of her half brother's head.

He reached up and swore violently before turning to Sam and reaching for her neck. "They shoulda taken care of you and your goddamn mother at the same time."

No one had noticed Sharon at the far end of the foyer. "Let go of her," she said. Even. Calm.

In her hands was the revolver from Thelma's nightstand.

Frankie pushed Sam to the floor a second before Jimmy bolted through the door, pushing past her half-brother to lunge at Sharon. His intention, he later claimed, was to wrestle the gun away from her.

Francella stepped in front of her son just as Sharon pulled the trigger. Only Thelma saw that Frankie had retrieved his own revolver. He was pointing it at Sharon.

Thelma moved to strike his arm away just as Sam rolled upright and banged into Thelma's shins, causing her to stumble into the line of fire. A gun discharged—once. Twice. As the smoke lifted, Francella and Thelma were on the floor, blood seeping across the white tiles.

FORTY

Sam, Miami, 1978

SAM MADE IT TO HER FEET, WOBBLING, ACUTELY AWARE that the dangers of sabering were overblown. Peggy raced into the foyer, wedging by as she yelled something incomprehensible. Her stepmother knelt beside Francella, either in conversation or resuscitation, Sam couldn't have said which—it sounded like she was underwater. The gunshots must have distorted Sam's hearing.

"Thelma!"

Sam did make out Peggy's cry as she dropped to her knees, cradling her best friend's head in her hands.

Something about the muffled scene sharpened Sam's focus. Eyes moving from point to point as she'd been trained, she noted that Thelma's revolver—the one Sharon had nicked from her nightstand—was beside Jimmy. Clearly the weapon that had been fired on Thelma. Frankie hadn't moved. The .45 still in his hand had obviously discharged into Francella.

The smoke had not fully cleared by the time Agent Miller appeared, probably because of the cramped space. A wiry fellow in a seersucker suit, hair off the collar, he had gray eyes, gray hair, and a deep tan. He was not what she would've expected. More Barney Fife than James Bond.

It occurred to Sam then that all she needed was one witness to suggest premeditation and she could frame this as first-degree. That can be me, she thought. *I'm a witness here.*

"They came in brandishing weapons, Agent Miller, sir," she said by way of hello. "Said they wanted payback for our little TV stunt." She gulped for air. "Frankie and Jimmy showed up with the intent to kill us."

"You're so full of shit," Frankie yelled, pointing his gun again before a swift blow from Agent Miller put him on the floor, where he crawled toward his mother's body.

"For Chrissakes, somebody call an ambulance," Peggy screamed.

Still at the far end of the hall, Sharon broke away to call emergency services. *Wash your hands,* Sam thought at her with all her might.

"Frankie, you need to stand up right now and move away from your weapon."

Maybe not so Barney Fife. Sam realized then that her hearing was back, and she had never felt more alive.

"Miller," Frankie began. "Listen, this is obviously—"

"Shut up. Get on your feet, and put your hands behind your back." Agent Miller pointed toward Thelma's living room. "Jimmy. Sam. You two, go in there, sit down, and shut up."

"But—"

"Not another word, Frankie," Miller warned. "Go on. Everybody but her." Miller indicated Peggy. "Soon as that dispatch goes out, the police will come. Hopefully, the ambulance gets here first."

Sam was about to protest. She could be of use here. For the first time ever, she was reading a crime scene, her training drowning out her nausea. She had to make sure Jimmy took the fall for Thelma and Frankie went down for murder. *They shoulda taken care of you and your goddamn mother at the same time*, he'd said. Confirmed her hunch—her mother's death had been Francella's doing. *But why kill...* Sam couldn't finish the thought if she was going to keep the pain of it at bay.

"Agent Miller," Jimmy interrupted her thoughts. "I'm his attorney. I—"

"I know who you are, Jimmy. Are you hard of hearing or what? Both of you, get out of this hallway."

In the living room, Jimmy took Thelma's chair. *Naturally*. Sam dropped onto the couch. She hadn't noticed before how the space was set up for conversation. Almost like a meeting room, with two long couches facing each other and stuffed armchairs at either end.

"You looked good on TV," he said.

"You asshole," she hissed. "I'll tell you what was in my mother's letter if you tell me who killed her," she heard herself saying, negotiating with a criminal. This whole episode was going to take a long while to unpack.

Jimmy rolled his eyes. "Like I care now. You think you're gonna frame me for killing Francella DiGruppo, you're nuttier than I thought you were."

Sam squinted at her ex-husband. "It's our word against yours. And you're a proven liar."

"I'm an attorney." Jimmy lifted his chin and shook out his cuffs. "Big difference. Trust me, you won't get away with this."

Sam looked away. "Jimmy Fontana, I swear to God...."

"Are you threatening me? Because I can use that too."

"What did I ever do to you?"

After an exaggerated once-over, Jimmy looked toward the hallway. "It's what you stopped doing for me, babe."

Now, she met his gaze without flinching. "Oh, you are going down."

"Sam, look, if you were my client, my advice would be to stay the hell out of this," he said. "Your mother was trouble. It was just a matter of time for her."

The wail of an ambulance siren broke their standoff. There was nothing Jimmy could say that would diminish Sam's view of her mother. Whatever secrets she'd kept for the Giancarlos, whatever dirt she had on them—she'd more than paid the price. What Sam had to do now was forgive her mother for leaving.

At last, Sharon joined them in Thelma's living room. "I stayed on the phone with 911 'til I heard the sirens," she said as she took the seat next to Sam. She leaned across her stepdaughter's lap. "I didn't think it was possible for my opinion of you to sink any lower. For once you've proven me wrong, Jimmy Fontana."

"Don't even bother with him," Sam said then lowered her voice. "Did you...." She cast a pointed stare at her stepmother's hands, fervently hoping she would pick up the clue to wash off that gunpowder. "Do you need to go to the bathroom?"

Sharon smirked. "All taken care of, pet."

She truly was remarkable. "We're agreed on who shot who?"

Sharon nodded. "But that's the least of it."

They were going to burn the Giancarlos to the ground.

FORTY-ONE

Thelma, Miami, 1978

THE HOSPITAL TELEVISION FLICKERED SILENTLY, ITS images washing over Thelma in waves of blue and gray. Despite the morphine fog, she was trying to keep up with the news in Havana, watching without sound as was her habit. Twenty years of reading faces across a crowded club had taught her to see the truth beyond words, the stories told beneath the surface.

Today's report showed Coast Guard boats in the Straits of Florida, circling like tired dancers. The newscaster's lips moved in practiced concern, but Thelma knew that one drug bust was not the real story. The real story was secure with Sam. Page after page documenting how women were brought into Cuba, never to be seen again. Women that society seemed only too ready to discard.

Now that Thelma's network was no more—the cook who hid passport photos in bread loaves, the cleaning woman who smuggled out messages in dirty laundry, the small fishermen whose cargo holds doubled as escape hatches had all gone underground—there was time to build a real case.

The bullet wound in her shoulder throbbed, a sharp reminder of her foolhardiness. She'd gotten reckless, going to the news media like she was Kathleen Young. That damn reporter. She was uninterested in the plight of Cuban women. She wanted the gotcha sensationalism of capturing Sal Giancarlo's daughter—Havana's Original Mafia Queenpin, read the chyron —on film. As if her real work was nothing more than a subplot bound for the cutting room floor.

Onscreen, the segment switched to footage from the press conference outside the Miami field office. Thelma reached for the remote with her good arm, turning up the volume.

"...largest cocaine seizure in Florida history," announced the FBI spokesman, the camera lingering on the neat rows of evidence bags. "The Bureau wishes to thank our partners at the Drug Enforcement Administration and the Central Intelligence Agency for their assistance in this multinational operation."

The television shifted to footage of Frankie being escorted into court—the same steps where his father's heart had given out —head high despite the handcuffs. The arrogance in his posture was pure Sal. The reporter's voice continued over the images. "Francis Giancarlo has been released on bail pending trial. His attorney, Jimmy Fontana, denies the drug charges, attributing them to, quote, 'a vendetta against the Giancarlo family.'"

Released. Of course. Thelma balled her hospital gown in her fists. Sam's attempt to hang first-degree murder on her ex had never gotten any traction, proving Frankie had inherited more than just Sal's swagger.

A quick cut showed the outside Thelma's home, crime scene tape fluttering in the breeze as the reporter read on. "Sources confirm that the shootout occurred at this Bayside mansion, owned by Thelma Miles, daughter of the late crime boss Salvatore Giancarlo and half sister of Frankie Giancarlo. While authorities are not releasing details at this time, they have confirmed that the death that occurred was accidental and unrelated. No charges have been filed in connection with the shooting."

They cut to a commercial, and Thelma hit mute before the "Brush your breath with Dentyne" jingle began. She wished she could brush her brain. In three minutes of airtime, the stage had been set for Miller's narrative, which he'd put to her as a promise "to keep the family drama separate from their drug bust." A point he'd made with surprising insistence.

"What about Sharon?" she'd asked.

"Self-defense, plain and simple," Miller had said, not quite meeting her eyes. "Mrs. Fuchs has been officially cleared. Text-book case."

"And Frankie?"

Miller's face had hardened then. "Your nephew is being charged with drug trafficking and racketeering. The shooting incident is… peripheral."

Peripheral. Thelma's chest tightened. "Women who don't matter," Francella had said. Now, she was dead, and Thelma had been shot, both of them collateral damage in the larger game being played. Yet there was a certain relief Thelma could not deny. No one would look too closely at the history—her history—that had led to that moment in her foyer. Victory, she'd learned through hard-won experience, was rarely absolute. It came pockmarked with concessions. Her secrets could stay buried in Cuban soil.

A parade of sunshine icons marched across Florida during the weather report. She shut off the television, but there was no shutting down the questions that loomed. Now that his connection to Frankie was exposed, what would happen to Carlos Gonzalez? Why had he been released in the first place?

Did it mean Castro's government would protect him or sacrifice him to maintain diplomatic relations?

Would she and Kathleen be able to rebuild their network, or was her cover blown too? There hadn't been time to warn her. Some contacts would disappear into the machinery of the Cuban state. Others would be too frightened to continue. Twenty years of work undone in a day's broadcast. What would happen to the women still trapped?

The throbbing in her shoulder intensified, but Thelma resisted the call button. Pain was clarifying. It reminded her that despite everything, she was still here. Still breathing. Still capable of rebuilding.

Footsteps in the hallway pulled Thelma from her morose self-reflection—measured, military-precise steps that still made her pulse quicken after all these years. George Wright hadn't lost his pilot's bearing.

She turned to find him standing at the room's entrance, shy almost, the light from the window catching the silver at his temples. The years had carved deeper lines around his eyes, but they beheld her with the tenderness that had once convinced her they could build a life together, something good. Those days were long gone.

"You look terrible," he said.

"You should see the other guy." Neither laughed.

"They said you were awake," he said, hovering at the threshold.

"Christ, do I need to pay off the uniforms at the door now?"

"Ah, but your money is no match for the Wright name."

"Thirty years later and you're still gloating about how right you were to stay away from my family?" The words came out sharper than she intended, but the morphine had taken off the brakes. The hurt he'd caused her, the hurt she'd caused him. All of it was there at the surface.

George's jaw tightened—she'd forgotten how he did that when he was angry. "I came because I heard you'd been shot. Because despite everything, I still—" He broke off, running a hand through his hair. "What were you thinking, going on television like that?"

"I was thinking about stopping a drug ring." She met his gaze.

"Really?"

The sensation of anger bubbled somewhere inside her, like a distant memory. This was the allure of intoxicants, this distance. She wanted to ask what ulterior motive he suspected, but the phrase "ulterior motive" eluded her.

"Because that's not what Sam said," George continued, moving into the room, close enough that she could smell his aftershave.

"Sam? What did she tell you?"

"She said her mother had uncovered a prostitution ring in Cuba. You got women out. That you've been helping women get out all this time."

"Goddamn her." Thelma gazed toward the ceiling. "The whole point of going on television was to keep the focus on Frankie's drug business."

"But Thelma—" His laugh was hollow. "Why do you think she told me?"

"Now, it's a quiz?"

George sank into the chair beside her bed. "Can we start over?"

Thelma had to force herself to breathe normally. Of course her ex-husband didn't mean start over. "Sure."

"First of all, I was wrong." The words hung in the air between them. "I thought you were just like your father, that you couldn't escape that life. But you weren't running rackets. You were saving people."

Thelma's laugh turned into a wince as pain shot through her shoulder. "Isn't that rich? George Wright, finally approving of my life choices. Well, I hate to break it to you, but I didn't do it for your approval."

"I know." He leaned forward, elbows on his knees. "You did it because it was right. Because you saw something wrong and decided to fix it, consequences be damned." His voice softened. "Like you always did."

"Don't." She turned away, blinking back sudden tears. "Don't act like you know me now. You left."

"And you let me go." His voice cracked. "But I never stopped loving you."

The words she'd waited decades to hear twisted like a knife. "You never looked back. Not once in all these years."

"I looked." George's face was stripped of pretense now. "I even tried to get you into rehab. You refused. Then nothing. I'd see you in the papers on some arm or another—"

"Please. They call you Senator Playboy in op-ed cartoons."

George crossed the room to look out the window. "Look, I didn't come here to rehash ancient history."

"Why did you come?"

"Agent Miller called me."

Of course he had. Senator Wright chaired the Senate Committee on Foreign Relations. "Why am I not surprised he blew my cover too?"

"Thelma, I'm trying to tell you we've been working together for years. Pushing through visas. Back channeling comms. I didn't know... it was for your network."

A yawn escaped as Thelma rubbed her eyes. *Am I dreaming this?*

"I think we can nail Gonzalez."

Thelma sat up quickly. "Oh, ow!" she cried.

George rushed to her side, and for the first time in almost

three decades, he took her hand in his. Gently, so gently. They stared into each other's eyes as a quiet settled between them, not entirely comfortable but honest—the first honest silence they'd shared since she'd brought Sal to Havana.

A sharp rap sounded at the door. Agent Miller. "Sorry to interrupt this little reunion, but we've got incoming," he said, face grim. "The Soviets have a diplomatic flight at dawn. A 'refueling stop.' But it's loaded with diplomatic pouches, and they're bringing twice the normal crew rotation. This could be Gonzalez's next move. We need to act on this intel now."

Thelma tried to push herself up, but George's hand on her good shoulder stopped her. "You're not going anywhere."

She opened her mouth to argue, but he continued, "Just tell me what needs to be done. I'll handle it."

Their eyes met again, and suddenly she was back in their first weeks in Havana, before his accident, before Sal's arrival, before the Bird.

"Earth to Thelma?" Miller prompted. "Your latest reports from the nightclub, Soviets who've been hanging around. Do you remember any specifics? Names, dates, anything your asset has given that could square up with those visa applications."

The room swam as Kathleen's intelligence reports floated through her memory—the cultural attaché who requested the same table, the trade delegate with his endless stack of travel documents. But she didn't want to put her former boss in danger either. Miller had burned her sources before.

"And what do my people get in return?" Thelma asked, her voice icy. "Last time I handed over names, your people were nowhere to be found when my contact needed extraction."

Miller had the decency to look uncomfortable. "This is different."

There had been a time when Thelma believed her greatest rebellion would be escaping her father's criminal clutches, but her true insurrection had been weaponizing the system against itself, using their own passageways to free the women it tried to consume. What she'd not fully grasped until now was that the battles would never end, that justice would never be a zero-sum game.

Studying the two men before her—George, his self-righteous certainty burning bright, and Miller, with his shadow-world pragmatism—it occurred to Thelma that there were no clean hands in this work. Only the courage to keep reaching into the muck. And sometimes, the devil you knew was better than the one waiting in the wings. A freed Carlos was a threat she couldn't ignore even if it meant playing Miller's game one more time.

"I'm going to need a pen," Thelma said, blinking away the cobwebs. "For you, Miller. Because none of this blows back on my people, and you're going to put that in writing. Not just your word."

Miller nodded, producing a ballpoint.

She scooted upright. "George? The third drawer of my desk has a false bottom. In it, you'll find a file marked Havana Girls. Miller can take you."

She watched him follow Miller out, her heart racing faster than any pain medication could control. The years of misunderstandings and hurt that stretched between them might never be bridged, but seeing George walk toward danger, she let herself believe in the possibility of healing. But not now. Now, there was work to be done. There was always work to be done.

FORTY-TWO

Sam, Miami, 1978

THE SEPTEMBER MORNING WAS ALREADY THICK WITH humidity, making Sam regret the blazer she'd chosen for her first day, but some occasions demanded a certain formality. She pulled into her reserved parking spot at the Carlyle Institute, still not quite used to the feel of the new-to-her Volvo's leather seats against her legs. Six months ago, she'd been calculating if she could make rent on her teaching assistant's stipend. Now, she had an actual savings account.

She paused at the entrance to the gleaming six-story building, its windows tinted against the Miami sun. The security guard smiled, holding the door. "Morning, Ms. Fuchs."

Sam smiled back, proud to have reclaimed her last name.

Inside, the blast of air conditioning hit her like a wall of relief. The lobby smelled of fresh coffee from the café where researchers gathered between projects. The rubber soles of her penny loafer pumps padded across the terrazzo tiles as she made her way to the elevator, her new security badge clipped to her lapel: Sam Fuchs - Senior Research Fellow, Behavioral Analysis Division.

"Sam?"

She turned to find Ed Torres by the elevator bank, looking out of place in his university tweed. He wore the same boyish look of surprise she remembered from that Christmas party, right before he'd kissed her behind the coat rack. As if he hadn't expected to run into her at her new place of work any more than he'd expected to make a pass at her in the office. His wedding ring was conspicuously absent.

"Ed." She kept her tone neutral as she swiped her badge to activate the elevator. She was happy enough to see him, but she didn't want him getting ideas. "What brings you to Carlyle?"

"I was hoping to catch you for a quick chat." He shifted, uncomfortable in the corporate setting.

The elevator dinged, saving Sam from looking at her wristwatch. It was not quite eight thirty in the morning. She wondered how long he'd been waiting as she stepped inside, holding the door. After a moment's hesitation, Ed followed.

"Listen, I know this might seem out of nowhere, but Janet and I—we're not together anymore. I've been thinking a lot about that night, about us, and—"

This was not out of nowhere. She'd been aware of his feelings. "Ed." She turned to face him, her voice gentle but firm. "You know I value our friendship. That's why you were the first person I called after... when I got to Miami."

His face fell slightly, and her dread rose. The elevator doors opened. Sam stopped in the frame to keep them from closing. "You didn't end things... not because of...."

"Oh no, no. That was some time in the making. But I thought, after you turned to me like that... I don't know."

Beads of sweat dotted his forehead. This was why she was better off not dating. Not that she'd ever date a married man who got drunk and made out with women who weren't his spouse. That behavior didn't bode well. "Well, last spring? That was a different Sam. Now?"

The doors tried to close despite Sam's half-in, half-out stance so she ushered her former officemate into the hallway.

"A different Sam. Sure, sure." Ed pushed his glasses closer to his face. "Anyway, congratulations on your new job. I'll miss you at school."

A twinge of guilt flickered in her chest until she remembered—she alone had been forced to leave the university. Ed's name would be on Filmore's research paper even though they'd done the same work on it, except for the admin responsibilities she'd had. He also made thirty percent more for his share. But that was before Carlyle. It would take him a while to catch up to their current pay gap. Though he would. And when it came time to graduate, he'd have his pick of FBI jobs.

"I'm sure we'll be in touch, Ed."

She watched him retreat toward the stairs before she headed down the hallway to her corner office. The room was exactly as she remembered from her meeting with the director last week— floor-to-ceiling windows with a view of the bay, sleek modern furniture, and enough space for a small conference table beside her desk.

Six months ago, she'd sworn she'd never again make the mistake of filling her workspace with personal items. No family photos, no little tchotchkes, nothing that might have to be swept into a box at a moment's notice. It had been a promise born of humiliation, of trying to protect herself from future hurt.

Now, she opened her briefcase and removed a silver frame containing a photo of her and Abby standing in front of their freshly painted house. Next to that, the hand-tinted photograph of her mother from the St. Pete *Times'* official bio, fierce and proud. Her breath caught as another myth collapsed—her father hadn't chosen Sharon over her mother. He must have believed that the less she knew about her mother's involvement with the mafia, the safer she would be.

Was that what had kept her classmates away while she and Sharon sat shiva?

Tears threatened Sam's mascara. She blinked them back as she pulled from her bag the glass paperweight Thelma had given her. The mere act of placing it on her desk changed her mood entirely as the globe caught the morning light, sending rainbows across her desk. She was not the same woman who'd left the university, promising to keep herself small. That woman had been desperate to prove herself. No more. Sam Fuchs was the woman who'd single-handedly destroyed the burgeoning drug cartel operated by Frankie Giancarlo and Carlos Gonzalez. She was systematically building awareness of human trafficking through her research, ensuring the issue would never be so easily ignored.

Now that she'd purchased Jimmy's share of the house and painted it pink—just like Helen and Archie Young—she had nothing to prove to anyone except herself.

The knock at her door came just as she was arranging the last of her books on the shelf. She didn't need to turn around to know who it was. Agent Miller had a way of making his presence known without saying a word.

"Settling in?" His voice carried the same dry amusement she'd grown accustomed to over the past months.

Now, she did turn, taking in his characteristic rumpled suit and the briefcase she knew contained more than just papers. "I thought I had at least until lunch before you showed up."

"Nice view," he said, ignoring her comment as he crossed to the window. "Better than that basement office they had you in at the university."

"I earned it."

"Yes," he agreed, turning back to face her. "You did."

She waited, knowing what was coming.

Her work on the Giancarlo drug bust had bought her position at Carlyle and freedom to finish her dissertation running her own study—"Our Daughters in Danger: The Mafia's Human Trafficking Framework." But even with the help of her mother's article—revealed to Sharon during Francella's final moments—Sam's study would take years. All she had was the story and that unfinished letter. At least she had her own research assistants to lean on.

"This one's a bit delicate," Miller began simply. "I'm going to need you to come with me. Remains of a political prisoner have been identified near Frankie Giancarlo's cabin. What's left of it anyway."

"I knew it," she said but without any joy. "Wait, would this...."

"Put that cocksucker away for life? Yes." Agent Miller looked thrilled. "And it will point right to Castro's regime. Come on. I have files that can't be removed from the office."

Sam glanced at her mother's picture, the determined set of her shoulders. Then she picked up her coat and dabbed on some lipstick.

"Lead the way, Agent Miller."

FORTY-THREE

Thelma, Havana, 1979

THELMA'S ROOM AT THE HOTEL HABANA LIBRE overlooked the bay, moody and gray on this January afternoon. After that morning's mind-numbingly dull drive-by of Viñales Valley—still striking for its lush green mountains but ruined by the tour guide's hectoring on the virtues of Castro and the evils of imperialism—she and Cora had been deposited back at the hotel in time for happy hour. If Thelma was going to break away, it had to be now.

"Cora, darling?" She heard the pleading tone in her own voice, how she still longed for the girl's forgiveness.

"Oh my God, look at this." Cora stomped out of the bathroom bearing a graying bath mat like it was the Maltese Falcon. She had her mother's supercilious expressions down pat, especially the way her nostrils flared at the particularly egregious signs of decay. She also shared her mother's sharp tongue, as if determined to prove she belonged anywhere but where she was. "This thing still has the Hilton logo on it!"

Thelma lifted her cheeks, unsure how to respond. The reminder that the state had taken everything pained her, yet she couldn't deny the urge she felt to defend the city. Havana had changed, yes, but hadn't they all?

"Let's hope the cocktail hour is an improvement," Cora said before covering her mouth. "Sorry, Auntie TT. Will that bother you, going to the bar?"

The apology jolted Thelma from her comparison. Having been raised by nightclub owners in Cuba then swept into a makeshift family held together by pretense, Cora didn't have to prove she was an outsider. More to the point, Kathleen never would have apologized.

"Honey, I've been around plenty of cocktail hours, and nobody does them like, well, at least like they *used* to in Havana," Thelma said. "Let me brush my teeth, then you can go ahead and finish freshening up. I need to nip out and see if I can find some fresh pantyhose. I got a snag."

"Fine." Cora raised an eyebrow, another gesture that was pure Kathleen. "I'll wait here and admire the mildew. You go and call Georgie."

Leave it to Cora to come up with a better excuse. Her blond perm had almost grown out entirely, and her Giancarlo heritage was unmistakable, from the thicket of dark hair atop her nearly six-foot frame to her dubious convictions.

When Thelma reemerged, she joined Cora at the window. Below, Havana stretched out like a faded photograph, beautiful and melancholy. The city was cleaner now, as various reports had indicated, but there was a stillness to it that felt wrong. She remembered these streets pulsing with life, music spilling from every window.

"That one there is the Bird of Paradise." Thelma pointed at a flickering sign, a pink neon heartbeat in the skyline. She'd chosen that sign herself, back when the club was her whole world. "Remember?" She watched Cora's reflection in the glass, but there was no response. "We'll go tomorrow, when we have some free time in our itinerary."

Cora was silent. It had taken some convincing to get her to Cuba, but she'd recognized the danger her mother was in. She might not have greeting card love for the woman, but she didn't wish her dead. And whether she realized it or not, Cora was the ace up Thelma's sleeve.

Thelma threw out a feeler. "Your mother always did know how to keep things running."

The younger woman's face tightened. "She wasn't much for keeping family together though, was she?"

The words hung like a pall between them. Thelma reached into her pocket for her cigarettes but stopped. She didn't have any. She'd promised George she was quitting. Instead, she pulled out a pack of gum.

"We all made mistakes back then." Thelma unwrapped a stick. "Me more than most. If Helen and Archie hadn't stepped in...."

"And Doris before that," Cora added quietly. "Before...."

Before I left her alone on New Year's Eve, before the revolutionaries stormed the club, before the fatal shots were fired, the ones I never heard, but still, they echo through my nightmares.

The room filled with shadows, but neither woman moved to turn on the lights. Finally, Thelma squeezed Cora's hand. "I'll be back in a jif," she said. "Or if you decide to hit the reception, I'll find you there."

Thelma's feet carried her automatically through the winding alleys to the Bird of Paradise. The names of the streets were different, but they were in the same places. The club's exterior was like a well-preserved corpse—clean but lifeless. No signs of renovation or decline, just a well-swept stasis. The hot-pink neon bird that had once seemed the height of glamour now looked tired, its wings frozen mid flight.

Inside, the bar reeked of stale smoke and forgetting. The tables were empty. Only a handful of Russians occupied the stools, their harsh syllables echoing in the empty space. The red velvet curtains Doris had chosen so carefully were faded to the color of old blood. Even the stage looked smaller, diminished by time or perspective or both.

Thelma had been so busy calculating the impact on Cora, she'd failed to consider how this visit might shake her. The Bird was where Carlos Gonzalez had blackmailed them, where George had handed over annulment papers, and where finally, Helen and Doris had told her about their plans for Cora. The memory of that night was still fresh: Doris's gentle voice, Helen's practical arrangements, the realization that they'd created a family while she'd become the one thing she'd always vowed she would not—*just like her mother*. Unable to care for a child.

Realization dawned—rock bottom wasn't the end of her story. "We don't regret the past," Ruby had often reminded her over the years, before the cancer took her. "We see how it can benefit others."

Standing here now, at fifty-two, Thelma felt this wisdom in her bones. The Bird of Paradise was a building, not an indictment of her failures. A waypoint in a longer journey. She thought of the women she'd helped escape over the years, the lives she'd touched. The club had been a cocoon, not a coffin. Here in Havana, she'd not only learned to dream but to make those dreams a reality.

"Thelma Miles!" Kathleen's voice, unmistakable after all these years, carried across the empty club. But something was off. She sounded too loud, too bright. Her silver hair was swept up elegantly, her posture textbook perfect, but there was a warning in her eyes.

"You made it! And during business hours too!" she said,

voice still booming—Thelma now understood—for the benefit of unseen ears. "How fortunate we could accommodate your change in schedule! Come. Let me show you."

She ushered Thelma back toward her former office with the efficiency of someone practiced at managing uncomfortable situations. The moment the door closed, Kathleen pulled her into a fierce, if brief, hug.

"Have you lost your mind?" she hissed, stepping back. "The Bird is on every official tour roster. You can't walk in here without a minder!"

"We have free time in our schedule here in Havana," Thelma said.

"That's because they have eyes everywhere." She looked around her office. "No one will hear us in here. I sweep it regularly." She stopped her scan and quirked an eyebrow at Thelma. "You shouldn't be here."

"I had to take the risk," Thelma said. "Surely you sensed something these last few weeks. The network's been compromised but we can still get you out."

Kathleen's face went still. "We?"

"I'm here with Cora."

The color drained from Kathleen's face. "You brought my daughter to Cuba? Now?"

"She needed to see you. And you need to tell her—"

The door burst open. Cora stood in the frame, her face a storm of emotions. Behind her, the murmur of Russian voices wafted across the bar. Inside the faded office, the three women stared at each other, like Cuba itself, the past and present facing off as the clock ticked forward.

FORTY-FOUR

Kathleen, Havana, 1979

WHEN THE WOMAN APPEARED AT THE ENTRYWAY, Kathleen's first inclination was incredulity. Who was this enormous creature in the halter top and shiny pants who dared burst into her only private space? As quickly, Kathleen knew. This stunning creature was her daughter, all grown and looking nothing like any child of Lloyd Young. Between her height and her coloring, she'd never have passed as Lloyd's child. A surge of relief stormed through her, relief that she'd never had to field such questions. Shame followed immediately.

Kathleen wanted to go to her and draw her close, but her daughter's accusatory stare kept her rooted. Her instincts took over. "Shut the door."

Cora stepped inside, showing a bit of her aunt. No one would confuse that girl for a dancer. She was curious whether her daughter could sing or if Archie had inherited all the musical talent. Communications with Thelma had always been brief. Coded. When it came to the children, there was no room for lengthy updates, merely the basics: Archie and Helen, alive and well in St. Petersburg. Bertie, missing since his last divorce. Cora, running a music business at Sun City.

Closing her eyes, Kathleen chanted to herself. *I am aware of my heart and my mistakes, and I love them all. Forgiven. Forgiven. Forgiven. Om shanti.* Like her physical asana practice, the mantra was something her guru had given her that she'd decided to keep.

"What's the matter with her?"

Kathleen's eyes popped open. Cora was glaring at Thelma, pointing a thumb in her mother's direction.

"I wasn't expecting...." Kathleen started.

"Me neither," Cora cut in. She remained standing while Thelma sank into one of the visitor chairs.

"Darling." Kathleen held out her arms as Cora crossed hers.

"Did you think you two were the only ones capable of tailing someone?" Cora asked.

"I understand." Kathleen indicated the sofa. "But we don't have much time. No one out there is going to think you're here on business dressed like that." Another twinge of guilt flared for the criticism. This was what she'd been avoiding all these years, these constant reminders that she was unfit to parent this child. Forgiven, she thought, the short version of her mantra.

She took a seat, patting the cushion beside her, but Cora stayed on her feet. The pain of this rejection was tempered by her fear that someone could rush the door at any moment.

"So?" Cora looked back at Thelma. "Why did you come here without me?"

"Sweetie, honey," Thelma said, "you saw those letters. Your mother is being watched."

"As are you, I'm sure," Kathleen added. "If Cora was able to follow you so easily then—"

"Let's cut the crap here," Cora said. "Kathleen, when that nutjob Sam Fuchs blew up the Giancarlo's cabin, it compromised your network. Frankie Giancarlo is in jail, as I'm sure you are aware."

Kathleen was not aware that Cora's uncle was in jail, nor was she prepared for her daughter to call her by her given name.

"Meanwhile, Castro is losing his shit again," Cora continued. "We need to get you back to the States."

Her tone reminded Kathleen of her eldest son but with one critical difference—Bertie would not have seen past his anger to help anyone but himself.

"Are you listening?" Cora asked.

The question was valid, Kathleen knew. She'd been staring, glassy-eyed and unfocused, for much of the girl's tirade. Her concern for their safety hadn't lessened, but the decades of grief and shame overtook such considerations. Her daughter wanted her to return home?

"Of course I'm listening, darling." Kathleen smiled, not her business mask but the one of motherly reassurance she'd worn with her sons when they'd gone into detail about goings-on at school. "There's just so much to take in."

As in those days, the part of her that didn't hear what was being said was lost in worry. Albeit a very different set of concerns. In Havana, her presence served a purpose beyond atonement—she had positively changed people's lives. She didn't have to but did, simply because it was the right thing to do. What good could she do by going back to the States? Providing intel on her patrons was easy.

"The cocktail hour at Habana Libre starts in forty minutes," Thelma said quietly. "We're expected."

If she returned, the possibilities were not really so mysterious. She could repair the damage she'd done. Unless she couldn't.

Cora snorted. "Wouldn't want to miss a government-sanctioned happy hour lecture on Castro's five-year plan. Scintillating."

"The musicians are quite good actually," Kathleen found herself saying. "I hired most of them myself."

"Oh, yawn. Give me Van Halen or Blondie. This big band shit is so tired."

She paused, studying her daughter's face. "You're in the music business now, aren't you?"

Something flickered in Cora's expression—surprise, perhaps —that Kathleen knew even this much about her life. "Was. Sun City's finished. The FBI's been sniffing around *all* the Giancarlo operations." She shrugged, a gesture so familiar it made Kathleen's chest ache.

But now was not the time for sentimentality. "Well, the party isn't the point. You must make an appearance, or it will be reported."

"She's right, sweetie. That's how this whole thing works," Thelma said. "We're here because George was able to pull some strings. We have to stay on the right side of this tour."

And I have to stay on the right side of you two to get you out of my office, Kathleen thought. Staying in Havana at least allowed for the possibility of helping more women escape. She'd been away from home for far too long. There was nothing for her in the States but more anguish.

"Where and when is the meet?" Kathleen asked. Might as well move this along.

"We've arranged with—"

A fist pounded at the door. "*Otkryt'*!"

All three turned to the rattling door handle. If her people sent their own, that could only mean one thing. They'd been made. No surprise, really. Cora had followed Thelma easily, and her daughter didn't exactly fade into the background. She hoped they hadn't found her diaries.

The angry barrage of consonants that ensued were threats

to break the door down. The time for decisions had passed. "This way," Kathleen whispered. "Now."

After shoving the window open, Kathleen urged the girls through, managing to shut it behind her as she heard wood splitting. "Heels," she called out.

They slid off their shoes and hit the alley running, Kathleen taking the lead. "We need to split up," she said over her shoulder. "Three different taxis."

"We're not separating," Cora said, but Thelma cut her off.

"She's right. Less conspicuous." Thelma's voice was steady despite their pace. Kathleen realized she hadn't seen her light a cigarette.

"Where do we meet?" Thelma asked.

A bullet sparked off the wall beside them. Someone must have a clear shot from the office window, but more shots would draw too much attention. They had mere minutes before the streets filled with police.

Kathleen steered them down another alley. "Mariel Port. One hour from now. Your driver will know how to get there. If you're followed, keep moving, and try again in an hour. But after that, we have to leave."

Thelma nodded, heading off in another direction. As she and Cora headed down another back alley, Kathleen spotted a taxi. She grabbed Cora's arm. "You take this. Back streets only, no Malecón."

"But—"

"No." She squeezed her daughter's arm, recognizing that this was the first contact they'd had since 1947. For a moment, she saw innocence in her daughter's face, same as the baby she'd left behind, swaddled and sleeping. "We were just shot at. Do you need more convincing?"

With a stomp of her foot, Cora shook her head. "That's not what I mean. What I mean is... are you really coming?"

Kathleen dropped her arm to face her. "Of course, darling." Her smile was bright.

"Cut the crap, Mom."

Kathleen's heart melted. *Mom.* Maybe they could—

"I know a bullshitter," Cora said, finishing her sentence.

From the corner of her eye, Kathleen saw the cab drive on. *Dammit.* Fuel shortages meant less traffic on the roads but also fewer cabs.

"I get it. You don't want to face what you've done," Cora continued. "But you need to get over that. Especially now. Auntie TT told me about what you've been doing. I wish I felt better about it, but I'm pissed you spent your life helping everyone *but* me."

Men shouted in the streets. Fragments of Russian and Spanish—descriptions being passed, directions given. Coming closer. Kathleen clasped her daughter's shoulders, looked her in the eye, and made up her mind on the spot. "I will be there. I promise. I won't let you down this time."

Without waiting for a reply, she grabbed Cora's hand and pulled her toward the old city walls. "Take this one," Kathleen said. "Don't argue. Go. And here." She removed the scarf she kept at her neck, her last vanity. "Cover that hair. It's easily spotted."

Opening the door, she practically pushed Cora inside. Before Kathleen could reach into her bosom for the pesos she always kept there, her daughter leaned forward and, speaking rapid Spanish to the driver, pressed forward more than enough to bribe him. The cab pulled away.

Kathleen took a moment to admire her daughter's prowess before checking her watch. Fifty-three minutes to go.

Heading deeper into the old city's maze, Kathleen reckoned she had ten minutes to pick up scarves and blouses for them all before she needed to be in her own cab. By then, every cabbie in the city would have heard the alert, but she had enough pesos to make any driver brave. Besides, an old woman—which she had to remind herself she was—rarely attracted notice. It was how she'd gotten away with brazenly collecting intelligence all these years.

The night sky was settling over Havana when at last she slid into her taxi. The first stars appeared over the harbor, clearer now than eighteen years ago because there were fewer working lights to compete. This had long been Kathleen's favorite hour, when the darkness softened the peeling paint and crumbling cornices. She watched the familiar streets blur past, knowing she'd never see them again.

Her hands were shaking. Not from the running or the gunshots. For nearly thirty years, she'd convinced herself that staying away from Cora was the right choice. That her work made up for leaving because it mattered more than any single person. She knew better. Men might do the same kind of thing every day, but that didn't make it right.

Disguises in hand, she checked her watch again. Thirty-five minutes remained to make a forty-minute drive. "*Rápido*," she told the driver, reaching into the front seat with a stack of pesos. "*Por favor.*"

She'd thought she was prepared to stay. She'd thought a lot of things. But she hadn't been prepared for the way Cora looked at her. Not with hatred or love or forgiveness. Only questions. Questions she'd have to answer, if they all made it to the seaport alive.

FORTY-FIVE

Thelma, Havana, 1979

THE PHONE BOOTH REEKED OF DIESEL AND DESPERATION. Thelma kept her voice low while she hunched over the receiver, as if her body could shield her words from the evening breeze carrying them across Havana Harbor.

"Emilio, it has to be tonight," she insisted, watching fishing boats bob in the harbor. "Tell Miller I don't care what it costs. Have someone waiting at the usual drop, three miles out from Key Biscayne."

The connection crackled. Emilio's voice came through in fragments. "... risky... Coast Guard... need more time...."

"We don't have more time." Thelma's knuckles whitened around the receiver. "We need to move out tonight." She didn't add the thought weighing equally heavy—*I still have to find a boat to get us there.*

A long pause, then: "Midnight. Signal with three short flashes, two long."

"Thank you," she said as she exhaled, but the line had already gone dead.

Thelma hurried back to where Cora waited behind an abandoned shipping container, the blond ends of her hair tucked under a scarf that did little to disguise her. The girl leaned against the peeling wood, arms crossed, the picture of impatience. So like her mother.

"Well?" Cora's foot tapped an anxious rhythm on the wooden planks.

"There's a boat waiting offshore, but we need to get out of Cuban waters first," Thelma said, scanning the docks. The evening fishing fleet was returning, small vessels puttering into their berths like weary old men into familiar chairs. "We need to find a captain willing to take us."

"For the right price, they're all willing," Cora snapped.

"Not necessarily," Thelma said, watching a border guard boat cut through the harbor. "Castro's men are looking for defectors. One wrong move, and we'll disappear into Villa Marista."

"Where they'll feed us grapes?" Cora's face puckered. "What's the big rush?"

"Villa Marista is the Cuban state prison," Thelma whispered, looking over Cora's shoulder. "From the response to our meet with your mother, I'd say they've connected more than a few dots. Castro does not take kindly to agents of imperialism."

"Where *is* Kathleen?" Cora's voice hardened. "She promised she'd meet us here."

Thelma's stomach twisted. "She'll come. Your mother always has a plan."

"Like her plan to abandon me for thirty years?"

The bitterness in Cora's voice made Thelma wince; at least she was speaking quietly. "That's not fair."

"None of this is fair!" Cora hissed, gesturing to the darkening harbor. "I'm still indebted to Frankie because my uncle Bertie is an idiot. I'm getting shot at by Russians for something I didn't do, and now, my mother vanishes—*again*—the moment things get difficult."

Thelma grabbed Cora's belt loop, putting her fingers to her lips as she pulled her closer while a security guard marched past. "Look at me," she said, waiting until Cora's furious eyes met hers. "I understand your anger. But right now, I need you to focus on getting out of here alive."

"We could shoot our way out," Cora muttered. "I know you have that gun."

"And then what?" Thelma asked, her voice sharp with barely controlled concern. "We murder some poor fisherman who's just trying to feed his family? Some young soldier who probably believes he's defending his homeland? Would that make you feel better about your mother?"

"Don't psychoanalyze me," Cora snapped, but there was a flicker of something vulnerable beneath her anger.

Thelma softened her tone. "Listen to me. I watched Doris die on that dance floor because someone thought violence was the answer. I've seen what happens when people decide other lives don't matter." She squeezed Cora's hand. "We're getting out of here but not by becoming the monsters we're running from."

Something in Cora's expression shifted. "Fine. What's the plan?"

Thelma peered around the cargo box. The last of the fishing fleet was limping in, nets empty, decks hosed down. One boat caught her attention, smaller than the rest, its blue paint fading, a single figure at the helm.

"That one," she said, nodding toward it. "The captain's alone. Probably independent, not part of the cooperative."

"How do you know?"

"Look at his boat. No state insignia. No crew. The cooperatives always have crews."

They watched as the fisherman tied up his boat, movements practiced but weary. He looked to be in his sixties, weathered as driftwood, his clothing patched, but his boat was clean.

"Let me do the talking," Thelma instructed, reaching into her bra to extract a wad of American dollars. "Stay close, but keep watch."

They approached as the man was securing his boat for the night.

"*Buenas noches, Capitán,*" Thelma called softly. "Poor catch today?"

The man turned, suspicion etched in the lines around his eyes. "The sea gives what she gives," he replied cautiously.

Thelma moved closer, keeping her voice conversational. "I knew a fisherman once who said the best fishing is at night, away from prying eyes."

The man stilled, his gaze flicking between Thelma and Cora then to the harbor. "What business brings you to these docks, *señoras?*"

"We need to bless the sea," Thelma said, a known code that had served her network for years. "For a safe journey."

Recognition flickered in the man's face. He looked to the sky, assessing the darkness. "The weather turns bad tonight. Not safe."

"We understand the risks," Thelma said, pressing the money into his calloused palm. "And we can make it worth the trouble."

The fisherman glanced at the cash before quickly tucking it into his shirt. He kept his expression neutral as a patrol boat drifted past. It didn't seem as if they'd raised any alarm, but they couldn't be too careful. "I have engine repairs," the captain said. "One hour. Then I must test the repairs in open water."

Thelma nodded, understanding his message. "We'll wait on the north end. For the repairs to be completed."

The man gave a single, almost-imperceptible nod then turned back to his work.

As they walked away, Cora whispered, "What about my mother?"

Thelma kept her pace steady, though her heart raced. "We'll wait as long as we can," she promised, scanning the docks for any sign of Kathleen. "But if she doesn't come...."

"We leave without her," Cora finished, her voice flat.

An hour crawled by as they huddled among cargo boxes stacked near the dock, Thelma repeatedly glancing at her watch. Every approaching footstep, every creak of the pilings sent Thelma's pulse racing as she pictured Kathleen's silver hair and confident stride emerging. But that hope grew thinner with the waning moonlight.

Finally, they spotted the small fishing boat easing toward their position, running dark. The captain gestured. It was now or never.

"We can't wait any longer," Thelma whispered, her tone leaving no room for delay.

Cora's eyes glistened in the dim light, but her voice was steady. "I know."

They slipped onto the dock, moving silently toward the idling boat. The captain extended a hand to help them aboard, his expression grim as he scanned the harbor behind them.

"Take off your shoes, and mind the nets," he said, already turning toward the helm. "Quickly."

As Thelma helped Cora onto the gently rocking deck, a movement on the dock caught her eye—a figure emerging from the customs house, moving with purpose toward them. Thelma's heart lurched.

A figure approached, stepping into the pool of weak light cast by the dock lamp. But it was not Kathleen, not a woman at all. Wondering if there was cause for concern she looked toward the captain, but he showed no sign of concern. Thelma willed herself to slow her breath, calm her heart.

They rode on in silence, sitting on the gunwale toward the rear of the boat. They'd scarcely been on board for ten minutes when the engine slowed. From where Thelma sat, the waters were dark. "What's wrong?" she called.

"One more passenger," the captain said.

"What the—" Cora began.

Thelma shut her down with a look. "Who is joining us, señor?"

The captain's leathery face revealed nothing. "I know nothing. I say nothing."

Considering she didn't know the captain's name and he hadn't asked for hers, Thelma wasn't about to argue with that policy. She craned her neck but stayed put as a motorboat drew up alongside the other end of their boat, bumping the hull moments before Carlos Gonzalez appeared.

Despite his limp—a permanent reminder of the workover he'd gotten courtesy of Sal Giancarlo's men—he moved with surprising agility, his expensive shoes finding purchase on the deck. He was alone, which could only mean one thing.

"Leaving without a goodbye?" Carlos asked as he came into focus, his forehead higher than when she'd first met him, though he still sported the slim mustache that had been the fashion before his imprisonment.

Cora leaned toward her aunt. "You know that guy, Auntie TT?"

Thelma's heart fell into her lap, so hard she thought sure everyone on board would've heard it. The girl had given herself away so easily. She stood, ready to protect her niece at all costs.

"*Gloria a Dios!*" Carlos cried, raising both hands to the sky. "Two in one."

Cora heaved forward, but Thelma pushed her back in her

seat. "Not so fast, Carlos. Think about what you're doing. You'll bring a whole force down on your head." Even as she said the words, they rang hollow.

Carlos laughed. "Boats go missing all the time. And we all know how helpful your government friends are when—"

She felt her purse jerk away from her shoulder as Cora yanked it open and withdrew her .38 special, sending one of Thelma's shoes clattering overboard. "No," she cried, as much from the wrongness of it as the pain. Thelma carried her purse on the side that had taken the bullet.

The boat seesawed, causing Cora to lose her balance. Carlos reached for his own gun. Tracking his revolver's trajectory to where her niece scrambled at her feet, Thelma caught a flash of yellow in the corner of her eye—the brake release. She glanced again at Carlos, his pricey shoe tucked neatly inside a coil of rope. With a swift kick, she sent Cora away from the netting as she tripped the lever.

Carlos's eyes widened as the rope at his leg unspooled, tightening around his calf as he tried to hoist himself in the opposite direction. But it was too late. The net was dragging him under the railing. He reached for the rusted steel bar. Somehow, his pistol was still in his other hand. From half overboard, he took aim. Thelma looked into her purse, grabbing her last weapon—her shoe. With no hesitation, she stomped to the rear deck and whacked his hand, wielding her heel like a hammer. He released his grip and disappeared into the black swirl as the captain made his way to the back of the boat.

He said nothing as he watched his net finish playing out. Finally he announced, "We trawl. You never know what you will catch." Then he turned and walked back toward the wheel, and the boat resumed on its way.

By now, Cora was on her feet. "Holy *frijole*," she said, smiling broadly. "That's what I call taking care of business."

But Thelma wasn't smiling. She grabbed her old .38 from Cora's hand, the one Artemis had given her all those years ago in her father's office, and launched it into the water. "Not one word of this to anyone. Ever. Understood?"

"But—"

"Cora, this is not a discussion. Nothing good can come from *that* business."

FORTY-SIX

Sam, St. Petersburg, 1979

THE DON CESAR'S TERRACE HELD THE LAST BREATH OF sunset as the couple said their I dos. The timing was perfect as they turned and waved at the crowd, framed by a watercolor wash of coral and gold over the sparkling Gulf of Mexico. Yet somehow, amidst all the splendor, the bride managed to be the only thing you wanted to watch.

Sam melted into the crowd, watching servers in crisp white jackets weave through the guests bearing trays of Harvey Wallbangers and whiskey sours, the cut crystal glasses catching the fading light. Such a sharp contrast to her courthouse ceremony, an event followed by a potluck at her friend Ginny's.

Reflexively, she did a quick check. *Nope.* That feeling was not about missing Jimmy but a simple reflection on her life experience. Her therapist would have been proud; they'd done a whole session preparing for this event. Sam was surprised she'd been invited. "Lillian insisted," Thelma had reassured her. "She was fond of your mother, and she just *had* to meet the woman who brought George and me back together." The ceremony had ended, and Sam gravitated toward where she stood talking with Peggy and Helen.

"That dress!" Peggy gestured with her champagne flute toward the beach. "And that train. Maeve would have turned that thing into a whole collection for Florida Girls. Remember how she could squeeze three costumes out of a bedsheet during the war?"

"Who's Maeve?"

"Clothing designer out of New York. Kathleen Young's personal dressmaker. She hired her to develop the Emporium's clothing line," Thelma said. "She was wonderful."

"Until they had a falling out," Peggy said. "That didn't help the business."

Helen tsked. "That was years before the store closed."

Sam hadn't meant to bring up a sore subject. "I wonder who designed Lillian's dress," she said.

"Christian Dior," Helen said.

"Skylar looks as good as when we first met him back in Vegas," Peggy said.

Sam looked toward the water, but the groom was long gone. She'd seen old photographs of him, but he was more handsome in person. She wondered how old he was. How old Lillian was. What their ages said about her own chances for finding love again. Does that count as looking? she wondered. She hoped not. "When did you meet him? Phil," she asked.

The women exchanged glances, and she knew. Had to be another story.

"Back in '45, was it?" Helen looked to Thelma and Peggy for confirmation, and they nodded. "But I didn't meet him then. I was already in Cuba. By the time I saw Lillian again, they were already heading to divorce court."

"Oh come on, Helen. First of all, that's not true. She stayed with us when we first found George. They didn't divorce 'til he was coming home." Thelma took a sip of her club soda. "And you can't deny... that ceremony was so moving. Did you see their faces when they said their vows?"

"Mmm. Let's hope he keeps them this time," Helen said.

"Geez, Helen, what's with you?" Peggy asked.

Sam wondered too. As she recalled the headlines—the co-stars, the dancers, the endless parade of temptation—both had done their fair share of damage over the years.

"Did you break up with—" Thelma asked.

"I don't want to talk about it." Helen shook her empty glass. "Anyone else need a refresher?"

"People change," Thelma said, lifting her glass.

Jimmy sure did. Dammit. That was definitely giving her ex headspace. *These are just thoughts. I can explore them at an appropriate—*

"Mother!" Abby materialized beside Sam, her face flushed with excitement, looking impossibly grown-up in the Laura Ashley dress she'd insisted on. "I can't believe you actually know Lillian Montgomery. Isn't she like way younger than you?"

The women's laughter rippled across the terrace. Before Sam could protest, the opening notes of Chic's "Dance, Dance, Dance" pulsed through the evening air, and Abby was gone.

"What happened to my baby?" Sam sighed, watching her fourteen-year-old daughter spin to the music. The caterers had removed the guest seating, turning the whole patio into a dance floor.

"Speaking of." Thelma's voice dropped slightly. "Has anyone seen Cora?"

The question hung like an overripe fruit. Sam had heard all about their night in Havana—finding Kathleen, the Russians, the hours of waiting that led nowhere. Until Thelma, desperate to get Cora out safely, found a fisherman to bribe. Cora had not taken her mother's second disappearance well.

"I don't get why she's mad at her," Peggy said. "She could be dead."

Again, the glances. Sam had assumed Kathleen Young was dead, that this would be the best case scenario for her. Unless... "You don't think—" Sam began as George Wright appeared.

"Time for family photos," he announced, extending his elbow to Thelma.

"Sweetheart, we talked about this," Thelma protested.

"Aw, c'mon," Peggy said. "Georgie wants to show you off."

"If you're not going to be in those pictures, I will." Helen moved toward George's arm.

"Okay, okay," Thelma said, her face softening as Helen and Peggy made shooing motions.

Sam watched them go, thinking how George had the air of a man who couldn't believe his good fortune. He wasn't wrong.

A burst of flashbulbs on the beach sent the security team scrambling. Sam watched the paparazzi jostling for position, remembering something her father had told her—"Your mother always said, the same people who complain about the press are the ones who devour every last Hollywood scandal with their morning coffee. All the while claiming moral superiority." She sent up a silent thanks to her mother and father both for what they'd given her, for the lessons they'd taught her, even for what they'd left unsaid.

The reception moved indoors for the dinner service. Sam and Abby found themselves at a table draped in heavy damask, seated with some third cousins. Thelma and George were positioned at the long table with the family at the front of the room, but she'd lost track of Helen and Peggy.

"Ladies and gentlemen"—the DJ's voice boomed through the ballroom—"please welcome Mr. and Mrs. Phil Skylar!"

"That's Phil Skylar and Lillian Montgomery, darling!" Lillian's famous contralto carried over the applause. "The only thing I needed to change was my outfit." She presented herself with a flourish, now wearing something sleek and very modern —maybe a Halston? Sam couldn't tell one designer from the next, but this was a stunner, catching the light like liquid gold.

Over dinner, she made polite noises about the meal—they'd spared no expense on the carved prime rib, potatoes Romanoff, and asparagus drizzled in hollandaise—but the rich food wasn't to her taste. The time came at last for the couple's first dance. Strains of Debbie Boone's "You Light Up My Life" filled the room as Lillian and Phil swayed together on the dance floor. The melancholy came on strong.

There had been no dancing at her post-wedding potluck, just grocery store cake on paper plates and good old-fashioned getting drunk. She breathed in deep, reminding herself that she was responsible for her own happiness, that healing had to come before love. The knowledge sat in her chest like a stone.

The DJ dropped Rod Stewart's "Da Ya Think I'm Sexy," and the mood shifted. Couples filled the dance floor. When Abby leapt up to join them, Sam winced but stayed firmly planted. She tried keeping an eye out but lost her daughter almost immediately in the swirl of bodies. By the time "Boogie Oogie Oogie" came on, Sam was tapping her feet, unable to resist the joy of music.

"May I have this dance?"

The voice was deep, warm. Sam looked into eyes the color of coffee, set in a face alive with anticipation. Her heart did something complicated in her chest. "Have we met? I don't—"

But somehow she was already moving, standing up to join him, her body betraying her mind's careful defenses. They danced through A Taste of Honey. Then the Bee Gees. And KC and the Sunshine Band. Sam kept meaning to step away, heed her resolution about healing, but then he'd smile, and she'd forget why that mattered. Surely, if you had to be fully whole and healed for romance, very few couples would exist. Love itself was a balm, no?

"Ladies, gather 'round!" Lillian's voice cut through the Cars. "Time to throw the bouquet!"

The DJ cut the music to a pulse as the women were pushed to the front. Sam did not want to be in this queue, but it was too late. White orchids arced through the air, spinning in slow motion under crystal chandeliers. Muscle memory took over, and she found herself reaching up as a movement across the room caught her eye. She turned to face it, the bouquet forgotten.

The flowers landed in Abby's twitching hands. But her daughter, sensing something in the suddenly charged atmosphere, immediately passed them to the person beside her —Cora, whose face held the kind of fury that could fuel a thousand wars. *Where had she come from?*

The DJ started playing "Le Freak," once more luring dancers to the floor. But not Sam. Her eyes followed Cora's to a flash of satin. A split second later, she saw Thelma grab hold of Kathleen, urging her toward an exit. She lost them in the sea of moving bodies. Her dance partner, too, was nowhere in sight. But, for perhaps the first time in her life, she felt no anxiety around his absence. She and Lucas, as he'd introduced himself, would reconnect.

FORTY-SEVEN

Thelma, St. Petersburg, 1979

JOINING THE WRIGHT FAMILY CONSTELLATION WAS AS awkward as Thelma feared it would be. Lillian's parents had passed, but Homer Wright—George's father and sworn enemy of Thelma's father—was there as the family patriarch. She tried standing at the edge, but George pulled her toward the center as the photographer's flash popped. She was grateful her dress was the color of autumn leaves. Otherwise, she would have visible stains at her armpits.

Throughout the ordeal, George's hand at her waist felt both anchor and question. Then he was called away for bridal party pictures. Thelma was considering her escape options when a voice called out.

"Miss Miles."

Homer Wright. His voice carried the patina of age, stretching thin despite his lingering authority. He beckoned her aside with one liver-spotted hand. "A moment?"

The old man had grown fragile, she noticed, as if time had finally caught up with his outsized presence. His tuxedo, impeccably cut, nonetheless hung loose at the shoulders. The commanding stance that had once filled boardrooms and beaten back strikers had softened into something more fragile.

"I've been meaning to tell you," he said, his eyes cloudy with cataracts and something that might have been regret. "When I heard about Sal passing on the courthouse steps... well, it wasn't right, how things ended."

The words hit her like summer lightning—unexpected, illuminating, gone before she could be sure they'd happened. She studied her former father-in-law's face, searching for calculation. He was nothing if not a strategist and still whip sharp. But she found only honest befuddlement, a genuine desire to make peace before his own time ran out. This was, she understood, Homer's version of an apology. His biggest grudge with her had only ever been over whose daughter she was. *The fool.*

Ruby's voice sounded in her head: "We don't punish people with the truth, honey. When we use the truth as a weapon, it becomes a bomb rather than a lantern, destroying rather than illuminating." At nearly ninety, Homer Wright might not have earned any right to peace, but Thelma had.

"Thank you," she said simply, letting the weight of unspoken years settle between them like dust. It was the perfect exit cue.

The DJ's voice cut through her contemplation as she strode toward the reception. "Ladies and gentlemen, Mr. and Mrs. Phil Skylar!"

"That's Phil Skylar and Lillian Montgomery, darling!" Lillian's correction sparked laughter that rippled across the room like wind through palm leaves.

"May I have this dance?" George appeared at her elbow, his senator's polish barely concealing the earnest boy she'd met thirty-some years back in Wright Pharmacy, the drugstore Lillian's parents had owned.

Her gaze fell to his extended arm, the offer that carried decades of waiting. Wanting.

Under strings of fairy lights, they moved in time to Stevie Wonder's "My Cherie Amour." George's cologne mixed with the Cuban cigars that had been offered at the men's place settings, a scent that had also followed her through every memory of these last decades.

"You're not going to believe this, my love."

They stopped dancing. Ric Ocasek had begun singing "Just What I Needed" as Thelma looked into George's eyes. Anything she had to say about Homer Wright's almost apology vanished in a surge of adoration. How had she lived without him all these years? His love. His counsel. Yes, even his reproofs. Maybe especially those.

"Marry me," he murmured. "You know I'm crazy about you. And I know you're crazy about me."

How many years had she longed for George to come back? To ask this very question? Decades, really. But... what if it was marriage that had ruined them? "Love, I want to spend the rest of my life with you. But...."

George pulled something from his pocket. "Before you finish that thought, here." He dangled a gold chain before her, revealing a brilliant blue gem that caught the sunset. His grandmother's sapphire necklace. He'd kept it all these years.

WITH THE UTMOST TENDERNESS, HE TURNED HER ON THE dance floor to fasten the clasp behind her neck. These were not the same urgent hands that she'd finally brought into her bed these past few nights since she'd been home from Havana, but she knew them well. Of course she would marry him.

Before she could answer, movement flickered in her peripheral vision. Across the dance floor stood Kathleen Young, elegant in vintage Balmain, her silver hair piled in a crown atop her head. Before Thelma could process the full implication that Kathleen was not only alive but back in the States, she caught sight of Cora's face, a storm warning in a sea of chartreuse taffeta.

Beside her, a pile of white orchid petals and ribbon littered the dance floor. She must've ended up with the bouquet, thought Thelma, momentarily amused that could have happened. She knew for a fact the girl never wanted to wed.

The young woman standing beside Cora, who couldn't have been a day over sixteen, dropped to her knees to gather up the bride's flowers, bringing Thelma back to reality.

"Excuse me," Thelma said to George, already moving away. Years of managing volatile situations at the Bird had taught her to read the signs of impending chaos, but any fool could've spotted this trouble. She reached Kathleen moments before Cora and wrapped her arm around her old friend's waist with practiced casualness.

"The powder room here is divine," she said loudly enough to be heard over Sister Sledge. "You'll want to see it."

"I can't believe she wore them," Kathleen growled, responding to some outrage Thelma could not begin to fathom.

At least she didn't put up a fight as Thelma hustled her from the ballroom. "Who? Wore what?" Thelma asked. "What are you talking about?"

Kathleen's reflection met Thelma's in the mirror, carrying echoes of another night, another confrontation. "Lillian whatever her name is now. She's wearing my emeralds."

FORTY-EIGHT

Kathleen, St. Petersburg, 1979

KATHLEEN'S SENSES WENT INTO OVERDRIVE AS THELMA steered her into the Don CeSar's ladies' lounge. But her attempt to ground herself in her reflection failed, overcome as she was by the ostentatious luxury of the gilt fixtures, pink marble, and ornate chandelier. This entire journey had begun with Lloyd's hare-brained Million Dollar Party, and she suddenly recalled that she'd hoped to host the event at this very hotel. But the Don's rooms had been commissioned for the war, and they'd settled for the Vinoy.

That was the night Cora's father bid on Thelma.

Her lipstick, she noticed, had seeped into the crevices above her lip. Grabbing a service towel, she wiped the color from her face then faced Thelma. Her eyes, Kathleen noted, were still that extraordinary amber color but less pronounced within their nest of wrinkles. They were also full of questions. "I'm sorry. I owe you an apology."

Thelma arched a single eyebrow upward, and Kathleen burst out laughing.

"No, that wasn't it," she said.

Their moment was cut short as the door burst open, and in

stormed Cora, squeezing past Thelma to get in her mother's face. "Your emeralds? You disappear for six months. We think you're dead. And you show up here worried about your *jewels*? You really are a monster."

She turned slowly from the mirror to face her daughter directly. Her daughter had inherited Matteo's height and coloring but also the Young family's proud bearing, despite her attempt to hide it under that hideous lime-green dress and rebellious slouch. For a fleeting moment, Kathleen felt as if she was looking at herself through her own mother's eyes.

Sorrow coiled around her heart. What must Cora think of her? Had Thelma counseled her over the years, advised her to expect the worst? Kathleen couldn't blame her if she had. Admittedly, she'd thrown Thelma to the wolves all those years ago. But that was ancient history, and she herself had been the one to become embroiled with Matteo Giancarlo.

"As I was just saying, I owe Thelma an apology."

"Thelma?" Cora spat. "Jesus Christ."

Thelma leaned against the wall, eyes darting between mother and daughter, clearly uncertain whether to intervene. Kathleen touched her shoulder. "All those years ago, I should have given you your freedom. I'm sorry I didn't."

"My what?" Now it was Thelma's turn to look incredulous. "You mean you should have cut me from the Florida Girls team?"

"What about me?" Cora cut in. "Who cares about the rearview anyway? It's not like that can change. Right here, right now, you show up after months—"

"Young lady," Kathleen said, smoothing her hair in the mirror, "you might believe that thirty-two years of life entitles you to an opinion, but it's better to remain silent and be thought a fool than to speak and to remove all doubt."

Her daughter's face puckered as if she'd sucked a lemon

wedge. Kathleen recalled the girls in Havana cooing over her and suspected the worst had happened—Cora had been terrifically spoiled. Perhaps that explained why she was single. Kathleen couldn't imagine any other reason.

"You asked why I was worried about my emeralds." Kathleen returned to her reflection. "The jewels brought it all back."

Cora turned to leave, but Thelma grabbed her wrist. "You have every right to be angry, but trust me. If you walk away now, you'll regret it. I'd give anything to talk to my mother again. You may not get the chance again."

She looked at her mother, frowning at Thelma as she pulled her arm back. "Fine. But—"

"Cora, darling, you deserved a mother who could be there for you. After Lloyd died, I couldn't." She smoothed her hair even as she cursed herself for going all wistful. It had become a regular occurrence since her seventieth, and she could do without it. "In every way, I did to you both what was done to me, and I didn't see it until I saw Lillian in my coming-out set."

Thelma and Cora exchanged a look, each shrugging slightly.

"That geometric pendant Lillian was wearing? The one that looks like it walked straight out of a Gatsby party? I wore that to my own debut, back when art deco was called contemporary."

"Okay," said Cora.

Had no one taught her the virtues of patience? Young Thelma had displayed a lack of it. Pity. Cora was getting a little long in the tooth for it. "The necklace, earrings, wide-strap bracelet. Those were my grandmother's. Designed to prop up a young girl's marriage prospects."

The powder room door opened again, and a smart-looking woman joined them. She looked from Cora to Thelma, clearly sensing the tension.

"This is Sam Fuchs," Thelma said. "Imogene Fuchs's daughter. Sam, this is Kathleen Young."

Sam's eyes widened slightly. Kathleen couldn't help but see, between the woman's carefully coiffed hair and perfect manicure, she bore little resemblance to the reporter she'd known. Then she spoke.

"So you're Kathleen Young," Sam said, her voice a near replica of her mother's.

There it was, Kathleen thought. That same intensity. "I take it you're upset with me too?" Kathleen asked.

Sam's mouth dropped, as if she was, indeed, about to share a grievance. But something in her eyes shifted, an understanding passing between them.

This moment, Kathleen would later realize, was when she truly accepted what she'd done. The anger directed at her was justified. She had deceived and manipulated and worse. But she'd made her choices, some terrible and some merely necessary. Dwelling in remorse wouldn't undo the deeds. Life demanded she move forward even if the stains of her past were still visible to those who knew where to look. Her redemption wasn't in forgiveness, after all, but acceptance. Of what she'd done and who she'd become.

"If you're not going to speak," Kathleen said to Sam, "then I'll finish my story."

Sam shrugged, plopping into a chair in the corner. "Sure."

"Lillian's mother had always envied the set." Kathleen motioned to her neck and ears. "When my husband worked at Wright Pharmacy, we attended functions together, her sitting there in the second-rate diamonds that her husband—the wrong Wright, as I used to call him—could afford."

"Still not getting how this connects," Cora said.

"I'm sorry Mrs. Y— I mean, *Kathleen*. I'm not following either."

"When we left to set up Sun City Emporium, that man refused to give Lloyd back his Forever Young formula. Said *he* owned it. So I went and bought our freedom. In exchange for my grandmother's emeralds, he let us keep Forever Young."

She looked between Thelma and Cora, awaiting the light-bulb moment. It didn't come. "Don't you see? Thelma, when it was clear that the Giancarlo's support rested on your making the team, I did what I had to do to keep you from leaving."

Thelma's eyes brimmed, but she didn't speak. This was not getting easier.

"And when I left Cora with you—I didn't do this on purpose, not exactly—I took away your choice to start a family. Just like I never had any choice when it came to starting a family."

Cora let out a furious snort. "I was a mistake. I get it."

"No, my love." Kathleen thrust her arm forward, causing Cora to shrink away, but she continued on, retrieving her handbag from the floor. Opening her bag, she withdrew a stack of diaries bound in faded blue ribbon. "These are for you."

Cora stared at her mother's hands but didn't move. "What about Havana? What happened there?"

"Ah, well," Kathleen said, placing the journals on the counter. "By the time I got to the port, they were waiting. Someone must've talked. I had to duck into a produce truck. Hid under a crate of plantains while they searched the city."

"Oh my God," Thelma said, moving closer.

"That night, I made it to Cuatro Caminos where I found a taxi driver who's ferried papers for us over the years. He got me to the state-run print shop my housekeeper's cousin runs, where I hid in a back room for a few weeks."

She closed her eyes, seeing the image of Fidel in fatigues, fist raised, emblazoned with the words ¡Patria o Muerte, Venceremos! Homeland or Death, we will win!

"Hey! Kathleen!" Cora snapped her fingers.

Does she think I fell asleep? Kathleen wondered.

"How did you get out of Cuba?" Cora continued.

No point in fanning the flames, Kathleen figured. "Yes, well... Catalina—that's my housekeeper—she went to my quarters as if nothing had happened. Cleaned the apartment, answered questions when the police came." Kathleen's voice softened with admiration. "They watched her, of course, at the market, church. But she knew how to move through a city under surveillance.

"Anyway, she knew where my papers were and brought them to me. I merely had to bide my time until I could join up with a group of tourists from Mexico." She shook her head. "That took months."

"Are you saying that everyone on the tour was in on it?" Thelma asked.

Kathleen leaned back, slapping her thigh with delight. "That's just it. Nobody noticed another silver-haired old lady in a shapeless dress and sensible shoes." She pointed at the journals. "Those diaries you dismissed? Catalina got them to me in Mexico two weeks later." Kathleen's fingers trembled slightly as she touched the ribbon. "Twenty-six years of entries. You see, my teacher forbade me from corresponding when I first arrived, so I started putting my thoughts on paper. Everything is here, everything I wanted to share with you."

Cora's expression changed, a flicker of something that might have been understanding crossing her face. "You risked your housekeeper's life for your old journals?"

"I begged her not to go back," Kathleen said. "But she told me—" Here she had to pause, compose herself. "Her mother had died before she could say goodbye. Insisted some words needed to be passed on, that they can never come too late."

She gripped the bundle to her chest then held it out to Cora. "I want you to have these in case you ever want the whole, unvarnished story." Her voice broke slightly. "But all you really need to know is that I always did the best I could for you, for Lloyd. My boys. For a long time, that meant staying away. I'm sorry for the hurt I caused you."

Her words hung in the air, raw and honest. She pressed the books into Cora's hands, watching her face without expectation. She truly had no idea how her daughter would react now.

Without warning, Cora tossed the books onto the counter and flung herself into her mother's arms.

Kathleen's body went rigid with shock before she slowly, carefully, circled her arms around her daughter. Over Cora's shoulder, she met Thelma's tearful gaze and Sam's surprised one.

"I'm still mad at you," Cora mumbled into her shoulder.

"I know, darling," Kathleen whispered, her hand finding its way to stroke her daughter's hair. "I know."

FORTY-NINE

Thelma, St. Petersburg, 1979

THE FIVE WOMEN EMERGED FROM THE LADIES' LOUNGE like survivors of a shipwreck—disheveled, emotional, but somehow buoyed. Thelma lingered behind the others, watching as Kathleen kept one arm around Cora's shoulders. The gesture was tentative, as if she feared her daughter might bolt still, but Cora was leaning into the embrace, if only slightly. No wounds could heal in a day, but walls could collapse in an instant.

Sam caught Thelma's eye, and she offered a small smile, an unspoken understanding between them. Having lost their mothers at a young age, the reunion they'd witnessed felt profound. "Your mother would be so proud of you," Thelma said softly, her vision blurring as they hugged.

"There's the bride," Kathleen said, nodding across the ballroom, alive with music and laughter. "I suppose I should go congratulate her."

Under crystal chandeliers, couples twirled to Natalie Cole singing "This Will Be" as waiters circulated with fresh champagne. But Lillian was easy to spot, holding court near the cake table, the emeralds still gleaming at her throat. They did go with a surprising number of looks.

"You sure?" Cora asked, her first protective gesture toward her mother.

"I've survived far more than an awkward conversation with a potential enemy," Kathleen replied with a wry smile.

As they approached, Lillian's eyes widened in recognition. "Kathleen Young! My God, I heard rumors... Well, I can hardly believe it! Here you are!" She embraced Kathleen with champagne-fueled nostalgia, air-kissing both cheeks.

"Best wishes for a wonderful life together, Lillian," Kathleen said. Her eyes lingered briefly on the emerald necklace. "Those jewels look stunning on you."

Lillian's hand flew to her throat. "Oh, eureka!" she cried, still exaggerated with drink. "Mummy said these had been in the Wright family for generations. But I saw you give them to my dad at the drugstore. Well, I don't know about *give*. It looked more like a robbery." She laughed. "That has been bugging me for years."

"You do them justice, Lillian," Kathleen said diplomatically. "They were meant to be worn."

Lillian fingered the pendant. "If you want them back—"

"No," Kathleen said firmly. "They're part of your history now."

Thelma watched this exchange with a mixture of amusement and respect. The Kathleen she remembered would have claimed those jewels without hesitation. This Kathleen seemed to understand what truly mattered.

A warm hand settled at the small of Thelma's back, and she didn't need to turn to know it was George. She reveled at his touch.

"I've been looking for you," he murmured close to her ear. "The dance floor's calling our name."

"One second." Thelma tapped Kathleen's shoulder. "Will you be all right?"

Kathleen smiled at George, who offered her a mock salute with his first two fingers. "I think we'll manage. You two go. Enjoy yourselves."

"We're going to have to do a full debrief with Miller—"

"I know," Kathleen said with a playful shove. "Now, go."

As they stepped onto the dance floor, the DJ switched to Earth, Wind & Fire's "September." George's hand found hers, and together they moved with the music.

"So, Kathleen made it back," he said, glancing over her shoulder. "I wasn't sure I believed Helen when she told me."

"That woman has been through hell and back."

"Haven't we all?" George's eyes met Thelma's, years of shared history reflected between them.

Across the dance floor, Thelma spotted Sam dancing with a tall man she didn't recognize. Sam's face was transformed, years of tension melting away as she laughed at something her partner said. The man's hand rested lightly on the small of Sam's back, his eyes never leaving her face as they moved.

"Who's that with Sam?" Thelma asked.

George glanced over. "Lucas something. One of Phil's cousins, I think. They seem to be hitting it off."

"Good for her." Thelma smiled, genuinely pleased. After everything Sam had been through, she deserved some happiness.

As they swayed to the music, Thelma realized she hadn't actually answered George's proposal earlier. In the chaos of Kathleen's appearance and Cora's fury, it had slipped away unacknowledged. She touched the sapphire at her throat—his grandmother's necklace, a symbol of everything they'd lost and found again.

"You know," she said, meeting his gaze, "you never got my answer."

George raised an eyebrow. "To what question?" he teased.

"Ask me again."

He pulled her closer, his voice low in her ear. "Would you marry me, Thelma Miles?"

"What about your career?" she asked, surprising herself.

George laughed, a satisfying rumble against her chest. "I've held my seat since '58. My constituents will love you."

"As much as you?"

"No," George said, turning serious. "That's not possible."

Thelma laughed. "Then yes. Of course I'll marry you."

The song changed to something slower, and Thelma caught sight of Kathleen sitting with Helen, their heads bent together in animated conversation. Nearby, Cora stood with the other young people, glass in hand, throwing glances Kathleen's way with an expression Thelma couldn't quite read—curiosity mixed with wariness, perhaps.

They all carried scars—some visible, others hidden beneath elaborate facades. But tonight, surrounded by friends who had become family, Thelma sensed something she hadn't felt in decades: peace.

"What are you thinking about?" George asked, following her gaze.

"The past," Thelma admitted, looking into his eyes. "And the future."

"And?"

She smiled up at him, this man who had waited for her through years of separation, pain, and growth. "And I'm thinking we've earned this," she said, kissing him as the music played on.

THE END

🔥Continue the Queenpin Chronicles🔥
Loved *Havana Girls*?
Start from the beginning or keep reading:

📘 *Florida Girls* — **Book 1**
When the mob hits Florida's Gulf Coast,
these wartime showgirls hit back.
Grab it now: tinyurl.com/FLG-ALL

🎲 *Vegas Girls* — **Book 2**
What happens in Vegas... doesn't always stay there. Especially
when the girls run the game.
Continue the story: tinyurl.com/getvegasgirls

Already read them all? You're ready for what's next...

🕵️ **NEXT UP: *Steel City Critic***, *a dark psychological*
mystery set in 1990s Pittsburgh.
When the local theater critic is poisoned, the woman he
replaced—Jessica Greer—becomes the prime suspect. As
evidence mounts, she begins a desperate investigation,
untangling artistic rivalries, false personas, and buried secrets
lead to a terrifying realization.
Get word first: tinyurl.com/SteelCityNews

Reviews help bold books get noticed:
Leave a review for *Havana Girls*,
go to llkirchner.com/reviews

FIFTY

Epilogue: Excerpts From The Library Of Kathleen Young, 1947-1978:

Trivandrum, India - February 25, 1947

Guruji tells me I must learn to love and I've no clue what he means. Does he sense that I'm more than a little in love with him? His deep brown eyes seem to know everything about me, my sorrows. My sins. I cannot imagine life before him, a hollow and vapid exercise in materialism.

And yet... it can be difficult not to regret leaving it all behind. Guruji insists I mustn't. For the most part, I don't. Any pain I have caused my children is nothing compared to what could have been if I'd stayed another moment. I shall return before the year is out and young Cora shall hardly know the difference. The boys are grown and gone now themselves, not of an age where they've any interest in dear old mother.

I am lonely, but feel the stirrings of independence. As if I *am* India, for there is great ruckus following the prime minister's announcement that India shall be free of colonial rule. I feel nothing if not aligned with the shedding of shackles. Though I am the only woman allowed to study here, I am at home.

Trivandrum, India - July 15, 1947

I have angered Guruji today. We were having lunch in the open pavilion when a local woman collapsed outside, her water jug shattering on the stone path. Monsoon season has begun and so I recognized the symptoms quickly—cholera. Before I could think, I was on my feet and rushing to her side.

Marcus chided me. "Her people will help her," he said.

There was only one reply I could think of as I knelt beside the woman, a regular lesson of Guruji's. "We're all her people, no?" I wanted to add, *Om shanti, chucklehead*, but managed to keep that particular thought to myself. Though Guruji himself can be quite sharp, it is his primary critique for me.

The woman's name is Priya. Her eyes were so sunken, her skin paper-dry. The other students—Marcus, Thomàs, the rest—they were all backing away. Afraid.

"We're heading back to the shala," Thomàs announced.

The fools, cholera is not contagious through casual contact. Still, I kept my composure, asking them to bring me a coconut from Suresh at the corner before they left. I pressed some rupees into Thomàs's reluctant hand.

I got Priya to drink the coconut water—it's rich in potassium. All that time toiling away with Lloyd on that tonic finally proved useful.

Walking to her home took nearly two hours, slowed as Priya was by her illness. She lives in a tiny adobe hut with five children and no soap in sight. Her oldest daughter speaks some English, thank heavens, so I could explain about boiling water for drinking and cleaning.

When I returned to the ashram, Guruji was there waiting. His face was calm but his eyes steely. He accused me of elevating my own importance. Of spiritual pride. Of failing to respect local customs. Your ego grows even as you claim to diminish it, he said. Is that true?

I burned with shame as he spoke. And anger. And confusion. All of which suggests some merit in his words. Nonetheless I must return to Priya's tomorrow and show her family how to turn her so she doesn't develop bedsores. I'll bring soap.

Cora is constantly in my thoughts. I'd like to think she would be proud. Eventually. She would be fifteen months old now. Walking, perhaps. Speaking her first words. Does she wonder where I am? Does she ask for me? I know that Thelma and the girls are caring for her far better than I could right now. This is why I'm here, to become the mother she deserves. Not the broken woman who could barely care for herself let alone a baby after Lloyd died. My anger would surely have rotted any child. I have begun writing her letters about my experiences, something to share when she is grown.

This setback is, like all things, temporary. I shall redouble my efforts.

Trivandrum, India - October 3, 1947

Guruji is sending me away. He says I need deeper practice. Less distraction. I need to learn how to practice with less effort.

I've no idea what he means. I do suspect, though, that he may be jealous. Once I'd helped Priya, women from nearby villages began to seek me out for treatments. More often than not I offered simple hygiene lessons, but it has meant that visitors to the ashram were looking for me, not him.

I shall miss the jungle paths I've come to know so well. Even the beaches. I never went to the beach in Florida, but here I am drawn to the calm waters, which I've been told have healing properties. Though I sense they offer as much healing as our old Forever Young tonic—which was rich in vitamins and vital nutrients to be sure—I love nothing more than a morning swim after meditation.

Perhaps this is why I am being punished.

"Too much agitation of the mind," the head sadhu told me upon arrival. "You must learn stillness before movement can have meaning."

Guruji did not come.

Since getting the news, my mind feels anything but still. It races constantly, circling back to Cora, to Sun City, to Lloyd. I don't know exactly when I will leave, or where I'm headed. The longer I wait, the louder my thoughts become.

Sometimes I stare at the waves, watching their ceaseless ebb and flow and thinking about how life continues without my permission or participation. What am I becoming here? What am I leaving behind?

I tried writing to Thelma again, but I don't believe my letters are being sent. I haven't heard from any of them since the beginning of Monsoon season. When I asked the ashram attendant, he said that "attachment to outcomes is the source of suffering."

What I realized is that I've only just begun to understand these teachings. Small wonder Guruji has said nothing about training me as a teacher in some time.

Lhasa, Tibet - December 25, 1948

Cora's birthday. She would be turning two today. Or was yesterday Christmas? The days blur here in this remote monastery where I've been sent for "advanced study."

It's been a year to the day since Guruji summoned me to his hut. I was certain then he was finally sending me home. That he'd given up on me as a student. Instead, he told me I must continue my studies.

Though I am now certain that Guruji never intended for me to teach, I have learned the lesson he meant for me. When he sent me off to pack and I discovered all my letters to Cora had gone missing I collapsed, sobbing and pulling at my clothes like a madwoman. In that moment of absolute grief, I saw how I remained tethered to my former identity as wife and mother and even businesswoman. I was so proud to be accepted into this community, even as I knew it was in no small part because of what I brought financially.

Beauty continues to reveal itself to me. The monastery clings to a mountainside overlooking a valley dense with jungle. The nuns here observe complete silence. Though no one has ordered me to do the same, I do the same. What choice have I? To whom would I speak? I know no Tibetan, and my Hindi is rudimentary at best.

I've started a letter to Cora for her birthday, but I can't seem to finish it. What can I possibly say to explain this absence? What words could bridge this growing chasm?

Lhasa, Tibet - January 17, 1949

Two years since I left Cora in Cuba and I've been pondering what brought me to Guruji. For most of my adult life, I was convinced that running Sun City while raising my children was extraordinary, but I was just fulfilling another set of expectations. But who am I without those roles? What remains when everything familiar is stripped away?

The isolation is profound. Sometimes I wonder if I'm disappearing entirely, like a leaf skittering across these ancient stone walls.

Today, during meditation, I felt a moment of complete unity with the world around me. The mountains, the jungle, the birds wheeling overhead—it all seemed part of a vast, breathing whole that included me but didn't center on me.

Is this what Guruji wanted me to find? If so, why does it feel so hollow?

Lhasa, Tibet - June 17, 1949

No sleep again tonight. I went to the meditation pavilion before dawn, but couldn't settle my mind. Instead, I sat on the ledge, watching the full moon illuminate the valley below.

From this vantage point, I could see the mountain trails where traders move through the darkness. Yaks loaded with wooden crates—opium bound for China, I suspect.

I've had no word from Guruji in half a year. No letter, no instruction, no sign that he remembers my existence. I've written to him three times, asking for further guidance or permission to return home. No response.

The truth is crystallizing with terrible clarity: he never intended for me to become a teacher. Perhaps he never intended for me to leave at all. Women like me—Westerners with financial resources—are valuable to ashrams and monasteries. We bring money, prestige, and free labor. Why give us the keys to the kingdom?

I feel as if I've been sleepwalking for the past two and a half years, and now I'm finally awake. The question is: what do I do about it? I have no passport (surrendered to Guruji for safekeeping), no money (donated to the ashram), and no obvious way out of these mountains. The nearest American consulate is hundreds of miles away through territory I can't navigate alone.

There's nothing that will undo my choice to leave Cora. That pain I must carry with me always. But I might still salvage something from this journey—authentic knowledge I can share without the trappings of guru worship and unquestioning obedience.

I will bide my time. Watch. Listen. Look for any opportunity. My survival skills haven't abandoned me, even if my common sense flew off. Lloyd always said a sucker was born every minute. I never thought that would be me.

Lhasa, Tibet - March 12, 1950

Everything has changed overnight.

I woke before dawn to shouting—real shouting—in a monastery where no one has raised their voice in the two years I've been here. The sound of splintering wood sent me scrambling from my sleeping mat just as heavy boots pounded down the corridor outside.

My door burst open and three soldiers stormed in, rifles raised. Their olive uniforms and red stars told me everything I needed to know even before the leader barked something in Chinese.

"American," I said, raising my hands. "I am American."

They brought in a young man with glasses to translate. "You are American citizen?" he asked in halting English.

"Yes, from California," I replied, keeping my voice steady despite my racing heart. "I'm here studying yoga and meditation."

After translation, the leader's stern expression softened slightly.

"The People's Liberation Army is now in control," the translator explained. "You will come with us for questioning."

I nodded agreeably. Liberation from what? By whom? But I knew better than to ask such questions. "May I gather my belongings?"

As I gathered my few possessions, I heard more shouting

and crashes throughout the monastery. Then the nuns began to chant—an urgent, swelling sound unlike their usual measured tones.

Then came gunshots. The chanting stopped.

I didn't flinch. These years in ashrams and monasteries have taught me true non-reactivity, if nothing else. I simply stood straighter, clutching my bundle in steady hands.

These men held power now. And if there was one thing my life as Kathleen Young had taught me, it was how to navigate power. I followed without hesitation. Whatever came next, it had to be better than slow disappearance in this stone prison on a mountainside.

Lhasa, Tibet - January 3, 1952

I feel like I've graduated. After eighteen months in this dreadful "re-education" camp, I've caught the eye of a visiting dignitary. He's Russian, one of our allies. But then, technically, so were the Chinese. But finding me in Tibet, an American no less, they have not been kind. Though I suppose the fact I wasn't murdered with the nuns against the outbuilding says something.

I'm hopeful. Though I don't know any Russian, unlike my Chinese hosts, the head of the delegation speaks English perfectly. We can communicate directly. He saw me in my thin robe, meditating outdoors in no apparent sign of distress, and I was able to assure him I could teach Soviet athletes these feats of endurance. He seemed intrigued.

If I can escape this place, I shall find a way to an American embassy. I'm sure of it.

Moscow, Soviet Union - November 3, 1952

Today I moved into my own apartment in a building reserved for "Foreign specialists" in the Ostankino district. The furniture is heavy and dark, the heating works most days, and I have indoor plumbing.

Training their athletes has been strangely comforting, the fulfillment of my initial desires. And yet, it's nothing like Guru-jii's teaching. I've simply combined yoga postures with athletic drills, stripping away anything spiritual. It seems the whole country has no use for God, but it's difficult to know. Beyond the language barriers I sense a great secrecy. Nonetheless, I am beyond grateful that the Chinese were happy to be rid of me, an inconvenient reminder of their invasion.

I have a handler now, Comrade Petrov. He speaks perfect English—educated at Cambridge, apparently, though he never mentions spending time outside of Russia. He tells me that I must have a sponsor to visit the embassy, which I find perplexing. And yet, I am now forty-five. I feel the fight is leaving me.

Nonetheless, I've written Thelma again today. Comrade Petrov promises to send my letters, though I have my doubts. I've included my Moscow address, begging for news of Cora, who would be nearly seven now. Has she started school? Does she remember me at all?

Moscow, Soviet Union - September 15, 1953

A miracle! A letter from Thelma arrived today—heavily censored, with entire paragraphs blacked out, but unmistakably from her.

What I can piece together is both heartbreaking and confusing. No word of Cora or Helen or George. Only Doris. She and

Thelma remain in Havana, running what she carefully refers to as "the business." Is the Bird of Paradise no more? Between the lines I sense she is both warning me and trying to tell me something important. Especially in the last sentence, which was only half untouched—*When the time is right, you will find your way.* The rest was blacked out.

Whatever has happened in Cuba, it warrants near total censorship.

I cried for hours after reading it. My first confirmation in nearly four years that any of them remember me. They surely think I abandoned them; I haven't been able to send mail let alone financial support. But perhaps I haven't been entirely erased from Cora's life.

I wrote back immediately, but understand now that even if my response reaches Thelma it will be near incomprehensible. I kept it deliberately vague, focusing on my teaching work here and expressing gratitude for any news of Cora.

Petrov picked up my letter personally, watching my reaction with undisguised curiosity, asking if I'd had good news from home. When I risked mentioning my daughter he seemed surprised. He too has a daughter, in Leningrad. It was the first personal detail he'd ever shared.

What I cannot imagine is what goes on in the lives of people here. To a one, my athletes, many quite young, are separated from home. When I asked a gymnast she simply shrugged and said this was best. It's as if the whole country endorses what I've done. Perhaps evil is only in the eye of the beholder.

Moscow, Soviet Union - October 30, 1956

Four years in the Soviet Union now. Four years of teaching Soviet athletes while gathering intelligence about possible escape routes.

There was no bread again today.

Much as I want to go, getting out of the USSR isn't my only problem. As an American citizen "re-educated" by the Chinese who has lived in Moscow for years, I'd be viewed with deep suspicion by U.S. authorities. But I can't simply go to an embassy. There isn't one. I am behind what I've heard whispers of, something called an iron curtain. Mercifully I can write these entries in French, or the KGB might've come for me already. The Soviets are not our allies, far from it. They are our enemies in something called the Cold War, something I feel I battle every day they refuse to turn on the heat in our building. I was too long in isolation from world events to understand when I first arrived, and my shame has only grown.

Moscow, Soviet Union - July 4, 1959

Independence Day back home. And perhaps for me?

As we prepare for Rome 1960—though I was informed I will not be permitted to attend the Olympics—I was taken to a new facility to work with our gymnastics team. Among the staff there was a Cuban athletic trainer, part of a cultural exchange. We spoke briefly during a break. Carefully at first, when I mentioned I'd been to Havana, then with growing animation he spoke of the revolution.

Revolution? In Cuba? I asked when this had occurred, and he eyed me with suspicion before saying it had been this year. In January. Once he realized my confusion was genuine, he asked how long I'd been in Moscow.

Seven years. The length of time shocked even me.

He nodded slowly, saying that much has changed. Then he asked if I might be interested in their cultural exchange program.

Somehow I managed to stay in my seat, but my mind raced.

Cuba! Would Cora still be there? I'd only had a handful of heavily redacted letters over the years, none with any mention of a revolution, or Cora. Thelma always had been clever, they'd likely have cut off our correspondence otherwise. She must have been getting at least some of my letters.

Regardless, I must approach this opportunity with caution. Make it seem like the Soviets' idea. Perhaps suggest that my training methods could benefit their new Cuban allies.

This is the first time in years I've felt a flutter of genuine hope.

Moscow, Soviet Union - January 15, 1961

How fitting that today I received confirmation: I'm being sent to Havana in two months as part of a business consultancy. Today is the very day, back in 1947, that I left Havana. Cora is fifteen now. Such a difficult age for me. Hard to imagine I was about to meet the love of my life, my Button, my Lloyd.

My entries have been sporadic of late because I did it. I finally managed to break my clavicle. The plan was to break my left arm, but I couldn't do it. I tried punching a wall, only to end up with bruised knuckles and multiple scratches. I tried getting drunk and throwing myself off the kitchen counter, but I'm trained to fall so I kept curling to protect myself. Finally I had to do it sober and then get drunk. And it turned out to be my right clavicle, so I don't know if this will be legible as I must write with my left hand. But that's probably for the best.

Comrade Petrov delivered the news; I put on my bravest face as if I hated to leave, even as I reassured him that my background in business was the best service I could give to the cause now. We agreed that we must make a success of the Cuba example. I've played it so carefully, planting the smallest of hints about my background running a business, training showgirls, and my brief stint in Hollywood. All the while careful to sound as if I abhorred capitalism. Before I lived here, I didn't know what capitalism was apart from the American dream. And while the materialism of it has proven pointless—chicanery aside, Gurujii taught me many valuable lessons—I've seen what happens when a government holds all the power. Wealth and the means of attaining it is controlled by the politicians with no regard to individuals outside the privileged class. We are less than human. We are commodities.

But I mustn't get bogged down now. I must get to Cuba. Find Cora. Thelma. Doris. I don't know what will happen from there, but as Gurujii used to say, *I am aware of my heart and my mistakes, and I love them all. Forgiven. Forgiven. Forgiven.*

I've begun studying Spanish with fanatical dedication, working with a Cuban doctor at the sports institute. I credit writing in French all these years with my ability to pick up the language. By the time I arrive in Havana, I'm hopeful that I shall be able to converse. I'm already better in Spanish than Russian.

Three more months in Moscow. After more than a decade of captivity—first spiritual, then political—the end is finally in sight.

Havana, Cuba - April 3, 1961

I was right that everything has changed. Even so, it's in ways I never anticipated. The entire island is on high alert due to something the officials are calling a missile crisis. American warships are blockading Cuba, and there's talk of possible invasion.

The conditions, too, are deplorable. Far worse than what I experienced in Russia, which I thought of as quite Spartan.

Now I'm in a converted hotel sharing a dormer style room with the female handler I've been assigned, Olga. She is terribly suspicious of me, but I suppose that's her job. I will win her over, and hope that no more roommates arrive.

The biggest shock of all came when Olga took me to the business I was to run. None other than the Bird of Paradise! What has become of Thelma? I wanted to march straight to the last address I had for her and Cora, but all the street names have been changed. How on earth did my letters reach her?

Fortunately, given my post, there was nothing odd about me poring over books and letters and scraps of paper in the Bird's office. We are reopening—without any fanfare whatsoever—for Russian tourists. None of the natives can afford to come. Though the food and drink is of low grade.

I scarcely know what to make of what's left, but I shall use the opportunity of hiring local entertainers to find out. It's especially difficult, I want to run, shouting in the streets. Instead I must be patient. Wait. Watch. Pounce.

* * *

💋 Want more Queenpin?

Find every book, plus secret stories at:
llkirchner.com/books

📖 If you enjoyed *Havana Girls*, a quick review on your preferred site will help other readers find it:
👉 llkirchner.com/reviews

NEXT UP: *Steel City Critic*

When the local theater critic is poisoned, Jessica Greer— the person he replaced—becomes the suspect. As evidence mounts against her, she begins a desperate investigation, untangling a

*web of artistic rivalries, false personas, and buried secrets that
lead to a terrifying realization.*
A darkly gratifying suspense set in 1990s Pittsburgh.
Part of my forthcoming *Steel City* series.

📮 Join the Insiders List. 🔥 **tinyurl.com/SteelCityNews**

Also By L.L. Kirchner

Nonfiction Memoirs:

Blissful Thinking — The decade I spent searching for spirituality in gurus, ashrams, and other people.

Lady Creature — I hoped moving to Qatar would change everything. Until it did. A true story.

* * *

The Queenpin Chronicles:

 Florida Girls — Book 1

When the mob hits Florida's Gulf Coast,

wartime showgirls hit back.

Vegas Girls — Book 2

What happens in Vegas... doesn't always stay there. Especially when the girls run the game.

Full catalog at llkirchner.com/books

Author's Note

The inspiration for this book came from the characters, a diverse group of women all experiencing an awakening.

Sam/Sally—the name. Sally was the name I thought would work as a forgettable kid's name, a throwaway from book 1. But then Imogene roared into the story and I had to work with the storyline as it had begun. Imogene *could* have had another child, but that didn't fit with her narrative.

Sam wasn't having it either.

This character showed up wanting to be called Sam. Once I'd written a fair bit, I tried to change the name back to Sally, but then I had a problem I had not considered in book one— Salvatore Giancarlo. Sal.

Of course, most would discourage using Sal and Sam in one book. Though it *is* better than Sal/Sally. I trust my readers will not be thrown by this. I did try like hell to jam in a scene where this background could come out... Sally means Princess in Hebrew, which Imogene would never go for. Bill knew that, so he was pleased as punch when Imogene went for the name as she knew the word—as a witty riposte, aka, a conversational 'sally.'

As for the rest of it, from the accounts I've read of Havana during the mafia era, there was certainly human trafficking happening between the U.S. and Cuba. This was not limited to young American women, but for simplicity's sake that's the main representation in the book. The problem would have been much larger than one small shadow network could have solved so I picked a lane.

As for the switch, that was another eye-opening part of my research. One of Castro's crackdowns was on prostitution. However, the women who worked in that area weren't keen to labor on farms instead. According to historical accounts, many sex workers wanted to make better money doing work they knew. It made sense for Peggy to return to Vegas (she loved it there!), and I liked the idea of Thelma and company helping these women do what they wanted to do.

These stories are all meant to be about self-empowerment, and importantly, women working together to achieve forward momentum toward their goals. I don't know about you, but that's the story I need right now.

I'd like to use this space as well to thank the myriad people who have helped make this book possible. The brilliant editing team at Red Adept, Lynn and Darlene, for making sure this story held. Dana Sacco, whose careful read led to the prologue, which I think makes the book! And of course, my writing partner in crime, so to speak, Betsy Farber, without whom I doubt I'd have had the stamina to go on. And nothing beats the moral support I've gotten from fellow members of the Women's Fiction Writers Association and the Historical Novel Society, except the in-person gnashing of teeth I get to do on the regular with fellow authors and part of the journalism diaspora, Tamara Lush and Arin Greenwood.

None of it would be possible without my very best beloved husband.

About the Author

L.L. Kirchner is an award-winning screenwriter and Pushcart-nominated author whose life and work as an expat in Asia became the basis of two memoirs that combine humor with "her discerning eye" (Foreword Reviews). As an NPR interviewer said, her memoir is "like *Eat, Pray, Love,* but funny." Her writing has appeared in the *Washington Post, Salon,* and *The Rumpus* among numerous other outlets.

Drawing on her eclectic journalism background as a religion editor, dating columnist, and bridal editor, her work explores feminist narratives. Read more at her blog, IllBehaved-Women.com or LLKirchner.com.

She lives in Florida with her favorite husband and their best boy, Hartley.

On socials everywhere @llkirchnerauthor.

For Book Clubs

I bet you love your book club as much as I love mine. In honor of that mutual adoration, I've put together a discussion guide. Find it on my website,
LLKirchner.com/FOR BOOK CLUBS.

WANNA TALK ABOUT THIS BOOK?
I'd love to join your book club's discussion if at all possible! On that page, tap the "let's connect" button.